Praise for Le
Mercenaries...

"I can always trust Lexi Blake's Dominants to leave me breathless...and in love. If you want sensual, exciting BDSM wrapped in an awesome love story, then look for a Lexi Blake book."
~Cherise Sinclair USA Today Bestselling author

"Lexi Blake's MASTERS AND MERCENARIES series is beautifully written and deliciously hot. She's got a real way with both action and sex. I also love the way Blake writes her gorgeous Dom heroes--they make me want to do bad, bad things. Her heroines are intelligent and gutsy ladies whose taste for submission definitely does not make them dish rags. Can't wait for the next book!"
~Angela Knight, New York Times Bestselling author

"A Dom is Forever is action packed, both in the bedroom and out. Expect agents, spies, guns, killing and lots of kink as Liam goes after the mysterious Mr. Black and finds his past and his future... The action and espionage keep this story moving along quickly while the sex and kink provides a totally different type of interest. Everything is very well balanced and flows together wonderfully."
~A Night Owl "Top Pick", Terri, Night Owl Erotica

"A Dom Is Forever is everything that is good in erotic romance. The story was fast-paced and suspenseful, the characters were flawed but made me root for them every step of the way, and the hotness factor was off the charts mostly due to a bad boy Dom with a penchant for dirty talk."
~Rho, The Romance Reviews

"A good read that kept me on my toes, guessing until the big reveal, and thinking survival skills should be a must for all men."
~Chris, Night Owl Reviews

"I can't get enough of the Masters and Mercenaries Series! Love and Let Die is Lexi Blake at her best! She writes erotic romantic suspense like no other, and I am always extremely excited when she has something new for us! Intense, heart pounding, and erotically fulfilling, I could not put this book down."

~ Shayna Renee, Shayna Renee's Spicy Reads

"Certain authors and series are on my auto-buy list. Lexi Blake and her Masters & Mercenaries series is at the top of that list... this book offered everything I love about a Masters & Mercenaries book – alpha men, hot sex and sweet loving... As long as Ms. Blake continues to offer such high quality books, I'll be right there, ready to read."

~ Robin, Sizzling Hot Books

"I have absolutely fallen in love with this series. Spies, espionage, and intrigue all packaged up in a hot dominant male package. All the men at McKay-Taggart are smoking hot and the women are amazingly strong sexy submissives."

~Kelley, Smut Book Junkie Book Reviews

Long Lost

Other Books by Lexi Blake

ROMANTIC SUSPENSE

Masters and Mercenaries
The Dom Who Loved Me
The Men With The Golden Cuffs
A Dom is Forever
On Her Master's Secret Service
Sanctum: A Masters and Mercenaries Novella
Love and Let Die
Unconditional: A Masters and Mercenaries Novella
Dungeon Royale
Dungeon Games: A Masters and Mercenaries Novella
A View to a Thrill
Cherished: A Masters and Mercenaries Novella
You Only Love Twice
Luscious: Masters and Mercenaries~Topped
Adored: A Masters and Mercenaries Novella
Master No
Just One Taste: Masters and Mercenaries~Topped 2
From Sanctum with Love
Devoted: A Masters and Mercenaries Novella
Dominance Never Dies
Submission is Not Enough
Master Bits and Mercenary Bites~The Secret Recipes of Topped
Perfectly Paired: Masters and Mercenaries~Topped 3
For His Eyes Only
Arranged: A Masters and Mercenaries Novella
Love Another Day
At Your Service: Masters and Mercenaries~Topped 4
Master Bits and Mercenary Bites~Girls Night
Nobody Does It Better
Close Cover
Protected: A Masters and Mercenaries Novella
Enchanted: A Masters and Mercenaries Novella
Charmed: A Masters and Mercenaries Novella
Treasured: A Masters and Mercenaries Novella, Coming June 29, 2021

Masters and Mercenaries: The Forgotten
Lost Hearts (Memento Mori)
Lost and Found
Lost in You
Long Lost
No Love Lost

Masters and Mercenaries: Reloaded
Submission Impossible
The Dom Identity, Coming September 14, 2021

Butterfly Bayou
Butterfly Bayou
Bayou Baby
Bayou Dreaming
Bayou Beauty, Coming July 27, 2021

Lawless
Ruthless
Satisfaction
Revenge

Courting Justice
Order of Protection
Evidence of Desire

Masters Of Ménage (by Shayla Black and Lexi Blake)
Their Virgin Captive
Their Virgin's Secret
Their Virgin Concubine
Their Virgin Princess
Their Virgin Hostage
Their Virgin Secretary
Their Virgin Mistress

The Perfect Gentlemen (by Shayla Black and Lexi Blake)
Scandal Never Sleeps
Seduction in Session
Big Easy Temptation

Smoke and Sin
At the Pleasure of the President

URBAN FANTASY

Thieves
Steal the Light
Steal the Day
Steal the Moon
Steal the Sun
Steal the Night
Ripper
Addict
Sleeper
Outcast
Stealing Summer

LEXI BLAKE WRITING AS SOPHIE OAK

Texas Sirens
Small Town Siren
Siren in the City
Siren Enslaved
Siren Beloved
Siren in Waiting
Siren in Bloom
Siren Unleashed
Siren Reborn

Nights in Bliss, Colorado
Three to Ride
Two to Love
One to Keep
Lost in Bliss
Found in Bliss
Pure Bliss
Chasing Bliss
Once Upon a Time in Bliss
Back in Bliss
Sirens in Bliss
Happily Ever After in Bliss

Far From Bliss, Coming 2021

A Faery Story
Bound
Beast
Beauty

Standalone
Away From Me
Snowed In

Long Lost

Masters and Mercenaries: The Forgotten, Book 4

Lexi Blake

Long Lost
Masters and Mercenaries: The Forgotten, Book 4
Lexi Blake

Published by DLZ Entertainment LLC
Copyright 2020 DLZ Entertainment LLC
Edited by Chloe Vale
ISBN: 978-1-942297-22-2

This is a work of fiction. Names, places, characters and incidents are the product of the author's imagination and are fictitious. Any resemblance to actual persons, living or dead, events or establishments is solely coincidental.

Sign up for Lexi Blake's newsletter
and be entered to win a $25 gift certificate
to the bookseller of your choice.

Join us for news, fun, and exclusive content.

There's a new contest every month!

Go to www.LexiBlake.net to subscribe.

Acknowledgments

I want to thank everyone who helped make this book possible. No novelist writes in a vacuum. Though the words might be mine, the emotions and feelings behind the characters are always influenced by the people around me. I think it's why I write happily ever afters. I grew up around one, found one myself, wish for one for all of my loved ones. Some of us become obsessed with the things we don't have, but I was always fascinated by what was around me—love. So this is for the people I love, the ones who love me and surround me with strength. To my friends and family. To my readers. To the ones who started it all for me—to my mom and dad who taught me forever is only the beginning.

Prologue

Paris, France

What the hell was she doing here? It was one thing to kiss the man, to go on a couple of dates with him, but this was something entirely different.

Veronica Croft stared down at the street below and the question kept running through her head. She was alone in a foreign city with Steven Reasor, the pit bull of the neuro world. He was stunningly handsome—far out of her league—sexy as hell, and scary. People at Kronberg Pharma, where they worked, were scared of Steven, and she was worried it wasn't simply because he could fire them.

There were rumors about the man who was currently taking a shower after the short plane trip from Munich to Paris. Rumors that frightened her. Rumors that should have had her running away, not going on holiday with him.

Vacation. That's what they called it in the States. Had she been away from home so long she sounded European? Working alongside Brits and Germans and Swedes and French had taught her a lot, had forced her outside her South Texas roots. The girl she'd been mere years ago wouldn't have found the courage to leave the safety of her suburban home, much less take a year to work for one of the most innovative companies in the world.

The girl she'd been had also known that when a moth touched the flame, her wings burned away.

"How do you like the place?"

The deep voice sent a shiver down her spine that didn't have anything to do with fear. His voice fascinated her because she could tell so much about his mood from it. When it went deep and had a rough edge to it, he was angry. When he was bored, he sounded pretentious and intellectual. He sounded like that a lot, like the world wasn't quite enough for him, and neither was the person he was talking to.

And then there was that voice he seemed to only use on her, the one that made her heart melt.

Don't believe what they say, Roni. I'm not who they say I am. It's all for show.

He'd whispered those words in her ear a month ago after he'd pretty much flayed the doctor who'd cornered her at a party. He'd been drunk and gotten handsy, and thanks to Steven Reasor, he was no longer employed.

It had been the first sign that Steven might not be who he seemed to be, and that one incident had brought about the first crack in her barely-there armor.

Her mom always said she was too open. She trusted too fast and it burned her. She was afraid she was going to get burned again, and she couldn't seem to help herself.

She turned away from the scene outside where she could see the green of a park and tourists and locals walking by. The smell of espresso wafted up from the café at the bottom of the building. "It's beautiful. This is a nice neighborhood."

"This neighborhood is known as the first arrondissement," he explained. "One of the oldest, wealthiest neighborhoods in Paris. All the best shopping is here, and the Louvre is close by."

Yes, she'd already figured that out. It was part of the mystery that surrounded him. His place in Munich was fairly utilitarian. She had been surprised by how luxurious this space was. "It's an amazing apartment, but it makes me wonder how you afford it. Most doctors your age are still struggling to pay off medical school."

Yeah, there were rumors about that, too. She didn't believe them.

He had a rough exterior, but he wasn't some kind of criminal.

He could be incredibly sweet when he wanted to be. And god, he was beautiful.

She forced herself to stay cool and not to drool at the man. He'd come in dressed in nothing but a pair of jeans that clung to his hips. They showed off the fact that Steven liked to work out. A lot. She was around doctors all the time. One would think men and women in the medical profession would be in tip-top shape. One would be wrong. But not about Steven. He was six foot two, with a lean frame and broad shoulders. And abs. Lots of sculpted abs. Maybe she could handle the to-die-for body, but his face was damn near perfect, too. It was the face of an angel.

It didn't fit the man's reputation at all.

He grinned, a light expression she rarely saw. "It's not exactly mine, but that's another story. It belongs to a guy I sort of work with. Worked with. While I'm here in Europe, I'm free to come and go as I please." He took a step toward her, his golden-brown hair slick from the shower. "But I'm probably going back to the States soon."

That surprised her. "I thought you were riding McDonald's coattails all the way to the top."

A startled expression crossed his face, and for a second she could have sworn she'd hurt him. His lips curled up then and that split second of openness was gone, replaced with that gorgeous mask of his. "Hey, doctors have been doing it for decades. Centuries, really. We all climb on the backs of the great ones and then call ourselves giants. But no, I've got plans that don't include McDonald. Or Europe. I want a bunch of American food and an elevator that doesn't make me feel like I'm some kind of ogre."

She laughed at that. The lifts here could make a person feel like they didn't fit. "I miss crisp bacon. The pancakes at the cafeteria are pretty good, but why can't they actually cook the bacon? And the Brits…"

"Who the hell eats baked beans for breakfast?" Steven finished her thought. "And tomatoes. I kind of want a Pop-Tart."

"Me, too," she said with a grin. "And I swore them off a long time ago. I pretty much ate them exclusively during my undergrad years. Pop-Tarts and ramen noodles."

"And when I had some cash, I would buy the good mac and

cheese," he added, that grin still lighting up the room.

Sometimes they connected, and that was what kept her flying so close to the flame.

That and the fact that she was almost certain he was involved in something criminal. Not that he was behind it, but that he was going to get caught up in it. Something was going on at Kronberg. Maybe not at Kronberg as a whole, but definitely with Dr. Hope McDonald's group.

According to her sister, McDonald and her father might be doing things they shouldn't. Katie was certain there was a story here, certain she could blow up the pharmaceutical industry. Roni didn't intend to become an undercover informant. Her sister was a brilliant writer and an excellent investigator, but she also tended to believe every kooky theory the Internet put out in the world. The idea that a group of companies had formed a shadow agency that ruled the globe was one of her older sister's favorites.

But Roni had been worried about what was happening with Dr. McDonald ever since Rebecca Walsh had left. Dr. Walsh had been one of the smartest, nicest people she'd worked for here, and the fact that she'd quit without notice felt wrong to Roni.

None of which explained why she was standing here with the hottest, most potentially dangerous man she'd ever met. It didn't explain why she thought about him all the time, why he haunted her every fantasy.

"Yeah, they don't have as much processed food as we have in the States." It was a stupid thing to say and she was feeling completely awkward.

A long moment passed and he turned to her, his eyes warm for a change, but then somehow they always seemed warm when he looked her way.

"Why did you agree to come to Paris with me, Veronica?"

There it was. The deep, rich tone that got her every time. She could give him some bullshit excuse, but she thought they were past that now. "You know why."

"I know why I asked you to come with me. I don't know why you said yes." He stared at her for a moment as though he could see through her every mask. "Are you afraid of me? If you're here because you think sleeping with me will protect your job, then I'm going to go get dressed and we'll have a long talk. I'm not threatening you in any way. I know you won't believe this, but I want to protect you."

The crazy thing was, she did. He seemed to be two completely different people. There was the ruthless head of research and the man who softened when they were alone, the one who'd kissed her three nights before like he was dying of thirst and she was a tall glass of water.

No one in the world had ever made her feel the way this man had, and she hadn't been able to stop herself from exploring that.

"I'm not here because I'm afraid of you. If I was afraid of you, I would have said no. I would have made sure I was never alone with you." She'd had a few colleagues who she'd been wary of over the years. Somehow, despite his reputation, Steven hadn't been one of them.

"I'm glad to hear that because the last thing I want is for you to be afraid of me."

"I don't understand you," she admitted. "I get that you have to be stern at work. Our business can be a little cutthroat."

"You have no idea," he said quietly, his smile going dim. "At this level it's beyond ruthless, but I don't have to always be at this level. When I was younger, do you know what I wanted to be?"

She shook her head. It already felt comfortable. This was how it went with him. She was anxious until they started talking and she forgot who he was at work. "I don't know. A marine biologist? Don't we all want to be that until we figure out there are sharks out there?"

"An astute metaphor for our business, too. No, I always wanted to be a doctor. I wasn't the kid who played at being a fireman or police officer. My brother and his friends always played soldiers and I was the medic. My granddad was a doctor. He died when I was a kid, but I remember watching him. I would hang out in the office. He was a GP for a small town. I wanted to be one, too."

She couldn't see it. He was so ambitious. It burned there in his eyes. Being a general practitioner required a patience he wasn't known for, and it had next to none of the acknowledgement he seemed to crave. "Then why go into research?"

He stopped for a moment and then shook his head. "It doesn't matter now. What does matter is that we're here alone together.

Veronica, I don't want you to be afraid of me. And I don't want to be friends. I kissed you the other night because I couldn't help myself even though I know damn well I should."

"Why should you?" This was another thing she didn't understand. She thought he wanted her. She could sometimes feel him watching her with the focus of a predator, but he'd stayed away until very recently. He seemed like a man who went after what he wanted.

"Because you think I'm an asshole. It's not exactly the best place to start a relationship."

She couldn't deny it. He acted like an asshole most of the time, but she also thought there was something beyond his work persona. "Is there more to you than the man I see at Kronberg?"

He moved closer to her, obviously pleased to be able to answer the question. "Yes. A lot more, and I want to talk to you about it this weekend, but it has to wait. Can you trust me for one more day? I've got a meeting tomorrow morning. If that goes well, we're going to have a long talk. Everything changes if this meeting goes well."

Was he leaving Kronberg? Somehow the idea that he was getting out made her way more comfortable with him. "Are you interviewing?"

"I can only say that I'm definitely looking to go home to the States and soon," he said. "I would like for you to think about going with me." He held up a hand. "Again, no pressure at all. I can only promise you that I'll take care of you if you leave with me. I'll handle everything, including getting you out of Kronberg."

"My internship is only through the end of the year." She had another couple of months. She was already applying to hospitals back in the States. She enjoyed research but she missed having patients, missed the connection that came from dealing with people. She needed to start her life. This year had proven what she didn't want.

Unfortunately, it also proved what she did. Him.

"I can help you find a job. A good job." He shook his head as though clearing it. "We can talk about this later. Now I think I promised to show you around the Louvre. There's a nice café close. I think you'll like it. I don't know the city well, but I can show you around this neighborhood a bit."

There was something about the way he changed the subject that made her suspicious.

"Steven, is something wrong at Kronberg?" Was her sister right? Why else would he leave a job that many people would kill to have? Back in the States, he couldn't come close to the salary Kronberg had to be paying him. He would make less than half as a GP and likely work far harder.

He moved in, taking her space and leaning over to whisper in her ear. "We can talk about that tomorrow. Okay? I'll take care of everything, and that includes you. Trust me, Roni. I want to know one person in the whole world trusts me."

Her hands had come up, touching his torso, and she couldn't help the way her whole body heated at how close he was to her. His skin was soft and warm. He hugged her to him, one arm around her waist and the other coming to cup the nape of her neck. As if she was precious. Something to protect.

"No matter what happens, this thing between us, it's real. Don't forget that," he whispered. "What I feel for you is real. It's the only real thing in the world right now."

She should step back. She should wait until he'd told her exactly what he was planning to do, what was going on. But she didn't. She leaned into him, breathing in the scent of the soap he'd used, loving the way his skin felt against her own.

Why him? Why did it have to be him? She asked the question even as she felt her heart rate tick up. Being close to him, alone with him, was causing a definite physical response. Her whole body reacted to him. Her brain no longer mattered. He was difficult and complex and right. He felt right to her. "This is very real, Steven."

He winced, but the expression was gone so quickly it might have been an illusion. "I want you badly. I feel like you're the only good thing that's happened to me in years and years. I know I should wait, but I can't. I wanted you with me when I finish this."

"Finish?"

"Transition," he corrected. "I'm going to transition out of my horrible boss phase and figure out who I am again. Let's call it that."

She wasn't getting answers from him tonight. "You're a frustrating man."

His head came up and the sweetest smile crossed his face. This was why he was maddening. For every moment he was cold to a coworker, she got a private one where he was warm and made her feel safe. She'd never been the focal point of his bitter humor or the victim of his savage reactions. For some reason, the beast inside him had never swiped out at her.

What if the rumors were about jealousy? He was young and on the fast track. That could be frustrating for some people. He had the ear of the most important people at the company. There were plenty of people who would love to be in his place.

It suddenly didn't matter because his lips were hovering right above hers, and everything that was feminine inside her responded to the wounded-lion vibe he was giving off.

"I won't be," he promised. "When this is over, I'll be the simplest man you've ever met. I'll only want to love you, Roni. I've decided you're the prize I get for everything I had to go through."

Yes, all the alarm bells she should be listening to faded away. She was a prize? She was a silly girl from Galveston who had book smarts and not a bit of sense. She'd been a dreamer all her life, a romantic, and the idea that Beauty could change the Beast was still the bedrock of her fantasies.

She was on the edge with this man and the minute his lips touched hers, she knew she was in for a fall.

She wound her arms around his waist and let him lead her.

"I crave you," he said against her mouth. "I never thought I would find someone like you here. When I started this, I never fucking thought there would be more than the job."

She let her hands move up the strong muscles of his back. She wanted to believe everything he was saying, wanted to shove aside all her doubts. Truly brilliant doctors could often act like assholes when they were working. It was when they were alone that mattered. "You have to be nicer at work."

She said the words instinctively. If she was getting into this, she had to believe she could modify some of his behavior. Didn't lions get a little more tame when they took a mate?

She held her breath because he'd once told her they didn't talk about work when they were alone. It was his rule. They could talk about anything else, but not work, never Dr. McDonald. Would she see that bad side of Steven Reasor now?

He chuckled and his arms tightened. "Promise. I promise you're going to see a whole new me soon." He smoothed her hair back and seemed to get serious. "You're the only one who sees even the tiniest part of me, aren't you? You see some good in me?"

Oh, she'd found the part of Steven that melted more than her panties. This was why she couldn't hold herself apart from him. She did see something no one else saw, something that was only for her. "Yes."

He was a doctor trying to do good in the world. He was brilliant and young and he likely thought he had to be ruthlessly tough to get anywhere in their business.

What if he truly wanted to go back to the States and become a general practitioner? A sudden vision of them working and living together made the world seem happier than it had been before.

"I do," she said, staring into those sky blue eyes of his. Sometimes they could be like ice, but they were warm when he looked her way.

"You've kept me sane." He kissed her again, plastering his body against hers. "Tell me you want me as much as I want you. Tell me you came here so we can be together, so when we leave, we won't ever be apart again."

It was everything she'd dreamed of hearing from him. "I came because I couldn't stay away from you."

It was nothing less than the truth. She couldn't logic her way out of how he made her feel and she was sick of fighting it. If he left, she would go with him. She would bet on them. It was a gamble, and she didn't take many of those. This time, she would be all in.

His fingers tangled in her hair and he gently eased her head back, kissing his way down her neck. Her skin lit up and she let go of any reason she'd had previously to not do this. Since the moment he'd asked her to go to Paris with him, she'd been nervous about where it would lead. He'd asked her to keep it secret and she'd gone along because she hadn't wanted anyone to know about their relationship. She'd gotten good at ignoring him at work only to meet up with him for a private dinner or talk to him on the phone late into the night.

"I don't want this to be a secret anymore," she said. "I want them to know why you're nice to me. I want to be able to have lunch with you."

"Every day," he swore as he kissed her ear, nipping at the lobe. "When we're done here in Paris, I promise we won't have a single secret between us."

It would be good to walk in to work with him. If he got this new job of his, they wouldn't have more than a few weeks left at Kronberg, but she would be with him every step of the way. Even if they weren't in Europe, the medical world was a small place and they could have to work with some of the doctors again. She could start to let people know he wasn't the monster they made him out to be. "It'll be a fresh start."

He looked down into her eyes, one side of his mouth tugging up in a heartbreaking grin. "Baby, you have no idea. Now kiss me. Take me away from everything for a while. I only feel like myself when I'm with you."

And she was finding herself with him. She was definitely finding her sensuality with him. Her every sense seemed heightened as he leaned over and swept her into his arms. He strode through the gorgeous apartment toward the bedroom. There were two and he'd offered her the master, but she got the feeling they wouldn't be using the smaller one at all. He would be moving his duffel bag in before morning.

"I've wanted this from the moment I saw you," he said as he set her on her feet. His hands went to the hem of her shirt and he dragged it over her head before taking her mouth again.

The man knew how to kiss. His tongue surged in, sliding along hers, an invitation to dance. She couldn't refuse him. She wasn't sure if she would ever be able to refuse this man. Certainly not when his hands were on her. She didn't protest when he expertly unhooked her bra and cool air hit her skin. He tossed it away and his bare chest rubbed against hers. Her nipples peaked and everywhere he touched got warm and sensitive.

Late afternoon light streamed in through the gauzy curtains, softening everything it lit, including him. In this light he seemed younger than normal as he kissed her and led her to the bed.

She let him take control. This was what had been missing in all her past encounters. There was no awkwardness, no hesitation here. There was only Steven and what he wanted. It was easy because she did trust him. She made the decision, letting all her doubts fall away.

This was the right place to be and he was the right man for her. They would find their way.

But all that mattered now was the fact that he was pushing at the waistband of her slacks even as his tongue delved deep inside her mouth.

She needed to be naked with him. All her inhibitions were gone and only the desire to be with this man remained. Her clothes seemed to fall away and then her back was on the bed and he shoved his jeans off.

She watched with dreamy eyes as his cock came into view. Like the rest of the man, it was magnificent.

He stroked himself, his big hand moving up and down as he stared at her. "This changes everything. We're together now."

It was all she wanted, to get to truly know him with all his complexities, having time with him that they didn't have to steal. This was the start of their lives together. "Yes."

He moved between her legs, covering her with his body. "I can't wait. God, Roni, I need you so much."

He didn't have to wait. She was ready for him. She wrapped her legs around him, need driving her. All that mattered was one more kiss, one more caress, more of him.

She gasped as he thrust inside her. He filled her and warmth suffused her body. It was a heat unlike anything she'd felt before. She squirmed to accommodate him. It had been a long time since she'd been so close to a man.

He held himself still, dropping his forehead to hers. "Are you all right? Am I going too fast?"

They'd been moving toward this moment since the day they'd met. He hadn't moved fast enough for her. "I'm good. It's just been a while."

"I don't want to hurt you."

He wouldn't. This man wouldn't hurt her. He was hers and she was his. She cupped his cheek, emotion welling inside her. "You won't. Unless you stop."

She could have sworn his eyes sheened with unshed tears. "Only you would say that to me. One good thing. I found one good thing."

He didn't explain it, didn't need to because she understood. This job had been hard and now she'd found one good thing, too.

He settled in and his hips moved, sparking pleasure through her. It had never felt like this before and she rode the wave. She was so full, full of hope and life, full of him. He kissed her as he managed to hit the perfect place deep inside her, shoving her over the edge and into sheer sensation.

His body shook as he found his own pleasure and seemed to lose all his strength. His body pressed hers into the mattress, but she didn't care. This part wasn't awkward either. This part was like the rest of it—right.

"You won't regret this, baby," he whispered. "I'm going to take care of you. I'm going to be good for you. I'm going to be me again and I swear I'll do everything I can to make you happy."

It was all she could ask for.

He shifted off her but wrapped an arm around her waist and pulled her against him.

"When is your interview?" Their return flight wasn't until tomorrow evening. She wanted to do touristy stuff with him, especially if they were going back to the States soon.

"Interview?"

"For the new job?" Sex seemed to be an excellent way to distract him.

He chuckled. "Ah. Yes, there will definitely be one of those." He kissed the nape of her neck, seeming to want to drown himself in affection. "In the morning. Early. I have to go out tonight to grab a few things I'll need, but it should all be over by tomorrow afternoon, and soon I will get you crunchy bacon. I promise." He groaned and fell back. "Shit. I didn't… Sweetheart, I might have lost control…"

She turned and rolled against him, settling her head on his chest. She knew exactly what he was freaking out about. She hadn't thought about protection either, but luckily she was prepared. "I'm on the pill. It's all right."

He hugged her again and settled back down. "I promise I haven't had sex in a long time. Not since my last physical."

"Me either." She listened to the strong beat of his heart as she came down from the high of making love with him. That's what they'd done. She'd expected sex. She'd gone in knowing she would likely sleep with him. This had been so much more.

This was everything. This might be the rest of her life.

"Roni?"

"Yes?"

He smoothed back her hair. "Thank you for trusting me."

She let her leg drift over his, tangling them further. "I have questions, but yes, I trust you."

"And I'll have answers." He kissed her forehead. "But for now, I think I promised to take care of you."

His hand cupped her breast and she started to warm up again.

She lay back and let him take the lead. It didn't matter because they had all night long.

They had the rest of their lives.

* * * *

Roni checked the clock again. Four thirty. Five minutes later than the last time she checked. She'd been doing this for the last five hours and it was starting to drive her crazy. She checked her phone for what felt like the hundredth time. It was on. The ringer was on. The phone was charged and he hadn't called or returned her texts. Multiple texts. Increasingly panicked texts.

They needed to head to the airport in less than two hours and she had no sign of him.

She wondered if she should start calling hospitals but forced herself to breathe. It was okay. It was a job interview. They could take all day.

A job interview that would take them to the States. So why was he interviewing in Paris? And why had he left at dawn? Even if his appointment had been at eight he wouldn't have needed to leave so early.

He'd kissed her and told her to get some more sleep and then he'd walked away.

Without his laptop or his tablet. They were sitting on the table. They were also password protected, as she'd learned when she'd gotten desperate enough to try to read his emails so she would know where his interview was supposed to take place.

She stood in front of the big window overlooking the Tuileries Garden. She'd spent the morning exploring the beautiful park, thinking about how nice it would be to walk around with Steven's hand in hers.

Where was he? He hadn't called or answered his phone. She'd

taken the morning easy, but as the day turned to afternoon, a bit of panic had started to fill her.

Had something happened? There was a knot in her stomach, a knot of worry that he'd somehow gotten hurt.

Or she'd gotten played.

Roni took a deep breath and banished the thought. She wasn't falling into that hole. He wouldn't have left his laptop behind if he hadn't meant to come back. He'd made love to her all night. He'd only left her briefly to grab pizza and wine, and he'd ordered her to stay naked. The minute he'd walked back in, he'd shucked his clothes and they'd eaten and drank and talked until they'd made love again.

He wasn't playing her. No man could make love like that and not mean it.

He hadn't had to play her. She'd meant to go to bed with him. She would have done it without all the promises.

But the promises are what made it fun for him. A guy like that enjoys the game and you weren't playing it, so he found a way to make you.

She sniffled as her inner voice turned distinctly dark.

Why would a man like that walk away from a job with a major pharmaceutical company? From a team that's supposedly on the edge of some major accomplishments? That man—the youngest team lead in Kronberg history—that man wants to be a GP and marry a woman who barely qualified for the internship program? Who isn't close to his league looks-wise? You really thought that man would give it all up for you?

Or she could be positive. He was stuck. The interview had gone well and he'd been offered the job. The mystery job he hadn't wanted to talk about.

Damn it.

She stared out, trying to find some calm, but then she saw something that absolutely wrecked her.

A woman was walking up the street, her high heels not holding her back at all. She was a woman who knew how to walk in those expensive things she could probably use as a weapon if she needed to. She didn't since she had a big bodyguard with her, one Roni hadn't seen before.

Dr. Hope McDonald was walking down the street and there was

no question in Roni's mind where she was going. The big guy beside her had dark hair cut in a military style. He wore a suit that probably hid a gun. McDonald was a US senator's daughter and she rarely went anywhere without some muscle.

The knot in her gut twisted because there was zero way this was a coincidence.

McDonald and the big guy disappeared from sight as they walked into the building, but it wasn't more than two minutes before there was a knock on the door.

Maybe she could simply stay quiet and McDonald would go away. She had her ticket back to Munich.

Or something had happened to Steven and she was being a colossal idiot. She'd told him she was with him and she was wilting at the first sign of trouble. That wasn't the kind of partner she wanted to be.

She ran to the door and threw it open. It didn't matter that the head of the project was about to know she was sleeping with the lead researcher. All that mattered was finding out what had gone wrong. "Dr. McDonald? Has something happened to Steven?"

Hope McDonald was a lovely blonde with green eyes that managed to constantly look cold. Even when she was smiling there was an emptiness in the doctor's eyes that unnerved Roni. It was probably why McDonald had gone into research. There was something off-putting about the woman that would likely lead to anxiety in any patient she worked on. She said all the right words, acted empathetic, but Roni always thought it was an act.

Some people said the same thing of Steven Reasor.

"Why don't you let me in, dear?" Hope didn't wait for her to move, merely stepped around her and entered the apartment. She glanced around the living room, her gaze calculating. "This isn't as posh as I would have thought. It needs a feminine touch."

"Dr. McDonald? What are you doing here? Do you know where Steven is?" He hadn't wanted to tip off McDonald about the interview, but she was too worried to keep her mouth shut and it was far too coincidental that the doctor would show up just as Steven seemed to disappear.

Something is wrong at Kronberg. Something dangerous is going on and I don't want to see my sister in the middle of it, Katie had warned her.

Had Steven been in the middle of it? Why had Rebecca run? Had she left for the same reason Steven had been trying to get another job?

"Of course I know where Steven is," McDonald said, finally facing her. "He's back in Munich. He left after our meeting this morning but he won't be there long. I had to have this little interview with him here in Paris. Such a lovely city."

His meeting had been with McDonald? But he'd said he was leaving Kronberg. "Why would you interview Steven? He already works for you."

"This is a promotion, dear. He's going to head my Argentina office. I've got an interesting project going on down there at Kronberg's Buenos Aires subsidiary." McDonald sighed, not paying any attention to the big man behind her. He was staring straight ahead, no expression on his face. "I wanted to talk to him before I approved his transfer."

"He said he was going back to the States."

She frowned and her eyes rolled. "He's such a bastard. If he weren't so good at his job, I swear I would fire him. I knew he was up to something when he insisted I come and pick up the rest of his things." She glanced at the guard. "Robert? I believe that's his laptop and tablet. Get those, please."

The big man picked them up along with the duffel bag Roni had put on the table when she'd decided to look through Steven's email. He silently slipped them inside and zipped it up.

Dr. McDonald's focus was back on her. "So he didn't mention that he was leaving Germany and going to South America? I suppose he also didn't bother to tell you he won't be coming back for at least a year."

Her heart dropped. "No. He didn't." None of this made sense. "He bought round-trip tickets. Why would he do that if he wasn't coming back with me? And why would he send you? He could have texted."

She shrugged. "It's his game, dear. And I assume he sent me here as a message. Not for you. For me. I've been neglectful and he wants me to know it. I've been busy and I haven't paid attention to him. He gets jealous and he wants me to be, too."

She hadn't thought her heart could sink any lower, but the

implications of her words struck out like a slap. "You...I didn't know."

"Well, we can't advertise our relationship, of course. I'm his superior. Our relationship is somewhat out of the ordinary. He needs his little games to feel like a man. You know the type?"

She didn't. She didn't understand anything at all. Why would he do this to her? What was the purpose? How could he have looked at her the way he had? Like she meant the whole world to him.

Dr. McDonald seemed to take her silence as an opportunity to lecture. "He plays with women, Veronica. He needs to conquer. I'm sure that having a female as a boss doesn't help. Steven is quite aggressive when it comes to sex. When it comes to anything, really."

Tears pierced her eyes.

"You truly didn't know, did you?" She turned to the big man behind her and gestured to him. He stepped back outside. "It seems Robert is not necessary. I have to worry. It wouldn't be the first time one of Steven's perverse games went awry. I lost Dr. Walsh because of him. I hope I won't lose you, too. I promise, he won't be back in Munich for a long time. He's been naughty and I intend to rehabilitate him."

She was talking like it was all some schoolyard thing she should easily forget about. One thing had come through clearly. "He did this to Rebecca? He slept with her?"

"Oh, he spent quite a bit of time with her," she said with an odd smile. It was almost wistful. "At least I'm sure it felt that way to Dr. Walsh. You know it's all about perception in the end. But if you're worried that people will think less of you, I assure you they won't. Steven does this to everyone. Well, all the women at least. I thank god he isn't more open-minded or I wouldn't be able to keep a staff at all. Now I have to go. We're leaving in a few hours."

It didn't make sense. Except maybe it did. Why had she thought this could work?

Dr. McDonald stopped at the door. "I'm sorry, Veronica. You're quite good at your job. You could be a functional doctor if you had a lick of confidence in yourself. I'm sure the innocence you project, the meekness, only made him more attracted to you. He's a bit like the devil, that one. He likes to trick people, enjoys knowing he has the upper hand. I will admit, I like to play some of those games, too, and

Steven understands I'm better at them than he is. Do you need a ride to the airport?"

There was no way she was getting in that woman's car. "I'm fine. Thank you, Dr. McDonald. My flight doesn't leave until later tonight. I'll see you back in Munich."

She would decide what to do later. Even if Steven wasn't physically there on a daily basis, she wasn't sure she could work there. She would forever be waiting to turn a corner and see him there, feel the burn of humiliation as he smirked and walked past her like she was nothing.

"Suit yourself," McDonald said with a shrug. "You'll need to report to the new lead. I'm letting Kronberg bring someone in from their Bern office. Try not to let this one fuck you over, dear. Good luck."

The door closed behind her and Roni was alone again.

The silence suddenly seemed deafening.

Chapter One

London, England
Three years later

Roni stopped outside the room where she'd been told Steven Reasor now lay in a coma. It was so normal. Not the building. The building was some kind of rich man's paradise complete with a lobby that looked like it could be the front for a French bordello. And a garden in the foyer. If one could call the entire center of a building a foyer. There was probably some other term for it, but she hadn't spent the last several years learning about design.

She'd spent them trying to survive.

"Why should I believe you?" She winced because she hadn't meant to say the words out loud. Still, she turned to the woman who had shown up on her doorstep not two days before with the most incredible story. Kimberly Solomon was a CIA agent, if she was telling the truth—which Roni's mother was absolutely certain she wasn't. Oh, her mother believed Solomon worked for the CIA, but her mother didn't trust anyone at all.

The gorgeous blonde had made a pretty convincing case, including documents and photos and a bunch of knowledge she shouldn't have had. And the woman could call up a special ops team whenever she liked. The woman, who liked to be called Solo, glanced at the closed door and back to Roni as though she knew she was stalling. "I've shown you all the documentation I can legally offer. I've explained who I am and why we need you. I can't do anything else, Roni. You either have to trust me or not, and I understand how hard that is."

"I don't trust her and I know exactly who she is." The massive hunk of Viking DNA who'd greeted her when she'd entered the building watched Solo with suspicious eyes. Ian Taggart was a golden god of a man, and he knew all the right things to say.

You are safe here. I'm not the Agency and I won't allow Solo to steal you away. All I'm looking for is some answers to help my men. You are free to come and go as you please, but if you need protection from something, we are here for you. I don't know what Solo told you about us, but I promise no one is going to fuck with you here. We've got a room for you. If you need sanctuary, you have it.

The former Green Beret had said the words not ten minutes before and it had been right on the tip of her tongue to tell him yes, she wanted his help. She wanted to throw the entire situation into someone more competent's hands so she could finally have some kind of a life, but she remembered everything Steven had told her that day, how comfortable he'd made her feel before he'd cut her to pieces and left her pregnant and alone and in danger.

For her daughter's sake, she couldn't be a trusting fool anymore.

She was right back to staring at the door.

"Does she think there's like a lion behind it or something?" Taggart asked under his breath.

She could practically hear Solo rolling her eyes. "No. She thinks her ex is behind the door and she's not ready to see him again. Give her a minute, Tag. Or better yet, I'll stay with her and you can take your impatient ass to the conference room. I assume Damon has one. All the best sex clubs do."

They'd been needling each other from the moment Solo had walked her in the door. From what she'd heard, Solo had done something to this private security group they hadn't forgiven her for yet, and they all spoke the language of sarcasm. They continued to bicker as she stared at the door and utterly ignored the sex club joke. She didn't think about sex anymore.

She dreamed about it. She dreamed about the one man who'd shown her exactly how good sex could be, the one man she couldn't forget no matter how hard she tried.

Was Steven Reasor here? Was he lying in a bed behind that door?

"How did you catch him?" She hadn't asked all the pertinent questions. Solo had shown up with her convincing documents and much needed cash and Roni had made the calculated decision to go with her. Up until now Solo hadn't given away the fact that she had a secret daughter. It seemed like Taggart and his group had no idea Violet Croft existed. Not that anyone knew her real name. According to all the German records her name was Violet Fisher, daughter of Veronica Fisher. After what had happened to her sister, Katie, she and her mother had gone underground.

Taggart frowned, the expression doing nothing to mar his masculine beauty. "Catch him?"

"Yes, how did you catch Steven? I assume he ran when Dr. McDonald did," she said, taking a deep breath and stepping back. She wasn't ready to see him yet. She moved to the railing and looked out over the green space below. It was peaceful, but she'd learned that looks could be deceiving. "Was he injured when the CIA raided?"

Taggart snorted. "The CIA didn't raid shit."

"Only because someone didn't bother to bring us in," Solo countered. "And you're welcome."

Taggart squared off with the CIA agent. "For what?"

Despite the fact that Solo was almost six feet tall, she looked petite compared to Taggart. "For not being in a French jail right now."

"Yeah, because French jail would be so tough on a guy," Taggart replied. "I think I handled the authorities pretty well."

"Or a Colombian jail," Solo replied. "You remember that one? It wasn't Drew Lawless who got you out. That was Beck, and who do you think he called to make that happen?"

"Okay, I am willing to admit that I'm grateful for that one," Taggart allowed. "I was pretty close to becoming a prison wife. There are some big fucking dudes in Cartagena, and they're mean. Charlie would have broken me out, but not before I lost something precious. She would have taken me back, though. She told me I should absolutely accept dishonor before death. I think she only said that because she needs my diaper-changing skills."

They were starting to annoy her. "I can leave if you two want to keep the comedy hour going."

"I'm sorry." Solo backed off. "I'm anxious about being here. Tag is a massive jackass most of the time, but he's solid when it comes to his job. And you need to understand that Tucker wasn't captured in any kind of a criminal way. He was McDonald's prisoner."

She really should have asked more questions, but Solo had offered her a whole lot of cash for coming with her, and that cash might be able to get them all back to the States. It might buy them a new life. "Prisoner? He was her employee. Her favorite employee. Why would she keep him prisoner?"

"We were hoping you could help us with that," Taggart said, his frown deepening. "But you're wrong. He was definitely her prisoner. She experimented on him." He turned to Solo. "How much did you tell her?"

"I told her we needed her to identify Steven Reasor." Solo leaned back against the wall. "I have to work within certain parameters. A lot of what I know is highly classified. You don't have that problem. I mean what you know is absolutely classified but you don't care."

A single shoulder shrugged. "Not in any way."

"But I think she knows more than she's saying," Solo replied, her blue eyes serious. "I'm fairly certain she knows what Dr. McDonald was working on. Her sister was writing an investigative piece when she died."

"When she was murdered." She wasn't going to let anyone pretend Katie had been killed in a random street crime. "Assassinated might be a better word. Or executed. I don't have anything of hers if you're looking for her notes. I don't have them."

"No one is trying to take anything from you." Taggart's shoulders straightened and his eyes had softened. "I promise. I hope you come to trust us. Dr. Walsh has."

"Rebecca Walsh is here?" She hadn't seen Rebecca in years, not since the day she'd walked away. She'd read about Rebecca's accomplishments, but she hadn't reached out to her. Rebecca had been the one who'd gotten away free and clear. At least it had seemed that way. Dr. McDonald's reach went beyond the grave.

"You really didn't tell her anything," Taggart said, a bit of accusation in his tone.

"I wanted to leave it to you," Solo replied quietly.

"I have nothing to do with it," Taggart argued. "You wanted to leave it all to Ezra so he'll forgive you for what happened in Munich. You want to push your way into this mission so you can be close to him."

"You would do the same in my place."

Taggart's head shook. "Nope. I would never have picked my job over my Charlie, which is precisely why I got out. But I get it. Ms. Croft, I don't need you to identify Reasor. Dr. Walsh already has. The man you knew as Steven Reasor now goes by the name of Tucker. At some point McDonald turned on Reasor. She used an experimental drug to erase his memories and held him captive for several years. I'll let you read the files I have on him."

It felt like the world shifted and she couldn't find her balance. "She used the drug on him? What drug? I know about the time dilation drug, but that wouldn't cause memory loss."

Katie had found evidence that McDonald was working on a drug and therapy protocols for time dilation. It sounded like something out of a science fiction movie. McDonald had been developing a drug that tricked the brain into thinking time was passing more quickly than it was. It made the patient open to influence and suggestion.

It could be used to torture someone without ever harming them physically. A day would seem like a month, pain and fear made to seem endless.

Had Steven gone through that? Had Steven helped McDonald create a monster only to be fed to it?

"It wasn't the time dilation drug, though he was definitely put through that hell," Taggart explained. "She had a drug that affected memory, too."

"Is that why he's in a coma? The drug? McDonald supposedly died three years ago. He's been in a coma for that long? Or was it a side effect of coming off the drug?"

She hadn't practiced medicine in the last few years, but she remembered the dangers of testing new drugs. It was precisely why they didn't go straight to human trials, but then McDonald hadn't seemed to care much about other humans.

"He's only been in a coma for a few weeks," Tag explained.

"And it wasn't from the initial drug. He'd recovered physically from that and he was starting to get back a bit of his memory. While McDonald held him, Tucker was given another drug, one that completely erased his memory. McDonald used it in conjunction with the time dilation to build soldiers. Tucker was one of those soldiers. So was my youngest brother."

That made her catch her breath. McDonald had taken this man's brother? It had likely been her downfall. She'd only met Taggart a few minutes before, but she knew a dangerous predator when she saw one.

Now. Now she could recognize a dangerous man. It was because she'd been torn apart by one once. By the man behind that door.

"Tucker was a victim," Solo said.

She wasn't buying it. In this, she could instruct them. "I'm sorry to hear about your brother, Mr. Taggart. I can't imagine what he went through, but Steven was likely a part of it. I assure you he knew everything McDonald was doing. He was her right-hand man the whole time. There's an old Chinese proverb that fits Steven to a T. *He who rides the tiger is afraid to dismount.* He played with fire and he got burned. Steven liked to play games. If you've brought me here to exonerate him, you've wasted your time and I should head home to Germany."

There was a part of her that wanted that exact outcome. It was perverse. She'd prayed every day for years that she would get her life back, that she could return to medicine and take her daughter home, but now that she was facing it, there was a certain amount of dread that came with change. At least she knew what to expect from her life in Germany.

"We've brought you here to try to help figure out the last few days of Reasor's life," Taggart corrected. "I call it that because Steven Reasor effectively ceased to exist the day McDonald erased his memory. We're hoping you can fill in some of the blanks because Tucker can't. We need information concerning McDonald's experiments and the people who worked with her. We're fairly certain Tucker knew who supported her crimes at one point. I think he might have stolen that information. I'm not sure why, but he's my best bet. You knew him better than anyone else."

She knew how he kissed and what it felt like when he wrapped his arms around her and held her tight, the embrace promising protection. She knew he was a liar of the highest order. "I don't know how much I can help you. He didn't tell me anything. You should know that up front. If that changes Ms. Solomon's offer of cash and safety, then I should leave now."

"I told you she was touchy," Solo said under her breath.

"Whatever Solo offered you, she'll come through," Taggart explained. "She's a woman of her word. Mostly. If she doesn't, I can assure you my firm will take care of it. The Garden is the safest place I know of in Europe. If you want to come to the States, I'll make sure you're safe there, too. You and your daughter."

A chill went through her. She turned on Solo. "There's one promise broken."

Solo sighed and crossed her arms over her chest. "I didn't tell him anything, but I should have known he has someone watching me. Whoever it is, he's good."

"She," Taggart said with a smirk. "Nina Blunt is one of Damon's new hires. She's former Interpol. It was a team effort, though. Hutch caught you going into Germany and Nina did the groundwork." He seemed to sober. "This is too important to me and my men to leave this all in your hands, Solo. You've got people to answer to, people who might not do the right thing with the information if they got their hands on it. Ms. Croft, Solo didn't tell me about your daughter. Is the older woman traveling with you your mother?"

She nodded, not sure how she felt about anyone knowing about her baby. Maybe that was one of the reasons she was scared of going home. She wouldn't be able to hide Violet. "Yes. When my sister was murdered, she came over and she's stayed with me."

"I stashed them at my place in Kensington," Solo explained. "It's not far from here. I think they should be moved to The Garden, but Veronica wanted to check it out first. The mom is actually pretty badass. Former Army."

Taggart's brow lifted. "Good. Then we'll speak the same language. I'll want a dossier, but she's more than welcome." He glanced down at his watch. "We've got the group meeting in twenty. If you don't want to see him, how about we make our way to the conference room and we can start to get some details worked out."

Did she want to see him? Was she stepping on a land mine and praying it wouldn't go off? He was alive. She'd been numb up to this point, and there was a lot of comfort in that detached feeling. Would she be able to keep that distance if she looked at him, if this became real?

She stared at the door for a moment but then the choice was taken out of her hands. The door flew open and a man with reddish hair stepped out, a wild look in his eyes.

"Rebecca!" He yelled out the name and Roni could hear the thick Scottish accent even in the single word. He looked to Taggart. "I need Rebecca. She went to grab some coffee before I left for the meeting. I don't know what happened. Something's wrong with Tucker."

There was a beeping sound, the one every doctor in the world knew meant trouble.

She pushed past the Scottish man and into the room because either something was malfunctioning with the equipment or the man on the bed was dying.

Steven. He was right there. He was starker than he'd been, thinner, and his hair longer. But this was the man who had held her all night long, the man responsible for her pain, for the last few years of hardship.

For her daughter. God, was she going to watch her daughter's father die in front of her?

Taggart had the defibrillation unit in his hand.

She grabbed it and got to work.

Chapter Two

Tucker was in hell. Or heaven. He couldn't decide which.

The dreams shifted in and out. Dreams? He wasn't sure if they were dreams or reality bleeding into this place he found himself in. There were times when he could hear his brothers talking. Jax would be joking with Owen about some football match they were watching, the TV volume low in the background. He wanted to open his eyes and join them. They would be passing each other beers and munching on whatever snacks they could find. It would be nice and normal and he could pretend nothing had happened.

Or Robert would read aloud to him. The freaking news. *Why?* Tucker had asked inwardly. He was stuck in his body and Robert wanted him to keep up with current events? The least the man could do was read him something interesting.

Other times he was stuck in moments. Those were the times he wasn't sure about because it seemed real to him. He was there. He could see and hear and smell and touch. The best of times was when he was with a woman. Not some random woman, a very specific one. Veronica. Roni. He called her Roni right before he cupped her face and kissed her. He was so close. The feeling was there in his heart. He was close to having everything he wanted, and she was part of it. If he could get away, they could have a life together.

All he had to do was…

What was he supposed to do? He had something to do, something that would make everything else okay. Something that would give him back his life.

He had to remember. Had to remember. Had to remember.

The pain started. It flashed through him with white-hot agony that threatened to melt his bones and leave him ravaged. He screamed out, in pain, in rage, because he'd been so close. The memory was right there, right on the edge. It was a shadow he couldn't quite catch.

"I need you to stand back," a female voice said.

Familiar. Haunting.

So close. She was in his arms. She'd felt right in his arms and then he was running. Running from her but not the same her. There was an angel and a devil in his dreams. He ran from one. Ran to the other.

Why did the devil have to catch him? Why couldn't he have stayed in bed with his angel? Would that have fixed things? Or would it have gotten her killed, too?

He'd been killed. He was a dead man walking, moving through his days without a past to animate him, to show him the path. So many people depending on him and he couldn't remember his own fucking name.

Lightning flashed through him and he felt his whole body go stiff.

"Charging," the voice said.

Darkness. He was used to the darkness, but now there was a bit of light.

Did he want to find that light? The darkness wasn't so bad. He got to see her here, flashes of a time when he'd seen the possibilities laid in front of him. If he left, she would be nothing more than a flicker at the back of his head, something he tried to catch but couldn't.

He would look for her in every woman he met. When the tension got to be too much and he had to have a woman, he would pick one who looked like her, instinct leading him when memory could not. She was every woman he'd gone to bed with in the last few years.

But if he stayed here, he could be with her in those last few moments before the world had exploded. Time stopped here. He could choose again.

Another jolt of lightning and he realized he wasn't going to have a choice. He was being thrust into the light and there was no way to stop it.

But then he hadn't had a choice since the day Levi Green had walked into his life, had he? He'd been set on a path and nothing would take him off it. Not even falling in love with Roni.

Levi Green. He'd been there. He'd been with Levi Green in some city that wasn't his home. His home was green fields and mountains. His home was the river winding through the valley, but he'd been born again in a city awash with lights. And yet again in that lab, harsh light welcoming him into a world of pain and misery.

"I've got a rhythm." The voice sounded closer now.

"What happened?" Rebecca. He knew her voice. "Oh, my god. He was fine when I left."

"He had a cardiac event, an acute coronary syndrome. Has he been having trouble with his heart?"

He wanted to open his eyes because that voice was so familiar. Where had he heard it before?

"No. He's been solid," Rebecca said. "But we don't know what that damn drug did to him, and according to Levi it was the only dose so I can't even test it to figure out what was in it."

"He's telling the truth about that." The husky voice belonged to Kim Solomon.

"How can you be sure?" Rebecca asked.

"Because I was pretty much twisting his balls off his body when he told me," she replied. "Trust me. He would have given up anything to get me to stop. Is Tucker okay? Should we get him to a hospital?"

"Stephanie is on her way up," Owen said.

Owen. His brother. One of them. He had brothers not born of blood but of suffering and sacrifice.

Sasha had sacrificed to save Owen. He was down a brother.

He owed his brothers everything. The darkness would have to wait.

He blinked and stared up at the light.

He hated that fucking light. That light had always signaled another procedure, another dose of McDonald's medicine. Medicine to make her boys behave.

"Tucker?" Owen stared down at him, moving in front of the light and blocking it out. "Tucker? You're awake, mate?"

Rebecca was right at his side. "How are you feeling? We need to run some tests."

"I'm okay." He wanted to sit up but he was so tired. "What happened? Where am I?"

"You're at The Garden," Rebecca said. "You've been in a coma for three weeks. I need you to go slow. I still don't completely understand what's going on. You've just had a cardiac event. I'm going to have to study the reports to figure out exactly what happened. Ian, I need to clear the room. Steph and I will check him out and decide if we need to transfer him to the hospital."

"You know why that's a bad idea," Ian replied.

"I don't need a hospital." Hospitals asked questions and checked records and tended to let Interpol know when a red notice walked in. Besides, he was feeling stronger already. "Levi Green gave me a drug."

"Yes." Owen stood behind his girlfriend, nodding. "That fucker put you in a coma, but apparently Solo's been playing with his balls in a not-good way."

He'd always liked Solo. God, it was starting to come back to him. They'd been in trouble. Munich. He'd been in Munich at Kronberg and everywhere he'd looked he'd seen ghosts.

Robert. Robert had been with him. All of his brothers had shown up. Robert and Jax and Owen and Theo. Dante. Dante, the betrayer. Dante had been McDonald's attack dog, hiding in plain sight, pretending to be one of them. Dante had killed Sasha and Ari had killed Dante.

And then he'd felt the burn of the drug entering his system. Yes. He remembered. He'd been caught by Green. Green wanted the information they'd broken into Kronberg to retrieve—a list of all of the people who worked with McDonald. Green wanted the list so he could get his place at the CIA back. The Lost Boys wanted it because it might help lead them to figuring out who they'd been before McDonald had erased them from the world.

"Are you really okay?" Owen asked.

He would be if Rebecca would stop examining him. He'd passed out and stayed out for three weeks. His head was foggy, but he needed some answers. "Is everyone okay? The last thing I remember…Ari killed Dante."

"Yes, she saved Rebecca, but I'm so sorry we couldn't save you." Owen had gotten to one knee, giving Rebecca space to work, but it was obvious he wasn't going to leave. "But we didn't let that bastard get away."

"Hey, maybe we should let Tucker rest." Ian stood at the back of the room. "He's been through a lot and I want to make sure he's all right before he gets out of that bed."

He wanted nothing more than to get out of this damn bed. He had a million questions. "I want a debrief. I want to know what's been happening. Everyone got out of the building okay?"

He started to try to sit up.

Rebecca put a hand on his chest. "No. You stay where you are until I'm satisfied."

Normally a gorgeous woman telling him he couldn't leave the bed until he'd satisfied her would be a good thing. Not today. "I want to stretch. Let me get up and walk around. I don't feel weak."

"Well, you had a cardiac incident, so I disagree." Rebecca wasn't backing down.

"Besides, if you get up now you'll have to carry your pee bag with you unless you plan on ripping the catheter out," Tag said. "I know that sounds manly, but the girlie scream that will come from your mouth when you rip it out of your dick will be anything but."

He stared at Tag. Naturally his boss was here to add much needed sarcasm to an already surreal situation. "What?"

Tag shrugged. "You were in a coma. Rebecca here thought you still needed fluids. I personally would have taken a Darwinian approach and set you outside to collect rainwater, but she had to be all technological. When you're hydrated you pee. Again, I was willing to buy some puppy pads…"

Sometimes he hated his boss. "I get it. I'm going to need someone to very gently remove that. Not Rebecca."

She was like his sister. She'd probably seen him naked at this point if she was doing all the medical stuff. Yes, she was a doctor, but she was also living with his brother and that meant she shouldn't know what his penis looked like, much less have intimate knowledge of how to thread a tube through the tip of it.

He was going to fucking murder Levi Green.

"She's very gentle, mate," Owen offered.

Rebecca rolled her eyes. "I'm very professional, and you get to pick between me and Steph. We're the only ones I trust to do it."

"I could do it," Tag offered.

"I'll do it. After all, I'm a professional, too," a voice from behind him said.

The world seemed to stop at the sound. He knew that voice. Where did he know that voice from? It had seemed so clear only moments before. When he'd been in the dark place, he'd known more than he did in the light.

She stepped into his line of sight. She was petite, no more than five foot three, but she had curves. Rich brown hair skimmed the tops of her breasts, though he couldn't exactly see those because she was wearing a sweater. Wide eyes and generous lips. She was exactly his type. This was the type of woman he sought out again and again.

But she was frowning at him and he so wanted to see her smile. It was what he always wanted. He hated it when she was sad. But he couldn't be overt about it. He couldn't simply walk up to her and do nice things because he had a job to do and…

Pain struck his head, hard and fast. His vision went foggy as he tried to hang on. He'd seen it when he was dreaming. He'd seen her.

"Damn it," Rebecca said. "Tucker, I need you to stop thinking. Could we clear the room?"

He managed to shake his head and forced himself to focus because this was important. She was important.

He knew her.

"Veronica." He managed to say her name. This was Veronica Croft. This was the woman who haunted his every dream.

God, he hoped he hadn't hurt her.

"Hello, Steven." She was looking at him like he was a bug and she couldn't figure out whether to step on him or walk by.

He'd been happy with her. He'd taken her to bed and wrapped himself around her. For those hours she'd been his whole world and it was okay because he was almost done. He could get out and tell her the truth.

What the fuck was the truth? He screamed the question in his head because the answer slipped away.

"Tucker, calm down," Rebecca admonished.

"What's happening?" Stephanie Carter jogged into the room. She was The Garden's resident doctor. Tucker had worked with her many times, offering his own weird medical skills to her solid ones.

He would be able to open a practice when he was done. He was only putting it off for a little while. Just until he found…

He screamed as his brain threatened to explode.

"What's wrong with him?" Veronica asked.

He looked at her, needing to keep her in sight even if it killed him. "Don't be afraid."

He didn't want her to be afraid of him. Everyone else was. It was necessary, but he couldn't stand the thought of *her* being afraid.

Tag had a hand on her arm, ready to guide her away. "McDonald trained his brain to punish him when he tries to remember. It's bad and he's making it worse. We should get out of here and let the docs get him calm again."

If she left, he might not see her again.

He'd left. He'd walked out, but he'd meant to come back. He'd gone to meet…

A soft hand was suddenly against his cheek. "Hey, it's all right. You don't have to remember." She was here. She was sitting on the bed, her eyes softer than they'd been before. "Steven…"

"Tucker," he managed between clenched teeth because the pain was still ravaging him. "My name is Tucker. I'm not that fucker Reasor. Not anymore."

She bit her bottom lip and seemed to come to a decision. "All right, Tucker. It's okay. Let it go."

"Need to remember." If he could remember, he might get her back. He might figure out what he was supposed to do. It was always there, low-level anxiety in the back of his brain like a humming he couldn't get rid of. He was supposed to do something. People were counting on him. Lives were at stake and he was lying in bed.

Her hand smoothed back his hair. "No, you don't. Not now. It's all right. Let it go. We can talk about something else. Lie back down and let it go."

She was so beautiful. Her eyes were a golden hazel. Sometimes she wore glasses. Tortoise shell. They made her look like a sweet librarian. "Where are your glasses?"

Her eyes widened slightly. "I got contacts."

"His heart rate is normal again." Rebecca looked back at him from the machine she was monitoring. "Keep talking. I think you're calming him down."

Roni glanced her way. "This isn't fair."

He lay down but reached for her hand. "I liked your glasses. I always thought about taking them off and laying them to the side before I kissed you. I missed you. God, even when I couldn't remember your name I missed you. It's better now."

The pain was receding. He was tired again, but her hand in his felt so good. He threaded their fingers together.

"Nothing in his life has been fair," Tag said quietly. "I don't know who he was before, but he's a good man now. I'm going to move the meeting. We can do this tomorrow and hopefully Tucker can be there."

"Not until I'm sure he's okay," Rebecca replied.

They were talking, but he didn't care. She was here.

She looked down and there was a sheen of tears in her eyes. "This isn't fair."

But she didn't take her hand back. He wrapped his other hand around hers, trapping her because it might not be fair to her, but this was what he needed.

Even as he fell back asleep, he was warm for once.

* * * *

"You sure you want to do this?" Solo parked the Audi in the tiny garage connected to the small but luxurious apartment she owned here in London. It had been the first place they'd gone after the private jet had brought them here from Germany. "You can stay here for as long as you like. I'll take you back and forth to The Garden."

"I'm not sure of anything." Roni sighed, the events of the day playing through her head. She'd sat there for a long time, holding Steven's hand even as he'd fallen into a natural sleep. She should have immediately walked out, but she hadn't been able to do it. She'd sat there listening to the doctors talk about what had happened, staring at his face and wondering what he'd been through in the last few years. "I don't know that man."

Except she did. The man who had told her he liked her glasses and held her hand like she was a lifeline was exactly the Steven Reasor she'd fallen for.

This was not how she'd expected to feel. She wasn't sure what she'd expected beyond anger, but it certainly hadn't been compassion. More than that, she hadn't expected how warm she would feel the minute he'd touched her. He'd engulfed her hand with both of his and she'd remembered how safe this man could make her feel.

Did she not have the whole story?

"It might be good to keep some distance," Solo said, not moving to get out of the car. "I know Ian wants you to stay at The Garden, but I can handle him if you want to stay here. I'll go with you back and forth and your mom can keep Violet. Ian isn't going to mention her to Tucker right away. You have some time."

She shook her head. "No. If I'm going to do this, I should be there. Besides, I'll feel better if Mom and Vi aren't alone all day. Mrs. Knight showed me around. The building looks secure. And I was told I could work with someone named Jax to get me everything I need to eventually return to the States."

Jax, she'd been told, was some kind of genius with a computer. He might be able to help her with more than mere documents. She still had questions. So many of them, and it appeared the people Steven was aligned with might have answers.

"I think that's a good idea. I'll hand over everything I have on your case."

"Will you stick around?" She'd gotten used to Solo. She didn't trust the woman completely, but so far Solo had come through for her.

"For as long as I can," Solo replied. "You should understand they don't trust me. My ex-husband is in charge of the team Tucker's on. I had to do something they didn't like a couple of weeks back, and to say he wasn't happy would be understating things."

It had been interesting watching Solo deal with a bunch of very suspicious people. "So Taggart's right and you came after me as penance?"

"Pretty much." She opened the door. "Not that it's likely to work. Let's get you packed up. Have you decided what you're going to say about little miss sunshine? Or are you going to lie to him?"

She forced herself to move, opening the door as the garage closed behind her. "He's her father. If he'd lived, I would have told him about her. Likely in four letter words. Trust me. I meant to get cash out of that asshole. But then…"

"Your sister was killed." Solo tapped the code in to open the door to the townhouse. It beeped and turned green.

"And then I was told Steven died." She could still remember hearing that news. She'd been caught between rage and relief. There had been no closure for her, no moment when she could tell the man exactly what she thought. No moment when he could tell her why he'd done what he'd done.

Solo opened the door and stepped into the hallway that led to her ultramodern kitchen. "How did you find out Reasor was dead?"

"I kept in touch with one of my sister's friends. She wasn't interested in following up on Katie's story, but she sent along information about McDonald and her group." Her sister's friend had sent her the information quietly, and she'd been the one to tell them to stay hidden. Roni had tried to learn as much as she could about what Katie had been investigating. She didn't know everything. There was a lot she seemed to have gotten wrong, and she owed her sister. She needed to find the truth and hold people accountable. "Dr. McDonald was a pro. She even had a small newspaper in Argentina cover the story of his death."

"Yes, she had help, I suspect," Solo said. "Her father was a senator with ties to the Agency."

"Which is precisely why we shouldn't be working with a CIA agent." Her mother stood in the kitchen. Despite the fact that it was almost ten p.m., her mom hadn't changed into pajamas. Nope. There was no fluffy robe and slippers in her mom's closet. She was dressed in the utilitarian cargo pants and T-shirt she normally wore. The better to hide all her weapons. Sandra Croft had been a nurse in the Army, but she was more of a soldier now than she'd ever been. Since losing Katie, her mother had gotten infinitely harder. "But I believe I've made my opinion plain."

"You certainly have, Mom." They'd gone endless rounds over it. "You get your wish. We're leaving."

Her mom's shoulders dropped in obvious relief. "Good. I'll get Violet ready."

Roni braced herself for another fight. "We're moving over to The

Garden. I met with Taggart and he seems solid. There's a lot we don't know, and I think his group can help us. I've got a piece of the puzzle and he has several. I want to know what he does."

"I didn't mean we should trade one CIA operative for another," her mom said, her mouth a flat line. "I meant we should go back to Germany. I was making headway."

She was lying to herself was what she was doing. It had been a solid year since they'd had a lead to follow concerning Katie's death. No one cared anymore. But Taggart might, especially if she could prove Katie was involved in trying to take down McDonald.

"Taggart's not CIA," Solo said, leaning against the island. "He got out a long time ago and really, that was for the best. He's shit at undercover. The man is totally impatient and intolerant. I heard once he punched an informant because he chewed too loudly. He's better at shooting things. It fits his personality."

Her mother ignored Solo. "And that Knight fellow is former MI6. Former MI6 means he's likely currently associated with them. Do you understand what you're risking?"

"Mom, I can't hide forever. I can't pretend like no one will ever find me as long as I work in a tiny Bavarian town selling tourists Christmas ornaments." It was how she'd spent the last few years. "Besides, I don't honestly think anyone is coming after us, and maybe they never were. They got Katie. They don't care about us. I've wasted years and I'm not going to put Violet through more."

Her daughter would have to go to school soon. She couldn't exactly tell the authorities that her work visa was fake because she was certain someone was trying to kill her over her dead sister's investigation into Illuminati-like corporations, so her daughter needed a bodyguard while she learned her letters. Nope. That wouldn't work at all. It would all start to fall apart soon.

When she thought about it, Solo showing up on her doorstep had been a miracle.

Her mother was quiet for a moment. "We could go somewhere else. I can get us to South America. I have some connections there."

"Yeah, you won't stand out there at all," Solo said under her breath.

"I'm not hiding in South America. I want to go home, Mom. I want Violet raised someplace where we don't have to hide at all," she said, though she'd gone over this a million times. "I'm taking Vi and staying with Taggart and Knight until we can get this whole thing sorted out. I would like for you to come with me, but I understand if you won't."

Her mother sighed and turned. "I'll get ready then."

She followed her out because she didn't want to fight about this. "Mom, I'm sorry you don't agree with me."

Her mother turned as they reached the elegant living room. "Was it him?"

There was no question what she was asking. "It was him."

"So Steven Reasor is alive."

"I'm not so sure about that." She quickly went over what she'd learned about Steven's captivity. "Technically he's alive. He's been through some kind of medical testing. It affected his brain. He doesn't remember who he is."

But he'd remembered her.

"Or he's lying," her mom pointed out. "Wasn't he involved in McDonald's medical research? What if he decided the best way to get out of being prosecuted for his crimes was to become one of her victims? He could have been pretending all this time. Hide in plain sight. It's a very old tactic."

She didn't think so. "He wasn't pretending his heart attack."

That seemed to stop her mother in her tracks. "He had a heart attack? From seeing you?"

"No. He was having some kind of reaction." And he hadn't been faking the pain he'd felt when he'd tried to remember. She'd seen how his stats had fluctuated. He'd been in real danger.

And then he'd calmed down when she'd touched him. Like she was magic or something.

Don't be afraid of me.

The words had sounded tortured coming out of his mouth. He'd been so desperate in that moment that she hadn't been able to turn away from him.

He was still the most beautiful man she'd ever seen.

"Tell me you're not interested in this man, Roni." Her mother had the same look on her face she'd had the one time she'd snuck in after curfew as a teen. Disappointment. Disapproval.

"I'm not interested in being his girlfriend." She wasn't going down that route again, but if he was alive, she had to deal with some things. "But he is Violet's father."

Her mother's eyes flared. "He left her."

"No, he left me." She wasn't sure what to do but she knew she couldn't go back into hiding.

"I don't know if he left you willingly." At some point Solo had followed them, and it was obvious she was interested in the argument.

"He walked out willingly enough." He'd kissed her and walked away without looking back.

"I'm interested in piecing that last day together," Solo admitted. "So is Tag and the group. You're the only one who was there, but I've put together some of the logistics. I'm not entirely certain Steven Reasor meant to be on a plane to Argentina that day."

"Dr. McDonald was known for being capricious." Humiliation washed over her every time she thought about that day. "I think she wanted to get him away from me. They were lovers and she wasn't particularly happy he'd cheated on her with me."

Although she also hadn't been enraged. There had been a cold practicality to McDonald that day, but then it was normal for her. Shouldn't she have been angrier? She had been later. She'd been colossally angry a week later when she'd fired Roni.

Solo's face fell. "I'm going to hope she was lying about that. I don't think Tucker will be able to handle it if he finds out he slept with her. She's the devil in his mind. Look, I'm only asking you to give him a chance. He honestly has no memory of who he was back then. I'm suspicious about his entire persona. It's a mystery and one I intend to solve. I don't think he was at Kronberg to further his career. I'm worried he was there to investigate McDonald and got caught."

She didn't want to consider that he was innocent. If he was innocent, then he was tempting. "I doubt that. He liked his job and he was incredibly ambitious. I wasn't the only one he played nasty games with. Ask Dr. Walsh."

"He didn't sleep with her," Solo replied. "At least not according to Rebecca, but that's her story to tell. He did hurt her though. Did you notice that she was the one taking care of him? She's forgiven him because today he's one of the kindest, most loyal men any of us has met."

She hadn't had a chance to really talk to Rebecca Walsh. The doctor had been too worried about her patient.

"Or that's what he wants you to believe." Her mother wasn't going to let up. "But I can see my daughter needs closure. Let's hope she's doing this so she can move on. Not so she can fall back into bad habits. I'm not going to allow my granddaughter to be used by a psychopath. You should understand that here and now."

"I'm trying to explain to you that he's not a psychopath at all," Solo bit out. "I was there the day he went into the coma. He could have fought but he went willingly toward that damn needle because Rebecca was in danger. He was willing to trade his life for hers. Whoever he was before, you have to judge him as he is now."

Who was Steven Reasor now that he called himself Tucker?

"I didn't know him," her mother allowed. "I only know that he ripped my daughter's heart out and was likely involved in a group that took my other daughter's life, so you'll forgive me if I'm skeptical. If I find out he was involved in Katie's death, I don't know that I'll care about the fact that he can't remember."

She turned and walked away.

Solo shook her head. "Your mother is intense. I think she might have watched *Terminator* too many times."

She'd often thought her mother could have been a model for Sarah Connor. "We're all she has. She went a little crazy after Katie was killed. I don't know what she would have done if I hadn't needed her so badly."

It was a lie. She was fairly certain her mother would have wreaked bloody vengeance on anyone she'd even suspected of having something to do with her daughter's murder. Her mother would be in jail or dead if she hadn't had Violet to concentrate on.

"Yeah, I get that," Solo agreed. "I know this is hard on you, but I do promise this is a good group."

"I checked them out." She wasn't a trusting fool anymore. "I have some contacts and they verified what you said about McKay-Taggart. They're known for taking care of their people and their clients."

"They're white hats," Solo said with a sad smile.

"And you aren't?"

"My hat went gray a long time ago." Solo sank to her couch, sitting back as though the day had exhausted her. "I always mean to do the right thing, but I have to think about what is best for my country. That doesn't always leave me with clean hands. I can't pick and choose my morality. I have to make hard calls at times. But not once have I made one of those calls with anything but duty in my heart. Until you. I should have taken you straight to Langley."

"Why didn't you?"

Solo was quiet for a moment. "Because I think this is going to get messy, and you're innocent in all of this. That baby girl is definitely innocent. I can't protect you the way Tag and his men can. They'll protect you from everything. Even me, if it comes to it."

Because if the CIA decided to use her, Solo would be the one to facilitate it. She got that. She knew the agent had divided loyalties, but from what she could tell McKay-Taggart didn't. But their loyalty would be to the man they called Tucker. Where would that leave her if their interests diverged?

"Should I tell him about my daughter? I could lie."

"DNA doesn't lie," Solo replied. "That is Tucker's kid."

She'd forgotten or she'd gotten used to not thinking about Steven. She'd forgotten how much Violet was starting to look like her father. She had his gold and brown hair and god, she had his eyes. Blue and clear as the sky. It went beyond mere looks. She tilted her head the same way he did when he was curious.

Was she doing the right thing? "What if he tries to take her? What do I do if he tries to get custody? My greatest fear is he'll take me to court."

Solo snorted, an oddly elegant sound. "Oh, he's not going to court. He's wanted by Interpol for lots of crimes he sort of committed, but it was under duress, so that's not going to be a problem. And Ian would never let it happen."

"Tucker is his employee," she pointed out.

"Yeah, but you're his client, and he takes that shit seriously," Solo replied. "Earlier today I wrote Ian a large check. He would protect you anyway, but now he has the resources to do whatever he needs to do. His job is to protect you and your daughter and your mother. Come on. I'm trying here."

She took a deep breath and made her decision. "All right, then we're going to The Garden and I'll talk to Stev...Tucker about his biological child."

He wouldn't remember that he'd taken part in her conception, but he deserved to know because Violet deserved to know. Roni started toward the bedroom she'd slept in the night before, the one her daughter was sleeping in now. It would be all right. Tucker would likely not consider Vi his. After all, he'd said it himself. He wasn't Steven Reasor.

"You're making a mistake." Her mother stood outside the room she'd stayed in. She already had her bag packed, but then Sandra Croft traveled light.

"He's not faking it. If you had been there with me, you would know. No one can fake that. Someone tried to give him a cure and it went poorly. The man I met this afternoon, he wasn't the same Steven."

"Only because he's forgotten," her mom said ominously. "But anything that can be forgotten can be remembered. What if this cure takes some time to work? What if he wakes up and remembers exactly who he is? Then where will you be? I hope you know what you're doing. You're betting all our lives on this group."

Her mom knew how to make an exit. She walked away and Roni walked into the bedroom, looking for the one thing in the world that could truly calm her.

Her daughter.

Vi was asleep, her arms wrapped around the doll Roni's boss had given her at her second birthday. They hadn't had a party because they rarely had people to the small flat they rented.

Vi deserved a party. She deserved cake and friends and to be able to walk in the sun and not be afraid.

Tears threatened as she looked down at her baby. So much had gone wrong, but Vi was one good thing to have come from the mess she'd made. She had to do everything she could to give her a better life.

Don't be afraid of me.

He'd known her.

What if her mother was right? It didn't matter that Tucker was some kind of saint. He hid a devil, and the devil seemed to know her name.

A moth to the flame. She was going to get burned all over again. She just had to make sure her daughter survived.

Chapter Three

Tucker came awake with a hole in his gut. Hungry. He was so damn hungry. His stomach growled and he forced himself to sit up.

The lamp was on and all around him there was the soft sound of medical equipment beeping and purring. This wasn't his bed, but he often wasn't in his own bed. What had happened? He'd been having the strangest dream and then…

He was at The Garden and he'd been in a coma for weeks. He'd woken up and Rebecca had told him he'd had an incident with his heart and Tag had offered to pull a tube out of his dick. That felt way more normal than it should. Something hadn't been normal though.

Veronica. Roni had been here.

"Hey, stay calm, man. If those beeps get bad, they won't unhook you." Robert was sitting in a rocker to the side of the bed Tucker was in. "You've still got an IV and a whole bunch of attachments reading your heart rate, but I managed to talk them into taking out the catheter. Owen was right. Rebecca has a gentle touch. You didn't even wake up."

At least he'd been spared that humiliation, but he wasn't worried about his medical state. "Where is she?"

"She's having dinner with Owen," Robert replied. "Steph is around though. She's been checking on you."

"I meant Veronica." Had she left? Where was she? She'd been missing for years. He remembered that much. Finding her had been part of the mission they'd been working in Munich. The minute he'd heard her name, he'd known she was important to his own story. He hadn't been able to recall any of the pertinent facts about her, but there had been a feeling he couldn't deny. A hollowness. Like he'd always known something was missing and it now had a name.

Roni.

She couldn't be gone.

"Veronica Croft?" Robert sat down at the end of the bed. "I saw Solo bring her in. I haven't met her yet. I'm sorry I wasn't here when you woke up. I was with Ari visiting her mom. She's been under the weather. I should have been here."

"I'm sure you rarely left my bedside. You get to have a life, Rob. Do you know where Solo took her? Is she still here?" She had to be in London. If she left, he would lose her again, and he couldn't lose her. He had zero idea why, but he knew the most important thing in his life right now was getting close to Veronica. He needed to talk to her, needed to figure out why she was constantly in his dreams.

"I'm not sure. I got back and they told me what happened. I came in here to wait for you to wake up," Robert replied. "Solo took her and left a couple of hours ago. She's coming back in the morning. We're having a big meeting in the conference room and I think she's going to be there."

"I want to see her tonight." He couldn't lie in bed and wait. Too much could happen. He needed to know she was okay. Why had she been in hiding all this time? Why? God, he needed to know if she'd been hiding from him.

Robert stood, his brow furrowing in obvious worry. "I think you should take it easy. A lot has happened in the three weeks since you've been down. We need to talk about it."

Robert was the most reasonable of his brothers. If Owen were here, he'd already be plotting how to get them out of the building. But no, he had to deal with Robert, who always proceeded with caution. He didn't have time for caution. "How about you write me up a memo? Pass me that kit the docs left."

Robert sighed and put the small container on Tucker's tray. It was a good thing that Rebecca and Steph were always prepared.

They'd left exactly what he needed to get out of this place. He opened it and found the bandage and gauze that would make this whole process far less messy.

Tucker gripped the line that held his IV.

"What are you doing?" Robert's hands went to his hips. "Don't do that."

He eased the cannula out and thanked the universe muscle memory was a thing. He bandaged his hand with very little trouble. All that mattered was he wasn't tethered to this freaking bed. "It's fine. I know what I'm doing."

He stood on shaky legs and glanced around. This wasn't the bedroom in his apartment. He wasn't completely certain where he was. He wasn't in the clinic Stephanie Carter had put together, but then it was really only for minor accidents. They would have put him in a place suitable for long-term care.

He needed pants.

"Yeah, you're walking around with your ass hanging out." Robert followed him into the hall. "You planning on running around Chelsea screaming her name? It's a subtle play."

"I'm going to find pants and then I'll run around Chelsea very quietly screaming her name." The important thing was finding her and making sure she didn't disappear again. Although if he could find her and a cheeseburger, it would be a good thing. "Does anyone have Solo's number?"

Someone had to have it, right? Did CIA agents give out their numbers? Ezra probably knew where she was. He said he didn't want to have anything to do with his ex-wife, but Tucker was pretty sure the man knew where she was at all times. He would likely say he needed to know where the enemy was or some shit, but Tucker knew better. There was some serious drama that would play out between the two of them.

Robert strode beside him as he walked out into the hall. "I don't think calling Solo is a good idea."

He was right. If he called her, then she would know he was coming. "Yeah, I don't want to give her a heads-up. Smart thinking. I need the element of surprise."

"She'll be surprised all right," Robert agreed. "Everyone will be since you're supposed to be in bed. They'll be super surprised when you have another heart attack and die."

"I'm not going to die. I feel fine. Rebecca would have taken me to a hospital if I was in serious danger." He stopped because he wasn't exactly sure where he was. The Garden was a big building and he wasn't in the office section or the residential part. "Where's the elevator?"

Robert stared him down. "I thought you knew everything."

Tucker sighed. "Come on, man. I have to find her."

"Veronica? She's important?"

Tucker nodded. "Yes. I can't explain, but I know she was important to me."

"In a you-were-in-love-with-her way or a she-tried-to-kill-you way?" Robert's question was fair since he'd recently been through the wringer with his ex-wife, who'd also been the reason he landed in McDonald's clutches in the first place.

"I don't know. Maybe both." He couldn't be sure. The way his life seemed to go he'd been in love with her and she would turn out to be an assassin with a hit on him.

"Can we slow down for a minute and talk this out? You know nothing about this woman."

"I know I need to find her." How could he make Robert understand? "This voice inside me is saying I need her."

"Need who?" Jax came out of a door to the left. He carried a can of soda and smiled broadly as he caught sight of Tucker. "Hey, man. You're up. How are you feeling?"

And now he knew where he was. The basement halls all looked the same. Jax kept an office here. Jax was exactly who he needed. Owen might help him run up and down the streets looking for Roni, but Jax might actually be able to find her. "Hey, I need you to figure out where Solo would stash a guest. I assume she's a guest, right? Or did Solo like arrest her or something?"

She would be in a worse mood if she was stuck in a cell somewhere. But then of course she might be in a better mood if he rescued her. She might be more inclined to talk to him if he saved her. There was always a bright side to things.

"I think Solo's coming in," Jax said, holding up his phone. "I got a text from Tag a few minutes ago. He said I'm supposed to go down and meet Solo and escort her and our guests up. Penny got their rooms ready. They're in a two bedroom on the fourth floor. Not far from you, actually. Do we know who she's bringing in?"

"Not really," Robert said. "And that's a problem. We have no idea what this woman wants. She could want revenge for something Tucker doesn't even remember he did. Have we forgotten that we got shot up by the last woman who said she knew one of us?"

"She did know you," Jax shot back. "She was your wife. Who is this new chick saying she is?"

"I used to work with her at Kronberg. So did Rebecca." He wouldn't believe she was coming in until he actually saw her walk through the doors. She would have to come in through the garage at this time of day. "It's night, right?"

He didn't even know whether it was light or dark outside. There hadn't been a window in his room. Like there hadn't been windows in the cells they'd been kept in when he'd been one of McDonald's soldiers. He hadn't known whether he would walk out into the light or have cover of darkness. His body had lost its natural rhythms. It was one more form of torture.

"Yeah, it's almost ten p.m.," Robert affirmed. "Why don't we let Jax do what he needs to do and I'll get you something to eat. When he's done, Jax can come down to the kitchen and give us a report. I don't think you need to confront this woman until we know who she is and why she's here. I know Tag wants to question her, but I want to know what she's been hiding from for the last couple of years."

"Me." It was what he was afraid of. "She was hiding from me."

Then why had she shown him such compassion earlier? She could have walked away, but she'd stayed with him. She'd been holding his hand when he'd fallen asleep. She'd calmed him down and that was why he'd been able to relax.

He shouldn't have fallen asleep. He should have stayed with her.

He shouldn't have left her. She'd been the one sleeping that day. A flash of Roni lying wrapped in white cotton sheets whispered across his brain. Her hair spread across the pillows and her eyes closed as the early morning light caressed her skin.

"Don't go there," Robert said, staring at him like he knew what was going on in his head. "I think you should get back in bed."

The pain stabbed at him, but he took a deep breath and tried to let it go. He wouldn't find her there. If she was here, then he wanted to see her.

He turned and started toward the elevators.

"He's killing me." Robert groaned behind him and then he heard the sound of feet pounding as his brothers caught up to him.

"So we keep close and make sure she's not here to murder him. You know half this job is making sure one of us has backup while he's doing dumb shit," Jax said, falling in beside him. "I'm sorry I missed out on your ex. All the good drama happens when I'm not around."

"It wasn't good drama," Robert groused. "It was awful and a whole lot of people died and Rebecca got kidnapped and Tucker went into a coma."

"That last part wasn't actually your ex-wife's fault," Tucker pointed out. "It was Levi Green's, and we need to talk about him, too. I don't honestly remember much after he injected me. Is he alive?"

The man deserved a bullet, but his death would complicate things. Green might be the only person who could tell him the truth.

"That's one of the things we should talk about," Robert insisted. "Once you get back in bed."

Jax shook his head. "He's not getting back in bed, man. Tucker, we think Levi's alive. I tracked Solo putting him on a plane in Munich that went back to DC. I lost them from there because the CIA is pretty damn good at hiding their tracks. I believe he was taken somewhere to be debriefed. Hopefully in the harshest of ways. He hasn't resurfaced so I think they're either holding him or they've gotten rid of the problem."

"If they took him back to the States, they wanted to talk to him." Robert seemed to give up on getting him back to the room. "I have a hard time believing they would kill him. He knows way too much, and he'll likely work out some kind of deal. He'll be back when we least expect it. Has anyone asked Solo what she did with him?"

"I'm sure Tag did and I'm sure she told him shit," Jax replied. "The question is can we get Ezra to smooth talk her. She might tell Ezra."

"He's been in a bear of a mood since she betrayed us," Robert said. "You should be glad you missed that."

He sent Robert a glare. "I missed it because I was in a coma."

Robert shrugged. "You still got to miss it. I've been avoiding him. He didn't even smile at the wedding."

Tucker stopped. He'd missed a lot. "Wedding?"

Robert winced. "Yeah, Ari and I got married."

"So did Rebecca and Owen," Jax said with a smile. "Double weddings are a thing here. We had it right in The Garden, so you were kind of there. Not that we had the ceremony in your room or anything. It was in the actual garden part of The Garden. I thought we should do a whole *Weekend at Bernie's* thing and have you stand with us, but Rebecca put the kibosh on it. I had picked out an outfit for you including sunglasses and this awesome hat for the pictures. She said no. Something about keeping you hooked up to all the machines. Doctors never let you have any fun."

"You didn't even wait for me to wake up?" This team was his family. "It hasn't even been a month. Most people can't plan a wedding in a month."

Robert's expression had gone solemn. "We didn't know when you were going to wake up—if you were going to wake up—and honestly, after everything that went down, it was kind of a live-for-the-moment thing. Between what happened to you, and Sasha and Peter dying…I didn't want to wait."

Tucker took a deep breath. Sasha had died right in front of him. Peter had gotten out of the spy game and he'd still died. Dante had betrayed them all. Robert had needed an affirmation of life. They all had. "Yeah, I get that. But I hope you took pictures. Did he cry?"

Jax grinned. "Like a baby."

"I did not," Robert shot back. "I teared up once. It was my wedding. And I'm pretty sure this time my wife won't hand me over to a crazy doctor. I was emotional. And I missed my best man. I'm sorry I'm acting like a mother hen, but I've sat at your bedside for weeks hoping you would wake up."

He got it. "I know you were worried, but I have to find Veronica. She can fill in so many gaps. And if possible, I need to talk to Levi Green."

"I'm not letting him anywhere near you." Robert looked at him like he'd gone insane.

"He wanted me to remember for a reason. I think I worked with him. I had this dream that I was meeting him somewhere." And it had felt like a beginning. It had felt like he was starting something important.

"That doesn't prove anything except that the fucker is in your head," Jax replied. "A dream isn't a memory."

"He stuck a needle in your neck. Of course you had a nightmare about him. Given that we don't know what that drug was or how it was supposed to work, we can't trust anything it does to your memory." Robert pushed the button for the elevator. "Can you put on pants before we confront the next woman who might try to kill one of us?"

The elevator doors opened and Owen was standing there. A grin spread across his face. "You're up. Tucker, mate, you have no idea how we've worried. I thought you might be stuck in that bed forever."

"Is that why you posed him?" Jax asked.

Dear god, what had his brothers been doing? "He posed me? What the hell does that mean?"

Owen shrugged, holding the door open. "Seemed a shame to leave you like that. Besides, they're supposed to move you around a bit. Lying in one position is bad for a body. I just took it a bit further. Got costumes and everything. Don't worry. I took pictures. I made a book of them. I call it *All Tuckered Out*. Everyone gets one for Christmas this year."

It was good to know his friends had his back. Sometimes his brothers were assholes. But it was probably pretty funny. He was self-aware enough to know he probably would have done the same if he'd been on the other side. "I look forward to it. Now, I need to get down to the parking garage. Solo's bringing Veronica back."

She was coming back. Willingly. It was a good sign. Or was Solo forcing her back? Solo would do a lot to help her cause with Ezra Fain. She loved her ex-husband and had done some crazy shit to get his attention.

"Pants first," Robert insisted as he pressed the button for the floor they all lived on.

"I don't know, mate," Owen said as the doors closed and they started going up. "If we're worried she'll react to him like Rebecca did, him being in a johnny with his arse hanging out might make him less threatening."

He reached behind and pulled the gown together. No one ever gave him any dignity. "How long did she stay after I fell back asleep?"

"Not too long," Owen said. "Rebecca cleared the room pretty quick and she and Stephanie examined you and went over all the reports. They decided you were stable enough to keep you here."

"I feel fine." He felt tired, but then he'd been stuck in a bed for three weeks, and perversely that could sap a man of his strength. "Did she say anything?"

"No." Owen shifted slightly. Having the four of them in that tiny elevator was a lot.

It made him feel like a hulking ogre to Roni's delicate pixie self. She wasn't a tiny thing, but he was so tall he felt like she was petite. The elevators at Kronberg had been one of the only places where he could stare at her all he liked, though he had to be careful. There were cameras in there. There were cameras everywhere.

He took a deep breath and let the thought go. If he followed down the path, he would end up sick as a dog and Robert would haul him back to bed. He would miss his chance to see her.

"You okay?" Jax was staring down at him as the doors opened, revealing the familiar hallway that led to the rooms he'd been given when he'd come to live at The Garden.

"You went white," Robert pointed out.

"I'm hungry. That's all." If he admitted what was happening, they would all freak out, and he didn't want to be the patient again. He'd always been a shitty patient anyway. That's what his mom had told him. He didn't like to be in bed. He liked school and didn't want to miss class. Grades. He needed good grades to get into the best medical school possible.

"Then let's get you some food." Robert put a hand on the door to keep it from closing.

"I think we should talk to Rebecca about that. He hasn't had anything solid in three weeks." It appeared Owen listened to his girlfriend now. Wife. Rebecca was Owen's wife.

"I need to take it slow at first." He stepped out and then stopped because they weren't alone in the hallway.

"Jax, you meathead. What about *go down to the parking garage and help Solo* do you not understand?" Big Tag was standing in front of one of the apartments that was normally vacant. He'd propped open the door and appeared to be moving stuff into the room. Brightly colored stuff. Kid's stuff.

"Sorry, boss," Jax said, sounding entirely unsorry. "I got sidetracked. Tucker's up and he needs pants. You know how you always tell us to wear pants."

"I tell you to wear condoms," Tag replied with a frown. "But pants are good, too. Tucker, you need to be in bed. Jax, get your ass in gear. They'll be here any minute and I don't want to have to explain…"

Whatever Tag said next was lost because the elevator doors opened again and there she was.

Veronica Croft stood in the elevator, her eyes wide as she caught sight of him. She wasn't alone. Solo was there dressed in what Tucker had long ago decided was her uniform. Chic slacks, an expensive but toned-down blouse, and heels she could run in. The woman next to her was older and looked like she spent a lot of her time working out.

But it was the baby in Roni's arms that truly caught his attention.

Solo had a hand on the elevator door, keeping it open. "Tucker, you're up. Ian, I thought we were going to deal with the introductions in the morning."

She said it with the tight jaw of a woman who'd had her plans upended.

The whole room seemed to stop, everything going quiet and his vision focusing in on that child with her golden-brown curls and big blue eyes. She clung to Roni with one arm around her neck and the other hand waving. He knew there was conversation going on around him. Tag said something but he didn't quite hear it because the world had focused down to one thing.

"How old is she?"

Solo sighed and stepped out of the elevator.

Veronica followed her and the super-fit woman moved out as well, putting her body between Roni and Tucker.

He had the wildest urge to challenge her. She shouldn't come between the two of them. She was standing there like she had the right to keep Roni from him, but no one did. Roni was his.

"Jax, is it just me or is that kid the spitting image of Tucker?" Owen asked.

"Thank god I'm here for this," Jax breathed. "I've missed all the soap opera stuff. I thought they were enemies."

"Yeah, because no enemies ever threw down and made a baby," Owen replied.

He was usually the one standing in the background making snarky comments. It was obnoxious. He ignored them all, concentrating on Veronica. He apparently needed to ask the question again. "Roni, how old is that child?"

Her arms wrapped around the baby. "She's yours if that's what you're asking."

Well, at least he'd figured out what his relationship with her was. Tucker took a deep breath and made a big decision.

* * * *

Roni bit back a yawn as the elevator started to go up. It had taken longer than she'd planned to get ready. It was surprising since they hadn't exactly packed heavy. "You're sure we didn't need to bring the crib?"

"Trust me. The way these people breed they have lots of options for you," Solo assured her. "Violet won't be the only kiddo living here. The Knights have a son and if Tag stays here for any amount of time, expect his wife and all…I think it's like four kids now. I could be wrong. I swear Charlotte spits them out faster than I can count."

Would Vi be an only child? She hadn't really thought about it. All she'd thought about for the last few years had been surviving, but seeing Steven today had her brain on overdrive.

"I want to meet this Taggart person and make my own judgments," her mother said. "The Knight fellow, too. I take it this is an all-male group?"

"Not at all." Solo glanced at the display that showed them moving up the building. "They have several female operatives. This is the London office. Knight's wife often takes assignments. She's former MI6 but her specialty is languages. Carmen Vega is a new hire. She's ex-CIA. Nina Blunt is excellent at following people around. Ariel Adisa is the resident profiler. She got married recently. I don't remember if she changed her name or not. Probably not since Robert's last name is made up anyway. Maybe he took her name."

"Robert is one of the men found with Steven." It wasn't a question. She simply needed to remind herself that relationships here would be complex. Solo had told her there were five men still alive who'd been McDonald's soldiers. Two of them had recently died in the mission that resulted in Steven being in a coma.

Tucker. She had to think of him as Tucker. And she had to think of him as a stranger because no matter what her mother said, she didn't think he was tricking her. Steven Reasor was dead but his DNA was still walking around. Did she owe him anything at all concerning their daughter?

"Yes. They're all here," Solo explained. "Everyone who's left. Except Theo Taggart. He went back to Dallas after the wedding. We might think about moving you there if you want to go to the States. At least until we're sure you're safe."

"Dallas isn't our home," her mother said.

It could be. Any kind of a home would feel good. Any place where she didn't have to hide who she was. Any place where she could start over and try to build something for her and Violet. She wanted to get back to work, though she had no idea how she would explain the gap in her résumé beyond the fact that she'd had a baby. Explaining why her last employer wouldn't give her a recommendation would be harder.

The doors came open and she stopped thinking about the future because her past was standing right there. Steven was still wearing a hospital gown, but she would know that naked ass anywhere. Despite the fact that he'd been in a coma, his butt still looked amazing.

He wasn't alone. Ian Taggart was standing there surrounded by men. She'd met the red-haired Scot, but not the other two. They were both tall and strong-looking men, one with dark hair and the other a golden blond. Taggart seemed to be lecturing them all. "I tell you to wear condoms. But pants are good, too. Tucker, you need to be in bed. Jax, get your ass in gear. They'll be here any minute and I don't want to have to explain…"

Solo put a hand on the door. "Tucker, you're up. Ian, I thought we were going to deal with the introductions in the morning."

He sighed as he caught sight of them. "Sorry, Solo. The puppies got distracted."

Steven…Tucker stared right at her, his blue eyes going wide. "How old is she?"

She'd known he would likely ask about the baby, but he wasn't merely saying, "Hey, didn't know you had a kid." Nope. The question was asked with a suspicious "Hey, is that my kid?" tone. Wasn't he not supposed to remember anything? She was supposed to have the upper hand. She was supposed to get to spring this on him.

Maybe if she stayed in the lift, Solo would get out and the doors would close and she could go back down. She could walk out and get in a cab and not look back. How had she thought this would be easy? How had she thought she could hold up Vi and say, "Hey, she's yours but you don't remember and I understand, so will you help take care of her financially and we can leave it at that? As soon as I get a good paying job and can use my real name again, I won't need help."

Did the dude with no memory even have money to help support a daughter he had zero connection to?

This was stupid.

Solo held the door open, blocking option number one. There was nothing for it. She stepped out.

The Scot said something that had the big blond guy grinning as though he'd found a spectacular show to watch. Blond guy said something about a soap, but she didn't pay attention because her mother was placing herself bodily between her and Tucker.

She watched his jaw tighten and for a second he looked like his counterpart. There was that ruthless will she'd always associated with Reasor. He didn't like anyone getting in his way, anyone getting between him and what he wanted.

"Roni, how old is that child?"

A simple question and yet there was so much tension in the words. She could lie. She hadn't even considered it until this moment. He'd been dead so she hadn't had to consider it.

Her brain whirled in those few seconds. She could lie. No one would believe her since Vi looked so much like her father. Then they would go through a ton of tests and the truth would come out anyway. Or he would accept it and not care. She could tell him the truth and he could still not care. She would be alone, but that was all right because she wasn't about to trust him again. Even if he'd forgotten everything, the core of a person didn't change, and he was still lurking in there, the man who'd used and left her.

"She's yours if that's what you're asking." There, she'd said it.

He stopped for a moment.

"What are you doing, Veronica?" Her mother turned her way.

"I told you I wasn't going to lie." There had been far too many lies between them and now he would explain that he didn't consider Vi his since he was no longer the man who had fathered her.

"See, this is why I tell you all to wear condoms," Taggart said under his breath. "You never know when that fun night is going to suddenly grow hands and feet and need a diaper change."

Tucker walked straight up to her and stared at Violet, a look of wonder in his eyes. "She's beautiful. Can I hold her?"

"Of course you can't hold her," her mother snapped.

But Vi was already reaching out to the new guy. Her daughter was leaning toward him like he wasn't a stranger at all. She grinned, showing off her pearly baby teeth and making grabby hands. She liked it when tall people held her. Yeah, that was it. She couldn't possibly know this was her dad.

Tucker raised her up and father and daughter considered each other for the first time.

She took a step back because it seemed like such a solemn moment.

"You don't know this man." Her mother leaned in, lowering her voice. "We know nothing about him."

He was Violet's dad. Wasn't he? He was acting like it. Her gut was in a knot. What if she was making a horrible mistake? Again.

But she needed him. She needed to figure out what had happened to her sister so they could all move on. Hiding wasn't working anymore and if Solo could find them, then someone else could, too.

She was out of options.

"Aren't you supposed to be supporting her head?" The Scot moved in behind Tucker.

"She's not a baby. She's a toddler," Taggart said. "They're way worse. You missed the screaming, crying part, Tucker, but it looks like you managed to make it for the rough part. She's mobile enough to do some serious damage."

But his lips had curled up as though he didn't mind.

Tucker pulled her in close, his arms supporting her body as she started to pat his face. "What's her name?"

"Violet."

"Like the flower. That's pretty. Hello, Violet. I'm your dad."

"And I'm her grandmother." Her mom moved to stand in front of Tucker. "I'm Veronica's mom. We never met before because you used her and left her behind."

Tucker's jaw went tight. "I don't know about that. I think there's more to it. I get these flashes…I think I loved her."

"That's awfully convenient," her mom said. "You left her behind and now you need her, you suddenly love her. It must be nice to wipe the slate clean. Where's my room? Unless you're planning on moving in with him now that he's back?"

Taggart pointed to the door behind him. "Right in here. It's a two bedroom. Why don't we get you settled in before you start wreaking bloody vengeance on my men? Jax, you want to help me set up this crib?"

"No." The golden-haired man named Jax shook his head. "I'm waiting to see what happens next."

"What happens next is I kick your ass if you don't give them some space," Taggart practically growled. "Come on, people. Robert, why don't you go get Tucker some pants?"

Tucker's gorgeous face turned pink as they were left alone in the middle of a hallway. "I'm sorry about the hospital gown. I woke up and I didn't want to miss you."

"Why? According to Solo you don't really know me. I can take her back if she's heavy. You just woke up."

He held her close. "She's not heavy at all."

"You haven't been well." Something about him holding their daughter made her antsy.

A sad expression crossed his face. "Here. I wouldn't want to drop her."

He passed Violet back to her.

She took her daughter in her arms. "She's not usually up this late."

"Why did you come back? If you think I did all those things to you…what did I do to you, Roni?" He was so heartbreakingly gorgeous and there was a wealth of worry in his eyes. "Did I physically hurt you?"

He'd broken her heart, but that wasn't what he was asking. "You never hit me or anything. You didn't get physical with anyone that I knew. You were gentle around me."

"We were together." He said the words like he was tasting them, getting used to the flavor.

Of all the scenarios that had run through her head since the moment Solo had told her Steven Reasor was alive and not at all well, never once had she imagined this one. He looked like he wanted them to have been together. Not like he would accept the simple fact, but like he would be disappointed if they hadn't had a relationship. She hadn't lied about Violet. She wasn't about to start now. "Not really. We knew each other at work, spent some time together outside of it, but I wouldn't call us friends. We spent one night together and then you left. You didn't even say good-bye."

He stepped back. "That doesn't jibe with what's in my head. When I think about you, it's not guilt that I left you. It's happiness that I got to be with you. I can see you in bed. I was looking down at you and the feeling I got…I wanted to finish what I was doing so I could get back to you. I had to finish something." His hand went to his head. "It's right there. It's clearer than it was before. I think those drugs he gave me are starting to work."

He'd paled the way he had earlier in the day. When he tried to think about the past, it made him ill. Someone had done this to him. A sweat broke out over his forehead.

"Hey, you're going to scare Violet." She kept her voice even because she didn't want to scare her daughter either.

He looked up and though his jaw was tight, he seemed to breathe easier. "I don't want her to be afraid of me."

"I know." Roni rubbed her baby's back as she settled down, obviously tired from all the late-night activity. "You were always worried about that. You told me I was the only one who wasn't afraid of you."

"At Kronberg?"

She nodded. "Yes. You were known for being pretty tough on people. Most of our colleagues were afraid of you because you wielded power pretty freely. I was the only one you were somewhat nice to."

"We were friends?"

How did she want to explain their relationship? She'd thought about it on the flight from Munich. "Not exactly. I was attracted to you. I was pretty naïve and it was my first time out of the States, my first big job. I wanted to see something in you that might not have been there. I wanted to think I could change you, that you could care about me so much you would change your ways. Beauty and the Beast syndrome. I'm not naïve anymore. I need you to understand that I'm here to see if you can help me, not to restart a relationship."

"Yes," he said simply.

She wasn't sure what he was assenting to. "Yes?"

"Yes, I'll help you," he said with a nod. "Of course I'll help you. What do you need me to do? Have you been hiding from me? Am I why you walked out on your internship? Because I won't hurt you. I don't know what I said or did to make you feel that way, but it won't happen again. Never. I'll do anything I can to help you and Violet."

He sounded so fervent she wanted to believe him. But she'd been burned too many times to not be suspicious. "Just like that? Shouldn't you ask for a DNA test?"

What could he get out of this? He had to be playing some angle.

"I don't need one," he replied. "You said she's mine. She feels like she's mine. Besides, even if she wasn't, I would still help you."

"I don't understand."

He was quiet for a moment, his eyes on Violet. "You show up and offer me some kind of a future, some even murky link to a past I might never remember. I'm going to take it. It's like I managed to start this tiny fire and now I need to nurture it. If I take care of it, I might have something warm in my life."

She didn't want to think about how those words made her want to melt. She wasn't supposed to be this easy. She was supposed to question everything this man said or did. "I told you I'm not interested in a relationship."

"You aren't now, but I'm her father and I'm going to help her and you. That means I'll be in your life as much you'll allow me to be, and I don't intend to waste this chance."

He wasn't listening to her. "There is no chance."

A ghost of a smile turned his lips up. "I bet you always thought there was no chance that you would see me again. Things change. So do people."

That was where he was wrong. "Steven…"

"Tucker," he corrected in a deep voice. "My name is Tucker and I'm not that bastard Reasor. I'm starting to wonder if I ever was. I've been letting the idea that I was some kind of monster eat me alive inside for months, and I'm going to stop. I'm going to live the life I have right now, and that includes you and our daughter."

"I wasn't asking you to be a part of her life." This was not going the way she'd thought it would, and his reaction was throwing her for a loop.

"Then what were you asking me for? Because, sweetheart, if it was cash, I'll give you everything I have, but it won't be much," he admitted. "Oddly enough, guys who can't remember their real names or have any proof that they even exist don't make a ton of money. McKay-Taggart pays us, but I haven't saved a ton. When McDonald wiped my memory and turned me into her slave, she apparently took all my assets, too. Unless you know something I don't. Did I like own the place I lived in? Ever mention a big bank account maybe no one else knew about? Did I have a safe?"

He was being entirely frustrating. "I wasn't going to blackmail you. I was going to ask you to help support her while I try to figure out if I can get my career back on track. That was all I was going to do. I want to get back into medicine if I can. It's a demanding profession, and I can't ask my mom to watch her all the time."

She hoped once they got back to the States and found a new normal that her mother would want to get back into life again. It wasn't good for her to spend every waking hour living out her paranoia.

He stepped up and put one big hand on Violet's back, a tender look coming over his face. "I think I could be a good stay-at-home dad. All the kids treat me like a jungle gym. I'm also pretty much a big kid myself. Not that I can't be responsible. And I bet Tag chipped me again. I cut out the last one because we were going into Kronberg and didn't want the CIA guys to be able to follow us. But if I know Tag, he probably put it in my butt or somewhere it won't be easy to get to, so you'll always know exactly where I am. I'm sure he'll give you the code if you adopt me."

"What?"

"Sorry. I was kidding about the adoption part, but Tag jokes about us being puppies a lot. I told you I didn't bring much of value to the table. Having a locator chip is one of the pluses. Unless you think it's a negative, and then I can cut it out. Wouldn't be the first or even the second time. If I can find it." He frowned but it only made him look adorable.

Like Steven had been when they were alone, when he let go of that ruthless will of his and his smile came from somewhere deep inside, some well of sweetness in the man.

What if the drugs that had been used on him had burned away all the hard parts of his personality, leaving him with all the sweetness and light?

Was his dark side gone or merely clinging to him like shadows, waiting to take over again?

"I should go inside." Standing out here with him was disconcerting.

"You should get some rest but know that I'll do whatever you need me to do, Roni. I'll figure out how to get us the money we need. I can probably sell some plasma. Do you think the drugs fucked up my plasma? Shit. I said fuck. And shit. I probably shouldn't cuss around the baby. I'm going to shut up now." His hand came out, cupping the side of her face. "Except to say this. I missed you, Veronica. I didn't know your name, but I missed you."

She was tearing up and she'd promised herself he wouldn't get to her. She took a step back. "This was a mistake."

He stayed where he was, giving her space. "Sorry. I won't touch you again if you don't want me to, but that felt right. I'm not supposed to think about my past. That can get me in trouble, so I've started following my instincts and every instinct I have makes me want to get close to you, to be around you, to protect you."

"I only need some help to get back on my feet." He was infinitely more dangerous than he'd been before. Or maybe she wasn't as far from that naïve girl she'd been as she'd thought. Maybe that dumb girl had been waiting for him to show up again and touch her like she was precious.

The elevator doors opened and a familiar woman stepped through. Rebecca Walsh hadn't aged a day. She was lovely and still had a thing for cardigans. Her hands went to her hips as she took in the man in his hospital gown. "Owen texted me that we had a problem. Tucker, what about *you're not supposed to get out of bed* do you not understand?"

"You know my memory is shit, Doc. I mean, it's bad. It's faulty," he said with a wince. "I'm going to get better about the potty mouth thing."

Rebecca turned her way and seemed to force a smile on her face. "Hello, Veronica. We didn't get to talk earlier. I'm glad you're okay. You disappeared off the face of the earth."

"And you left without saying good-bye." Or warning her. She'd thought they were friends. Not the closest of friends, but at least friendly.

"I'm sorry. I didn't mean to leave everyone without an explanation, but things happened so quickly." Rebecca's face fell. "I would like to explain that to you, but it's a long story."

"I doped her up with a time dilation drug and scared the holy hell out of her and she wasn't sure what was real and what wasn't," Tucker said. "She freaked out and ran."

A shiver went up her spine.

"Okay, maybe not such a long story." Rebecca stared at Tucker, considering him. "But now I'm not certain why you did it. Being around you the way I have has made me reconsider. I think you might have been trying to force me out of McDonald's team to save me."

Good, he'd tried to save Rebecca but left her behind for Dr. McDonald. Now that she knew a bit more about the doctor's experiments, she had to wonder why she'd been spared. Had he thought about that when he'd left her there?

Or had that been the day he'd been taken?

Don't believe what they say, Roni. I'm not who they say. It's all for show.

What had he meant? At the time she'd thought he meant his outward asshole was in place to show everyone he was in charge. He was young to be in his position, and he wasn't the first leader who overdid his boss persona.

What if he'd meant something else?

She'd recognized one of those men who'd stood near Tucker. Her eyes had lingered on him, but it wasn't until this moment she realized who he was. The dark-haired one. She needed to see him, to make sure her memory wasn't playing tricks on her.

That last day had been playing in a loop through her head ever since the moment she'd realized Steven was alive.

"We should talk about all of this tomorrow," Rebecca was

saying. "Maybe we can have breakfast. I can fill you in on everything I know. I promise I won't hold anything back this time, Roni. For now, Tucker needs some rest and I need to run a few more tests. I'm worried his cardiac event was connected to something I'm missing."

"I want to put my daughter to bed," Tucker insisted. "Then I'll let you do whatever you like, but I want to say good night to her and make sure she and Roni have everything they need."

"Daughter?" Rebecca's eyes widened. "Oh my god. I didn't know. I thought you were playing with fire, but I didn't realize you'd actually slept with him."

Violet yawned, giving her mother the perfect excuse to get out of this conversation. She needed some distance, needed a night to think about what had truly happened. Steven was back and she didn't know how she felt.

What if he hadn't meant to leave her that day? She'd believed Dr. McDonald, but McDonald was a liar and a criminal. What if he'd really had a job interview and McDonald had taken him into custody to protect her research? Had that been why the dark-haired man had been at her side that day?

Solo had said they needed her to put together those last days in Munich and Paris. She hadn't once considered that the reality she knew could be false.

What if he'd meant everything he'd said to her? What if he'd kissed her and promised to come back to her and she'd listened to a woman she knew was evil? She hadn't even questioned McDonald, hadn't tried to contact Steven to confirm he was a jerk.

She hadn't seen him again. According to everyone he hadn't even gone back to Munich to clear out his apartment. He'd simply moved to Argentina.

Who did that?

"Veronica, are you all right?" Rebecca was looking at her. "You went a little pale."

"Are you okay?" Tucker was right back to her side. "She's been through a lot today."

"You have, too," Rebecca argued. "You need to be careful until we're sure that drug Green gave you isn't still having an effect."

The door to her room came open and Solo strode out, Taggart hard on her heels.

"What do you mean someone's trying to break into your place?" Taggart asked. "Like right now?"

Solo pressed the button for the lift. "I don't know. I only know my perimeter alarms went off and I need to figure out what's going on. No one is supposed to know I'm here in London. I assume you didn't send someone to loot the place."

"Of course not. All my puppies are accounted for. I'll go with you." Taggart looked over at Tucker, pointing a finger his way. "If you don't follow Dr. Walsh's orders, I'll let Owen tranq you. He's been practicing. You've gotten to talk to your girl. She's not going anywhere. Get back to bed. Your daughter doesn't need to lose her father to a heart attack right after she's found him. Ms. Croft, your mother is going to be a pain in my ass. Tell her someone will walk her through our security protocols in the morning. If you need anything, call Damon. Everyone get to bed. We'll sort this out in the morning."

The doors opened and Solo stepped in. "I'll be back tomorrow. Don't worry. You're safe here."

"What's going on?" The dark-haired man from before walked up and he was carrying clothes on hangers. A shirt and jeans, sneakers in his other hand. He was a spectacularly handsome man, but then McDonald had surrounded herself with those.

"You were there." She was sure of it now. She rubbed Violet's back, the motion as much for her comfort as the baby's. "You were McDonald's bodyguard on the last day I saw Steven. You showed up at his flat with her. You took his things, his laptop and tablet."

The dark-haired man looked stunned. "I did what?"

"Robert?" Tucker turned his way. "God, she's right. You were there. I was there. I can remember everything was green and the sun was starting to come up. There was a grave. I was…I had something to do. How did I know you? I knew you."

She watched in horror as Tucker went white and fell to the floor.

Chapter Four

Tucker paced, the early morning light illuminating the conference room. Was Veronica awake yet? He wasn't sure what he wanted. He wanted her to be able to rest, but he also wanted to see her. He hadn't stopped thinking about her all night. Even as the docs had run every test they could on him, his mind had been on his *V*s—Veronica and Violet.

They were sweet and innocent and he knew he should hold himself back. He wasn't innocent. He had blood on his hands. He'd done bad things, things he couldn't even remember doing. He should help them and then walk away.

He wasn't going to do it. He was going to win her over and before she figured out what was happening, he would be in her bed, sitting at her breakfast table and taking their daughter to daddy and me classes. If her mom didn't murder him in his sleep. Also if he didn't get arrested and thrown in jail.

Minor problems. He'd gotten around far worse.

"You should sit down," Robert said from his chair. "If one of the docs catches you walking around, you'll find yourself right back in bed."

One coma, a minor heart attack, and a fainting episode and suddenly he was an invalid. "I'm fine. I just needed to eat."

"According to Rebecca, hunger wasn't the problem," Rob

pointed out. "She thinks it's all tied to the way the drug worked on your brain. Your whole system goes haywire when you try to remember."

He understood what Rebecca and Stephanie had been talking about. There was a chemical reaction in his brain that hadn't been there before. His neuro pathways were attempting to heal themselves in a way no one understood. He was some kind of walking medical miracle. Or a time bomb that could explode at any moment.

"I can't not think about it. Veronica needs to know what happened. She's important, Rob."

"I get that, and I'll do anything I can to help you," he replied. "I talked to Ariel last night. She wants to try hypnosis again. I know it didn't work the first time but…"

He didn't need a *but*. "I'll do it. I'll try anything, man."

He hadn't betrayed Roni. He knew it deep in his bones. There was something else here, some truth that was waiting be uncovered, and it would explain everything. "I'll even let Rebecca stand right there with her paddles in hand in case my heart goes wonky again."

"You know Rebecca wasn't the one who shocked you. She wasn't there at the time. Veronica did it. At least that's what Owen said. He told me she stepped right in and told Tag to get out of her way and brought you back from the brink."

He touched his chest. How close had he come? Would he be here if she hadn't decided to show up at exactly the right time? He couldn't see it as anything but the universe telling him she was important. "She was a good doctor."

He hated the fact that he didn't know how he knew that, but he let it go. He wasn't going to spend this day sick. He wanted to spend it getting to know his daughter.

God, he had a daughter.

"I'm sure she was. Kronberg goes after the best," Robert said. "She must have been great in her interviews. Technically she didn't fit the profile they usually went with."

"What does that mean?"

Robert sat up, leaning his elbows on the big table. "Jax has a fat stack of information on her. We've been studying her for months."

"I know. Everyone hoped she was the one who had the information we need." They'd headed to Munich because they believed Kronberg Pharmaceuticals had Dr. McDonald's records, specifically notes that would lead them to their true identities. But they'd also discovered that a list of every person in the medical, political, and military fields who had known and supported McDonald's research had existed at Kronberg.

Tucker wanted that list. Tucker thought he might have had that list at one point.

"I find it interesting that of all the interns Kronberg ever hired, only Veronica came from a state school," Robert said.

"There's nothing wrong with state schools. When did you become a snob?" It wasn't at all like Robert. And Veronica was smart. She might not be the wizard of the neuro world like Rebecca Walsh, but she had a good head on her shoulders and she would be a great doctor someday.

They would work well together. They could open a practice and…

He took a deep breath and let it go, but it was there. He hadn't been planning on leaving her. He'd been planning a life with her.

What had happened to kill those plans?

"I'm not a snob, but the directors at Kronberg certainly were," Robert explained. "Look through the dossiers of the other employees. Harvard, Stanford, Oxford, the Karolinska Institute, Cambridge, the list goes on. The University of Texas at Houston is not their typical hunting grounds when it comes to interns. As far as I can tell, she's the only state school intern in twenty years."

He didn't like the sound of that.

The door came open and Ezra Fain walked in, his laptop in hand. He nodded Tucker's way. "Good to see you up and about. How are you feeling? I read Rebecca's report."

He'd read it, too. He wasn't getting back in bed. Well, not unless Veronica went with him. "I'm fine. I feel fine."

"Yeah, you'll feel fine right up to the point you die," Ezra said, sliding into his seat. "You need to listen to the doctors. We've all been worried about you."

There were things they hadn't talked about. Well, he hadn't talked about. "Did you…what did we do with Sasha?"

Sasha. Obnoxious, snarky, sometimes mean Sasha. But Sasha had been his brother, too.

Robert's jaw tightened as he leaned back. "We had him cremated. He's in a safe storage place right now. When we figure out who he was, I'll take his family the remains."

"No movement on that?" he asked. "He might have had a daughter out there."

"Until we figure out a place to start from, I don't know how we find his daughter," Ezra said with a sigh. "Charlotte Taggart has connections in Russia. She's put out some feelers, but we don't know how old the kid would be. We don't know who the mother is. It's a needle in a big haystack. Don't think it's not on my mind. We owe Sasha. It's one more reason for us to find the key."

The key being the other half of McDonald's notes, the ones that had the actual names of her victims. Hope McDonald had thought herself clever. She'd coded the files she'd kept with her, giving each subject a Latin name. They'd managed to match up a few of them via medical records. Robert was a subject she'd called *Ex Novo*. Built from nothing. She'd erased Robert entirely and built him back up to be her soldier.

Tucker rather thought he was the file titled *Damnatio Memoriae*. He'd looked the phrase up after they'd found the files. It referred to a practice in Roman times when an enemy would be stricken from all official records, all paintings and references to the person outlawed. It was a way to eradicate everything about a person.

Like he'd been eradicated.

It was something one would do to only the greatest of enemies. He kind of liked the idea that he'd been McDonald's enemy.

The doors came open again and Tucker held his breath. And then let it go because Solo walked through followed by Ian and Damon, who seemed to be arguing.

It was good to know some things never changed.

"I don't know that it's a good idea to let the CIA agent stay here," Damon said in his upper-crust British accent.

"Where do you want me to go? My house has been compromised." Solo's eyes went straight to her ex-husband. "Did Tag bring you up to speed?"

Ezra was suddenly endlessly fascinated by whatever was on his laptop screen. "I know someone breached your perimeters last night, and it sure as hell wasn't me. Are we sure it wasn't some guy trying to pick you up for a date? We all know you can forget your responsibilities. Maybe it was a fellow operative delivering the latest plans to fuck my life up."

"I don't need an operative for that. I can do it all on my own," Solo shot back.

"Yeah, it seems to be what you're best at." Ezra was looking at her now, a fire in his eyes like he hadn't expected she would fight back and he was ready. "How's your boyfriend?"

"Levi Green is not my boyfriend." Solo bit off every word. "He's not my friend. He's a man with information that can help my country. The last time I checked it was your country, too."

"We serve our country in different ways," Ezra replied. "Actually, I don't serve it at all since Green got me burned. I always thought it was Green. Now I wonder."

Solo's eyes narrowed. "You can't honestly believe I'm the one who got you fired. After that clusterfuck of an op in Mexico, I was the one who had to clean everything up. I worked overtime to make sure no one put a hit out on you."

"Or you set everything up," Ezra argued. "Isn't that one of your plays? Set up a problem so you can solve it and then the person you solved it for will forgive you for anything because you're so kind to have helped him?"

She pointed her ex-husband's way. "I have never done that."

Tag groaned. "Get a room and have hate sex and don't come out until you either kill each other or fuck the other one out of your system. I'm too old for this shit. We don't know who was at Solo's last night, but I suspect whoever it was, he or she was a pro. Damon, I'm putting her up here so I can keep an eye on her. Also, so she'll owe me."

Solo laughed, a bitter sound. "You already owe me more than you can repay, and you put me in the room next to the kitchen. Someone was playing K-pop and burning toast at six a.m. It's not much of a favor."

"You do understand that if we let her in, she'll steal the prize at the end of this," Ezra pointed out. "It's what CIA operatives do. It's a class we all have to take. *How to fuck over your friends 101*."

"I wasn't fucking over anyone," Solo said with a long sigh. "I did what I had to do. If you had killed Levi, they would have come after you and honestly, he does know things we need to know. He's been working this a hell of a lot longer than I thought he was. He's been involved for years."

"And yet you didn't see it," Tag accused. "He was your colleague, but you didn't figure out he was working his own angle?"

Knight snorted. "I'm going to move a bit so the lightning doesn't strike me."

Solo glared Tag's way. "I have two words for you. Eli Nelson."

Ezra snorted and covered his smile.

Tucker felt his eyes go wide. Eli Nelson had been Big Tag's Levi Green. He'd been a Collective agent who'd also worked for the CIA. Nelson had been the reason Tag left the Agency. Ian's wife had been the reason Nelson likely still had body parts floating around the Arabian sea.

Tag turned a nice shade of pink and then sighed. "Fair. All right, Solo, you want to prove you're one of the good guys, what have you figured out about Green and his involvement?"

Solo's face fell. "Not a lot. He won't say much about it except that he wants to cut a deal. He's been willing to talk about a lot, including the fact that several members of the Agency and other intelligence units knew what McDonald was doing before and after they closed The Ranch. We all know there was a group within the Agency that knew she was using soldiers to experiment on. He won't give me names."

"He might not know them," Ezra said. "Oh, I have no doubt he knows some of them because he's likely been working for the fuckers, but he won't give them up. He gives them up and he loses his only safety. The people you're working for don't have an appetite for execution. He knows that."

"Are we talking about the president?" Tucker remembered that much. Solo was working for President Hayes, if the rumors were true.

She looked to Ezra.

Ezra rolled his eyes. "Take her silence as a yes. We have to assume the president wants to clean house, but he needs help. He needs proof. If Levi thought it would help him, he would pass over a list of names."

"It would help him." Tag let his big body sink into the chair next to Ezra. "But only if it was backed up with proof. Hayes isn't going to let Levi make up a list of names."

"I think I knew him." Tucker said the words, careful not to concentrate too hard about Green. "In my head I can see myself meeting him, but I think it was before."

"Or he worked with McDonald," Knight said. "We've been piecing together a timeline. I can place him in Europe shortly before McDonald fled. The question is what made her leave."

"Kronberg got scared," Robert replied. "According to the interviews we did in Munich, something happened that made Kronberg shut her project down. They wiped everything clean in the course of a night. Now we know they kept notes on her research and copies of their donors, but they aren't held on their campus. At least according to what Solo told us about the files we found."

"The main thing I found on those files was the information that led me to Veronica," Solo explained.

That tidbit had Tucker's attention. "Why was Roni even on their radar?"

Robert leaned forward. "Yes, I'm interested in that, too. She doesn't fit their profile."

"I don't know, but they were watching her," she said. "I know Veronica and her mother thought they were hiding, but Kronberg knew exactly where she was. There was surveillance footage. Probably from an in-house PI. I think they're the ones who were crawling around my place last night."

"They were smart enough to stay away from your cameras," Tag said. "I'm worried we're dealing with more than an investigator. That's why I think we should either bring Solo in or ship her back to the States. Tell me something. Did you pay Green back for slapping the shit out of you in Munich?"

Ezra's head came up. "He did what?"

Oh, Tag was such a bastard. He knew exactly what he was doing. He was sure Solo had wanted that part left out of the official report. Ezra hadn't been in the room when Solo had confronted Levi after giving herself up to his mercenaries to buy them all some time. She'd spouted some sarcasm Levi's way and Levi had reacted poorly. He'd slapped her hard enough to make her head snap back. It had been the first time Tucker had understood how evil the man could be. Apparently, Robert had told Tag everything that had happened. Tag was making sure Ezra knew and letting Solo see exactly how he would react. He was meddling. Unfortunately, Tucker approved. "Yeah, that was rough. I couldn't believe he smacked you like that. You were completely helpless."

"He did what?" Ezra's voice was low but there was no mistaking the menace there.

"Oh, he smacked the hell out of her." Robert threw in with them. "Just bitch slapped her hard. I was surprised you didn't notice the handprint on the side of her face that night."

"I'm betting she tried to keep it from him," Tag said.

"He fucking hit you? Physically?" Ezra turned to his ex-wife.

"Well, I had said something about him having a tiny dick at the time," Solo mentioned.

Tag's head shook and he sat back.

Ezra chuckled but there wasn't a hint of humor to it. He stood and picked up his laptop. "Well, you would know all about that. If you'll excuse me, I'll grab a cup of coffee and go down to help Jax. I would like a report of anything discussed here today. If you need me, you know where to find me."

Solo looked up. "Beck…"

He walked out without looking back.

"I lob you an easy one and not only do you swing and miss, you kind of throw the bat in his face," Taggart said.

"Which is precisely why you should stay out of it, you meddling old man," Knight said under his breath.

"I didn't…" Solo groaned. "Levi wasn't my lover. He was my drunk mistake. How long do I pay for this?" She shook her head. "Nope. I'm not going there right now. Tucker, you said you remember meeting Levi, and Damon's intelligence places him in France before McDonald left for Argentina. Didn't you find out that you took a trip to Paris around that time?"

"I don't know. That's what Arthur Dwyer said." Arthur had been a colleague at Kronberg.

Robert shook his head. "No. He said he saw you at the airport. He didn't see you in Paris."

"But he saw me get on a plane with Veronica."

"This should be easy to clear up," Knight said, getting up and heading for the door. He opened it briefly. "Please let Ms. Croft in when she gets here," he said to the receptionist before coming back to his seat. "We've got other things to talk about. I'm hearing rumors that MI6 was upset that you're not sharing intel, Solo."

"I don't have intel to share," she replied. "Look, I know you all think I have this sacred document, but it wasn't in the files the boys found when they raided Kronberg."

"The files you stole," Tag pointed out.

Solo threw her hands up in obvious surrender. "The files I stole because I'm the worst person on the face of the earth." She started to push her chair back. "It's obvious I can't make any headway. Consider Veronica a gift. I'll leave you all be."

Tag sighed and leaned toward her. "Hey, I'm sorry. It pissed me off, but I do understand what you did. Ezra would have killed that son of a bitch and then he would be in a world of hurt because the Agency wouldn't have looked the other way. I'm worried that we're going to find some Agency names on that list."

Solo nodded and sat back. "I am, too. I'm worried that Levi's set up a system that protects him and fucks Beck over if anything happens to him."

"He told you that?" Damon asked.

"Not in so many words," Solo said. "The insane thing is I really have tortured him. I think the bastard likes it."

"Give me five minutes with him," Tag offered.

"You would be surprised what he can take and not talk," Solo said. "And how reasonable he can sound. He's probably making a deal even as we speak. Anyway, you want to know what was on the intel we got from Kronberg. What I got was years of financial records and some sketchy business practices. I've got proof that Kronberg knew their erectile disfunction meds could cause testicular cancer, but other than giving that to a reporter, I don't see how it helps us here."

"I want to talk to Levi Green." He knew Green had the answers.

Solo seemed to consider it. "We would have to go back to the States. I would like to get him in a room with Tucker and see if he slips up. And Robert. He seemed to know a whole lot about Robert's situation."

"I would definitely like to know if he has any information about my family," Robert said quietly. "I've had my mind on other things, but I'm getting to the point where I need to know if what Emily said was true."

Emily Seeger had explained that Robert had a mother and a brother, both of whom had died. Levi Green had dangled the tempting possibility that they were alive and he knew where they were. Someone had done a damn fine job of wiping them off the face of the earth.

Like they'd done with him. *Damnatio Memoriae.*

It was hard to believe someone hated him so much.

The door came open and his world seemed to come to life. Roni walked in wearing jeans and a green sweater that brought out the gold in her eyes.

He immediately moved to hold a chair out for her. "Hey, good morning. Did you sleep okay?"

She seemed almost startled to see him there. "No. I slept terribly, but I'm fine. I want to get this done so we can all move on."

He did too. Oh, he was absolutely certain she meant move on from him, but it wasn't going to go that way. "Sit down and we can all talk. Can I get you some coffee?"

She stared for a moment and then seemed to find her voice. "Sure. I could use some coffee. My mom is with Vi. Is that okay or do you need to talk to her, too? Mom didn't work at Kronberg. She came over to Germany when my sister died and then we realized we were in danger, so she stayed."

Oh, he had so many questions about that. He hadn't been given the dossier on her yet because he was too fragile to read or some shit. "Sit. I'll take care of you. Now what happened to your sister? I'm assuming this wasn't a natural death."

He moved to the small buffet that the London crew always set out when they were having a planned conference. Theresa—who had been known to listen to some K-pop and usually had toast first thing in the morning—set out coffee, tea, and pastries for the morning meetings and tea and sandwiches for the afternoon ones. He poured her a cup of coffee and added a bit of cream and two sugars. She liked it sweet. She would want the cream cheese Danish.

"She was murdered," Roni said.

"According to the reports it was a fire," Taggart argued. "She was working late at her office in the bottom of a very old building and there was a gas leak. The resulting fire killed three people, including

Katherine Croft. She was a freelance journalist who specialized in investigative reporting. She particularly liked to catch corporations misbehaving."

His stomach turned at the thought of what that must have been like for Roni. She'd been alone and pregnant at the time and mourning.

Had she mourned him? Or merely hated him?

"I don't believe for a second that it was an accident, Mr. Taggart," she said as he placed the cup and plate in front of her.

"And why is that?" Ian asked.

"Because an hour after my sister's building blew up, I received a message that if I ever talked about what I knew, they would do the same thing to me."

Tucker's knees went weak and he forced himself to sit.

Bad had just gotten worse.

* * * *

The coffee was exactly how she liked it. Not too much cream. Probably way too much sugar. And she would have fought over the Danish.

You like it sweet because you're sweet, sweetheart.

She'd laughed at his goofiness and then sobered quickly because they'd been walking to Kronberg when he'd said the words to her and she hadn't been allowed to do what she'd wanted to. She'd wanted to kiss him before they split up for the day, before she spent long hours trying to ignore that something was wrong with the company she worked for.

She remembered that she'd been surprised he knew how she liked her coffee and that she was always disappointed because all the cheese Danishes would be gone by the time the interns got a turn at breakfast.

Could he really remember her though McDonald had done her best to wipe clean every semblance of his life? Why would she be the one thing that came through?

Unless he was doing exactly what her mother accused him of. Lying. Pretending. Covering his own ass.

She didn't want to believe it, but she rather thought that was her hormones talking and not her brain. Because he was still the most beautiful man she'd ever seen and she'd sat up all night remembering how he could make her feel.

Beloved. Desired. Sexy as hell. Wanted.

Alone. Empty. Hollow.

"That isn't in my notes," Taggart said with a frown as though the worst thing that could happen was for his notes to be wrong. "I never heard you were sent some kind of warning."

Or perhaps the man was simply used to the world obeying him. According to Solo he was kind of the boss of everything here.

"I didn't realize you had notes," she replied before sipping her coffee. Tucker had taken the seat next to her and she didn't miss the look that had crossed his face when she'd talked about the message she'd received. He'd gone pale and for a moment she worried he was going to have another fainting spell.

But he'd sat down beside her and his hand had come up on the table almost as though he would cover her hand.

She'd moved slightly away from him and he'd sat back.

"Ian always has notes. He's always prepared," Tucker explained. "He doesn't often get caught off guard."

"Oh, I can think of a couple of times I've been caught off guard and it cost us all." Tag turned to Solo. "I take it you knew all about this development."

"Only because I've already interviewed the Crofts," Solo replied. "I told you I'd found out a couple of incidents I thought we needed to investigate. The pieces of this particular puzzle don't seem to fit, but I think we need to look at them all again. We've missed something."

She didn't like her sister being called a puzzle piece, but she understood the way an investigator's mind worked. Her sister would have said the same thing. "Katie had been investigating Kronberg for a long time before she died. I didn't even realize she was working on a story about them until I got hired there. My sister was older than me and she was pretty much wholly devoted to her career. I didn't talk to her often, and neither did Mom. When my mom mentioned she should look me up because I was in Germany, my sister got upset."

Tucker frowned. "Your sister was investigating Kronberg before you got the job?"

She nodded. This was one thing he wouldn't know even if he did remember his old life. She'd played Katie's job close to the vest. She almost never talked about what her sister did for a living. "She'd been living in Europe for a couple of years at that point. She often got published by French and German news outlets. She was fluent in German. Mom was stationed at Ramstein for most of Katie's childhood. I spent a couple of years there, but she moved us to Texas when she left the Army."

Tucker looked at the man who'd been there the day he'd left her, the man who'd probably been with him as he'd left for Argentina. They shared a long look that made her wonder.

"What?" They were obviously having a whole conversation made up of eyebrows rising and heads tilting. They had oddly similar gestures.

The dark-haired man nodded to Tucker.

"Rob thinks your internship might have been out of the norm for Kronberg," Tucker began.

The door opened again and Rebecca was followed by the gorgeous Scot who Roni had learned the doctor had recently married.

"I'm sorry I'm late," Rebecca said with a frown.

"We're not late. They started without us." Owen held a chair out for his bride before sitting beside her. "We're a good ten minutes early."

"I was hoping to get to talk to Dr. Croft," Rebecca admitted. "Big Tag doesn't usually slide into his seat until two seconds before he's supposed to be here, and then he often sleeps with his eyes open."

"Not when he's attempting to meddle in someone else's marriage," the British man with dark hair said. Knight. Damon Knight. "Then he's bright and early."

"You're welcome, married man," Tag shot his way.

She got the feeling this group could devolve quite quickly if she let them. "Why was my internship odd?"

"What are you talking about?" Rebecca asked.

"Something about my internship at Kronberg has set off alarm bells for Tucker and the other one," she said, looking to the man across from Tucker. "Ron?"

"Robert," he replied. "I go by Robert, though I've been told my name is Russell Seeger."

Something about the name sparked a curiosity. Memory was a

funny thing. Even when one's hadn't been wiped, it could still play tricks on a person.

"I was told you remember seeing him," Taggart began. "Robert, that is. You saw him in Paris?"

She shook her head. "I'll talk about it after they tell me what it is about my internship that bugs them."

Tucker's jaw tightened. He hadn't changed his tells. His jaw always formed that hard line when he didn't want to do what he was about to do.

"If you expect me to trust you at all, I need some honesty," she prompted.

He turned her way and she got the feeling this was another of those times when he would like to touch her, when all she had to do was reach out and he would take her hand in his.

She couldn't do it.

"You aren't the usual candidate they look at," Tucker began.

"She was an excellent intern," Rebecca argued.

Tag held out a hand. "No one is saying she wasn't good, but Robert has been looking into Ms. Croft's background and he and Tucker have spent the last year studying Kronberg and their practices. Let's not get sensitive. I'd like to hear them out."

She sat up, bracing herself. "I would, as well."

"Robert mentioned that Kronberg could be a bit snobby when it came to their intern program," Tucker began, obviously picking his words carefully.

"I went to a state school." She could guess where this was going. Did they think she hadn't considered this? At the time she thought she'd hit the lottery, but later on she'd known there had been a more sinister purpose to the invitation. "Kronberg recruited me because they knew my sister was investigating them. They wanted to use me against her, or they hoped I could be a reasonable voice my sister would listen to."

"Did they approach you about your sister?" Damon asked.

"She was mentioned in my last review, but it was more of a reminder that I signed a nondisclosure agreement and I couldn't share information with her. It wasn't until after she died I thought they brought me in to keep a close eye on the situation with my sister. I wasn't there for my talent."

"You were quite good," Rebecca insisted. "Before my world exploded, I thought about looking you up to take a job at the Huisman Foundation with me."

"It doesn't matter if I was good enough or not." She didn't allow herself to dream anymore. "The truth is they came after me because my sister was investigating them. A representative from Kronberg prodded me to apply, and that's not how they operate."

"But they do," Rebecca insisted. "They recruited me."

"You are a star in the neuro world. Everyone knows you'll get a Nobel one day," she pointed out. "I was in the top fifteen percent of my class at a state school. I had good grades and references, but nothing stellar. I should have realized there was something odd about it, but all I could think of was I would get to work with some of the best doctors in the world and I would get to do it close to my sister. Hell, my German wasn't even very good."

Though it was much better now. Living in Bavaria and having a desperate need to fit in had made her fluent. She'd spent long hours perfecting her accent so no one would question the odd shop girl.

Except she didn't have a reason to hide, according to Solo. They'd known where she was the whole time. It made her sick to her stomach. She'd wasted years and they could have taken her when they wanted to. It was one of the reasons she'd decided to come in.

That and the fact that no matter how much she denied it, she'd wanted to know if Steven Reasor was still alive.

She still wasn't certain, and that was a problem.

Solo had her tablet in front of her, and her fingers worked the monitor. "I'm sending you all the report detailing the interviews I've already done with Roni and her mom. She wasn't directly threatened with her sister, but I think it's obvious the bigwigs at Kronberg are still worried Katie Croft left behind information Roni could use against them."

"It's been years," Roni said. "If I had something, I would have used it by now. I would have used it to protect my daughter."

"What exactly made you decide to hide your identity? Was it just the threat? Or was there something else?" Taggart asked.

She didn't like to think about that day. She hated it now because it might have been the day she'd made a huge mistake. "Hope McDonald fired me herself. It was the last time I saw her."

"Can you walk us through that timeline?" Tag asked. "We've got some information on her movements, but I would like to hear it from your side."

"It was a week after Steven left," she explained. "This was the week after I saw her in Paris. She came to where Steven and I were staying and explained that he'd taken a job with her in Argentina."

"And I was there." Robert was watching her intently.

"Yes, I think she brought you in case I freaked out on her or something." She'd asked for honesty and she intended to give it back to them. Even when it hurt. "She showed up with Robert, though he didn't say anything."

"Yeah, we weren't there to talk," Robert agreed. "You realize, of course, that I don't remember this at all."

She nodded. "You didn't do anything beyond stand behind McDonald and when she asked you to take Steven's laptop and tablet, you made sure you had them. Like I said, she told me Steven wouldn't be coming back to Germany with me. She basically told me I was stupid to have believed that Steven truly wanted me. She implied that Steven was using me to make her jealous, and then she said she would see me back at Kronberg."

Robert leaned forward. "Tucker, just because she said it doesn't mean it's true. You know we've never found anyone who would say you were her lover."

She glanced toward Tucker and he'd gone a pasty white, his eyes on the table in front of him as though he needed a moment to gain his composure.

"I never saw McDonald be affectionate with you," Rebecca said. "Not once. I did see her flirt with a lot of men, but not you."

"We could have been hiding it since she was my boss," Tucker said, his voice tight.

"Or she could have been lying so Veronica was so angry she didn't ask questions," Knight pointed out.

"We all know she was good at manipulating people," Taggart added.

"It worked." She was starting to wonder if she hadn't made a horrible mistake. "I didn't ask any questions. I went back to work and hoped I didn't bump into Steven again."

"Why were you in Paris with him?" Taggart asked.

"Because I thought we were starting a relationship. He told me he was interviewing for a job that would get him out of Kronberg. He said he wanted to go back to the States and this job would make that happen for him. We spent the night together at an apartment he said he used when he was in Paris."

"She's given me a general description of the place," Solo offered. "It was close to the Tuileries Garden, so that narrows it down a bit. I'm hoping I can find the actual building because I would love to know who owned the apartment."

"That would be helpful." Taggart turned his attention back to Roni. "So you spent the night with him and he went to his interview the next morning. Did he say anything before he left? Did you go with him? Were you supposed to meet him? He didn't tell you who he was interviewing with?"

"If he was close to taking a job in the States, he would have been far along in the interview process," Rebecca mused. "At the level he would have been looking at, he likely would have multiple interviews. He could have done the initial interviews on the phone or over the Internet, but there would be several in-person meetings. Had he been gone a lot in the weeks prior?"

She had never thought about that. "No. Steven was married to his job. I was there for almost a year and he didn't even take weekends off. McDonald would come and go, but Steven was always there. It was a surprise that he wanted to go to Paris for the weekend. He left the apartment before dawn. At the time I didn't think much about it. He was always a careful man and he was never late, so I thought he was being proactive. But now that I think about it, he didn't have a suit with him. All he had was a duffel bag. He wouldn't have carried a suit in a duffel bag."

"I'm not a fan of suits," Tucker said with a weak laugh. "So I was obviously lying about what I was doing."

"I think we can say that's a safe bet," Taggart agreed. "He was gone for too long, wasn't he? Did you try his cell?"

"I did. Many times," she admitted. "I got worried when he didn't show up that afternoon. Then McDonald and Robert were there. She basically threw a bunch of lady aggression in my face, told me she pitied me, and walked away with all of Steven's things. I shouldn't have let her take his stuff."

She'd missed a chance. She should have hidden his computer the minute she'd seen McDonald walking up to the building. Her sister would have. Her sister wouldn't have been so worried about her tender feelings that she'd stopped thinking at all.

"You should have done exactly what she wanted you to do." Tucker leaned her way, a serious look on his face. "If McDonald thought for a second that you knew something you shouldn't have, she would have taken action. She would have either killed you or wiped your memory and left you with nothing. I'm glad you gave it up. You being safe is all that matters."

The man knew how to say all the right things. He was looking at her, his face so earnest. As she'd watched him last night and this morning, she'd been struck by how open he seemed. Where Steven had been shuttered emotionally, only giving out glimpses of what he was feeling when they were alone, Tucker was an open book. His emotions played across his face with no mask to hide them.

"Thank you for all the feels, Tucker," Taggart said with a shake of his head. "You're going to let her walk all over you. Back to the actual matter at hand. When did you see McDonald next?"

"About a week later." Everyone was making notes now. She'd spent so much of the last few years of her life trying to go unnoticed that being the center of attention was unnerving. "It was two days before my sister died. I hadn't talked to Katie in weeks though. I'd been ducking her calls because I didn't want to explain how I'd screwed up my love life. I was pretty depressed. McDonald showed up at the lab and I asked if Steven was with her. I wasn't asking because I wanted to see him. I wanted to avoid him, to tell you the truth. I was still pretty raw. She had the angriest look in her eyes. She told me he was done with me and walked away. I took that to mean I was fired. I'd asked to move teams and they'd told me no. I'm ashamed to say I walked out. I was unnerved."

"That seems sudden. Is there anything else you remember about her that day?" Knight stared at her as though he could see inside her head.

"She wasn't herself." She could still see the crazy look in McDonald's eyes. "I know she'd spent a lot of time upstairs in the corporate offices. When she came down, she didn't talk to anyone but me. She ignored everyone else, even people who tried to talk to her."

There was something else. Something that hadn't seemed important at the time. "Someone said her father was with her."

"You didn't tell me that." Solo's eyes had widened.

"I'm sorry. I didn't think it was important until now," she explained. "And I didn't see him, but I remember Arthur Dwyer talking about it. He was in some of those meetings. You should talk to him. I would be surprised if he isn't still at Kronberg. I think he took over for Steven."

Rebecca sighed. "We did talk to him and he didn't bother to mention he was in those meetings. He did tell us he saw you with Steven at the airport."

"How would he have seen us?" That didn't make sense.

"He said he was at the airport," Rebecca replied.

There were some things she definitely remembered. "Oh, he couldn't have been. We left on a Friday afternoon. We went straight from work. Arthur got angry with me because I wouldn't stay and help him with an experiment he was running. I know he turned in his findings so there's no way he was strolling around the airport. That particular experiment would have taken him all weekend, and he would have to babysit it. And there was no way he would have seen us together at the office because Steven made sure we left at two different times. Anytime I saw Steven outside of work, he was careful no one would catch us."

Taggart grinned, a baring of teeth that could only be called predatory. "Oh, I'm interested in talking to Dwyer myself. I would love to know why he lied about that. I think we'll have to go a bit deeper on that man. But thank you, Ms. Croft. This helps us with a timeline. Did you know anyone who spent time in Argentina?"

"There were three other members of her original team who went with her, but I wasn't close to any of them. After McDonald left, Arthur's group then became the lead team working neurology at the Munich office. I never talked to anyone at Kronberg again." She looked around because there was a tension in the air she didn't understand. "What?"

"From what we can tell, everyone who went with McDonald to Argentina is dead," Rebecca said quietly.

"Or mind wiped," Tucker added. "When you look at it that way, I was lucky."

"You're the only person who worked directly with McDonald in those last days who still has a heartbeat and a functioning brain," Taggart pointed out. "And now you're out in the open."

"And someone figured out where my London safe house is the same day I move you to it," Solo pronounced grimly.

Someone was looking for her. She'd placed them all in danger again.

Chapter Five

Tucker knocked on the door to Roni's apartment and hoped she would actually answer. The morning's conference had turned into a whole afternoon of questions from Ian and Damon and Solo. Ezra had rejoined the group and gone over every second of those last few weeks.

Not every second. She'd glossed over the time they'd spent in bed. According to her, they hadn't left the apartment in Paris the whole day they'd spent there. He was fairly certain they hadn't been watching television.

They'd been busy making a baby. Violet.

The door came open and Roni's eyes went wide. "Hey. Is everything okay? They said they didn't need me again until tomorrow."

"I wanted to come by and see if you needed anything." He held up the box he'd had delivered moments before. "Like a pizza. I figured you hadn't had time to stock your kitchen."

She breathed through her nose and a dreamy look came over her face. "Tell me it's pepperoni. American pepperoni, and not those pepper things you get when you order pepperoni over here."

"This is all-American pepperoni, and it's from my favorite pizzeria in the city," he explained. "Trust me. We've tried them all.

One of the cool things about losing your memory is getting to try all the foods again because you have no idea what you like. Although I tried kale and that wasn't so cool. I decided to discount all hard-core greens at that point. But I did experiment with about a thousand ways to eat a pizza."

She took the box and turned, leaving the door open so he followed her inside.

And stopped because Violet was in a playpen, her hands on the top of the wall and her whole body bouncing. She was wearing a pair of footie pajamas, her hair in pigtails, and she was so cute his heart nearly stopped.

This was why Tag kept Charlotte pregnant all the time. He'd been around a lot of kiddos, but Violet was different. Violet was his.

Her mother didn't know it yet, but she was his, too.

"I was hoping we could talk."

"Didn't I do that all day?" She disappeared into the kitchen.

"I wanted to talk about Violet." He stared down at her. There were a couple of toys at her feet, including a worn stuffed bunny that had definitely seen better days.

The vision of an old stuffed bear hit him. He could see it. They'd called the bear Stanley. It had been his older brother's. His brother. He had a brother and his name was…

"Hey, maybe you should sit down. Are you having another episode?"

He shook it off. Or tried to. His head was starting to pound. His daughter was staring up at him as if she knew something was wrong.

He didn't want to scare her. "I should go."

"Sit down." Her hand found his and she tugged him back toward the couch. "Let the memory go. That's what Rebecca said you need to do. Let it go and think about something that's happened to you since you came here."

She'd asked Rebecca about her protocols when it came to him? Maybe she was curious. She was a doctor. It was one of the things that had brought them together. He loved how she worked with the people around her. But he believed firmly that she didn't belong in research. She would be so good with patients. They would love her. They would trust her.

"You're still thinking about it," she said in a low tone.

He was on the couch next to her and suddenly she eased him down, letting him lay his head in her lap. A soft palm eased over his forehead and then he could feel her fingers on his scalp.

Yeah, he wasn't thinking about the past anymore.

"Sorry." He hadn't meant to break down in front of her, but that seemed to be all he could do. "The memories are coming faster now, but they're not complete. They're little visions. I can remember that I have a brother but I don't remember his name."

"You called him Ace, though I got the feeling that was a nickname."

Ace. His brother. Their mom called them Ace and Bub. "What else did I say about him?"

"Not much. You didn't talk about your family except to tell me they would like me and I would meet them when we went back to the States." Her fingers moved over his scalp as she looked down at him. "Is it any better?"

He closed his eyes, letting himself simply be in the moment. "I'm getting there. Thank you."

He didn't want to break their contact.

"You wanted to ask about Violet? What do you want to know?"

"Everything. Were you mad when you found out you were pregnant?" He meant everything. He wanted to know it all—the good, the bad, and the rightfully angry.

"Oh, I was beyond angry. I was also scared. My sister had been killed and I had gotten that horrible message that I could be next. I realized I couldn't go home."

"Why? I would think it would be easier to hide in the States."

"I was afraid to get on a plane, to go through an airport. It's so easy to find a person. I was scared to go anywhere with security cameras. My mom had friends in a small town in the Bavarian Alps. They found us a house and we spent a lot of money getting not-so-legal documentation. An EU passport is a powerful tool. I can pretty much run anywhere on the continent if I need to without too much security."

"So Violet was born in Germany?"

"Yes. She was born in a small hospital in Oberammergau. I worked there in a shop," she explained. "Mom worked at a grocery. When I gave birth, I got paid time off. It was nice. I liked being home with Vi, but I want to work again. I want to go home and get back on track."

"What was she like?"

"She was an easy baby. At least that's what my mom tells me. Violet rarely cried. When she was born I had to ask the doctor if she was healthy because she was so quiet. They put her in my arms and she looked up at me and I realized we were going to be okay. As long as we had each other, we would be all right."

He turned and looked at her. Tears shimmered in his eyes. "I didn't leave you, Roni."

"You remember?"

"No, but I know I didn't want to leave you. I know deep in my gut that I was trying to get us out. I can't promise you that I wasn't involved in what McDonald did. I pray I wasn't and I had some different reason I was there, but I know everything changed when I met you. I was getting out. I was getting us both out. I can't remember the hows or the whys, but when I get a vision of that day, I wasn't leaving you behind."

"Are you better now?"

And his sweet time was done. He eased himself up. "Much. Thank you. You should eat."

She stood, smoothing down her T-shirt. "Yeah. Do you want some? These are nice apartments. Does everyone who works here live here, too?"

Good. She wasn't kicking him out. "I would love a slice. And yes, for the most part. There's Nick and Hayley, Brody and Steph, Damon and Penny, of course, though they also have a country house they spend time at. Nina lives in a single. So does Walt. I share with Rob…I guess I don't anymore since he got married. Without me. It's rude. Who gets married when his best friend is in a coma? Can I pick her up?"

Roni set two plates on the table and hesitated for a moment. "I guess so. Sure. She's doing the grabby hands thing, so she'll likely insist now."

He hesitated. "She's so small."

Roni moved in, bending over and lifting Violet into her arms. "She's really not. She's tall for her age and she's a solid kid. She's not delicate, as you will learn when she decides to climb all over the place. You can hold her."

He found his arms suddenly full of sweet baby girl who immediately started patting his face.

"You should watch her. She will stick her finger up your nose," Roni said with a grin. "Do you want a water? I would offer you a beer but the lady who brought us bread and milk and stuff did not bring beer, and that is a mistake when it comes to my mother. She's way easier to get along with if she's had a few."

"No, baby." He gently moved Vi's finger away from his nose and evaded her eye poke. "Your mom does not like me, I take it, and yes, I'll have a water, and yes, I'll get you some beer."

She opened the pizza box with obvious relish. "I never drank beer until I went to Germany. Now I love it."

"There's a bar downstairs, but it's not open tonight." He sank down into his chair, Vi standing on his lap.

"Nose. Nose." His daughter grinned at him.

He touched her nose. "Violet's nose."

"She's learning parts of the body," Roni explained. "I'm teaching her in English and German. *Die nase.*"

Vi touched his nose again. "*Nase.*"

"She already speaks more languages than me. How did I work in Germany and not pick up any German?"

"Because everyone spoke English in the city. I've been out in the country. Almost everyone speaks English there, too, but if you want to fit in, you speak German. And my mom hates everyone. Everyone except Violet and me. But she does hate you in particular since you deflowered her darling girl and left her knocked up."

Violet was trying to climb up his body. "Not willingly. I mean I was totally willing to do the knocking up part. Not the leaving part. Wait. What? Deflowered?"

He'd been her first? She'd been mature to be a virgin. She'd gone all the way through medical school. Had he been a virgin?

Violet was a monkey determined to sit on top of his head. He gently pulled her down and she started right back up again.

Roni was grinning, her face lit with amusement. "Well, she's my mom. She didn't know about all my fun times in college. I'm teasing you, Ste…Tucker."

He liked how she was looking at him, how she was teasing him.

All day she'd been somber as she answered all the questions the different operatives asked. It was good to see her more relaxed. Violet tried to haul herself up by his hair. He winced and stood. "She really likes to climb."

"Told you." She sobered as he started to pace. "What do we do now? I came here because I thought this was going to be over. But it seems like someone is still watching me. How do I handle it? I don't even know who it is. Obviously, I think it's probably Kronberg, but I can't walk in and ask to speak to management."

He'd wondered if she'd been planning on leaving as soon as she could. "You stay with us while we figure out what's going on. We're trained investigators. I assure you Jax is already working on the problem. If for some reason my team has to move, you stay here and be safe."

"Why would you have to move?"

"Ear." Violet tugged on his ear.

How to explain this to her and come out sounding at all like a man who should be trusted with a child. "After I became Tucker, I joined the group of McDonald's men. At some point Kronberg turned on her or she turned on them and she needed cash. We were trained to rob banks."

"Ah, so you're a wanted man." She reached for her second slice. "Solo mentioned something about Interpol. Are you trapped in this building?"

He was trapped in so many ways. "I don't go out a lot, but earlier this year we realized that the Agency was starting to apply pressure. We needed to move around to keep the heat off Damon. We spent some time in Colorado and then Toronto and Munich. Huh, I just realized everywhere we go one of us gets married. It's only me now since...well, Munich was hard on my team."

They'd lost Sasha. They'd lost Dante. Yes, he'd betrayed them all, but he'd been around for so long it was odd to not see his face.

Everything was changing. His brothers were moving on and finding their lives. They were all married, and he knew Jax and River were talking about having a baby.

He had a baby. She was currently laying her head on his shoulder and yawning.

"So at any moment you could be arrested?"

He was such good boyfriend material. "Yes, and you should know that. If anyone comes for me, you pretend you don't know who I am. If we're together, I'm a guy you recently met and you know nothing, and thank you officer for saving me from the dangerous man."

"That seems cold."

"No, it's smart. You're more important." He found a rhythm that seemed to have Vi calming down. She patted his chest and her eyes closed.

Roni stared at him for a moment. "I wish I could believe you're real."

He chuckled. "I just told you I'm wanted by a whole bunch of different authorities and you worry I'm not real? I have no real memory of my past, one of my fun nicknames is Dr. Razor, and according to Rebecca I could pass out or have a cardiac episode at any moment. I'm pretty fucking real. I said fuck. I'm sorry. Don't listen to me, Violet."

"They called you Dr. Razor because anyone who got into a verbal argument with you felt like they'd been in a knife fight," Roni explained. "You were kind of an ass. They liked to say you could cut pretty deep with words. You didn't need a scalpel."

If only he could believe that was the true reason he had that nickname.

"I cared about you," Roni continued quietly. "I think I might have been in love with you, but you hurt me so badly. I understand that you might not have meant to do it, but you also didn't tell me anything was wrong. You did lie to me. You weren't going on an interview."

He wished he knew what he'd been thinking at the time. He had one real thought. "I hope I was trying to protect you."

"But you left me ignorant. You left me so I couldn't protect myself because I didn't know what was going on. I still don't know what's going on."

"I don't know what I was thinking at the time. I think I was trying to protect you. Or maybe I was trying to protect me. Maybe I didn't want you to know all the things I'd done. I can't be sure and I might never be sure. But I promise I'll do everything I can to help you and our daughter. I made a mistake back then. I won't make the same one again. I'll tell you everything."

"You don't know me. That sounds like a dangerous thing to do."

That's what she didn't understand. "But I do. I know you. I don't recall your middle name or where you were born, but I know you're good. I know you like to help people. I know that when I kissed you I felt safe. Isn't that odd? I can't remember the first time I kissed you. I couldn't tell you where it happened or what you were wearing, but I know how I felt."

"My middle name is Ann and I was born in Galveston," she said with a little smile.

"I don't have a middle name. I'm not even sure if Tucker is my first name or my last name," he admitted.

"Honestly, it's probably not your name at all," Roni replied, relaxed again now that they had gotten the emotional stuff out of the way. "But I like it. Somehow it suits you. It's way better than Razor. Yikes."

He'd never liked it either, and he wondered if that dark part of his soul was still lurking somewhere.

The door came open and Sandra Croft strode in. She was dressed for the gym, her toned body in leggings and a tank top. She stared at him, one hand on her hip before shifting her focus to Roni.

"Did you listen at all today? He's got a red notice from Interpol."

Roni pushed her chair back. "For something he didn't really do. Well, he did it but then had his memory wiped, so I don't know that it should count. Do you want some pizza?"

"After a two-hour workout?" Sandra's brow had risen in an aristocratic way. "Of course. I'm starving. You're sure he's okay with Violet?"

"He's already wrapped around her finger," Roni replied, getting another plate.

Sandra looked him over as though sizing him up and finding him wanting. "That would be an excellent way to get into your good graces and potentially use you."

"Mom, she did that thing where she tried to put her finger in every orifice of his face then pulled his hair and basically treated him like a jungle gym and he was perfect with her. She's now drooling all over him and he hasn't even tried to put her down. He's cool."

There was drool? It was all good. He was typically not great with bacteria, but they shared DNA, so Violet's drool was basically his. "I wouldn't hurt my daughter."

"You hurt mine," Sandra replied simply.

Yeah, Sandra was going to be a hard sell. "I also brought her a pizza."

Sandra stared at him and then the faintest hint of a smile broke through her grimness. "Well, then all is forgiven, I suppose." She held out her hands. "She's down for the count. I'll put her in bed. And that better be pepperoni pizza."

He had zero illusions that Sandra was suddenly okay with him, but maybe they could reach a cease fire. "American style."

He handed off his sleeping daughter and turned to Roni as Sandra disappeared into the larger of the two bedrooms. "Does she have everything she needs?"

"My mom? All she needs is a utility knife and a water bottle and she can take over the world. The paranoia is simply a part of her soul," Roni quipped.

"I was talking about Violet."

Roni set another water bottle on the table and he vowed silently to stock the place with beer because if he was eating regularly with his could-be mother-in-law, he was going to need it.

"This place is well stocked," she said, sitting back down. "Penny Knight brought us extra training pants. Her son is potty training, too. Luckily Vi won't care that they're all blue."

"Would she rather have pink?" He could find a way to get pink training pants. He could totally shop on the Internet.

"That's the thing. She doesn't care," Roni said. "As long as she has Mr. Bunny, she's cool. She's a chill kid. I often wonder if all the drama surrounding her somehow made her calm and accepting."

"She takes after me," Sandra said, walking back in and sitting down at the table. Everything about the woman spoke of a military-like economy of movement. "I don't panic. Ever. I have a cool head. I like to think before acting. I've found it always helps to be prepared for everything. You never know when you might need to take action."

She said the last with a pointed stare his way. He wondered how long she'd been plotting revenge. "And it also is good to figure out if the person you might want to take action against wasn't really just an idiot who got caught in a trap not of his own making."

Sandra huffed and turned back to her daughter. "They've got good facilities here. I worked out with that big blond man. He's an asshole."

"Mom, try to get along," Roni said with a frown.

"Oh, if I was twenty years younger I would definitely get along with him. I would climb that man like a tree and make my nest where it counted, if you know what I mean."

He thought he might, and it scared him.

"Mom!"

"I'm old not dead, and that man is beautiful," Sandra said with a chuckle. "Actually all of you are. Including all you idiots who got mindwiped. I can understand why you did him, baby. He's got those soulful eyes that make girls stupid. I bet he's got abs, too."

"Everyone has abs." He wasn't sure how he felt about being objectified. Which was weird because he usually didn't mind. But this was Roni's mom.

Sandra snorted. "Yeah, they are not all the same. You should come down and work out with me tomorrow, Roni. I think the Brit is going to be down there."

"You know they're all married, right? Everyone. Except me. I'm not married. I'm not even dating anyone." He was not mentioning the fact that most of his female experiences since he'd come out of captivity had been with hookers.

Sandra shrugged. "Again, I can look. I wouldn't touch a married man, of course, but I have needs."

"Can we not talk about your needs?" Roni practically begged.

Sandra ignored her daughter. It was obvious she was going to try to make the new guy as uncomfortable as possible. "So, what's up with all the crazy stuff out in the garden part of the building? Those benches are weird. And why are they hidden?"

"Because they're spanking benches and they're hidden because they make scene spaces." Luckily, he wasn't easily made uncomfortable.

The room seemed to go still, both women staring at him like he'd grown horns.

Finally, he had the upper hand. He knew he should step back, but it was good to take the lead on something. It almost never happened. "Yeah, The Garden's a sex club every weekend. And sometimes on

Thursdays. Don't worry. There's a nursery and the subs all take turns with the kiddos."

He picked up his slice and took a bite. His appetite was totally back.

* * * *

Two hours later Roni stared out over the lush greenery below and tried not to think about whether or not Tucker spent time down there. It was quiet at this time of night, though it wasn't even eleven. Apparently, this group kept their kinky stuff to the weekends. And some Thursdays.

Of course he spent time down there. Why wouldn't he? He lived here. He was a gorgeous man who likely had a sex drive, and there was a sex club. Where people had sex. Where he'd probably had sex.

It had been a long time since she'd had sex.

"Hey, are you all right?"

She winced and turned to see the man she'd been thinking about as though she'd managed to conjure him. He'd stayed for dinner, explaining the BDSM lifestyle to her mother. Yeah, that had been uncomfortable for her. Mom and Tucker seemed to have a great time. He was still in the jeans and T-shirt he'd been wearing earlier, but he carried a beer in his hand.

"I needed some air," she replied and held out her hand. "And I'm going to need that."

He'd said he would give her everything.

He passed her the cold beer without a single complaint. "Sure. I went down to Rob's for a couple of minutes. Okay, I went to Rob's because I knew he had beer and your mom is a lot. I think she's planning to do something terrible to me, and it might involve not-fun torture."

Because he was interested in the fun kind of torture.

She took a long drink and then realized that her lips were touching where his lips had touched, and that did something for her.

She turned away and went back to staring at the lush green below. It was beautiful, like the man who moved in beside her, and like that man, she didn't understand it.

"Did I freak you out with the BDSM stuff?"

"Yes." She'd promised honesty.

He took a deep breath. "When I came out of captivity, I was out of control. I might not have looked that way on the outside, but I was angry and confused and violent in my head. I know BDSM sounds like it's all about sex, but it's not. It's about control and trust and communication, which I wasn't great about when I got out."

Of prison. He'd been in prison and punished in ways she was only beginning to comprehend. Why would he turn back to violence in a place that should be loving? "I would think having been tortured that you wouldn't want to have anything to do with it."

"Torture is a funny word. I guess it's like any word. It is what you make it." He pushed off the wall. "I'll make sure you know when play nights are and you can stay in or I can have you moved to one of the apartments at the bottom of the building. You can't see anything from there."

She also wouldn't be able to see the beauty below her. She wouldn't be able to see him as often if they weren't living on the same floor. "All right. Then what does the word mean to you?"

He stopped and she was worried he wouldn't answer her. Finally, he leaned back over, looking down, his hip brushing against hers. "Oh, torture can be hideous. Trust me. I've been worked over by some of the finest pain givers in the world, and I was on time dilation drugs so it lasted for what felt like years. But there are forms of torture that can be sweet, and we use the word the same way we use the word *play* or *submissive*. The women and men who submit here typically aren't submissive in their vanilla lives. They use it as a form of relaxation, a way to let that piece of themselves be expressed. Some use submission as permission to enjoy themselves. The torture in that case isn't torture at all since it's something they choose, something they enjoy."

She hadn't considered what role he would want to play. He'd been so in control when she knew him, but it was apparent he'd changed a lot. "Are you the submissive?"

He grinned her way. "No. I prefer the dominant side. I know. I'm so sweet you wouldn't expect it, but there it is. You are not the first person to ask me that question." The grin faded as he sobered. "I need the control during sex. I need it to feel safe and I need my partner to trust me so I feel…human, I guess. Worthy."

"Worthy?" She wasn't sure how spanking someone could make him feel worthy.

"Having someone trust me makes me feel good. I was out of control in the beginning. BDSM gave me some of it back. It let me bring out a part of my personality in a controlled, negotiated way where I know the boundaries and the rules. In the beginning I had a mentor who wouldn't allow me to hurt anyone. Now I would never do it because I'm in control. I wouldn't ever want to lose the trust of the people around me."

She shook her head. "I guess I don't understand it because I don't have those tendencies."

"Really?" He made a sound, the one that let her know he didn't buy what she was selling.

"What?" She turned to look at him.

He shrugged slightly. "I'm just saying most women have tendencies when they let themselves."

"What is that supposed to mean?" She hadn't even wanted sex for years. Not since him. First she'd been far too angry with him to want any man. Then she'd lost her sister and she'd been pregnant and scared. The only reason she was thinking about sex again was that she was somewhat safe. It didn't have anything to do with him.

"What do you want from sex?" he asked.

She took another drink. She knew she should walk straight back into her apartment and avoid this incredibly inappropriate line of discussion. It had been one thing when he was explaining St. Andrew's Crosses to her overly curious mother. There had been humor in that.

This was different. There was clear sensuality to his words, and his eyes were warm on her. Though they were standing in the hall, they were alone, and the garden below made the whole setting somewhat romantic. Very romantic. She shouldn't talk about sex with him.

"Pleasure, of course." She hadn't had physical pleasure in a long time. She hadn't even touched herself. She'd gotten so caught up in being a mom that she forgot she was a woman.

He straightened up. "Of course. And what else?"

"Why does there have to be something else? It's a biological imperative."

"I'll tell you what I want. Everyone wants an orgasm. It's easy. I can use my hand for that. What I want, what I've been chasing for the whole time I can remember, which isn't long, is connection. I want to feel close to someone. I want to give pleasure as much as I want to receive it. Sometimes more. That's where the worthy part comes in."

Oh, how she longed for the secretive Steven. He'd been mysterious and closed off and he had nothing on the man in front of her. This man could rip her apart if she let him, and she couldn't bring herself to not respond. "All right. I want connection, too, but it has to be the right person. I think I find that connection more in the kissing and the holding than in the actual sex."

He frowned suddenly. "Did I...I didn't give you an orgasm, did I?"

He went from intense and sexy to goofy and somehow still sexy in a heartbeat. It was fascinating to her. It made her smile. "I had an orgasm. Several, actually. You were good in bed, but there wasn't anything weird about it. It was straight-up sex."

He was right back to serious and sexy. "Then I wasn't on my game."

"I said it was good."

"And I'm saying it can be better," he insisted. "So you say you don't have any of these tendencies, but let me run you through a scenario. What if you had a partner who you trusted fully. You know this man won't hurt you so for an evening you offer to do anything he asks of you sexually."

Now she saw his game. "That sounds pretty good for him."

"Only because you don't understand what it means to be a Dom. At least not the way I prefer to play. This dominant partner would think about the way he's going to play with you for a long time before your date. He would plan how the evening would go. He would watch you for long periods of time, observing what pleases you and what doesn't, what turns you on and what you can live without. He would try to make sure everything was set up properly so all you have to do when you join him is obey."

"I don't like that word." Sometimes she felt like she'd been far too obedient in life. But then again, her sister had defied the world and she wasn't here anymore.

He shook his head. "Again, you're hung up on words. Obey is

tricky here because the obedience must be given. It has to be consensual or it means nothing. No one can force you to obey. In fact, in our world if you withdraw consent, it's my duty to stop and ensure your comfort and safety."

"Even if that means walking away?"

"Especially in that case. So this man you trust will have likely spent days thinking about you. That would be part of the thrill for him. He would enjoy thinking about how he could bring you pleasure. He would know that sometimes a woman needs permission to be sexual. He would create a space where there's no shame, where she can explore the limits of her sexuality because he knows that shame is the enemy of pleasure."

"I've explored. I'm not a virgin." She'd had some crazy college nights.

"You've explored your fantasies?" His voice had gone low. "Or have you even allowed yourself to fantasize at all? What did you like about me in bed?"

She was oddly comfortable talking to him and that made her anxious. "This is weird."

"Not in my world," he said with a wistful sigh. "You want to know what happens in the garden below? A whole lot of it is talking. How can you know what you want if you never ask, if you never let yourself acknowledge that it's okay to talk about this?"

She didn't like the fact that he was making sense, but then she was mostly flustered at how nice it was to be with him. And what did it really hurt? They were only talking. "Fine. I'm not some kind of prude. I liked the way you kissed me."

"How did I kiss you?" The question came out with an aching curiosity that hit her right in the heart.

He couldn't remember something that had been important to her, a moment that had changed her life.

"I don't know. I guess I liked the way I didn't have to think when you kissed me. It wasn't awkward. You would put your hand on the nape of my neck and I would feel petite. I liked that. I liked how big your hand was and how I could follow your lead."

"Like this?"

His hand slid over her neck and her whole body lit up. It was right there—the impulse to let herself relax and follow his lead.

"Yeah, a lot like that."

He stared at her for a moment, the heat palpable between them. And then he withdrew his hand and she could breathe again. "If I were your Dom, I would set up a scene where you were completely helpless. I would tie you down and you would be forced to accept whatever I gave you. I would touch you everywhere, letting you know that at least while we're playing, your body belongs to me. I would run my hands everywhere and when you least expected it, I would give your nipples a nasty twist. The pain would flare, but it wouldn't last. It would only serve to make your nipples exquisitely sensitive when I decide to lick and suck them. You wouldn't be able to fight me in the beginning and in the end, you wouldn't even think about fighting me. You would be my plaything, and that's all you would need to be."

She was back to not being able to breathe. This intensity had been a large part of Steven's appeal. He could be so ruthless about his work and he would often turn that singlemindedness on her, and that was when she felt like she was the only woman in the world. No man had ever looked at her like he had, like Tucker was now.

"The first time you kissed me we were at the lab. It was after hours and I'd stayed behind because I was finishing up some reports for Dr. Walsh. There were a couple of doctors there who thought they could mess around with me. One in particular made a nuisance of himself. He was married but he thought the younger women were all fair game. That night he'd stayed behind, too, and he was coming on to me. Hard. You walked in and he pretty much peed himself after you were done with him."

"Did I hurt him?"

His question came out measured so she couldn't tell if he wanted the answer to be yes or no.

"Not physically, but he didn't touch me again. Anyway, afterward you stayed while I finished up. You said you wanted to walk me out to my car. I thanked you and we ended up talking." She could remember how grateful she'd been to not be left alone. "It was the first time I saw you as something other than the ambitious doctor who handled things for McDonald. You stayed way longer than you had planned, and I felt bad for keeping you. You told me it was okay because it might be the only good thing you'd done for anyone in months. I don't know what made me do it, but I went up on my tiptoes and kissed you. It wasn't much. It was barely two seconds. When I moved back, you told me that wasn't a kiss. You asked me if you could show me what a kiss was. And you did."

He'd been careful with her, making sure she was all right.

Rather like he'd explained he would be now. He'd been careful right up until he'd been sure she was with him and then he'd taken over. Then he'd taken her someplace she'd never been before.

"Show me."

She came out of the memory at the sound of his command. *Show me.* That was what he'd said to her that night.

She could come out of the memory because it was hers. That moment was there in her brain and she could call on it for the rest of her life. It was something so personal. Her memories were the sum of her soul. It struck her forcibly what he'd lost. What she'd lost. That memory had truly been theirs, a shared history that should have connected them for the rest of their lives.

Now she was the only one who knew what it had felt like that night. He was right there. He was standing in front of her asking for that connection again.

She went up on her toes. "Thank you. I didn't want him near me, but I don't feel the same way about you." She let her lips brush his, the bare meeting of flesh that came from a woman who wasn't sure of what she'd wanted then. Of what she wanted now. "And then you shook your head."

Tucker shook his head and took the beer from her hand. He set it on the ledge and turned back to her. "Oh, that wasn't a kiss. Let me show you how I kiss. Will you let me kiss you, Roni? I think about kissing you all the time."

So close to what he'd actually said. She would take it. "Yes. Please kiss me."

The air seemed to go out of the room and her vision focused in on him. It was like the rest of the world fell away. It was exactly as it had been that first night with him. Something had fallen into place when he'd looked at her and she'd known nothing would be the same.

If he kissed her again, they would have that connection they'd lost.

His hand went around the nape of her neck, sending a delicious warmth down her spine. He pulled her slightly, drawing her close in an easy show of strength. He brought their bodies together and her breasts brushed against his chest. His free hand wrapped around her waist and she took a moment to look into his eyes.

They were the clearest blue. Something about his eyes had always dragged her in. Even when they were cold, even when no one else had been able to see the emotion behind them, she hadn't been fooled.

"I want to believe. But I don't want to want to believe," she said quietly.

"Because it would be easier if I was the bastard you've spent years believing I was. I know. Roni, I can't imagine I was easy to care for then. I'm not easy now. But for however long we get together I want to try to be with you. We can take it slow and find a way to be friends again."

She sighed at the thought because he was going to pull away and that was the last thing she wanted. Now that she was here and alone with him, she knew she couldn't lose the chance to explore this side of the man. "We were never friends."

She moved in and kissed him. It wasn't what had happened that night, but that was all right. They were making a new memory, one no one could take away from them. It might all go to hell tomorrow, but she would kiss the father of her child again. She would have this new memory of him.

Tucker groaned as her lips met his and his hands tightened. He took over the kiss and she followed his lead, wrapping her arms around him and letting every reason to not do this fall away.

His mouth took hers, devouring her in the best of all possible ways. Comfort. She'd found comfort and safety in his arms. It was precisely why his leaving had been so hard a betrayal. No one had ever made her feel like Steven had.

And she wanted that again. In that moment, she couldn't even lie to herself.

His fingers wound in her hair, tugging lightly to guide her. His tongue slipped in, dominating hers, and she realized he'd been right. They'd been in dominant and submissive positions even then. She simply hadn't known what to call them.

Would he have taken her further if they'd had longer together?

Would he have eased her into a sexual relationship where he took control and she was able to find a place where she was comfortable with herself? Where she didn't question if she was doing something right because he would tell her and they would find a way?

Was this why sex had been so good with him? And what would sex be like with this version of the man?

"God, I remember this," he said against her lips. "I remember how good you felt in my arms. I remember that this felt like home, and I hadn't been home in so fucking long."

He kissed her again and she held him tight, emotion welling inside.

"Veronica? I'm sorry to interrupt but Violet woke up. She's asking for you. I can tell her you're busy."

She practically jumped back at the sound of her mother's voice. She was absolutely certain she was a bright shade of red. Violet was awake? She was in a foreign place and she'd woken up and her mom wasn't there. Of course she was scared. What was she doing? He'd been back in her life for a single day and she was ready to give it up?

"I'm sorry. I'll be right there." She turned to Tucker. "I should go."

"Do you need help?" His hair was mussed because at some point she'd run her fingers through it. It was soft and she liked that it was slightly long. It framed his gorgeous face. "I could rock her."

They were moving way too fast and he was right. His life was complicated. She hadn't come here to fall madly in love with the man she'd thought had ruined her life. She'd come to build a new one with her daughter. She shook her head. "No. I should get to bed. I'm...this was..."

"A mistake?"

She nodded.

"I accept that, but Roni, it's one you're going to make again and soon. I'll see you in the morning. I want to have breakfast with my daughter."

Was that a good idea?

He continued. "I might not be able to be in her life later. The unselfish thing to do would be to stay away, and I would if she was older. But she's so young. Can't she know even for a few days that her father loved her?"

"She usually gets up around seven. I don't know what I have for breakfast," she admitted.

He'd placed much needed space between them, as though he knew how close she was to simply running away. "I'll be here at seven with breakfast. I'll handle everything. And Roni, thank you for letting me know her. I'm down the hall if you need anything."

He walked away and Roni turned to her mom. "It didn't mean anything."

Her mother's eyes rolled. "Sure it didn't. That boy. He's good. Damn, even I wouldn't have been cold enough to turn his hot ass down."

"Mom." She rushed inside and found Violet crying. "I'm sorry, baby girl."

"No, I'm sorry," her mother said as she walked in. "The situation might not be what we thought it was. I talked to Taggart and despite the fact that he's a massive ass, he's also solid. He's willing to stand up for the kid. I shouldn't have interrupted you but it's habit. I'll try to go easier on him. But, sweetheart, even if he's everything they say he is, even if he didn't leave you willingly…"

"He's still dangerous." She finished the sentence, reading her mother's mind with ease.

Violet clutched at her, but her little head had turned as though she was looking to see where the new guy had gone.

Tucker was dangerous for all of them.

Chapter Six

Four days later, Tucker sat back in his chair and put a hand on Buster's head. "She tried broccoli for the first time last night and it did not go well. Neither in the eating process or the digestive process."

Robert chuckled. He occupied the desk across from Tucker's. All of the Lost Boys shared a single big office space when they were in London. "I think Ari and I will hold off on the kiddos for a while. They're cute, but I want to avoid diapers as long as I can."

"I'm not going to be able to," Owen complained. "I'm terrified of nappies, but Rebecca's got that look in her eye. She knows Jax and River are trying. And I saw her playing with Vi and Ollie the other day. All of the sudden she's asking what do I think would be a good name for a kid. She was not amused when I told her I liked the name Ten Years Down The Line. I'm worried but then I think if Tucker there can have a kid, I'm probably okay. He's a baby himself."

He sent Owen his middle finger. He was settling in nicely to being a father, including watching over her while Damon's boy sized her up. Yeah, he had his eyes on Oliver Knight. Though she could do worse. Ollie would be well educated, and Damon was both wealthy and polite. When they eventually got to Dallas, though, he would watch those Taggart boys.

"Hey, he's been a doting dad," Robert pointed out. "He spends all his free time with Roni and Violet. Have you made any headway with Roni? She seems to have opened up a bit. I saw her downstairs having lunch with Rebecca and Ariel."

"Rebecca and Roni had a breakthrough," Owen admitted. "It involved wine, and then they yelled at each other for not talking when things were going bad at Kronberg. I thought I should break it up at one point, but Ian said it was how women worked things out. There was a lot of crying and then the tequila came out and now they're best friends."

It was the emotional equivalent of guys punching it out.

He and Roni needed to do the same thing, though it wouldn't involve punching. It would involve getting nasty, though. The tension between them was building and had been since she'd kissed him so sweetly and then he'd eaten her up like a starving man. He just needed more time.

"Explain the delay again," a deep voice said, reminding Tucker why he had a hundred-pound dog seeking his comfort.

The big mutt who had followed Jax and River halfway across the globe rested his head in Tucker's lap. Normally he would have stayed close to Jax, but Jax was currently being interrogated by Ian, who was anxious to get home. Buster had an excellent sense of self-preservation.

Ian loomed over the resident computer guru. "Why is this taking so long? You've had days to do a simple job. Do I need to bring Adam over?"

Jax's head tilted up to look at their boss. "I thought Adam was working for himself now. I don't know that he can drop everything to come over and fake a couple of IDs for you. That's like asking Michelangelo to paint a portrait of your dog."

"Fine," Ian said, his jaw clenched. "I can bring Hutch over if you can't do it."

He had to give it to Jax. His brother was cool under pressure. "I thought Hutch was holding down the actual paying work while Adam's company is searching for Robert's mom."

"I told you I would help with that." Robert stood at his desk. "But I also don't want to put her in danger. We don't even know if she exists. She could be dead for all we know. My brother, too."

"That's not what Green said," Jax pointed out.

"Green lies." Robert sat back down, his eyes going to the screen.

Tucker wished he knew what was going on in Robert's head. He didn't want to talk about the family his former wife had described. Despite the fact that Levi Green had told them Emily Seeger hadn't been lying about Robert's mother and brother, Robert didn't want to talk about the potential of finding them.

Jax seemed to understand Robert needed a moment. He looked back to Ian. "Do you want to pull them off important work so they can forge a couple of documents? I'm waiting on the right tools. This is a delicate thing, Tag. Especially considering we're dealing with a baby and an elderly woman."

"Elderly woman my arse," Owen said from his desk. "She talked me into sparring with her yesterday and then she kicked me in the balls. Bloody hell. She said ISIS wouldn't play fair and they wouldn't care about my future baby-making prospects. I tried to tell her I wasn't planning on going up against ISIS anytime soon."

Tag pointed Owen's way. "You should always be ready to go up against ISIS. Sandra Croft is the most awesome thing I've found in a long time, and I want to recruit that woman. I think she could make an excellent operative if we could get her to stop calling everyone an asshole. And Jax, I'm going to tell her you called her elderly."

Jax proved there was pressure that could faze him. He paled considerably. "Hey, I was only pointing out that we don't usually have to move women like her. We don't normally move whole families. I have to have a cover story and I have to deal with the baby and… Tucker asked me to slow things down."

He groaned. Fucking tattletale.

Tag had already turned on him and Buster whimpered and shifted away. "I knew it was you. Listen here, you little shit, I can't go home without them. They want to go back to Dallas and I can't send them out without an escort. I have a pregnant wife and three kids. Do you understand how pissy the wife gets when she's left alone with three kids for two weeks because I'm waiting on Jax to do his damn job?"

"I'll go with them." It was what he wanted to do. He needed to move around a lot. Why couldn't this move be to Dallas for the time being? "You can leave tonight and I'll go when everything's ready. I can help out around the office and get them settled in."

"Or you could go to jail and be extradited to any number of countries."

Tag was being overly dramatic. "It's only four countries. That's a specific number. Four whole countries in the world want to throw me in jail. One of them is New Zealand. How bad could that be?"

He didn't remember robbing that bank in Auckland, but he was sure it had been a polite crime.

"Yeah, well the other three aren't known for hobbits," Tag shot back. "I haven't spent years of my life trying to keep you alive so you could get tossed in a freaking gulag in Siberia. Am I clear?"

He'd been clear all week. It was frustrating. He wasn't going to let Roni leave without him. He couldn't lose Violet. "That is my child. Tell me you would let Kenzie or Kala go alone? Anything could go wrong."

"Which is precisely why I'm escorting them, and Solo is going to monitor things so I've got a heads-up if we need to change plans. We're going on a private jet." Tag seemed to rein himself in. "I get that you're worried, but I think it's safe for her to go. I think it might be safer for her than staying here, and you should know that I've talked to Ezra about moving you guys again."

That had them all sitting up.

"What?" Jax said.

Tag held a hand up. "I'm worried because I think German intelligence is sniffing around MI6. Solo has information that places two known German operatives in London at MI6 headquarters talking to the new boss. And we all know both agencies are interested in you. Kronberg has a new VP. You remember Arthur Dwyer? The one who we're pretty sure lied about seeing Tucker and Veronica at the airport, but he definitely knew they'd gone somewhere?"

"I remember he watched my wife's arse and breasts the whole time he was having lunch with her," Owen said with a frown.

"Yeah, well, he's gone from research to the corporate top floors, and I think that can't be a coincidence." Tag stared at him. "I think it's a matter of time before MI6 puts the pressure on Damon to give you up, and he won't. What do you think that will mean?"

It meant trouble.

The door came open and Ezra strode through. He stopped when he realized everyone was looking at him. And frowning because he hadn't said a damn thing.

Ezra turned to Tag. "You told them? I told you not to tell them until I had a plan in place."

"Why the hell do we have to move?" Jax asked, standing. Buster sat at his side. "I've moved my wife three times in the last year. You know we're talking about having kids."

Ezra pointed a finger his way. "Which is precisely why you shouldn't have gotten married. You knew what would happen when the heat was on us again. River knew exactly what she was getting into. Robert and Owen are free to stay here. You and Tucker will come with me. I think whoever was checking out Solo's place the other night was intelligence."

"I don't understand why they would come after us at this point. You're working with MI6 and the CIA," Robert pointed out. "You've been feeding them intel on us the whole time."

"In order to protect you." Tag's arms had crossed over his chest. "Damon and I have been working with trusted members of those teams. Damon's old boss recently retired, and it wasn't his choice. We think one of the reasons they forced Nigel out is because they want someone who will put more pressure on us. I would fight, but the truth of the matter is I *am* harboring two fugitives. I was able to get the charges against my brother and Robert resolved because of the countries those charges came from. I haven't been able to do the same for the secondary team."

Because McDonald had used them far more than her alpha boys. Because she'd been willing to risk them in a way she hadn't with her favorites.

"And would that change if Tucker and I offered to fully cooperate with the Agency?" Jax asked. "Would the Agency be able to get them to back down?"

It was funny because a few days before he wouldn't have even considered it since it would mean medical tests, and he didn't trust the Agency as far as he could throw it. But now, the thought of being separated from Roni and Vi made him sick. If there was even a chance they could have any normalcy at all, he would take it. "Yes. What if we were willing to do whatever they asked in exchange for full pardons or the promise to fight any extradition attempts?"

"River and I will be perfectly happy in Bliss. We don't need to leave the country again," Jax said, his eagerness apparent. "Tucker's more than welcome to come with us. Or he can stay in Dallas. I'm done with leaving home."

He would have options if he could get his name cleared. Or at least the promise that he wouldn't be arrested and tossed into some international jail. He could have a relationship with his daughter, and he was desperate enough to use that to forge a new bond with Veronica.

He wanted her. He needed her. She was the one and he needed time to make her see that they worked. She'd softened up enormously since that first meeting. She let him stay at her place until it was time for Violet to go to bed. He ate most of his meals with her. She cooked and he did the dishes and Sandra told him all the ways he was doing it wrong. Once they'd watched TV afterward and he'd sat beside her. It had been a British show about ghosts trying to get rid of a couple in their home, but he hadn't really watched it. He'd watched her laugh. He'd watched her lips curl up and her chest move.

She hadn't let him kiss her again, but it was coming.

Then he would be coming. But only after she came.

He couldn't do any of that if she was in Dallas and he was holed up in Liechtenstein or some other European country with cheap hotels and not a ton of security. Yeah, it probably wouldn't be Liechtenstein.

"You don't understand what you could be getting into," Ezra said, a grim set to his face. "I don't know what they want. I know what Solo says, but she's not working directly for the Agency in this case. I've told you there are factions in the CIA, and they don't change the way a president does. Hayes is up for reelection."

"He's probably going to win," Robert pointed out.

"But if he doesn't, we have no idea how the other guy would handle our case." Tag continued Erza's line of thought. "Or if he even would handle it at all. Most presidents take a hands-off approach, hence places like The Ranch existing. They don't want to know what the Agency is doing so they don't get any blood on their hands. You could go into this and it could be fine for a couple of months, then there's a regime change and suddenly you're worth more dead than alive."

The Ranch had been a secret facility deep in the woods of Colorado. According to the records they'd found, he was fairly certain he'd been there, working with Hope McDonald. Would he end up in a place like that? Would he deserve whatever he got there? He knew Jax didn't.

"You can't do it." Robert moved to stand next to Owen. "You have to give us time. We can find out what happened to that intel. If we have the intel—that list of everyone who knowingly worked with McDonald—then we've got the advantage. We can handle this. I think you had something to do with it, Tucker."

"We all do," Owen agreed. "We think you figured out exactly what was happening and you decided to go to the authorities. Maybe that's what you were doing that day you disappeared. We've got some leads to follow. And Rebecca and I will go with you. Wherever you go, we'll be there. She won't even question it."

Because Rebecca had become a part of the team. Rebecca would put her career on hold, place herself in danger, do anything it took to stay with them.

Did he want that life for Roni and Vi?

No, but he also didn't want them out in the world on their own. He didn't want his daughter to wonder what had happened to her father for the rest of her life. She should know that he fought for the right to stay with her and her mother.

"How long do we have before you're going to move us?"

Ezra seemed to breathe a sigh of relief. "I think we should do it next week. I'm putting Rob on logistics. But you should understand that I am going to try to convince Rob and Owen to stay here. We'll move faster as a foursome than in a big group."

"Not going to happen," Rob said.

"Even if I wanted to, Rebecca won't let Tucker go without a physician," Owen explained. "She doesn't like the idea of him working so soon. She definitely won't like him traveling."

"I'll minimize it as much as possible," Ezra promised. "I'm worried that the Agency seems to be here in London. That's three intelligence groups. I don't like it."

"Solo would know if something is about to go down. Wouldn't she?" Jax asked. "She would warn us."

"Only if it suited her purposes." Ezra moved toward the desk he used. "I worry she's staying here to keep an eye on us in case we do move."

"And I worry that your emotional state won't let you see an ally when she's standing right in front of your face," Tag shot back. "She's the one who told us she thinks MI6 is working with German intelligence and might be ready to make a play."

"Which is exactly what she would say if she wanted to distract us so she could make her own play." Ezra kept on walking.

"She's had access for a long time. If she was going to make a move, she would have made it," Tag said with a long-suffering sigh. "But your butt is so hurt it's affecting your vision."

Ezra set his laptop on the desk. "Fire me, then."

"I didn't hire you in the first place." Tag's eyes rolled before turning back to Tucker. "Let Jax know it's okay for him to do his job. I would threaten the hell out of him, but he's not going to move until you let him. I trained you too well. The puppies have a pack and they're tight."

Tag had been the one to get them out of that hell they'd been in. He'd only been there to save his brother Theo, and Tucker knew well that most men would have done the job and turned the rest of their sorry asses over to whoever wanted them. Not Ian Taggart. At great personal expense, he'd given them a place to stay. He'd put himself in the crosshairs when he hadn't had to. He trusted Tag. He owed Tag.

"Jax, it's cool." It turned his stomach but if Tag said this was what needed to happen, he would be patient.

"It's already done," Jax admitted. "I'm actually brilliant at what I do."

Tag ignored Jax's lack of humility. "Thank you, Tucker. I promise I'll take care of them. We'll leave for Dallas the day after tomorrow. I've got some friends at customs and immigration who I'll let know we're coming."

Which meant they would probably not look so closely at the documentation Roni, Vi, and Sandra would be flying under. They would be safe with McKay-Taggart.

"I'll also make sure she's got a safe place to stay. Adam's offered up his guest house," Tag explained. "We'll give them twenty-four seven security, and that also means zealously guarding your territory of all invaders foreign and domestic, and other men who sniff around your chick."

Tag was a giver. "She'll need that for a while, but if I'm gone for months, maybe years, you have to help her move on."

He didn't want her to move on, but he had to face the fact that he might never be able to be the kind of husband and father he wanted to be. He might spend the rest of his life on the run. It might end up being a short life.

Tag put a hand on his shoulder. "I know I haven't sorted this out yet. I know I've shot down every plan you've come up with. But I promise it's not going to be years."

He'd had a lot of ideas he'd thought could help, including having them all spit into one of those DNA test things and putting them online to see who they matched with. Tag had pointed out that DNA was one of those things the cops probably had from their various crimes and that they wouldn't hesitate to use it against them even if they'd only been wanting to find out how much Norwegian blood they had.

"Solo is right about one thing," Tag continued. "This whole mess is coming to a head and we've got to hunker down and get through it. I want you to try hypnosis again. I know it didn't work with Ari, but Kai has had some success with it. When you're settled, I'll send him out to you."

Because the keys to the kingdom might be locked in his fucked-up brain. That was what killed him. He was very likely the one who could give them the bargaining chip they needed. Someone had stolen those files and it was probably him. He'd gone into the Kronberg building and he'd known exactly where the files should have been. He'd known where the safe was hidden. When he'd worked there, he'd been a researcher. How else would he know where the secrets were held if he hadn't been the one to take them?

"I'll do whatever you think is best, but I want to talk to Levi Green, too." He needed to find out what Levi knew. Yes, he could be lying, but at least that would tell them something.

Ezra stood back up. "I doubt that's going to happen. Unless Solo pulls some serious strings, there's no way they'll let any of us close to a high-value prisoner."

"I don't know how long he'll be of high value if he doesn't talk. Solo says he's been holding out," Tag explained. "He still has some influence with the agency. My question is why is he holding out? If he gave them the information they wanted, they would cut a deal with him."

"What if I'm the only one who knows? What if I was working for him and I was going to meet him that day?" He'd thought about it a lot since he'd learned Green was supposedly in Paris the same day. What if he'd fallen in love with Veronica and realized he needed an out? What if he'd been willing to cut a deal to hand over valuable information to the Agency in exchange for not getting his ass prosecuted for international crimes? "It's why I should talk to him."

"I'll run it past Solo," Tag offered. "I'm only going to agree if we can work out a deal where we share the information with the Agency, but they don't get physical custody of you."

"And I'm going to be there," Ezra said. "I'm not letting him anywhere near a bunch of Agency assholes without backup. If he goes in, we both go with him."

"Agreed." Tag nodded toward the door. "Can I talk to you in private?"

He was going to get dressed down for asking Jax to hold up Roni's documents. He could handle it. It was nice of Tag to not do it in front of everyone. And it didn't matter because she would be gone soon. She would be on a completely different continent and so would his daughter. He followed Tag out but he couldn't really feel his feet.

Tag walked to the end of the hall before turning to him. He glanced back down toward the office. "I don't think those fuckers can hear us here. We need to talk."

"I'm sorry about holding you up."

Tag waved that off. "I do get it, man. No, we need to discuss something else. I'm giving you two nights to get her in bed and brand her."

That wasn't what he'd been expecting. "What?"

"I'm not talking about an actual brand, though Kori totally let Kai do that to her. It was a weird night. I offered to do Charlie and she promised if I touched her with hot metal in an attempt to put a *property of* sign on her body, she would torch my dick. I believe her so I dropped it. No, I'm talking about an emotional and sexual brand. I've watched her a lot over the last couple of days and she wants you. It's obvious she's not over you. So, give her something to hold on to and by something I mean your dick. You have to be good at it, man. I know you've practiced because I paid for your hookers."

He glanced around. "Hey, let's not say the *h* word while Roni's in the building. And I didn't sleep with most of them. I was looking for connection."

"Then they overcharged," Tag complained. "They should have a cuddle rate. You do realize you always picked the one who looked like her, right? Every single one of those women looked something like Veronica Croft. You didn't mean to leave her. Or am I wrong and you're spending every night at her place so you can be with your daughter? That's fine, too, but if that's true you shouldn't implement the plan."

"I'm crazy about Roni. I want to marry her." He knew it deep inside. "What plan? I didn't realize there was a plan except you're going to take her back to the States."

"The plan where you fuck her so well she's still waiting for you when you get to come back to the States. That plan. You need to make your move."

There was a scenario Tag wasn't thinking about. "And if I don't get to come back? If I never clear my name? Then all I'll have done is hurt her again."

It was the last thing he wanted to do. It was precisely why he hadn't even thought about pushing her. He wanted her, wanted every minute he could get with her, but it might only bring her heartache in the end. Hadn't he brought her enough of that?

Tag groaned. "I knew you'd do the martyr thing. You have that look in your eyes, the one that says I'm not going down fighting. It's stupid. I'm telling you a life secret. Don't go down at all. You don't go into a mission saying I hope this works out but maybe I shouldn't give it my all because it could go wrong and someone might get hurt. Fuck no. You go in believing fully that you will win the day. You will win the girl. In this case it's more like winning back your baby mama."

He winced. "I don't think we should call her that."

Tag shrugged. "Everybody will call her that. I'm planning on introducing her to everyone in Dallas as Tucker's baby mama. If she doesn't like it, she can marry you and then I'll introduce you as Veronica's husband. See, this is complex psychological manipulation. I'll handle that part. You do the easy part. Fuck her so well she can't imagine fucking anyone else. Do you need a playlist? It's not actually a list. It's more like a single song set to play over and over again, but it gives you the perfect thrusting rhythm."

He was not listening to Guns N' Roses while he made love to Roni. He would close his eyes and see Big Tag's head or something. No. Yuck. And he wasn't making love to Roni. "I'm not trying to be a martyr. I'm trying to hurt her as little as possible. I obviously fucked up the first time. It's not fair to do it to her again. If I can get us what we need and get back to her in a reasonable amount of time, maybe we can try."

Tag frowned his way. "No, what's not fair is to treat her like she's some prize to only be won if you survive. She's not. If there's one thing I've learned it's that our women, our wives, the ones we would do anything for, need to be more than a freaking prize. If you love her, you tell her and you give her the chance to choose what she wants to do. You trust her enough to know her own mind and to decide if she can be a partner to you. You don't walk away from your partner because she might get her feelings hurt if you die."

He was deliberately misunderstanding. "I'm not walking away because my job is dangerous. I literally have people who would like to cut me open and see how my brain works. She's in danger around me."

"I think she's in danger whether you're around or not. Tucker, think about it. According to her she's been safe for almost three years. She comes out of hiding and suddenly someone knows where Solo's secret house is? They've been watching her. They know she was there the day you went missing. Hell, it could be about whatever her sister found out. Someone thinks she knows something."

His gut clenched. "Then we have to protect her."

Tag's eyes rolled. "That's what I've been trying to say."

"No, you've been telling me to take her to bed." Which was all he wanted to do. He wanted to wrap her up and never let her get out of bed. Except when Violet was hungry. Or needed a change. Or got fussy. He understood that his courtship was going to involve a lot of baby bodily fluids.

"Exactly." Tag nodded like he was happy he'd finally understood.

Tucker hesitated. "I don't want to ask. I really don't, but what do you mean?"

"I mean she'll trust you more if you show her how much you care about her." Tag seemed to get serious. "I mean if she cares about you, she'll want that memory. There's this thing from an old poem and it makes me gag even to say it."

He knew exactly what Tag was talking about. And he was absolutely going to force him to say it. "What's the saying? I'm sure I never heard it."

Tag groaned. "Fine. 'It's better to have loved and lost than to never have loved' or something like that. It means life is short. Drink the beer. Fuck the girl. Love her. Let yourself love her. Give her the chance to love you. You don't know if you'll get another one. And, man, if you tell anyone we had this talk, I'll kill you."

But only after he'd made his play for Roni. Maybe Tag was right and he was trying to martyr himself. It was better for her to know how he felt. It was better for Roni to know he'd loved her even if it all fell apart. It was better for Violet to know her dad had fought to keep them all together.

Even if they couldn't physically be together.

He could have two nights with her. If he could convince her to give him a chance. Tonight was a play night. The Garden would be lit up and she was curious. He could use that. And he had practiced. Not that he would ever tell her those stories. Ever. "All right. I'll try."

Tag seemed to breathe a sigh of relief. "Thank god because the last thing I needed was you being all emotional. Excellent. If you can get her to come to play night, that would be a place to start. I won't be there. I'm being a perfectly good boy and I'll be on the computer having a family meal I can't eat and yelling at my kids so they don't forget me. They put the laptop in my place and I sit there. Sometimes Bud licks the screen and hits the camera and I get to watch them all through a haze of dog saliva." Tag sighed and walked toward the elevators. "I need to get home."

He watched as Tag walked away. It was a mere moment before Robert was in the hallway.

"'It's better to have loved and lost'?" Robert said with a shake of his head. "I can't believe he said that."

"Jax has that superhearing thing on, doesn't he?" He hadn't mentioned to Tag that Jax might have modified his computer to help them hear and see what was going on in the hallway.

"Oh, when he realized Tag was giving you his version of the dad talk, he recorded that sucker for humanity. I think he's already making a song out of it," Robert revealed. "But I'm glad you're going after Roni. I think you should. Tag is right. You don't know when you'll get another chance. And I'll talk to Adam. I should try to find them."

His family. His mother and his brother, who might or might not exist. Who might or might not be alive.

He held out a hand. "I'll do anything I can to help you find your family."

Robert took it. "And I'll do anything I can to help you keep yours together."

It was a promise between brothers. That was all he could ask.

* * * *

It felt good to sit in the courtyard with friends having lunch. How long had it been since she'd gotten to do something normal?

Granted she'd only known Ariel for a few days, but Robert's wife was lovely and already felt like a woman she could get close to. Rebecca and she had patched up things the other night in what Ariel called the Great Tequila Peace Treaty. They'd both made mistakes and they'd both been afraid.

It was time to find some bravery.

"How are things going with you and Tucker?" Ariel asked in her lovely British accent. Her hair was in its natural curl, forming a halo around her face. "Has he put the moves on you yet?"

Yeah, maybe bravery would have to wait. "He's getting to know Violet."

"I won't ever have a Violet if your mother keeps kicking my husband in the balls," Rebecca said, her hand on the glass of rosé she was enjoying. "I had to hold a bag of frozen peas to his crotch, and you would not believe how much he whined. Balls are delicate things."

She winced. It was not the first time Rebecca had mentioned her mom and Owen's sparring session. "I talked to her. She's not allowed to spar with Owen anymore. I'm so sorry. She can be intense."

"She can be insane," Rebecca said with a shake of her head.

"And you're avoiding the question. Has Tucker not been trying to hump your leg? I find that difficult to believe. I've never met a man who needed physical affection more than Tucker."

Was that why he constantly wanted to hold Violet? Why he would get down on the floor and play dolls with her? He was a tall, muscular man and he didn't seem to mind at all when a tiny girl tried to put a plastic tiara on him.

He was heartbreakingly good with her daughter. Their daughter.

"You know why that is, and he wasn't the only one," Ariel chided. "Owen humped more than your leg the first chance he got. Like five minutes after he met you."

"It was hours," Rebecca corrected. "But yes, it was that first day. Being stuck in an elevator can be frustrating. We both needed some affection, but I understand what you're saying. Continue."

Ariel grinned at her friend and did as she'd asked. "Like I was saying, all the lads craved affection. Jax was all over River the night he met her." Her grin faded. "Robert was the stubborn one, but then he'd been out longer than the rest of them. I suspect Robert was treated better. Not that any of them weren't tortured, but McDonald seemed more invested in Robert's group. She treated the group Tucker was in like animals she experimented on before giving her drugs to humans."

Roni looked down at the lovely salad in front of her and knew it would taste like ashes in her mouth. Every time she thought about what had happened to Steven, the events that had turned him into Tucker, she wanted to be sick.

"I'm sorry," Ariel said. "I know it's hard to hear, but you should understand what he went through if you're going to have a relationship with him. Even if it's only to co-parent. I hope you intend to co-parent with him. I think it would be hard for him if you denied him visits with Violet. Tucker bonds quickly and he's intensely loyal. Once he got himself kidnapped by Ukrainian mobsters and let them torture him because his friend's girlfriend had been captured and he wouldn't let her go alone."

"He had a tracking device in his arm," Rebecca explained. "By letting himself be taken, he led Big Tag and the group right to where Stephanie was being held. He saved them."

He'd willingly walked into more torture? Well, he'd mentioned the tracking device was a plus…

"But he couldn't have known they wouldn't simply shoot him and leave his body behind," Ariel pointed out. "He was willing to take that risk. I say it was because he was loyal to Brody, but I think he would have done it for anyone. He's that kind of a man."

"He was willing to take that stupid drug to save me." Rebecca sniffled and took a deep breath. "I hate Levi Green."

She'd heard a lot of people hated Levi Green.

"Tell me about it." Solo stood in the doorway, a plate in her hand and a bottle of water shoved under her arm. "He sucks."

She stood there, half in shadows, and looked like she wanted to join them but was uncertain of her welcome. Ariel gave her a half smile and looked Rebecca's way. Rebecca was suddenly intensely interested in that wine.

"I was just grabbing a sandwich," Solo said with a nod. "You guys have a nice afternoon."

She'd noticed Solo didn't seem to do much more than work, talk on the phone about work, and argue with Ezra Fain, who she called Beck. She seemed lonely. It was sad since the CIA agent was bright and fun to be around. It was obvious she didn't feel welcome.

"We're having lunch, too." She'd been that girl waiting in the shadows, hoping she wouldn't have to eat lunch alone. "You want to join us? Penny was supposed to but Ollie's fussy and she's worried he's got an ear infection."

Solo was in that seat faster than Roni could pick up the wine to offer her a glass. A bright smile lit the operative's face. "Thanks. I've spent the last few days eating at my desk. They put me next to the security guard's bathroom. There's something wrong with one of them. I'm sure of it. Either that or Beck's setting off stink bombs. I wouldn't put it past him. It smells nice out here."

Rebecca sighed. "I'll make sure it wasn't Owen. He's still a touch upset he didn't get to murder Levi."

"Sorry," Solo offered. "I know it doesn't help."

"No one died," Ariel pointed out. "And we wouldn't have even gotten into the room to save Rebecca and Rob and Tucker if it hadn't been for you. You know I understand why you did what you did. So do Damon and Big Tag. We know the position you were in. You could have waited until Levi was done and then taken him. You didn't have to risk your mission."

"Of course I did." Solo sat back. "I'm human and not whatever the hell Levi is. And I'm sorry about what happened to Tucker. I didn't know what Levi was going to do. I wouldn't have risked him if I had. But I was worried Levi would damage the data. Can we go back to talking about whether or not Roni's going to throw down with the sweetest of the puppies?"

"I invited you over here so I could avoid that question." It was funny how she'd lost the will to prevaricate. Since she'd made it to The Garden, she hadn't been able to moderate herself the way she normally would. She didn't even want to. Years of hiding had taught her the value of being honest.

Solo grinned. "You shouldn't avoid it. I meant what I said. Tucker might seem like the runt of the litter, but he's all kinds of awesome."

"He is not the runt." He wasn't that much smaller than the men he called his brothers. "Just because he's not three hundred pounds of muscle doesn't make him a runt. He's very strong and tall, and he makes me feel delicate."

Rebecca sat back. "Ah, there it is. There's that look of longing every single one of us had before we snagged our man. The good news is I think Tucker really wants to be snagged. You shouldn't have too much trouble. Show him your boobs. It's what I do to Owen. Well, when he can function properly because no one kicked him in the balls."

Her mother was a menace. "Obviously we have a connection, but it's complicated."

"Because he's a wanted criminal with no memory of his past and you got burned by another version of him and worry if he gets his memory back, he'll be evil again?" Solo asked.

"Yes, that's terribly complicated." Ariel put her fork down. "Is that what you're worried about? That Tucker will become Reasor again?"

It was always there in the back of her mind, but she questioned if that was even a problem. "I know he had a bad reputation, but I saw a side to Steven I don't think anyone else knew. I think I might have made a mistake in not questioning Dr. McDonald. Why would he have slept with me and left me? I get why, but he showed no indication that was what he was planning. Those last few days, he seemed more tense than usual. He was upset by something."

"Well, he'd made sure I left," Rebecca said. "Though now I see that bit of terror actually saved me. Dr. McDonald planned to transfer me to the Argentina facility. I assume that's when she would have offered to bring me into her unethical experiments or done something to me so I couldn't have talked. At the time I thought it was because Steven didn't want me taking his place."

"But you were never in competition for the same job." It was what she hadn't understood about those rumors, the ones that pitted Steven and Rebecca against each other. "Dr. McDonald would never have put you over Steven anywhere but research. She needed Steven to keep everyone in line, and you wouldn't have even been tempted to play that role."

"I wouldn't have. The job in Argentina was strictly research the way Dr. McDonald explained it." Rebecca seemed to think for a moment. "She told me I would have my own lab and I would have all the funding I wanted. Not once did she imply I would be over Steven. She was giving me the key to the kingdom when it came to my own research, but I wasn't taking over from Steven. And now that I think about it, he was there at that meeting. I guess he could have not believed Dr. McDonald."

"Or he knew what would happen to you if you got on that plane to Argentina." It was becoming more and more clear in Roni's mind. At least she thought it was. Memory was a funny thing. It could be influenced by any number of forces, and certainly emotional states. But it felt right to say the words. "Did he try to convince you not to go?"

"We had a conversation about how the conditions would be and what I wanted for my career," Rebecca said. "But I didn't like him. I didn't let him talk to me often. I would pretty much come up with any excuse to not talk to him. I can't remember what happened that afternoon. I was planning on telling McDonald I wasn't going to go."

"I've read all the reports on that day," Solo said. "I can tell you what I think happened."

Rebecca nodded. "I'd like to hear. Owen has his own thoughts, but I worry they're influenced by his love for Tucker."

"When I look at those reports, take in your part of the story and what Roni's told the group, I come to the conclusion that you likely had a conversation with McDonald where you turned her down. According to your phone records, you called your father that day and your computer records show you looked into flights home."

"I know all of this," Rebecca said. "My dad was sick. I think I was going to see him."

"Then why did you buy a one-way ticket?" Solo sat back. "I have better connections than Big Tag no matter what he thinks. This particular one isn't connected to the Agency. My family connections are wide and far reaching. I pulled your credit card records from that day. You bought a one-way ticket, not an open-ended one. You were leaving. Something happened that day that led you to buy that ticket."

Rebecca shook her head. "I don't remember buying a ticket until two days later, after I recovered. Damn it. That drug they gave me screwed with my short-term memory and I didn't look into what I'd been doing earlier in the day. Steven wanted me gone. Why would he drug me?"

"What if he didn't?" Ariel mused. "What if McDonald was the one who drugged you, but Steven took over so he could control it? He did want you gone, but what if it wasn't for the reasons everyone assumed?"

"He told me we wouldn't go back," Roni said, so much falling into place. "That day in Paris, he made it sound like we might not even bother going back to Munich, but he'd bought a return ticket."

"Because he'd already seen what McDonald did to someone who tried to leave," Rebecca concluded. "What he did to me was horrible, but the truth is that whole time is vague, and given how McDonald could manipulate memory, I have to question everything that happened. I've lived with Tucker for months and I don't see the same man. It's like he's wearing Reasor's face. He's sweet and funny, and my husband trusts him completely."

"He was sweet and funny with me." She remembered those moments so clearly. "Not when anyone else was around, but honestly, it always felt like he was playing a role and I got to see the real man."

"I've worked with a lot of terrible people," Solo said, her eyes intent on Roni. "It's the nature of my job. I have to trust my instincts or I can get into trouble. I would trust Tucker. Almost immediately. I would actually worry about him because I don't know that he would be worried about his own safety. He would put others ahead of himself. Ariel could explain this better, but there's a nature component to personality. You know nature versus nurture."

"What she means is simply because you take away a person's memories doesn't mean he or she suddenly becomes something they're not," Ariel explained. "I know we joke about how they were a bit like toddlers, but they had obvious personalities and they each reacted to what they went through in different ways that tell me a lot about who they are at their cores. I think Tucker either got caught in something he wasn't prepared for and lost his way or he was undercover."

"But the Agency would have had records," Roni pointed out. "Who else could he have gone undercover with?"

Solo actually choked a little at those words. "He could absolutely have been working for someone in the Agency. We're not some happy family who gets together for reunions and catches up. We've got secrets on top of secrets, and we're not always working toward the same goal. I haven't been able to get Levi to tell me whether or not he was working with Tucker. He says he won't say a thing unless I put them in the same room together, and he wants immunity. From everything."

"But if Tucker was working for Levi Green, wouldn't that mean he should get immunity, too?" She hated the idea of him being hauled away in handcuffs.

She hated the idea of not seeing him, of him not sitting across the breakfast table trying to get Violet to put the banana in her mouth instead of smashing it all over her face.

She hated the thought there wasn't a chance for them to be a family of any kind.

"The problem is we're working with countries that aren't necessarily friendly to the States," Solo explained. "Some of them are, and if we got the State Department involved, yes, we might be able to clear things up for him. But right now, in the eyes of the Agency, Tucker and Jax are ways to manipulate Big Tag and Damon."

She felt her brow rise at that.

Solo held up her hands. "I'm being honest. I'm not saying I would do it. But you should know that I've talked to Ezra, well more like at him since he won't actually talk to me. I told him I think it's time to move Jax and Tucker."

Rebecca sat up. "What?"

"Where will we go?" Roni had thought they would be here until they were ready to be moved to the States.

"You will head to Dallas with Big Tag as soon as Jax can get your paperwork done," Solo explained.

"Why are you only talking about moving Jax and Tucker?" Rebecca asked. "We're a team. I'm not staying here while they're hiding somewhere. Owen won't let that happen. We're safer together."

"I don't think so." Solo sat back as though she expected to be asked to leave. "I admire your loyalty, but Beck can move faster with Jax, River, and Tucker. I would suggest that they leave the dog but then I would be a terrible, horrible human being who loves neither dogs nor families. River's words, not mine."

"I'm not going with Tucker?" All she'd wanted when she'd gotten here was to go back to the States. Now the idea of leaving him behind was difficult to process.

"No." Solo drained her wine glass. "Things are reaching a breaking point. I can't tell you everything, but I'm worried that we're all in a dangerous place. After Levi's speech at Kronberg about how Tucker knows more than anyone can imagine, there's been a push to bring him in. As far as anyone knows he's still in a coma. But I suspect I set something off when I moved you here."

"You think someone doesn't like Veronica and Tucker being in the same place?" Ariel asked.

"Why would they care? I don't know anything." She should be excited at the prospect of getting on with her life. This was exactly what she'd wanted. She'd come so she could find closure with the man who'd hurt her so badly. Now all she wanted was a little more time with him. A little? She wasn't fooling herself this time. She wanted a lot more time with him. She might want a lifetime with him.

It was way too soon to think that way, but she did know that she wanted the connection with him. Even if he wasn't the one for her, he was Violet's dad and he always would be.

How could this be ending? It had barely begun.

He'd only kissed her once.

"Roni, are you okay?" Ariel was looking at her with concerned eyes.

She managed to nod.

"Tucker needs a doctor with him," Rebecca was arguing. "Honestly, so does River because she might be pregnant."

Solo groaned and said something about how much easier it was to deal with spies than women whose biological clocks were ticking out of control.

They continued to argue but all she could think about was where she would be in the world at this time next week. And where he would be.

Was she willing to leave things the way they were? If Ariel was correct and he'd been trying to do the right thing, shouldn't she give him another chance? She'd spent the last few years hesitant to trust anyone because she'd been so wrong about him. What if she'd been right? What if it had been her fear and insecurity that had allowed her to believe every word McDonald said?

A memory of the way he'd held her washed over her soul.

The women around her continued to fight about who was going where, but Roni sat back. She'd lost her appetite.

Chapter Seven

Roni stared out over the first floor of The Garden from her place four stories above. The lights and music floated up, an invitation to her. All she had to do was get in the elevator and she could be down there, joining the party. Was Tucker down there? This was his place, his club as he'd called it. How many times had he passed an evening in the club? How many women had he been with?

Would it be so bad to be one of them?

She'd spent the whole afternoon trying to figure out what she wanted. Tucker was leaving. She was leaving. They wouldn't be together in a couple of days. Would it be easier to not have a night with him? Or would she always regret it?

She stared down, unable to make a decision.

Was it rude to watch? No one had told her she had to stay in her room on what they'd called a "play" night.

"You thinking about going down there?"

She gasped and turned, her mother's voice startling her. "No."

Her mom was dressed for bed, wearing pajama pants and a tank top and looking more relaxed than she normally did. She'd actually settled into a nice routine here and seemed happier than she'd been in a long time. She liked being around the men and women of McKay-Taggart. She'd taken to working out with Big Tag and what she called the "Fucked-Up Ones." It was her surprisingly affectionate name for Tucker and his team. "Why not? I've thought about going down there. If only to see all those gorgeous men with their dicks hanging out. Do you think they hang out?"

Maybe it had been better when her mom had only been concerned about their survival. "I don't have a place down there. There's a whole lifestyle, and it's not mine."

"I think that's the whole point of their lifestyle. It doesn't have to be yours, but it's open to you. I find these people surprisingly tolerable, and I think part of it is that they've discovered a brilliant balance between hippy-dippy, live and let live, and knowing exactly when it's time to kick some ass. You don't usually find that. Even your Tucker."

When had her mom stopped referring to him as Steven? It had been days. Maybe after that first night when he'd so obviously been madly in love with their daughter. Tucker had not only taken all the shit her mom had piled on him, he'd made her laugh, speaking to her mom's surreal and often dark sense of humor.

"He's not mine."

"He's trying to be." Her mother leaned on the railing and looked down with a frown. "Damn Knight. He did a good job with the placement of those trees. I can't see much. Oh, hey. The hot Russian isn't wearing a shirt. I can objectify him. He used to be a bad guy."

She was going to start a whole TV show. *Moms Say the Darnedest Things*. "He was never a bad guy."

"He's Russian. He was a bad guy," her mom insisted, proving she wasn't the most tolerant of people. Apparently, though, all one needed to be a "good guy" was to work for an American ally and look hot without his shirt on. "Is it wrong that I understand him better than the Aussie? He walks in and says stuff and all I hear is shrimp on the barbie."

Roni groaned. "You're the reason everyone hates Americans."

Her mom simply grinned. "Yeah, it's because I'm so cool." She sobered. "Are you going to leave him?"

"I don't have much of a choice." She knew something her mother didn't know. "Even if I asked to stay, he wouldn't be here. They're moving him in a few days. I don't even know where. I don't think he'll know where until they actually get in a car or a plane."

How hard was that life on a man who so wanted normalcy? He obviously craved family life. He wasn't a loner. He liked to be surrounded by people who cared about him, and he gave that care back to them.

He was a good man.

He was an insanely sexy man.

Her mother seemed to think about that for a moment. "Maybe you should go with him."

It was startling. Enough that she felt her eyes go wide. "He's on the run. If I go with him, I could be arrested for harboring a fugitive."

"Well, I didn't say it would be easy," she replied.

"I have to think about Violet."

"I know you do," her mom said with a sigh. "You're a good mom. But you can't forget to be a woman, too. I know I did. After your dad walked out, I focused on two things—my career and you girls. I don't regret a minute of time I spent with you and Katie. God, you have to know I would do anything to have another minute with her. But I wish I hadn't been alone when she died."

Guilt swamped her. "I'm sorry."

Her mom shook her head. "Baby, you were mourning, too, but in a different way. And we were scared because you realized you could lose Vi, and I couldn't even consider losing you. No, I'm not saying you weren't there for me. I'm saying that it's a different kind of support you get from a lover."

She couldn't help it. She cringed.

Her mom rolled her eyes. "Get over it, baby girl. I had a lot of sex in my time. Good sex. Not any lately, and everyone here is married or otherwise taken. But trust me, I've thought about walking down there and seeing what it's all about. I could get into a man who needed some discipline."

She was ready to put her fingers in her ears and start singing loudly so she didn't have to listen to her mom talk about sex. "I think I hear Vi crying. I should go check on her."

Her mother sighed. "She's fine. Come on, Roni. Tell me you haven't thought about it. All joking aside, you're going to miss him."

She missed him when he wasn't in the room with her. She missed him when he was at work a few floors away. It hadn't been hard to fall into a routine with him, one where she depended on him. He was as reliable as any clock. He showed up on her doorstep at seven every morning. He almost always had some Danish or pastry he would offer her and then they would sit and have coffee and he would watch Vi smash food against her face. He would laugh and clean her up and kiss the top of her head before he left for work. At noon he often met them for lunch, and then at five thirty he came for dinner and didn't leave until long after Violet was in bed.

Why hadn't she moved closer to him on the couch as they sat watching television shows? She pretended to watch, but the whole time all she could think about was how close he was, how little time they had left.

How if she'd had some faith in him, he might not have lost his memories.

"Have you thought about the fact that while I was cursing his name, he was being tortured?"

Her mother's eyes softened. "Baby, you couldn't have saved him. From what I've read and heard about McDonald, it's highly likely that she'd already given him the drug by the time she came to see you. Even if by some miracle you had figured it out, you couldn't have saved him."

"I didn't even look for him. All I cared about was not being embarrassed if he came back to Munich."

"Do you know why I like that kid?" her mom asked.

"If you say something about his ass…"

A brilliant grin crossed her mother's face. "It's not bad, but I like him for other reasons. Reasons I never expected, and one of them is the fact that I don't think it would ever occur to him to be angry with you. I doubt he's thought for a single second that you should have tried to save him. Not because he wouldn't want to be saved, but because I genuinely believe that man would put you and Violet above his own needs. I realized it when he was close to vomiting and managed to make it through a diaper change because you were napping and he wasn't going to wake you up."

"I have a surprisingly sensitive nose," a deep voice said.

She turned and Tucker rounded the corner. He was dressed as he had been earlier, in a dark T-shirt and buttery soft jeans.

"That's not going to serve you well with Vi. She's a stinky kid," her mother said before leaning toward Roni and lowering her voice. "I know you think you might spare yourself some pain if you don't get close to him again, but I think you'll regret it. I think he's special, and you know I don't say that often. When you find something good in life, you grab it with both hands and you try your damnedest not to let go." Her mom hugged her briefly. "I'm going to bed. I'm spotting for Taggart in the morning. I don't want to listen to that man whine about me being late. 'Night, young folk."

"She's right, you know." Tucker moved in beside her, his elbows on the railing. "I don't blame you for anything. I should have told you then. I didn't mean to, but I put you in danger. So, I'm going to tell you now that they're going to move me in a few days. I don't know where, but if you want, I'll try to communicate with you. I'll make sure it's on a safe channel. I don't want to put you or Violet in danger, but I also can't stand the thought of not talking to you."

She couldn't stand it either. "Of course. You should be in her life as much as you can."

An awkward silence fell between them and she went back to staring at the space below. Had he come out because he was planning on going down to the party? Was someone waiting for him? A sub? That was what they called themselves. Subs. Rebecca and Ariel had answered some of her questions earlier in the afternoon, explaining without any self-consciousness how their relationships worked. She'd noticed Solo had gotten quiet during that discussion, and she hadn't thought it was because the woman was uncomfortable. She'd seemed deeply interested in the conversation.

"You can go down if you want to," she said quietly.

"I wasn't going down to The Garden. I was going to knock on your door. We didn't talk much tonight and we need to. I don't want to merely be in Violet's life. It's not only Vi I'm going to miss. I'm going to miss you like hell. I've missed you all along. I just couldn't remember who I missed."

They fell silent again. She wasn't sure what to say to those words. She'd missed him but that emotion had been wrapped up in anger, and she wasn't sure how to let it all go. The simple fact that she'd had no real right to be angry with him didn't make it all fall away. She was in a corner and she wasn't at all sure how to come out.

"Veronica, do you want me to leave?"

That wasn't the question. Life would be simpler if he'd stayed

Steven Reasor, if he'd stayed dead. She could have gone through the rest of her life hiding her heart away because once it had been broken. She could have concentrated on her daughter. She wouldn't have to confront all the complexities that came with caring for a man.

"Baby, you have no idea what you want, do you?" His voice had turned warm and she felt him move in beside her. "There's a part of you that wants to go down there, and a part that wants to run back into the apartment and use our daughter like a shield between us. I get that."

There was not an ounce of frustration in his tone, merely an acceptance of her state of mind. "I don't like feeling this way. I don't like being on a clock. I need more time."

"Yeah, I get that, too, but I've learned I have to work with what I have. I don't know what comes after this. Once they move me, I don't know when I'll see you. I haven't tried to do what I wanted to do. I haven't kissed you or held you. But you have to know I wanted to. I thought it was best if I didn't hurt you again."

"I think that ship has sailed." She turned to him, emotions rolling inside. "I think I'll miss you in a way I didn't before, and that's going to be hard. I'll worry about you." She already did. How would she feel when they were half a world away? "I don't know what to do. I'm utterly and completely paralyzed when it comes to you. I expected this would be easy."

"You expected you could walk in, identify my comatose body, and walk away without looking back. You thought you could get some closure. If I was a good man, I would give it to you. But I'm not. I'm not selfless enough to let you go. I'm going to make it hard. I want a place in my daughter's life, and I want a place in yours."

She let her head fall forward, the weight of the decisions she had to make hitting her hard. She had to weigh the danger that surrounded Tucker with what it would mean for Violet to know her father. She had to decide if he even was the man she'd fallen for years ago, or some new person wearing his skin.

She had to figure out if it mattered because she had strong feelings for this version of the man, feelings that went deep and ran true.

A warm hand covered the nape of her neck. "Tell me what's going through your head. Let me help you."

"It's too much." She wanted. She longed. She couldn't seem to let herself have him because every question she managed to answer brought up three more. "I can't decide. I want you to kiss me. I want to be with you, but I can't decide everything. I should know what I want, right?"

He shook his head. "No. You don't have to know everything right this second. You don't have to decide everything. We don't have to know what we're going to end up being to each other right this second. But we do have to decide what we want tonight. I want you, Roni. I want to remember what it feels like to make love to you."

She wanted that, too, but it seemed like a huge step.

"Hey, let me kiss you. That's all you have to decide this second. Let me kiss you and hold you and we'll figure out what comes next." He leaned over, his lips brushing the shell of her ear and sending delicious shivers down her spine. "Or you can make the decision to simply be with me this evening. Let me take control and you don't have to think of another thing all evening. You'll let me take care of you. You can stop me at any time, but my only goal for the whole night is to make you happy, to make some memories. I don't have many of those and I want so badly to have memories of you, of us. Roni, I'm leaving and I won't see you again for a while, but I also know that I won't be able to have any other relationships because somehow, now that I've seen you, I'm yours. I always was. Let me take care of you. Let me show you how good it can be to let me take control."

She was always in control. She had to be. She had to hide and protect. It had been years since she truly relaxed. What had her mother said? Comfort was different when it came from a lover.

He would be gone soon. She would have to sink into building a new life, finding a new self. Even if this was nothing more than good-bye, she wanted it.

"Yes."

* * * *

The minute she said *yes* his whole body seemed to come alive. He could have her. She'd given him permission and he trusted her to know her mind. He absolutely knew his. Tag's words had played through his head all day. She wasn't a prize. She was a partner.

Even if only for a night.

He'd had so little joy that he couldn't turn it away even if he would ache over her the rest of his life.

He let his hands sink in her hair, tugging it out of the scrunchie that held it. "I want your hair down. When we're playing, I want it around your shoulders. I want to be able to fist it and turn you this way or that. Do you understand?"

Her eyes came up and he could see plainly what he was saying had an effect on her. She wanted to sink into this, to be able to follow his lead without thinking. She needed to relax but couldn't give herself permission.

He could do that for her.

"Roni, do you know what I want you to do?"

She stared up at him. "What?"

"I want you to stop thinking about anything but me and what I'm going to do to your body. I'm going to touch you and taste you and do everything I can to bring you pleasure, to make you forget there's anything but the two of us in the whole world. For a few hours, we're going to tune everything out."

"Violet."

He shook his head. "Your mom is taking care of Vi. She's safe and happy and won't notice you're gone. And don't tell me you should tell your mother where you're going. While you weren't watching she made several incredibly juvenile hand gestures to let me know I should get you in bed at the earliest opportunity. I believe she thinks you need to get laid."

She turned the sweetest shade of pink. "Oh my god."

He couldn't help the grin that came over his face. "Hey, I'm glad she approves, otherwise I have no doubt she would cock block me in genuinely terrifying ways. So Vi is fine. Now come here. Do you want to go to my apartment, or do you want to play?"

"I don't understand what you mean when you talk about play," she admitted, the words coming out on a breathless tumble.

But she wanted to. It was there in her husky tone, and it was definitely there in the way her nipples poked against the thin material of her T-shirt. Luckily he knew exactly where to go. "Follow me."

He started down the walkway to the elevator, her hand in his. He could feel the blood thrumming through his body, beating in time with the music from below.

"Where are we going?" Roni asked, her eyes wide.

If he had more time with her, he would teach her that she didn't have to ask. He would be so good to her she would simply follow him, knowing anywhere he took her would be good for her. But he'd burned her once. "There are rooms downstairs. Privacy rooms. They're built for play, but we'll be alone. We have to walk through some of the scenes. Are you okay with that?"

He didn't want to shock her. It was normal for him. He'd seen so many butt plugs in his life they were a normal part of any landscape for him. But Roni was more sheltered. Everyone was probably more sheltered.

She glanced over as the elevator doors opened and she seemed to come to a decision. She tugged on his hand. "I'm fine if everyone else is. It's weird but it doesn't seem bad."

He pressed the button to take them to the club level before pulling her into his arms, bumping their bodies together. "It isn't bad. It's fun and it's taught me a lot about how to communicate. I learned very quickly that I was meaningless in life unless I was obedient. I was nothing but a test subject, and whether I lived or died didn't matter as long as I provided the doctor with data. But here I learned that nothing works in this world if I don't talk about what I need, if I don't tell the people around me what I think. I need you to talk to me. I know I said you didn't have to think, but you do have to feel."

"And that's what scares me," she admitted. "But I think I'm more afraid that you're the only man who ever made me feel this way before and if I don't take this time with you, I won't ever meet anyone who can make me feel again."

He kissed her, his mouth lingering on hers even as the elevator doors opened. "I promise no matter what happens that I'll do everything I can to get back to you and Vi. Now don't think about us being separated again. We're together tonight and that's what matters. And don't look too hard to your left because there's a lot of penises hanging out. A lot."

Her head swung to the left and she gasped.

"Hey, Roni." Owen grinned as he walked by. He had a plaid tossed over his shoulder. Tucker was certain at some point it had been wrapped around his body, but now it simply covered his left shoulder and not any part of his dick.

"Hi." The greeting came out on a squeak. "I'm glad to see your…parts survived my mom." She winced. "That came out wrong."

Owen laughed. "They've recovered quite nicely. You two have fun. I've got a Sassenach to plunder." He shook his head. "Ariel gave her those books. Don't let that one read. Women get funny ideas when they read."

He looked down at Roni, hoping the incident hadn't embarrassed her. She had a hand over her mouth and her eyes were filled with laughter. She let her head fall against his chest.

"We can never tell my mom. She'll want to be down here and I can't. I can't with her. I can deal with your brothers walking around with their willies hanging out, but not my mom."

He didn't think he could ever come down to the club if he thought his mother-in-law was there. And she wouldn't be a sub. Sandra would be ordering around everyone, whip in hand.

He'd just thought of her as his mother-in-law when he'd promised himself he wouldn't think past the night.

He leaned over and slid his arm under Roni's knees. She wasn't wearing shoes, only a pair of fluffy socks. Soon she wouldn't be wearing anything at all. He strode over the familiar path that wound through the beautiful indoor forest that formed the heart of The Garden. He moved quickly because he was breaking club rules, but he knew Damon wouldn't mind. They weren't going to be on the dungeon floor for long. Off to his left he saw Damon standing with his wife, Penny, watching a scene playing out in one of the spaces. The big Brit gave him a nod as he strode by.

"It's pretty here," Roni said, her arms around his neck. She seemed far more comfortable now that he was holding her. She looked around with eager eyes.

Getting acquainted with the dungeon would have to wait. He wanted her to himself. He wanted a night where there was no one in the world except him and her.

In the morning he would have to play his dangerous game. He would meet his contact and pass off the…

"Tucker, are you okay?"

He hadn't realized he'd stopped in the middle of the path. The whisper of that first night with her, the one in Paris, had slammed into him. If he let himself go, he would get sick and this would all be over. He would spend the rest of his time with her lying in a freaking bed, and he didn't want that. There would be time enough to force his brain to work when they were apart. He walked on, leaving the past behind. He hoped.

"I'm fine." There were frosted sliding glass doors that led to the privacy rooms.

Nina Blunt was sitting in the place where the dungeon monitor usually stayed. It was a small station in front of the hall that led to the privacy and specialized playrooms. From here it was like the club didn't exist. There was a big desk with security monitors trained on the entrances and exits of The Garden.

"So there are rooms to have sex in? Doesn't everyone live here?" Roni asked as he approached the station.

"Not everyone. There are plenty of members who don't live and work here. But you'll see why even the ones who do like the privacy rooms." He nodded Nina's way. "Which rooms are open?"

Nina was a pretty woman who'd come to McKay-Taggart and Knight straight out of Interpol. She wasn't dressed for play at all. She was in yoga pants and a T-shirt, like she'd come from the gym. Her auburn hair was in a high ponytail. "I think three is the only one being used. But I'm just filling in. The monitor tonight is also a security guard, and something's going on in the garage. I was told it was nothing to worry about, but still, here I am. Hello, Veronica. I see you didn't feel like putting on a bustier and heels. I don't understand why fet wear can't be more comfortable. I'm protesting until Damon declares yoga pants and trainers proper costume for the dungeon floor."

"We'll be in four." It was the room furthest from the dungeon. It was also the most romantic of the rooms. They each had a theme, played to some fetish, but the fourth room was simpler. It was still stocked with anything a top could want, but there was a gauzy feel that would appeal to Roni.

And to him.

"I will mark that down for when our friend comes back." Nina gave him a jaunty salute. "Carry on."

He did. He carried Roni right to the door and swept her inside.

"Oh, this is pretty." She looked around as he set her on her feet.

A large four-poster bed dominated the room. Dark wood contrasted with the luxurious dove-gray cover, and big, fluffy pillows hid the restraints he could use to tie her down.

"Tell me how I made love to you the first time." He knew he shouldn't dwell on the past, but he wanted his memories of her. Even if they were merely stories she told him. He'd learned about himself through her, about who he used to be, and it hadn't been all bad. He'd protected her. He'd had a heart.

He'd loved her. It was why he'd moved too soon. He should have taken his time.

"Stay with me." Her hands were on his cheeks. "Don't go wherever it is you go when that look hits your face. You're right about everything. We need this time together. Let me tell you. Rebecca said it helps if I tell you what happened. I was so nervous that first time."

"Because you were scared of me."

She shook her head. "No. Because I was afraid I wouldn't be enough. We had been dancing around each other. And then you kissed me for the first time and I knew I wanted to try with you. But I was still nervous when you asked me to go to Paris. I was afraid you wouldn't really want me. But you did. You told me I was beautiful and I believed you."

"You are beautiful. You are so fucking gorgeous to me." He let his hands find her hair. He loved how much of it there was, that he could get wrapped up in it. He loved the color and how it shone when the sun hit it.

"I was surprised at how different you were when we were alone. Not that you were mean to me when we weren't," she said. Her hands moved to his shoulders. "You could be short with everyone around you."

"But not you."

She shook her head. "Never me. You told me once I would get you in trouble. That you had a plan and I wasn't in it."

He seemed to have a lot in common with his former self. "But I couldn't stay away any more than I can now. Take off my shirt. I want you to touch me."

Her hands went to the hem of his T-shirt and she dragged it up and over his head. The minute her hands were on his skin he breathed a sigh of relief. He realized it had been days since he relaxed. Not since the last time he'd kissed her had he felt like himself.

He placed his hand over hers, holding it to his heart.

"You kissed me for a long time. You liked your hands in my hair then, too," she said, staring at his chest like she could find something there. Her free hand brushed over the worst of his scars. "I didn't realize it at the time, but you took control that night. I liked it because nothing felt awkward. You showed me what you wanted. You focused on me in a way no one ever had before. It wasn't like I'd never had sex, but it felt so different with you." She frowned suddenly. "You've forgotten everything. Do you know how…"

"Roni, I've had sex since I was rescued." He couldn't lie to her again. "I wish now that I hadn't, but I came out pretty damn desperate."

She shook her head. "It's okay. I can't imagine what you went through. You should know, though, that I haven't. My sister died shortly after you left…were taken, and then I was pregnant. I haven't had sex in years."

Because he'd hurt her and she'd grieved and she'd raised their baby. He kissed her forehead, tenderness welling inside him. "I'll take care of you for as long as I can. I'll be in your bed and in your life as much as I can. Let me show you. Take off your clothes for me and I promise you'll know exactly how I feel about you."

She hesitated.

He couldn't let her insecurity take over again. If he thought she was afraid, he would back off, but that wasn't what this was about. "Roni, we should put some boundaries into place. If things get to be too much, you tell me to slow down or to stop. I'll do it. But unless you say those words, I expect you to obey me."

Her nose wrinkled. "I don't like that word."

"Well, it's the only time I'll use it since any other time I'll lay down and let you walk those pretty feet all over me. You can order me around during the day and I'll complete every task you set for me. But when Vi's in bed and we're alone, you're mine. Now take off your clothes, baby. I want to see you. It's all I've been able to think about for days. Do you know what I do while Rebecca runs her millions of tests? I think about your breasts. I think about how soft they'll be against my palm. I think about playing with your nipples. I think about finally tasting that pussy of yours, and then Rebecca yells at me because I get hard as hell."

Her whole face lit up. This was how to handle her. She could be grim. She needed to laugh and let her light out instead of hoarding it because she was worried the world would go dark. She took a step back and there was a lovely blush to her face as she dragged the tank top over her head, revealing her breasts.

They were every bit as gorgeous as they'd been in his head. "Turn around."

She bit her bottom lip but did as he requested, giving him her back.

He moved in behind her and let his hands slide around her, cupping her breasts and dragging her against him. It was the easiest way to get his hands on her breasts, to surround them and feel them against his palms. He loved the shudder that went through her. "Did I touch your breasts that night?"

She moved against him, not in any attempt to get away. No, she slid her body along his as though trying to tempt him. "Yes. You touched me everywhere. You were incredibly thorough."

He could have told her she didn't have to do a damn thing to tempt him except exist. "Tell me how it made you feel."

Her head fell back as though she'd already surrendered completely. "Sexy. It made me feel wanted. I would go through the days working and studying, and somewhere along the way I forgot what it meant to have a life outside of work. I forgot I was anything but an employee trying to fit in. Then I would look at you and I would remember I had a body and a soul, and I wanted you to feed both of them. I knew you were the one who could. I tried to tell myself it would only be sex, but I always knew it was more."

He could feel the way her nipples had gone rigid. He memorized the softness of her breasts. Her skin was silky and warm and her breasts filled his hands like they'd been made for each other. "I assure you it was more for me. It meant so damn much to me that even her erasing my memory couldn't take you entirely from me. I knew you were important the minute I saw you."

"You told me then you wanted me the minute you saw me. You said I was the one good thing that happened to you."

"And you still are. I got lucky, Roni. I found a family here, but I haven't truly belonged until I opened my eyes and you were there." He let his fingers find her nipples and twisted them lightly. She gasped, a throaty sound that went straight to his cock.

"You pinched me." She sounded so surprised he almost laughed.

He eased off but licked the shell of her ear. "And how did that make you feel?"

"Horny, Tucker. Everything is making me crazy horny, and you know it."

He chuckled. Oh, she was fun. She would be so much fun to torture. "I'm going to do worse. Take off your pants and get on the bed. I'm going to tie you up."

Her gaze went distinctly suspicious. "You're going to make me wait, aren't you? Do you know how mean that is?"

"You were always impatient." He knew it somehow, but he didn't pursue the memory. It was knowledge that was written on his brain. Nothing more. The more he allowed himself to accept these moments, the more they came to him. "The best things in life take time, and if you don't do what I ask, we'll have to start talking about punishment."

Her lips curled up and he loved how relaxed she was now. "You're going to spank me?"

"Only if you don't mind me."

She shoved her pajama bottoms off her hips. "Fine, but only because I'm horny and I think you'll spend way too much time on the spanking. But later it might be fun." Her eyes found his, a serious expression taking over. "You need this now. You took control then, but I think that was your nature. This is different. You need this to feel safe, and I want to give that to you. You're safe with me. Tie me up. Do what you want to me. I trust you."

She turned and walked to the bed, every movement graceful. She laid herself down in the middle of the big bed and offered up her wrists.

This was exactly what he needed, what he'd been craving since that moment when he'd awakened and realized she was here with him. He'd needed her looking up at him like he was some kind of savior, like he was worthy. She was laid out like a feast for a starving man.

"God, you're beautiful." He stared at her for a moment before joining her on the bed. He pulled the first restraint out from its hiding place and slid it around her wrist, securing it.

"Sneaky," she said, watching him. She pulled against it, testing it.

He gently restrained her other hand and then eased off the bed. She might be impatient, but now that he had her here, he found he wanted to take his time. His cock was dying, but he was in control and he intended to show her exactly how focused he could be. He opened the door to the armoire, revealing how prepared Damon Knight liked his playrooms to be.

"What's that?" Roni asked.

"You can't play without toys," he replied. There were impact toys of all kinds, each one cleaned and cared for by the employees who worked on the club side of Damon's business. He wasn't going too far out tonight. He ignored the canes and floggers and whips. They would need far more time to talk and decide what she was interested in and what she couldn't handle. He selected the thing he knew she would enjoy.

He opened the packaging on the large feather.

"A feather?" Roni asked. "That's kinky but not what I expected."

He didn't intend to do what was expected of him. Not anymore. It would take a bold approach to get out of the web he found himself caught in, but he would do it all for her. "Close your eyes and keep them closed."

Her eyes shuttered and she seemed to relax. He climbed on the bed with her, leaving his jeans on because he didn't trust himself to take them off. He could only be so patient.

He turned the feather over so the pointed end was placed against the notch at her neck and he started to slowly drag it down her body.

Her eyes flickered open. "That wasn't what I was expecting."

He bet she wasn't expecting this either. He reached with his free hand and tweaked her nipple. "Close your eyes or I'll get a mask for you."

Her eyes drifted closed. He didn't need to see her eyes to know that anticipation was building inside her. It was there in the way she bit her bottom lip, in how tight her nipples were and how her legs slid against one another restlessly. She wanted and he intended to make sure she begged before she got.

He turned the feather over and let the soft side skim her skin. "How many times did I make love to you that night?"

She gasped as the feather fluttered over one breast and then another. "Three times. No, four. You didn't let me leave the apartment. You made me wait while you grabbed pizza and wine, and I wasn't allowed to put my clothes on. I stayed there in bed waiting for you."

"I was a strategic thinker," he replied, brushing the feather over her belly. Even if he'd been a bastard in those days, he'd had a few good ideas. He wanted to keep her naked as often as possible. She didn't need clothes around him. He brought the feather down to her pussy and let it brush over her bare skin. "You shaved. Did you do that for me?"

She squirmed slightly, holding on to the bonds that kept her in place. "I told myself it was because I needed to give a damn about grooming, but yes, I did it for you. I did it last night when I was pretty sure I wouldn't be able to hold out any longer."

He relished the idea of her running a razor over her pussy, making it soft and neat. "Did you shave for me the first time?"

She nodded. "I wanted to be sexy for you. Honestly, I'm not good at like trimming down there. Gardening is a skill I don't have so it's easier when I want to be pretty to shave that sucker all the way off. You seemed to like it then."

"Oh, so I got this sweet peach in my mouth then, did I? Did you like it when I ate your pussy?"

She was breathless, her hips moving as if they remembered what had happened that night. "Yes. You could do that again. You probably should do that so you can maybe remember."

She made him smile. "So I should eat this sweet pussy as part of my therapy. Is that what you're saying?"

She nodded, her lips curling up. "I'm definitely saying that. I'm sure your doctors would concur."

He moved down, shifting so he was between her legs. He could smell her arousal and it did crazy things to his cock. He needed to make sure she came because once he got inside her he wasn't sure how long he would last. Need pounded through him, but he couldn't give in. He wanted this time to be every bit as meaningful as the first.

God, he was competing against himself sexually, but damn if he didn't want to win.

He teased the feather against her pussy. "That was the night we made Violet."

He kind of wanted to do that again. He wanted to see her pregnant, hold her and take care of her while she carried their child. He wanted to be at her side, letting her break his hand when she delivered. He wanted those late nights where neither of them could sleep because their daughter had her days and nights mixed up.

"Hey, that is one hundred percent true, and you need to wear a condom because your sperm are serious. I was on the pill, Tucker. The pill. It's a pretty damn good method of birth control, but your swimmers got through all of it. I see that look in your eyes. You're thinking about leaving me another parting gift, but you better not put another baby up there until you can be with me."

Her eyes came open and she stared up at him, her hands in bondage and a bit of pure crazy in her eyes, and Tucker was able to let go of the sorrow that had welled. There wasn't a place for it here. This was their time to rediscover each other, and he knew exactly how he wanted to do that.

He set the feather aside. He had something else he could caress her with. His tongue. His fingers. His cock.

"I will remember that always. My sperm are just as insistent on finishing a mission as I am." He lowered himself down, placing his mouth right above her core. He glanced up and she was staring down at him, all the humor having fled in favor of pure desire. He'd told her to keep her eyes closed, but he wanted her to watch this.

He very slowly dragged his tongue over her pussy, gliding over her up to her clitoris.

A deep shudder went through her and he settled in. He relearned her taste and smell and the silky feel of her thighs clamping down around his head. He loved every desperate sound she made as he licked and tongued her. He took his time, letting her wash over his every sense. His cock throbbed, and he wouldn't be able to wait much longer. He gently thrust his fingers deep inside her pussy as he sucked on her clit. Her whole body went rigid and she cried out his name.

Tucker, not Steven. Tucker was the one who claimed her now. It was Tucker she would be with.

He got to his knees and shoved his jeans down, freeing his cock.

And then remembered he had to cage that sucker again. He fished the condom out of his pocket. He'd been carrying the damn thing around for days, hoping and praying she would trust him enough to let him in her bed.

"You were so eager the first time, too." She was staring at him. "I loved that you couldn't wait. Please make love to me."

It was a request he wasn't about to refuse. With shaking hands, he managed to get the condom on, tossing the wrapper to the side. "Yes, but then we slow down. There's a shower behind that door and I'm going to take you there and lick every inch of your body clean before I get you dirty again."

"And I'm going to get you out of those jeans and get my mouth on your cock," she promised with the sweetest smile. "You didn't let me do that last time. I think you should order me to suck your cock, Sir."

He groaned because if she kept talking, he would come before he even had a chance to get inside her. "You've got topping from the bottom down, but I think you're also a wise woman so I might have to follow your advice. God, you're beautiful."

She spread her legs and looked like a sex goddess lying there. She was in bondage, but she didn't look like a woman who wasn't in control. She was powerful and she knew exactly what she wanted.

Him.

Nothing in all of his life had ever made him feel the way that look in her eyes did.

He pressed himself against her pussy and vowed to do anything he had to do to get back to her.

Her legs wrapped around him and he thrust deep. She held on to the bindings, but her eyes were on him. He stilled inside her, savoring the sensation of all that heat surrounding him. He lowered himself on top of her, finding her lips and kissing her with need, the need to brand her while he bound himself to her, to possess and be possessed. To belong to her.

He groaned and positioned himself again, wanting to hit her clit with every thrust. He moved in and out, watching her every expression until he was certain he'd hit the right spot. When her breathing changed and her whole body tightened as though she was fighting to keep him there, he knew he could let loose. He thrust in, over and over, sliding against that one spot that could bring her the most pleasure, pressing down on her clit with his pelvis until her legs were a vise around him and she cried out all over again.

Then it was his turn. He felt his balls draw up and a tingling at the base of his spine. The world went soft around him and all that mattered was her.

He let go, the orgasm flowing through him until he couldn't hold himself up a second longer.

He slumped down, letting his head find her breasts.

This was his place. He'd finally found it. Since the moment he'd awakened to that bright light and all the pain McDonald could give him, he'd been looking for this feeling.

"I would put my arms around you, but you tied me up." Roni sighed, a deeply content sound.

He would have to fix that because he definitely wanted her arms around him. "I'll see what I can do about that, baby. We have a shower to get to."

"Good, because I think I have a feather up my butt," she admitted.

He started to laugh and then groaned because there was a knock on the door. He kissed the tops of her breasts. "This room is occupied. Go away."

This was what happened when non-professional dungeon monitors took over. He would bet Nina had run the minute the guard had come back without even bothering to mention they were in here.

The door came open and he cursed. "Hey, I said we're in here."

Nina shoved her way through anyway. "I know you're here. The problem is so is MI6. They're raiding The Garden and they're looking for you."

Tucker cursed again. His night in heaven had just gone straight to hell.

Chapter Eight

Five minutes later, Tucker's heart was still racing as he eased out the door, one hand in Roni's.

"They can't see us?" Roni stared at the glass doors.

"No, the glass in the doors are specifically made to look like they filter light, but they don't," he explained. "You can't even see shadows through them. When Damon said he wanted that part of the club to be private, he meant it. But obviously we can't go out that way. We open the doors and they'll know we're here."

"But we're trapped." Roni sounded shaky. She'd been calm but he could sense the panic bubbling under her surface. She was terrified.

He'd brought her here. He was the reason she was scared, but her hand was in his like he could save her.

He had to save her.

"There's always a way out," Nina said. "I've just got to make sure it's safe for us to go. Damn it. I forgot there's someone in room three. I don't know who it is." She was about to knock on the door when it came open and Solo walked out, her eyes wide as she realized she wasn't alone.

"I...I...It's got a sauna," Solo said, a tote bag in her hand.

"Steam is good for my skin."

"Is Ezra in there?" He'd always known they were probably doing it.

"No. He's not," Solo replied. "No one is in there. I really was using the sauna. Damon said it was okay as long as I didn't linger in the dungeon area. Ezra isn't there tonight. He was working with Big Tag on something. They told me I wasn't invited to their boys' club, hence the sauna."

"Well, while you were relaxing, MI6 decided to raid the club. I think we've figured out who was sniffing around your place the other night," Nina pointed out.

Solo's eyes went even wider. "No. Fuck. If they're here, they want Tucker. Is there a way out? Can they get in here?"

"I locked the doors when I realized what was happening," Nina explained. "but I have to make sure we can get out of here. Can you watch these two?"

Solo settled her bag on her shoulder. "Yes, but you need to know that if that's really MI6, they'll be able to get in if they want to. Where's Jax?"

Nina was backing up, moving to the end of the hallway. "Hopefully he's on the move. I got a code red on my cell a few minutes after I locked us down, so I have to think Tag knows what's going on. I'll be back. If it looks like they're coming in…"

Solo nodded. "I'll stash them somewhere and create a holy ruckus."

"I would rather have a gun than hide," Tucker said. He needed to make sure Roni was protected.

Nina shook her head and pointed to a space next to the guard stand. He knew it well since he'd taken many shifts working that particular station. From here he could see the security monitor. Usually it was focused on the exits and entrances, but Nina had switched it over, probably the minute she realized something was going wrong. "No. It's best we don't even look threatening if they catch us. What are you going to do? Shoot up MI6?"

That was the problem. That was precisely why Damon had his hands up. From Tucker's vantage point, he could see the boss talking to a man in a suit. Damon was calm, but there was no question about how pissed off he was.

Solo moved close to the monitor. "Can we get audio?"

Tucker flipped the switch that allowed them to hear.

"If you would allow my wife and the others to get dressed, we could have this conversation in a civilized fashion," Damon said. "Or is this how you conduct business since you took over MI6, Rupert?"

Nina put a hand on his shoulder. "I'm going to check on something and I'll be right back. Stay with Solo. You can't go out there. If they take you into custody, they don't need us anymore. I want you to think about that before you play the hero."

He nodded tightly and looked back at the monitor.

The man named Rupert was dressed in a tailored suit and despite the late hour, there wasn't a hair out of place. "I conduct business in an entirely different fashion from my predecessor, and that means I don't allow anyone to harbor dangerous fugitives under my nose. Nigel might have trusted you, Knight, but I do not. I don't care what's going on here. Have all the deviant sex you like, but you won't do it with criminals in the building."

Solo looked his way. "That's the new head of Damon's old division. Rupert Milbern. They were not friends. I knew they were getting impatient. I never imagined they would try something like this. Damon is going to be so pissed."

"I was unaware there were criminals here," Penny said, standing next to her husband. She was wearing a corset that pushed her breasts up and a teeny, tiny thong. "Damon, did you invite criminals to our party?"

Rupert frowned her way. "Now, Mrs. Knight, I was told you used to be an excellent agent. I suppose this is what happens when you consort with the wrong type. I'm talking about the men you call Jax Seaborne and Tucker Jones. Obviously those are aliases, but we can sort all of that out during our interrogations. If you surrender the men to me now, I won't hand you over to the police for conspiracy."

The minute his name was mentioned, Roni gasped and put a hand to her mouth.

"It's okay," he promised. "We can hear them but they can't hear us. It's going to be okay."

Damon was staring down Rupert. "You won't hand me over to the police at all. If you do that, you would have to hand over Jax and Tucker, too. Or are you planning on lying to the police? You're not here to arrest them. You want to study them. You're tired of waiting. What prompted this? And why is German intelligence here?"

It was Solo's turn to gasp. "Damn it. I knew they were talking. Beck's going to kill me. If I get you captured, Beck is literally going to kill me."

Tucker held a hand up to ask for silence. He wanted to hear what Rupert was going to say.

"Also unlike my predecessor, I find value in allies," the Brit said. "We're working with BND because they have some of the same problems we have. They keep getting caught in your bungling. What happened in Munich was unacceptable. Not only did your team give up the intelligence to the Americans, you got a former German agent killed in the process. And that wasn't the first time you've fucked the Germans over. Did you think they would forget what you did in Berlin?"

Roni's hand squeezed his.

"So this is some form of payback? Raiding my home, coming after my employees?" Damon was obviously trying to buy them all time.

Roni looked up at him. "What are we going to do? I can't leave Violet. I should go out there."

That wasn't going to happen. "If they get their hands on you, I'll do anything they ask, so if you go out there, I will, too."

Tears fell on her cheeks. "You can't. You don't know what they'll do to you."

They would question him. Likely they would be polite in the beginning, but they could use force if they didn't get what they wanted. They would test him. They would toss him to the wolves if he wasn't useful to them. "I don't know what they'll do to you either."

Her eyes had gone wide and she pointed to the screen. "Is that who I think it is?"

A shiver went up his spine as he realized who she was talking about. Arthur Dwyer stood in the background.

"Why would a representative from Kronberg be here?" she asked.

Solo's eyes had narrowed, a feral look on her face. "German intelligence is working with Kronberg. Bastards. We had a deal. We shared information with those assholes because they promised when the time comes, they'll help us take down Kronberg."

"This isn't just about me. This is about Roni, too. Fuck, they're here because they're worried two of their puzzle pieces got together and we're going to figure it out." So many things started to fall into place. "The whole time you thought you were hiding, they knew exactly where you were. They kept tabs on you and they kept tabs on me. They've kept to the shadows until now. Why? Because now we're together. They think we know where that list is. I stole it. You went with me to Paris where I was trying to hand it off to someone, maybe the CIA. McDonald convinced them at the time that you didn't know anything, but they still watched you. Now we're in the same place and they won't take the chance that we'll get the intel and run with it. Roni, if Kronberg is here, they want you every bit as much as they want me."

"I think he's right," Solo said.

"Where's Mr. Taggart?" Rupert was asking on the monitors.

Damon shrugged. "Probably halfway across the Atlantic. He went home."

So Tag was on the move. He hadn't been in the dungeon earlier. He'd been in the offices working and talking to his family on the computer, and according to Solo, plotting with Ezra. He would have been informed quickly if there was a problem.

The discussion continued but he turned to Veronica and put his hands on her shoulders. "It's going to be okay. No matter what happens, I'm going to get you out of this."

She took a deep breath and nodded. "Okay. But, Tucker, I don't know anything. I haven't been lying. I didn't even look at your laptop that day. It was password protected and then Dr. McDonald had Robert take it. I don't know anything and that means I'll be useless to them."

Oh, she wouldn't be useless. She would be a tool to get him to do whatever they wanted. They needed to get out of the building and regroup.

A woman in a suit stepped into the frame and whispered something in Rupert's ear that had him turning to Damon again.

"Would you like to tell me where Sandra Croft and her daughter are hiding? My employee found the apartment they're living in, but sadly we seemed to have missed them."

Roni breathed a deep sigh of relief.

"Ian got them out." Violet would have been Big Tag's priority. Having kids around meant every person in the building had to make those kiddos their first priority. Ian would have made certain Ollie was safe as well.

"Then Beck is likely trying to secure River and Jax," Solo surmised. She nodded, never taking her eyes off the monitors. "He'll do whatever he can to save his men. Tucker, tell me you left your phone upstairs."

He hadn't been thinking about the fact that someone could potentially track him. He'd left his phone behind because he hadn't wanted anything to interrupt his moment with Roni. "It's upstairs, but Solo, we've got the clothes on our backs. That's all."

"It'll be fine," Solo promised. "I assure you Beck's thought about this. He's planned for a worst-case scenario. It's what he does. He's going to get you out of here. He'll do whatever it takes."

Her faith in her ex-husband was a palpable thing.

"They got Vi out?" Roni was crying, but it was obvious she was trying so hard to keep it together.

He hauled her close. "Tag will protect her. He knows that she's the first priority. You and Vi are everything."

"Oh, no." Solo breathed as she watched the monitor. "Oh, no."

Tucker's heart threatened to stop as Jax showed up on the screen. His hands were restrained behind his back and he had a defiant look on his face. He was shoved along but managed to stay on his feet.

Jax. They'd caught Jax.

A sob came over the monitor and River ran into the frame, tears streaming down her face. "Please. He didn't do anything. Please."

"Oh, there are several governments who would disagree with you," Rupert said. "Mr. Seaborne, I think it's time we had a talk. This might go easier on you if we could also interview your friend Tucker Jones."

"And his girlfriend." Arthur Dwyer's voice was tinged with a German accent. His words were soft but they sent a chill through Tucker. "We would like very much to talk to Veronica Croft."

River was being restrained by another of the operatives, though at least they seemed to have some compassion for her. She was crying, looking to her husband like the world was falling apart.

"Since when is MI6 in the business of acting as mercenaries for corporations?" Damon asked, his voice as cold as ice.

That seemed to trip Rupert up momentarily. His expression went blank as though he'd never considered the possibility that anyone would view his actions in such a way. His expression went stubborn. "I'll work with anyone who will help me keep a potentially dangerous drug off the streets. Do you understand what could happen if our enemies gain control of McDonald's research?"

"I know Kronberg would like their research back," Robert said.

Rupert turned on him. "You should count yourself lucky you have friends in high places, Mr. McClellan, otherwise I would be bringing you in with Seaborne. I don't believe for a moment it wasn't you involved in those South American robberies. But I'm not allowed to touch you, and Mr. Shaw was the sad-sack idiot who got caught right before everyone was safe again. So I'm going to ask again, where are Tucker Jones and Veronica Croft?"

"I have to save him." He couldn't let them take Jax. This was everything they'd been running from since the moment they'd been rescued. This was the nightmare scenario. "Maybe they'll take me and let Roni go. She doesn't know anything."

"You don't know anything either," Roni argued.

Solo stepped in front of him. "I can't let you go out there. I know you're scared, but you're not thinking. We've got one way to save Jax and that's to give them what they want."

There was only one thing they could want from him. "The intel that I stole from Kronberg."

"The intel we think you stole," Solo qualified. "It's obvious that MI6 has been compromised. I can work this from a diplomatic angle. I can open talks with some people I know on that side. I'll let them know I've got you and I won't share anything with them unless they prove to me they're not going to hurt Jax. He'll be in a holding cell, but I can make sure they don't do anything to him physically. I will lie and tell them you know where the intel is but you're holding out on me. It'll buy us a couple of days."

A couple of days. They would only have a handful of days to ensure Jax didn't become someone's punching bag. Or their medical experiment.

He felt numb. How could everything have gone wrong in the course of mere minutes? His whole world had crumbled because he'd been stubborn. If he hadn't told Jax to hold off on Roni, Vi, and Sandra's papers, they would be safe in Dallas now. He and Jax likely would have been moved out of London, and Jax wouldn't be in custody. But no, he'd wanted time to convince Veronica he wasn't the selfish monster he'd been in the past.

Dr. Razor. Who made people bleed. Jax would be the one bleeding this time. His brothers were the ones in the line of fire, and he was in a nice comfortable hidey-hole.

Rob stood in front of Ariel, but she was whispering in his ear, likely giving him her assessment of everything that was going on around them. Owen was beside Robert, Rebecca behind him, both with their eyes on Jax and River.

He should be out there with them.

"Tucker isn't here, man," Jax said with a shake of his head. "That asshole left days ago. He took one look at that woman and his brothers didn't matter anymore. He suddenly had better things to do, you know. He didn't pay attention at all to our bro code."

Their code. Jax had been the first of them to get married. The code meant no one was more important than their wives. They had to pick their wives over everything and everyone else.

Jax was giving him permission to go.

"We all told him he should honor the code," Rob said. "But you know how men can get around a woman."

"They lose their damn heads," Owen agreed. "That's why we have the code in the first place. Real men honor it."

They were all telling him to go, to protect Veronica.

"That's not the intelligence I have," Rupert said with a frown. "The last I heard, he was in a comatose state and unable to be moved. I think he's still here. Fan out and check again. I want every single person in this building questioned. Please escort Mr. Seaborne to the cars. We'll question him at headquarters and then see what happens. There are several agencies who would love to speak with him."

River screamed her husband's name as they started to haul him out. "Let me go with him. I did it, too. I did all of it. I was with him."

Jax looked back, a desperate plea in his eyes. "Owen, please."

This was another part of their code. Owen had on a proper kilt this time and he looked somewhat primal as he wrapped an arm around River and hauled her over his shoulder. Rebecca was crying, too, as River fought to stay with her husband.

It was too much. Too much emotion. Too much fear. Too much guilt. His system threatened to shut down.

Rupert's men flanked out, some of them going toward the elevators. They would find Nick and Hayley in their cozy apartment, likely wrapped in each other's arms. They would find Walt in the lab either working on some project or trying to dominate the world via video game. Steph, Brody, and their son, Nate, were out for the evening. They would return home to a different world.

He'd brought it all down on their heads.

"The way's clear. We need to move." Nina was back and she wasn't alone.

"Tucker, don't you take another step near that fucking door. I already lost one of you tonight. I didn't get to Jax in time." Ezra was with her, a grim look on his face. He stared at Solo. "You were in the sauna? You okay?"

She nodded. "Beck, I'll fix this, but I can't do it if they haul me in, too. An American agent on British soil...they won't believe I was here visiting friends."

"Then you come with us and when we're safe, I expect you to do what you have to do to protect Jax," he said. "But now we need to move. The tunnels are clear."

He hadn't even known there were tunnels. He'd lived here for almost two years and no one had mentioned there were escape routes. Of course, they hadn't exactly needed escape routes until the Lost Boys had shown up since they hadn't been engaged in criminal activity before that.

Was he going to bring the whole company down?

"This tunnel leads to a parking garage in the financial district," Nina explained. "Damon has a small flat there and a car we can use. But we have to move now. We've got two go-bags. Ezra picked up his and there's always one in the tunnel."

Solo frowned. "Mine is upstairs, but I've got a couple of guns and my secure phone with me."

"Where's my mom and Vi?" Roni stepped forward. "I can't leave without them."

"Ian has them. We split up when we realized what was going on. They're in a secure location, but he can't get here," Ezra said. "He's holed up with them and when it's safe, he'll follow. But we have to go now."

He had to leave his brothers to the wolves? He had to leave his daughter behind?

Ezra stepped in front of him. "I know what is going through your head, but you cannot help Jax. We gain nothing by giving you up. They'll take him anyway, and they'll take Veronica. They'll use both of them to get you to do anything they ask. We've got to figure out if you stole that intel."

"I did." He sounded hollow to his own ears. "I know I did. I can see the thumb drive in my hand."

When he closed his eyes and thought about it hard, he could feel it there, feel the morning sunlight on his face, the hint of a breeze that had run through the city that morning. He'd walked down the street with a spring to his step because it was almost over.

"Then we'll find it and we'll bargain with it," Ezra said, jarring him out of his thoughts. "But we can't do any of that if they catch us. The only thing that will happen is they take the two of you into custody, and we will have absolutely nothing to bargain with." He pointed to the frosted glass doors. They shuddered as someone on the other side tried to open them.

"Mr. Knight," Rupert was saying, "I'm going to need you to open these doors."

"Tucker, should we open the doors?" Roni stared up at him. "If you think we should talk to them, I'll come with you."

Like River had tried to go with Jax. The trouble was Jax had earned his wife's loyalty. All he'd done so far for Roni was leave her alone and pregnant, and now he'd managed to separate her from their child.

They were going to have to run through London's underground like rats in a maze, and Roni didn't even have a pair of shoes.

All because he'd been impatient.

He glanced at the monitor and sure enough, the man outside the door now had several friends who looked ready to break it all down. He didn't have a choice. He had to put her first. He leaned over and shoved his arms under her knees, hauling her against his chest. He might have put her in this position, but he could make sure she didn't have to walk the path alone.

"Lead the way." He carried Roni toward the back of the hall where Damon proved he was always prepared.

As Tucker followed Ezra into the dark tunnel, he vowed he would find what they needed.

Even if it killed him.

Chapter Nine

Roni looked around the gorgeous country home three days later and wished she could enjoy it on an aesthetic level. She knew she should appreciate the stunning ceilings and the stained-glass windows, but all she saw was a million ways they were unsafe.

The smell of coffee permeated, hitting her nose and reminding her that she had barely eaten in days, much less had a decent cup of coffee.

But then what mother ate when she didn't even know where her child was in the world?

She stopped just before the hallway opened to the large great room. She could hear the sound of people talking. Ezra. And Nina. They were saying something about how no one seemed to have followed them, and Ezra had reprogrammed the security cameras to watch all the possible entrances. They'd even placed some new ones to watch the woods around them.

"Hey, I was going to see if you wanted some breakfast. Nina's making omelets." Tucker walked out from what appeared to be the kitchen. "I know it's been rough these last few days, but this is a safe place."

It had been beyond rough. First there had been the harrowing escape through London's underground tunnels. Despite the fact that

Ezra and Nina had promised her no one would be able to find the hidden door unless Damon talked, she still had held on to Tucker like a lifeline. All through the long trudge below, he'd carried her and she'd watched over his shoulder for signs that they were being chased. Every footstep Tucker had taken had put distance between her and Violet.

They'd made their way to the small flat that served as one of McKay-Taggart and Knight's safe houses. They'd stayed in the tiny one-bedroom flat until late last night when Ezra and Nina had decided it was safe enough to move to this massive house in the English countryside. She'd been told it was owned by a member of The Garden and was as safe as they could be.

"Have you heard anything about Violet and my mom?" It was all she'd been able to think about for days. She hadn't seen or talked to her baby since they'd fled The Garden.

The half smile that had been on his face faded. "I checked the message board we're supposed to use. Ian's got them on a plane back to the States."

"Without me?" They were going to be so far away. She'd never spent so much as a night away from Vi until two days ago, and now there would be a whole ocean between them?

Tucker's voice dropped low as though he didn't want the rest of them to hear what he was saying. "I would do anything to get you on that plane. Anything. Say the word and I'll turn myself in."

That was the problem. There wasn't anything to do. She took a deep breath, trying to quell the emotions welling inside her. She knew they'd done what they had to do, knew Tucker giving himself up wasn't going to help, but it didn't fix the anxiety and fear festering deep down in her gut. "No, of course not. That's absolutely not an option."

Nina's head popped around the corner. The former Interpol agent looked far cheerier than she had the last few days. "Hey, we have actual food that doesn't have to be reconstituted with boiling water. Do you want any veg in your omelet? I've got onions, tomatoes, and spinach to go with some lovely ham I intend to thank Clive Weston for the next time I see him. Truly the aristocracy lives so much better than the rest of us."

Weston. He owned the house they were staying at and she'd

heard it mentioned he was some kind of earl or something.

"I don't know that I want anything." She wasn't sure she could eat.

Tucker frowned. "Come on. At least you can have some toast. You need to keep your strength up."

That was funny because she wasn't sure she'd shown a lot of strength the last few days. She'd cried and felt sorry for herself. She'd asked endlessly about her daughter, but not about anyone else. These people had been kind to her, but she'd been caught up in her own misery.

He turned and followed Nina into the ultramodern kitchen. The rest of the house looked like Downton Abbey, but the kitchen was sleek and technologically advanced. There were big windows that let in the light. The kitchen felt normal and that made her wary. Solo was pacing outside, walking back and forth in front of the windows, her cell phone to her ear and talking animatedly. Again, normal. Normal scared her right now.

"Shouldn't she be inside?" The first day, she'd gotten a massive lecture on why she couldn't leave the flat.

Ezra glanced up from the laptop he'd spent endless hours on the last few days. It was supposedly secure and their only line of communications besides two burner phones they were only to use in extreme emergencies. She'd thought her life in Germany had been restrictive. Her mother had nothing on Ezra Fain. "She's under the awning. See how she stays close to the house? She's doing that so she can't be picked up on satellites. She knows what she's doing. Trust me. If there's one person in the world who knows how to take care of herself it's Kim Solomon."

Nina sighed as she flipped over an omelet. "I could be back at The Garden, but no. I had to go downstairs after a workout to grab a water because I was too lazy to stock my flat. Listening to the two of you bicker has been a life lesson, I tell you. How did you ever stay married for years?"

The faintest hint of a smile hit Ezra's face. "Because when she's good, she's really good." He seemed to shake the feeling off. "It will be better now that we've got some room. We won't be on top of each other all the time. How are you this morning, Veronica? Did Tucker fill you in on what happened last night?"

She was hungry for all the details. "He said Ian moved Vi and my mom. They're on a plane now? Will he tell us when they land? Is he with them?"

Tucker nodded. "Yes. He got them from London to Dublin. I have no idea how, but he's got connections. They're going out on a private plane his sister-in-law sent. They're going to land at a private airfield in New York and stay with Drew Lawless. That's Case's brother-in-law. Ian will go on to Dallas, but he's got bodyguards in place and a whole legal team waiting to see if anyone shows up on Drew's doorstep. They're safe, and Ian's going to find a way to let them call you."

It was far better for them to be on US soil. They had rights in the US they didn't have here.

Tucker stared at her for a moment. "I'll ask him to send the plane for you in a day or two."

"I don't think that's a great idea," Ezra said.

"For me? Not you?" She kept her attention on Tucker. He would be safer in the US, too.

"I can't leave. I need to be in Europe. There's every probability that I'm going to go to Paris as soon as Ezra and Nina decide it's okay to go," he explained. "I'll make sure you're safe first. Did the clothes fit?"

He was good at deflecting from the real point. She'd learned that over the last few days. That first night he'd held her while she'd cried, but then he'd slept in the living room, offering the bedroom to her and Nina and Solo.

She would rather have been on the couch with him. The previous night he'd tucked her into bed after the long drive and told her he needed to talk to Ezra. It had been hours before he'd crawled into bed and he'd seemed so intent on not waking her, she'd pretended to sleep.

He was feeling guilty. He thought he was the reason they were all in this position. She wasn't stupid. It was there in his every gesture, in the way he fell over himself if she wanted so much as a glass of water. She knew what his problem was. The trouble was she felt guilty, too, and she hadn't been handling it well.

"I don't know that I should leave you," she said. "Especially since it puts our daughter in danger again. I don't know what I would

175

do if I led them straight to the safe house. They're looking for me. Asking about my mom and Vi was incidental. They're safe. You're not."

"Neither are you." He put a hand on the table as though he needed it for balance.

This was the other thing that had been happening. He was getting sicker and sicker.

"Is it another headache?" She moved to his side.

"It's nothing."

That was what he'd been saying for days. She'd missed the signs that he wasn't well. She hadn't noticed Tucker wasn't eating until the night before when he'd refused the sandwiches Nina had made.

She tried to move in, but he dodged her, keeping the table between them.

"I think I should go lie down. I didn't get much sleep last night. Tell Solo I'll be ready if she needs me." He strode out of the kitchen.

Her heart sank. He was drawing away from her, and she might have missed her shot to keep him close.

"No matter what he says, he's not okay." Nina put a plate in front of Ezra. "Watching Jax get taken into custody gutted him. It's what they've been desperate to avoid."

"Yeah, well, knowing he's the reason his daughter is in hiding can't have been good for his state of mind," Ezra added.

"It wasn't his fault." That was the one thing she was sure of.

Ezra took a drink of his coffee. "Actually, when you think about it, it's Solo's fault. If she'd left you alone, Kronberg probably never comes after you."

Nina's eyes widened in what couldn't be mistaken for anything but righteous indignation. "You're the one who asked Solo to find her."

"No, I didn't ask Solo for anything," Ezra said with a shrug. "This is one more of her crazy stunts to try to prove to me she's changed. It happened to also lead to us being on the run and Jax in jail. That's how it goes with Solo. Everything she touches tends to turn to shit."

"I'm trying," a soft voice said.

She turned and Solo was standing there, her cell peeking out of her pocket.

Ezra frowned and hopped off his barstool, flipping his laptop shut. "You always do, Kim. And it always ends up going wrong. I've got a secure call with Damon in five. I'll be in the office. Thanks for breakfast, Nina."

Nina looked back, one hand on her hip. "Not that you actually ate it." She sighed. "I don't know why I try."

"I'll take it." Solo slipped into Ezra's seat and picked up the fork he'd left behind. "I've been living off scraps with him for years. Roni, I'm sorry. I was glad to hear Ian thinks he's got a safe spot to stash your mom and daughter. The Lawless building is secure and Drew Lawless has enough government contacts that the Agency will think twice about even approaching him."

That was good to know and even more reason why she shouldn't go. If they were safe, going to the States could only give the Agency or any of the intelligence groups a reason to think about upsetting the balance. And Ezra was wrong. "I don't blame you."

Solo smiled faintly. "It's okay. Beck can blame me enough for both of you."

"Why do you call him Beck?"

"Because that's his name. Becket Kent. Ezra Fain was his half brother. He was on a special operations team and he died on a mission I sent him on over Beck's very vocal objections." She said the words without a hint of emotion. As though she'd been over and over them so often, she couldn't quite feel them anymore.

Guilt. It seemed to be a thing today. "Well, I don't blame you for coming to find me. I know it might have been the catalyst that started this fire, but I think it was always going to start."

"Has anyone considered the fact that it's not Veronica that upset the fragile balance?" Nina asked, setting a tray of toast on the island.

"But they raided The Garden only a few days after I showed up," Roni pointed out.

"It takes more than a few days to plan something like the other night. I should know. I've been involved. It would have taken a while just to get MI6 and German intel on the same page." Nina sat down beside Solo. "I think the turning point was when the lads broke into Kronberg. That was when Kronberg realized they were sitting on a bomb that hasn't gone off yet, but it will. I think having Tucker walk back into that building is what made them move and fast. The fact that there was an Agency team there would have been icing on the cake."

Solo held up her fork. "Then see, still my fault. Although I would like to point out I was hauling in a rogue agent."

"And you coordinated with BND?" Nina looked expectant, though it was obvious she knew the answer to the question.

"No," Solo admitted.

Nina pointed her way. "See, there it is. But then Ezra wouldn't have either. It's the nature of your job. Secrets and obfuscation. I worked in a far more transparent place. I like the world better in black and white. But that's neither here nor there. The point is the lads woke this particular sleeping beast. Not Veronica. Levi Green pushed them to do it. So I say we stash the guilt and deal with the problem head on."

"That's what I'm trying to do," Solo said. "Now that we're here and have some space, I have a plan. But I need Tucker for this plan, and that means he can't make himself sick."

He was doing it for her. For her and Violet and Jax. He was trying so hard to fix the problem, but this wasn't something he could plow his way through. And being apart wasn't helping the situation.

He was spiraling and there was no one to catch him. From what she understood, he'd had the support of his brothers through everything. Since the moment he'd been rescued, he'd had those men to surround him and understand him. Then in the last few weeks he'd lost two of his brothers, one to betrayal and the other betrayed, but he had to feel both deaths. And now he felt like he'd abandoned Vi. He had to feel close to losing her, too. In some ways, he wanted to. Sending her away would be the final blow. Sometimes there was a relief that came with knowing you couldn't lose anything else.

She knew that feeling, but she couldn't let him push her out because losing her would be freeing.

She'd been in a state of numbness where only her own grief and panic had stirred anything inside her, but it was time to take control. Her mother would have already poked her enough that she would have come out of her shell. Her mother never backed down from either challenge or tragedy. Even when Katie had been killed, her mom was the one who'd realized the threat and acted to protect her daughter and unborn granddaughter. Her mother would do anything to protect Vi and honestly, she would put Sandra Croft up against a CIA team any day of the week.

It was past time to be more like her mother. Her mother would never let a person she loved drown in guilt.

She loved him. She'd loved him when he was Steven Reasor. She loved him as Tucker Jones. She just loved him.

"What's the plan?" She reached out and grabbed a piece of toast. She might not be hungry, but she didn't want to get weak, and that meant normalizing. It was time to be strong.

Solo looked up from her eggs. "Are you in now? I was worried you were going to be deadweight."

"I'm in and I assure you I might not be deadweight, but I will be a pain in your ass if you get Tucker into more trouble. I don't care what the American government wants. I only care about getting Jax free and finding a way to clear Tucker's name. Whatever his actual name is."

Nina's lips turned up in a grin. "Thank god. He needs someone to take him in hand."

Solo passed her the butter. "It's good to have another team member. I'm afraid the guys are super emotional. We need more solid logic. So yes, I have a plan. Now that we're in a safe location, I've called in some favors and I'm bringing in a couple of people I think can help Tucker remember. Rebecca told me she thinks the cure Levi gave Tucker is actually working. At least partially. He's been remembering more and more."

"Yes, he has, and before all that crap went down, he was handling it quite well. He was doing everything Ariel and Rebecca had taught him to do. He was letting it flow. He would talk about it, but he wouldn't try to force the memory," she explained. "The only times he would be tempted to was when he thought about his brother."

Solo sat up a little straighter. "His brother? I haven't heard he thought he had a brother." She sat back again. "Maybe you should wait to talk about this. You have to understand that I'm here on Beck's...Ezra's sufferance. He might not want me to know everything."

"I trust you." Solo had done nothing but reunite her family.

Nina nodded her way. "Go on. I'd like to hear about it, too. And

Solo's here. She's part of this and she didn't have to be. She could have walked at any moment. Is she doing it to try to get her husband back? Probably, but the good news is her husband would be super-pissed if she betrayed us. Ergo, we can trust her."

"Your way with logic is spot on," Solo said before turning back to Roni. "Now what's this about a brother?"

"He remembers a brother. He said his name was Ace. He can't see a face, but he knows Ace was older than him. I don't know if this helps solve the mystery of whether or not he stole that intel, but I know it's on his mind a lot," she explained. "Is there any way to find his family?"

"McDonald was excellent at covering her tracks." Nina crossed to the coffeepot and filled a mug. "We actually know what Robert's name is and we haven't been able to find his mother or brother. His wife has a small footprint, but it didn't lead to Robert."

"According to Levi, Robert's family might still be alive," Solo said. "But he's not talking about that to me. He got the data Jax found at a highly secret black ops site called The Ranch. I wasn't allowed to study that data. I suspect it had a ton of information on McDonald's subjects. It could be how he knew so much about Robert's family and what Tucker was doing. Or it could be complete bullshit. Levi lies and often."

"But even the devil knows that the best lie contains a hint of the truth." Nina offered her the mug.

Roni was more than happy to take it. She needed some caffeine. "So you think these people you're bringing in might help him remember?"

"That's what Big Tag thinks," Solo replied. "It's a gamble on my end, but it's one I've got to take. I don't care what Nina says. I don't think Jax gets hauled in if I hadn't brought you to The Garden. I owe River a lot. I like Jax. I can't let this stand. I have to fix this. And honestly, it was my agency that allowed McDonald to work. I want those names. I want to know who sold out Robert and Jax and Tucker. And all the rest. Justice might have been served on Hope McDonald, but there are still people out there who haven't paid their debt. I'm going to be the bill collector."

Solo's voice had gone cold and Roni was happy she was on that woman's team.

"How do I help Tucker?" There was still a fear in the back of her mind that Tucker remembering who he'd been could have terrible consequences, but she couldn't let fear rule her. He cared about her now. He'd cared about her then.

She had to have a little faith.

Solo seemed to think about that. "Mostly, you can get him to relax. It's going to be a rough afternoon and I think if he goes into this with a bad attitude, it might not work."

Luckily, she knew exactly how to get that man to relax. And maybe it would help her, too.

* * * *

Tucker stood in the bedroom he and Roni had been assigned to. He should have taken his own. It wasn't fair to ask her to sleep with him, and there were plenty of rooms in this massive place. Ezra wanted them all in one wing, but he could just deal with it. She'd only had sex with him once. She shouldn't be forced into a relationship she probably didn't want.

Couldn't want since he kept fucking up and getting her in trouble. He'd promised her he wouldn't lie to her again, but how could he know if he was lying now? How could he truly know what he'd been doing that day? What if he'd been using her as cover to do something nefarious? He'd spent hours going over and over everything that he could have been doing the day he'd been taken.

Everyone was optimistic that he'd magically seen the light and realized that what McDonald had been doing was wrong. Or that he'd somehow gotten recruited by Green either before or after he'd gone to work for McDonald.

What if he'd been covering his own ass? Or worse. What if he'd been selling McDonald out for cash? Didn't that sound more like something a man with the nickname of Razor would do?

"Hey, are you ready for that shower you promised me?"

He turned and there was Veronica standing in the doorway. She was wearing shorts and a T-shirt. It was one of three changes of clothes she had in the whole world. The only reason she had those was Clive Weston had his assistant drive them out before they arrived. She'd been forced to sleep in one of Tucker's T-shirts. It hung to her knees and made her look soft and sweet, and he'd wanted to wrap her up and promise her everything would be all right.

Then he'd remembered she'd spent the last two days crying because she missed her baby, and her own future was in question.

Wait. What had she said?

"I'm sorry. Did you need to take a shower? I can leave."

She gave him a sunny smile, a thing he hadn't seen out of her in days. "I wasn't asking you to leave, Tucker. I was asking you to join me. You promised me a lot out of that shower and then the world blew up and it seems to me you forgot."

She crossed the room, walking to him and going up on her toes. Her head tilted and her lips hovered close to his.

His cock responded, tightening and stretching like the fucker wanted to play. He couldn't play right now. Could he?

No. He couldn't. It wasn't fair to her. "Roni, you don't have to do this. I'll take care of you. You don't have to offer me sex."

She was suddenly flat footed again and her eyes had gone from soft to hard as emeralds and twice as cold. "Excuse me."

Fuck. What had he done wrong? Because he'd definitely done something wrong to put that look on her face. Roni was always sweet. She never lost her temper. Well, she hadn't before. She'd always been patient. "I was trying to explain…"

"Go on," she said as if she hadn't interrupted. "I would love to hear this explanation since what I heard was you saying our sexual relationship was based on me giving you my body in exchange for your protection. Like a hooker."

"No, baby. Not like a hooker. All the hookers I've ever met wanted cash. I don't have any cash. I can't offer it to you." He knew the minute the words were out of his mouth that he'd made another mistake.

Her eyes went wide, and that wasn't wonder in them. "You've been self-aware for like two minutes, but you already figured out how to hire a hooker?"

"They all looked like you."

She turned and her shoulders shook, her hand going to her mouth.

"God, Roni. I'm so sorry. I didn't mean for you to know," he said, his voice hoarse. "I'm such a dumbass. Please don't cry."

She turned and she was laughing. "Sorry, it's like when your baby's first word sounds an awful lot like *shit* and you don't want to encourage her. I blame my mom for that, by the way. She's got a potty mouth and she won't even try to fix it."

Was she playing a game with him? He stepped back. "What's going on, Roni?"

She wiped her eyes because she'd laughed so much she'd cried. "You're a little crazy, you know. So, hookers? I was raising your daughter and you were running around with hookers?"

That wasn't the whole story. "I was also getting shot at and trying to remember who I am. I got the shit kicked out of me a couple of times. And I have bad dreams. And sometimes I didn't actually sleep with the hookers. They can be nice to talk to."

Her expression softened. "Tucker, you didn't remember me. I can't exactly yell at you for cheating on a woman you didn't know existed. But I can get upset that you seem to think I'm using you for protection. I assure you, I can get protection. I'm not exactly without skills. I grew up with GI Jane as a mom. Do you know the only thing worse than a soldier? A soldier who also happens to be a nurse."

"You can't protect yourself from these people." He knew Sandra was capable, and she would have taught her daughter self-defense, but they were up against highly trained operatives with connections they couldn't even understand.

"I'm not sleeping with you because I think that's the only way you'll protect me. I know I've been a mess the last few days. I haven't been apart from Violet before and I didn't handle it well," she said, an unnecessary apology in her tone.

"You shouldn't handle it well. You shouldn't have to handle it at all."

She moved close to him again. "I don't blame you."

How could she not? "It's my fault."

Her hands found his chest, gently touching him like he was fragile and she didn't want to break him. "Did you ask for this? Did you ask the universe to take all of your memories and torture you? Because I'm damn straight sure I didn't ask for the father of my child to be taken away from me. I didn't ask for my sister to be killed and to have to hide for years. So the way I see it, it's neither of our faults. But the way we're acting now is."

"The way I'm acting?" He took a step back because if he didn't, he was going to get his hands on her and then they wouldn't have this very necessary talk. "I assure you I'm not acting. And you can't possibly know that this isn't my fault. We don't know what I was doing."

She sighed, an exasperated sound. "I don't care what you were doing."

"You aren't listening to me."

Her head shook. "No, you aren't listening to me. I don't care what you did then. If we find out you were leaving me behind, my question to you is going to be what do you want now?"

That was the real heartbreak of the situation. He knew exactly what he wanted. "You. I want you. I want you and Violet and hell, I want your crazy-ass mother as my family. But that can't happen because I'm going to ruin you. I'm going to ruin all of you. I love you so fucking much but everything I touch turns toxic."

"I'm not toxic."

"Your situation is."

"Only if we let it be," she insisted. "And I don't think Robert or Jax or Owen would say they're toxic, either. I heard you saved Stephanie Carter once."

That seemed like so long ago. He'd felt worthy that day. Right until the moment he'd learned he'd been called Dr. Razor because he cut so deep. It was then he'd realized how arrogant he'd been, thinking he could be the hero. "I was dumb enough to let myself be taken because I had a microchip. They had to chip me like a dog so they might be able to find me. I was nothing but a homing beacon."

A frustrated groan came from her mouth. "A homing beacon doesn't make the choice to save someone. It doesn't have to think about whether or not they'll die in the effort. Do you know what I've done the last few days?"

"Hidden in a too tight apartment and cried because you didn't know if your daughter was dead or alive?"

She rolled her eyes. "Before that. Since I came to The Garden, a couple of times a day someone would show up wherever I happened to be and they would plead your case. Oh, they didn't come out and say that's what they were doing, but I caught on pretty quickly. Robert talked to me about how loyal you are. Owen told me the story of how you helped him in those first days after he was dosed with

McDonald's drugs. You took care of him and you didn't even know him. He hadn't been in the compound with you for more than a day. Ariel and Rebecca tag teamed me with how amazing you are. Jax...well, Jax said he doesn't survive any of this without you."

She was forgetting a salient point. Jax was in hell because of him. "He still might not."

"They love you. Even the big guy and the scary Brit. You're worried that you're going to remember and you'll turn back into the cold, selfish, evil person you used to be. But I'm telling you, you were never that person. You were real with me. I don't know why you put on that act with everyone else, but you were real with me."

He wanted to believe her so badly. "How can you know that?"

She moved in again, putting her hands on him and looking up, her eyes intent upon him. "Because when you were at the bottom, when you were in hell and every moment was agony, you weren't selfish at all. You sacrificed. You gave. You made a family for yourself in the worst conditions, a family that still loves and supports you. Tucker, we're not defined by how we behave when times are perfect. It's who we are when we're half dead on the ground and everything seems hopeless that counts. I've been a mess for days, but it's time to take a cue from my mom and get up and fight. It's time to follow in the footsteps of the best man I've ever met. I'm not going to roll into a ball and forget that there are people who need me. At my worst, I want to be open and kind and strong and compassionate. I want to be like you."

Emotion welled deep inside him at her words. He wanted to be that man, wanted to know deep inside that he could be the kind of father and husband Roni could be proud of. He hadn't even known he wanted to be a dad, but now that he'd met Vi, he knew he couldn't fail her. He let his head drop to Roni's, the contact piercing through the veil of self-loathing that had threatened to swallow him whole since that moment he'd realized what he would cost them all. "I want to be good enough for you. I want it more than anything."

"Then come to the shower with me and let's take a few hours off. There's nothing we can do. You trust Ian Taggart?"

He nodded. "None of us would be alive without him. He and Damon...they risked everything to protect us. He won't let anything happen to our daughter."

"Then be with me. I'm going to go and get ready for whatever today holds. I would like very much to do that with you. If you can't, I understand. But you should know I'll ask you every day. Being together is a choice. I choose you, Tucker. I hope you can do the same for me."

She turned and strode into the shower.

Brat. She'd just put him in an impossible position. She'd basically said *I choose you. Please choose me, too.* Like they were kids and it was as simple as checking a box on a note he would pass back to her friend, and they'd giggle about it and everything was easy and innocent.

What wasn't innocent about the way he felt about her? The easy part was a given. They weren't kids and honestly, it wouldn't have been easy if they were. They were human and that meant everything was complicated.

He heard the shower turn on and a wave of longing hit him hard.

Was he treating her the way Tag had accused him? As some prize to be won. Earning her love had more to do with how he treated her, the priority he placed on her, than martyring himself.

Why would it be wrong to take what she was offering? If he gave it all back to her, what was wrong with accepting the comfort that would come from being close to her?

He hadn't even answered the question in his head before he was standing in the doorway of the magnificent bathroom, watching as she stepped into the shower. Steam was already pouring through the room and she'd swept her hair up. She was naked, her skin luminous in the natural light.

It had been morning, soft light flowing into the conference room. No one had turned on the overhead lights so there was practically a halo around the head of the woman staring out at the cityscape, the Frauenkirche's twin towers in the distance.

She'd turned and he'd stopped. Stopped breathing. Stopped thinking. Stopped doing anything but looking at her.

"Hi. I'm Veronica, the new intern. Everyone calls me Roni."

It had been right there on the tip of his tongue to tell her his name. His real name. He'd been ready to reach out his hand and introduce himself when...

The lights to the conference room had flickered on and that voice banged against his calm.

"We don't need interns in this meeting." Hope McDonald had strode in, every hair in place and wearing a Chanel suit that likely cost more than his mother made in a month.

"I was looking at the skyline. You've got an amazing view here," Veronica had said. Roni. Everyone called her Roni.

"Yes, and we've earned it by being the best in the building," McDonald said. "When you've worked your way up, you'll be welcome to stare as much as you like. Until then, your place is in the basement."

Her smile dimmed and she nodded, holding her notebook against her chest as she walked to the door. "Of course, Dr. McDonald."

"I'm Steven," he said as she brushed past him. "Dr. Reasor."

She gave him a hint of a smile and a nod as she exited the room and started back toward the elevators that would take her down where the sun wouldn't caress her skin.

"Interns. Well, we'll have to watch that one," McDonald said.

Yes. He would have to watch out for her. She didn't know it, but she was stuck in hell and that demon in front of him could tear her up.

He had to make sure she didn't.

"Tucker?"

He came out of the memory at the sound of her voice. For a moment, he'd been there. He'd not simply had a sliver of memory. He'd been there, like it had happened to him.

It *had* happened to him.

"The first time I saw you it was morning. You were in the conference room on the fifth floor. You introduced yourself to me. McDonald walked in and she was a bitch to you."

Roni stood in the entryway to the shower and seemed comfortable with her nudity, a soft smile playing on her lips as though she remembered, too. "She sent me to the basement because I wasn't one of the big boys. But I remember that you stopped me and introduced yourself. Everyone had warned me about you, but you were nice to me. You didn't look at me like I was something less."

He'd known even then that she was more. "I wanted to protect you from her. I knew she was bad. I wanted…I wanted to tell you my name. My real name. Steven Reasor isn't my real name, but I can't…"

She stepped out and put her hands on either side of his face. "Don't. You don't have to know right now. It will come to you or it won't, and forcing it will only make you sick. You're remembering and it's exactly what I said. You were always you. It's a puzzle that doesn't completely make sense yet. But when we put it all together, you're going to be you, Tucker. You're going to be the brave, sweet, amazing man I've come to know."

He'd wanted to protect her. He wasn't sure if that meant he was innocent or if he'd simply not wanted a pretty girl to get hurt, but he would take it. He might have become Steven Reasor at some point, but there was someone else beneath it all. Someone who cared about her.

He lowered his mouth to hers and let the memory slide away as their tongues tangled and his hands found her silky flesh. He didn't care that she was damp from stepping into the shower and she was plastered against his clothes. He wouldn't be in them for long. She was right. They needed this. He'd been wrong to think for a second that they should be apart.

He kissed her over and over, backing her into the shower. He managed to get his shirt off, tossing it to the side. Roni stepped back, going under the spray from the shower and managing to look both shockingly innocent and like a sex goddess all at the same time.

Because there was nothing not innocent about sex. Not when it was about pleasure and joy. Like all things in the world, it could be corrupted, but it was a joyful act. It was a necessary act because he wasn't whole if he couldn't touch her.

He shoved his jeans and boxers off. She didn't care about the scars on his body. She liked him. She wanted him. It was all he could ask.

He stalked into the shower after her, his sorrow and self-pity rapidly morphing into hunger. Days had passed and he hadn't felt close to her. He needed more than close now. He needed to be inside her, surrounded by her. He needed to know she was still his because he wanted so badly to be hers.

His cock was already hard and ready to go. He didn't care about anything with the exception of her. He felt feral as he towered over her. Roni's hands came out, stroking down his body like he was a predator she could soothe.

And she could because something in him eased the moment she touched him.

"I know things are stressful and you feel like it's all on your shoulders, but I'm with you. You're not alone. We get through this together," she said.

She'd made her choice. He'd given her every out and now he would take her at her word. She wanted him? Oh, she would have him. He would give her everything.

He kissed her again, bringing their bodies together. The water was warm, but she was so much hotter.

He gripped her ass, grinding his cock lightly against her belly. Her nails raked against his back and he happily took the little pain. She was here with him. She was right. They were in this together, and she was his partner. He owed her everything, and that included faith. Faith in his team, in them as a couple. Faith in himself.

"Tucker, I want to play," she said as he kissed his way down her neck. "I want to touch you. I didn't get to explore the way I wanted to. Please. We've only made love a few times and it was always about me. I want to explore you, too. I want to know every inch of your body."

She was going to make him crazy. He wanted to know exactly what she was talking about. "You want to touch my cock?"

She nodded. "Yes."

"Because if you touch my cock, I'll want you to suck my cock. I've been too impatient. You know I've wanted that always. I needed to show you how much you mean to me, and that meant giving you everything." He'd tied her up in the privacy room because he'd wanted to show her how he would treat her. Like she was a queen and he worshipped her.

"Then give me this. I need to show you how I feel, too." Her eyes were on him as she dropped to her knees.

His whole body tightened in anticipation.

She licked her lips as she wrapped her hand around his dick. He forced himself to breathe.

"Lick me, Roni." He'd felt such attraction to her that first day. It had shocked him. As though he'd thought there couldn't be anything good in the place he found himself in. She'd been sunshine in the gloom. She still was.

She stroked him and leaned forward, brushing her lips over him. Her tongue came out and dragged over his cockhead.

His eyes nearly rolled in the back of his head. Her mouth was soft. So fucking soft. His cock was rolled in hot, wet silk. Her tongue moved all over, not missing an inch of his dick as she moved her head up and down.

He hissed as her teeth lightly scratched against him, the tiny pain immediately flaring into pleasure. She started to move away, likely to apologize. He caught the back of her head and directed her to continue.

"Give it all to me. I can take it. Don't stop until I tell you to," he growled and flexed inside her.

Her eyes flared and she settled in again, her hands coming up to cup his ass. Her nails dug in lightly as though she'd figured out he didn't mind a bite of pain. He didn't. He kind of craved it, but only coming from her. It meant she was involved, so involved she wasn't thinking about anything but being in the moment with him.

She deep throated him and he knew he wasn't going to last.

"Baby, I'm going to come."

Her hands tightened on his cheeks and she sucked him harder.

She wanted him to come in her mouth. The thought of her drinking him down brought out something primal in him. She was his. She was making the conscious decision to put off her own pleasure so he could have this moment.

She stroked him with her tongue, lips caressing while her hands pressed on his ass, directing him to give to her. To give her everything he had.

The orgasm spiked through him, making him shudder even as she groaned around his dick. He let go, thrusting into her mouth and letting the sensation flow through him, binding him to her.

He was weak in the knees by the time she stood. There was the wickedest, sexiest grin on her face and she pointedly licked her lips.

"See, that was fun," she said, her voice going husky.

He was so in love with her. He kissed her, tasting himself on her lips. "Let's see if we can have even more fun."

Chapter Ten

Tucker walked into the great room as quietly as he possibly could. Something was going on. He'd heard a bunch of movement as he'd walked down the hallway. Doors opening and closing, feet scooting across the floors and harsh whispers. Whatever drama was going on, he wasn't a part of it.

How the world had changed. A few short weeks ago, he would have gone looking for the drama. He would have popped some corn and found the best seat he could to watch whatever was going to play out in front of him. Now he didn't have the time.

He was going to sneak into the kitchen, grab a couple of waters, and hope no one saw him before he could sprint back to their bedroom. He'd left Roni napping after a long session in bed. She hadn't slept well the past few nights.

It's better when your arms are around me.

He probably had the stupidest grin on his face. He ducked into the kitchen and Nina was sitting at the table, a book in her hand.

She took one look at him and shook her head. "Well, at least one of us is getting some. You know the worst part about being on the run? There's nothing to do except eat and watch telly and have sex with the incredibly handsome billionaire you happen to be on the run with." She gestured to the book in her hand. "And read a bit. For a stuffy nobleman, Clive's got some fun books. I'm on my third romance since I got here. Why can't I find my own hot, needs-a-woman-to-fix-him billionaire?"

He was going to keep Roni away from the library. He could totally give her a guy to fix. He was the king of broke-down guys, but he was also pretty actually broke, and she didn't need any ideas. "Maybe Damon can put you on bodyguard duty. You know, once we can all show our faces in the world again without getting arrested. What's going on out there?"

Nina glanced at the great room. It was open to the kitchen. "Not sure. Solo walked in about ten minutes ago and asked to have a word with Ezra. Then there was some door slamming and whispering on mobiles. Now they're both out in the garage. Maybe they're having sex, too. Everyone's having sex but me."

Another change. Weeks ago he would have been offering himself up to the lovely operative. He would have been giving her his most seductive smile and trying to coax her into giving him a try.

The thought was distasteful now and not because Nina wasn't wonderful. Because he belonged to Roni, and even flirting was off limits now. "Do we have any word on Jax?"

Should he be this happy when Jax was potentially being tortured?

Nina seemed to sober, too, as if Jax's very name was enough to bring them all back to reality. "He's still at MI6 headquarters and they're allowing Damon to see him. I believe that's Solo's doing. Apparently she's cut some kind of deal with them. Damon isn't being accused of harboring a fugitive at this time, but I get the feeling all that changes if we take too long. Solo can only hold out while they've got some patience. We're all at a standstill until she can deliver."

Until he could deliver. That was what she really meant but was far too polite to say. What Solo was trying to deliver existed only in Tucker's head, and his head didn't want to cooperate. "Is Ariel coming up? Ian mentioned something about wanting me to try hypnosis again."

"I think that's what all the drama outside is about," Nina explained. "I heard Solo say she's bringing someone in from London."

Maybe Rob would come with her. It would be good to see him.

Rob had a strange way of balancing him out. Jax might be his best friend in the world, but Rob was a steady influence on him. Rob always felt safe. It would be good to talk to Rob about everything that was happening with Roni. Rob would probably talk him out of doing stupid shit like asking her to marry him right now. Rob would convince him he should wait until he could at least get a ring. And until he didn't have cops across the globe looking to arrest him.

River knew what it felt like to have her husband dragged away in handcuffs. That thought sobered him entirely.

"I'm going to sneak back to my bedroom. Roni's napping and I don't want to leave her for long," he admitted. "Let me know if you need help with dinner."

"Can you cook?"

He shrugged. "Not at all, but I can add much needed sarcasm."

Roni could cook. She'd made dinner at The Garden. It had been simple but filling, and he'd adored those nights when they sat around a table together and talked about their days.

He missed Violet. He missed her sweet face and how she clung to him like he was worthy of being her dad. He'd barely known her for a week, but there was a hole inside him now that only she could fill. It was the same with Roni. He wanted his family together.

Was River sitting somewhere in London wishing she'd never met Jax? He seriously doubted it. She was at The Garden holed up with her big mutt, Buster, and praying for her husband's well-being. She would be grateful for every moment they'd had together and work hard to have more good days with him.

He wasn't going back to that old thinking. Roni had made her choice and now it was up to him to be worthy of her.

"Are you fucking crazy?" Ezra walked in from the hallway that led to the garage. He was wearing jeans and a T-shirt, boots on his feet. He immediately pivoted and turned to face Solo, who walked in behind him. "Do you know how dangerous this could be?"

"What other choice do we have, Beck?" The normally exquisitely dressed lady was dressed down due to the lack of a handy mall to outfit her for their hideout. She was in yoga pants, a T-shirt and sneakers, her mass of blonde hair in a high ponytail. "I have to do something no matter what the risk is. I've been prepping for this for days."

"There is no way to truly prep for this," Ezra shot back. "Unless this is all some scam. Are you in this with him?"

He should have moved way faster. The last thing he needed was to get caught in an Ezra/Solo throwdown. They happened way too often and went on far too long. He started to try to ease his way into the kitchen. Maybe there was another way to get back to Roni.

But a third person walking into the room made him stop in his tracks. Nina was suddenly beside him.

"Is that who I think it is?" Nina whispered the question.

The man who walked in would likely command whatever space he occupied. He had dark blond hair cut at a fashionable length, but there was no denying the man had a military air about him. He strode in, brown eyes focused on the argument playing out in front of him. His expression was completely shuttered, as though he didn't truly care about the outcome of the fight. He was merely waiting to see what he would need to do next, and he would carry that mission out with the same ruthlessness that had likely kept the White House in the current president's hands.

"Connor Sparks," Tucker whispered back like Sparks was Voldemort and no one should say his name aloud. Though Sparks had always played for the good guys. At least that was the way Big Tag explained it. When they'd first joined the London team, they'd been given a thorough class on the key political situations around the world, and part of that had included the men close to President Zack Hayes. He'd paid particular attention to Connor Sparks since he was not only one of the president's closest friends, but an intelligence officer.

"Yeah, that's what I thought. What has Solo gotten us into?" Nina stared at the scene in front of her.

Connor Sparks was a legend at the Agency. Mostly because almost no one at the Agency would admit he'd ever worked for the CIA. That's what happened when a CIA operative also happened to be close friends with a man who'd ended up being the president of the United States. Of course, the rumor was Solo had been working for President Hayes for a long time.

"You can't mean to do this," Ezra was saying.

Solo crossed her arms over her chest. "Do you have any idea the hoops I had to go through to bring him here?"

Ezra wasn't backing down. "Do you have any idea the hoops I'm going to throw him through? Hint, they will all be on fire and there will be a vat of acid at the end of them."

"Maybe we should talk about this, Solo," Sparks said with a frown.

Solo waved him off. "He's good at hyperbole."

"He's also not an employee," Sparks pointed out. "He was let go. He has no security clearance at all."

"I believe the word you're looking for is burned." Ezra turned on the newcomer. "Yeah, thanks for that, buddy."

Sparks held up his hands as though pushing back on the claim. "Hey, that wasn't my call. I don't technically work for the Agency anymore. I'm at the White House for the time being and work directly with the president."

"Then what are you doing here?" Ezra asked, staring at the guy.

If Sparks was intimidated at all, he didn't show it. "I handle things for the president from time to time, and this is a special case. President Hayes has taken an interest in this one. He doesn't like the idea of these drugs being out in the world. This happened partially on his watch, and he wants it cleaned up before there's a scandal and the world knows our soldiers were used as lab rats. The Brits and the Germans are willing to work with us."

"So you want the data in order to sweep the whole thing under the rug?" Ezra sounded like he wouldn't believe any answer he was given.

"We want to know who worked with the McDonalds. German intelligence wants to know who from Kronberg knew what was going on," Sparks explained. "There will be repercussions. They won't be public. Yes, we want to keep this out of the press, but we're not going to allow anyone to treat our soldiers this way."

"German intelligence brought a Kronberg employee with them." Tucker stepped out into the great room. He didn't like the idea that the Agency might sweep it all under the rug. He certainly didn't like the idea that they would go into this wide-eyed.

Sparks's expression softened and he stepped forward, holding out a hand. "You must be Tucker. Connor Sparks. It's good to meet you, and let me assure you the president is working on clearing your name."

"I don't know my name." He sighed, but he shook the man's hand. "But I appreciate anything you can do for me and my brothers."

"Jax is fine," Solo said. "I'm trying to make sure he stays that way. Damon is checking on him, and they let River visit him yesterday."

"Jax is in a holding cell," Ezra pointed out. "I assure you he's not fine."

Sparks stepped back. "Unfortunately, I can't get involved in freeing Mr. Seaborne. According to all our records, he doesn't exist. Neither do you, Tucker. It's why it's so important we figure out what happened and how she hid your identities."

"And if the CIA helped her do it?" Nina stared at Sparks.

"Then the Agency will have a shake-up they won't see coming," Sparks promised. "From the accent, I'm going to assume you're Ms. Blunt. Former Interpol. You have to understand why it's important the president isn't involved. Your own organization is actively looking for these men."

"Former organization," Nina replied. "And yes, if Interpol knew the president of the United States was even thinking about harboring men with red notices, there would be a scandal. I understand that, but I would be careful with MI6 and the Germans. I'm sure they're telling you Kronberg is helping with their investigation, but that's a major German corporation and that means they'll protect them like the asset they are."

"They don't want the list of names out any more than we do," Sparks said. "We can work with them or against them. Allies are funny things. They can turn on a dime, but sometimes it's best to keep them close. This is Solo's op. The president has complete confidence in her." He glanced down at his watch and then back to Solo. "You're sure you want to do this? I don't like the look in your ex's eyes. You know we expect him back in one piece."

"Then you should take him right back to the US," Ezra swore. "Because I can't assure you that he'll leave this house alive."

Tucker knew he was missing some important part of the conversation. He didn't think the "he" they were talking about was Sparks.

Solo sighed, a long-suffering sound. "I'll keep them apart. I've got a room ready for him. The owner of this place has some interesting hobbies. There's an actual jail cell in one of the rooms. I checked it out and it should hold him nicely."

"Hold him?" Something was going on that he didn't understand. "I thought you were bringing Ariel up so she can put me under hypnosis."

"She's on her way up here now," Solo said. "She and Robert are bringing up some more people Ezra won't like."

Ezra's eyes were like laser beams focused on his ex-wife. "What the hell have you done? Have you forgotten that these men are my responsibility?"

She frowned his way. "Talk to Damon and Tag. They approved the plan because it's the only way we keep MI6 from pulling out the big guns."

"They already raided The Garden," Ezra shot back. "How much bigger are those guns going to get?"

Sparks whistled. "You said he was a do-gooder, Solo. You didn't tell me he was naïve. I didn't know you could work for the Agency for that long and still be so innocent."

Solo turned to Ezra. "A lot bigger, and you know it. I promise you that everything I'm doing is to protect Jax and Tucker. And you."

All he knew was he wanted to work with Ariel. If this was about her getting to come up here, he was going to weigh in. "I need to figure this out. We know the intel is probably somewhere in Paris. At least we're certain that's where I lost it. I need something to spark my memory. The drugs Green gave me seem to be working, but it's not fast enough."

"Because you were never patient," a deep voice said.

A chill went up his spine and he watched as Levi Green was guided through the door by two men he'd never seen before. Guards. They were probably CIA agents and they'd been sent to transport Green here. His hands and feet were locked in heavy chains and he'd lost weight from the last time he'd seen the man. He looked lean and hungry, as if the past few weeks had robbed him of his ability to pretend to be anything but the predator he was. He'd never understood how much of Green's mask came from the clothes he wore. He normally was very stylish, presenting himself as something of a hipster with his pork pie hats and suspenders. He had a cool vibe he cultivated.

He hid behind. This was the real man, and his eyes practically ate Solo up. His hair was longer than usual, and it tumbled over his forehead as though he'd recently thrashed around. "Hello, Solo. I knew you would come for me eventually. You know, darling, you didn't have to put me in chains. I would have come willingly. Don't I always help you when you need it? When you're lonely and wanting, I'm always there for you."

Fuck.

Ezra had gone still. Not the kind of still that happens when someone's tired. It was the kind that happened right before a man committed a vicious murder.

Solo stepped between the men. "Spare me, Levi. You know why you're here. And I've got a nice cell with your name on it. Gentlemen, if you'll follow me we can get this exchange over with and you can head back to the States."

"I'm serious." Sparks was watching Ezra like he might lose his shit at any moment. "If you can't protect him, I need to take him back with me. He's been working with the Agency and he's got a surprising amount of intelligence we need."

"Because he's been playing everyone for years," Ezra said between clenched teeth.

"And you know as well as I do that if he's got the right information, he can buy his way out of a lot of trouble," Sparks said with a sigh. "He's got a deal. If he can help Tucker Jones find the information we need, the Agency will be willing to reconsider his incarceration."

A completely humorless laugh came from Ezra's throat. "Isn't that handy. He causes the problem in the first place and now he's also the solution. That sounds about right."

Sparks stared at Ezra, his eyes sharp as he took the former operative in. "He doesn't know?"

Solo's jaw went tight. "I haven't talked to him about it."

"Mr. Kent or Fain or whatever you choose to call yourself," Sparks began, "you should give her some more credit. She held the line on this one. She wouldn't give up your location so we can get this done unless we agreed to give you your job back. If this mission goes well, you'll be back at the Agency with full pay and benefits. You'll get your old job back and the records will reflect that your firing was in error."

"I don't want my old job back. And this is a mistake. He's got something up his sleeve and it will all go to hell in the end." Ezra turned and walked away.

Solo took a long breath as though banishing whatever it was she felt. "The deal still holds. I get you what everyone wants and Ezra, Tucker, and Jax get their records erased. They get a clean slate. What they do with it is up to them."

"Agreed." Sparks shook her hand. "But that man has problems. Problems you can't solve."

She sniffled slightly and a smile curved her lips up. "You only say that because your wife wants to set me up."

A brilliant smile came over Sparks's face. It completely transformed the man from dangerous to joyful. "She's got lists. I promise I'll go through them and weed out all the crazies." His smile dimmed. "Be careful with him."

"Beck or Levi?" Solo asked.

"Both," Sparks said with an almost pitying smile, as though he knew what it meant to be in a hopeless situation. "When this is over come out to the house. Lara's quite good at matchmaking. It's time to move on." He started toward the door he'd walked in through. When he turned back, the friendly guy was gone and the operative was back in place. "And Solo, you know what happens if he gets out."

She nodded. "You have to disavow any knowledge of the mission and I get to be the bad guy. The good news is I'm pretty good at that role. Just ask Beck."

Sparks nodded at the two men who had hands on Levi Green. At Sparks's nod, they released him and fell into line behind the boss, leaving Green standing there in chains, a smirk on his face.

"He's right about moving on, but he's wrong about letting his wife fix you up. Lara Sparks can't possibly know what you need," Levi said. "But I do. And I forgive you for hauling me in. You were only doing your job and I've been a bad boy. Tucker, it's good to see you up and about. I knew you would come through. So ye old memories aren't coming back as fast as we would like. We can fix that. Or should I call you Steven now?"

"That's not my name either." All in all, he would have preferred hypnotism to having to work with the man who'd pretty much tried to kill all his brothers.

Green's eyes flared. "Ah, so it is working."

"If that man knows everything, why doesn't he tell us what we need to know and we can all move on with our lives?" Nina asked.

"Where would the fun be in that?" Levi asked, holding out his chained-together hands. "Hello, we haven't had the pleasure of being introduced. I'm Levi Green. You can call me Levi."

Nina didn't take the proffered hand. "The fun would be in us all getting to go home."

"And miss spending time with my best girl? Never. This is foreplay for me and Solo. I'm a patient man. Why don't you take these things off me, baby? You know I'm not going anywhere. I intend to give you everything you want and then I'll get what I've been waiting for all these years," Levi promised.

"I'm not letting you out of the chains and I swear to god if you touch me, I'll make you regret it." Solo stalked over to him. "You're here for one reason and one reason only. You're going to help Tucker remember what happened and where he left that intelligence he stole from Kronberg. You'll do it because you were there."

"Oh, yes, I was. I was there far longer than anyone imagines. I was there in the beginning," Levi replied. "But merely telling him who he is and why he did what he did wouldn't spark his memory. We have to do this my way or no way at all."

His past was standing right in front of him and all he could think about was the fact that he didn't want Veronica anywhere near this man. Levi Green was toxic. He was like the devil, always looking for a way in, and once he got there he corrupted everything he touched.

I have a way for you to get everything you want. You'll be doing a service to your country, too. You've seen what she's doing. You've been affected directly by it. What would you do to get a little revenge?

The words floated through his brain. Insidious. They'd been insidious. He'd wanted to walk away but Green had gotten him. Green had convinced him he could get everything he needed if he only did this one small favor for him.

"Are you okay?" Nina put a hand on his arm.

Green's chains jangled. "See, being in the same room is helping, isn't it? You need me to walk you through it all. I can't simply tell you. You need to experience it because I have no idea where that intel is. I only know that you had it."

"I was meeting you that day," he heard himself say, but he was doing exactly what he wasn't supposed to do. He was looking deep inside. It was right there. He could feel the wind on his face, know how excited he was because soon he wouldn't have to lie to Roni anymore. He was going to get his life back. He was going to get his...

He'd been looking for something. Something important. Something. Or someone.

"You're close, aren't you?" Green was staring at him, a fascinated look on his face. "Dig a little deeper. It's right there, man. I gave you the drugs that should rebuild the connections."

His gut was starting to clench, pain pulsing through his head.

"Hey, you don't look so great," Nina said.

"Tucker, let it go," Solo ordered. "Ariel taught you how to handle this."

"You're almost there, man." Green egged him on, but the problem was he was right. He was almost there. It was so close he could taste it. "Reach for it."

"Tucker, what's happening?"

Only one voice could bring him out. "Roni?"

A low chuckle reminded him they weren't alone. "Well, that explains a lot. I assume this is Solo's doing? Hello, Veronica. Long time, no see."

Roni gasped beside him and her face flushed. "Lewis? What are you doing here?"

Solo looked to Roni. "You know him?"

Roni nodded. "He was dating my sister when she died. Was killed. Did he have something to do with my sister's murder?"

"If I did, I probably had help," Green said with a wink. "Shouldn't we find out who that was?"

Tucker's heart felt like it sank to his stomach because Green was staring straight at him. Like they had a secret.

God. Had he had a hand in killing Roni's sister?

His knees buckled and he stumbled toward the bathroom. He was going to be sick.

* * * *

Two hours later Veronica was still shaking as she sat down at the table in the dining room. The world seemed to have upended and she wasn't sure she liked where she'd landed.

Tucker reached out and slid a hand over hers. He was still pale. She'd chased after him, leaving Solo and Nina with the man her sister had introduced her to as Lewis Green. Her mind was still whirling, but at least Tucker seemed to be better now.

"All right, let's get this over with since we've got more company coming," Ezra said as he took a seat. "Did Solo tell you she's letting MI6 and the Germans send a rep up here?"

Tucker's hand tightened on hers. "What? Why the hell did we leave The Garden if we're inviting them to hang with us?"

Solo sat beside Ezra. From what Roni could tell they'd spent most of the last two hours yelling at each other when Ezra wasn't yelling at Big Tag on the phone. "We left The Garden so we would have leverage. We're now using that leverage to force better conditions. MI6 and BND have agreed they do not need to question Sandra Croft. She's being issued a new passport as we speak and we'll handle the records of her coming back into the country. Also, we'll deal with Violet's citizenship. She'll be granted dual citizenship and two passports, one US and one German. You understand what this means?"

Despite how upsetting it had been to see that man again, something good might come from it. "I can talk to my mom?"

Solo gave her a smile. "FaceTime with her. Let Violet see you. The deal I've worked out is that MI6 gets to keep Jax for now. We keep Tucker. All three agencies get to interview Levi Green. Robert and Ariel are on their way up here with a couple of representatives. They don't know where the location is, and they won't have freedom to roam while they're here. I've taken down any pictures or mementos they might use to identify the house. It's not perfect but it's all I've got and with any luck, between Ariel and talking to Levi, we'll figure out where that data is."

"And if McDonald took it with her?" Tucker asked.

Solo's eyes darkened as though she'd gone through that nightmarish scenario in her head way too many times. "We'll cross that bridge when we come to it. I'll figure out something that will satisfy them. I'm not going to let them take Tucker. And honestly,

Ezra already knows how he's going to break Jax out."

Ezra's lips quirked up in a feral smirk. "I have no idea what you're talking about."

"I'll help you if it comes down to that," Solo promised. "But if I can avoid a worldwide execution order on your head, I will. Now, Nina's babysitting. I gave her noise canceling headphones so she doesn't have to listen to Levi talk."

"You should have given her a cattle prod." Ezra seemed to perk up. "Hey, Weston's got some crazy shit in this place. It's like his dungeon in the woods. I bet he's got one."

"I bet he does," Tucker said with a smile that kind of scared her.

She shook her head. "Will someone tell me who this guy is? I met him twice when he was dating Katie."

Solo and Ezra shared a look she didn't understand.

"What?" she asked, a knot in her gut. Once again something was going on that she didn't quite understand. She was on the periphery with no real knowledge except whatever that look meant, it would likely rock her world.

Solo's face cleared. "Nothing at all."

"They think your sister might have been CIA," Tucker explained, his eyes tired. He'd had a rough afternoon. After throwing up for a while he'd lain in bed with the lights off and a cool rag on his head, trying to get rid of a migraine. She'd lain next to him, changing the rag every now and then, her head resting on his chest and listening to the steady beat of his heart.

"Katie wasn't a CIA agent." It was completely ridiculous. "She was a journalist. She had a degree and started working freelance as soon as she graduated."

"When did she meet the man you knew as Lewis?" Solo asked.

"It wasn't anything serious. At least not according to what Katie told me," she explained, trying to remember everything that had gone on at the time. It was a swirl in her brain. "She said he was a freelance journalist, too. They met while she was working on one of her corporate corruption stories. My sister had this crazy belief that the world was being run by this group of corporations. Like an Illuminati thing. I blame my mom. She's been into conspiracy theories since we were kids. I'm afraid my sister fell into that trap. Not that there aren't conspiracies in the world, but my sister can get a little crazy."

Tucker sighed. "It's called The Collective. Kronberg was a part of it."

"We're pretty sure Big Tag neutralized them the last time they tangled," Ezra continued. "He took out the head and we're hoping it takes them years to reorganize."

"Are you telling me The Collective was real?" She tried to make sure her jaw didn't drop.

"Yes, and I think Levi likely had some connections to them," Solo explained. "It wouldn't be the first time an Agency employee worked for The Collective. He could have done double duty, reporting back to both the Agency and his corporate bosses. If your sister was getting close to The Collective or what was really going on at Kronberg, they might have sent him in to keep an eye on her."

Now she was the one whose stomach threatened to revolt. Tucker squeezed her hand again. "Baby, you couldn't have known, and if she'd told me the same thing, I would have thought she was crazy, too."

How much had she missed? And how much had she been played on all sides? "We've already established that I was likely hired because my sister was investigating Kronberg. They were going to use me as leverage against her. But they never threatened her. Not that she mentioned. If you're looking for her old notes, I don't have them. Mom and I went through her things, but we couldn't find anything of value. Her apartment was burglarized two days after she died. Naturally the police don't have suspects."

"So we can assume Kronberg did it," Solo said. "They would have gone in and cleared anything that might have implicated them. I've tried to get Levi's records from the Agency but what they sent told me nothing. He was definitely in Europe around that time. I don't know what he was working on. I know he was meeting with key assets during that time frame, but the names are redacted. Dating Katie could possibly have been his way of hiding the fact that she was an asset."

"Also, we can't believe a word that comes out of Levi's mouth." Ezra sat back. "He lies like the rest of us breathe."

"He'll tell the truth if it buys him something," Solo insisted, but the words were flat as though the speaker knew she wouldn't be heard. "In this case finding that intel buys him a lot."

"And if what it buys him means the truth never getting out?" Tucker asked.

She hadn't thought about how that would affect him. He'd been tortured for years and his pain might be weighed against governmental secrecy and corporate profits.

There was a knock on the door.

Solo pushed her chair back and stared at Tucker, her expression completely open. "I don't know that letting this particular secret out does anything but hurt the country. I don't know that it was ever going to be allowed out in the open. But I promise you'll be free. I might not be able to give you the justice you deserve, but I can give you your freedom."

Somehow she didn't think Solo was merely talking to Tucker.

She turned and walked out.

Tucker leaned over. "Are you okay?"

Her heart ached for him. They'd had such a good start to the day, but reality was already infringing. She let her head rest against his. "I'm fine. It was a shock to see him again. I hadn't thought about Lewis in years. He disappeared after Katie died. I'm more worried about you. They want you to remember what happened, but it made you sick."

"Did I thank you for taking care of me?" His hand found her hair and he stroked her. "I'm usually the one playing doctor."

"You're not playing, babe. You are a doctor, and an incredible one at that," she replied. Sometimes she forgot how much he didn't know about himself. It wasn't natural and she needed to remind him. "You're smart and you know a lot about the workings of the human brain."

"I don't think neuro was what I wanted to do." He kissed her forehead and sat back up.

Now that she knew this side of the man, she was fairly certain he'd been honest with her that day in Paris. "You didn't. You wanted to be a GP like your grandfather. You told me you wanted to go back to the States and find a small town and be a general practitioner like he'd been."

He was still for a moment and he let go of her hand. He took a deep breath and stood. "I'm going to grab some water."

She looked back at Ezra. "Did I say something wrong?"

"I think he's trying to avoid getting sick again," Ezra replied. "You gave him a big dose of information and he wants so badly to chase it down in his head. I would bet he got a flash of something. It's okay. He knows how to handle it. Trust me. This is not his first time. But it's worse today because Levi's here. He can seem perfectly reasonable, you know. Levi, that is. When he wants to, he can be very convincing. That's why he's good at his job and he got away with it for years. He's going to keep getting away with it if Solo has her way."

"What are our other options?" She wanted what Solo was offering. Solo offered her a way to get out of this tangle and get back some normalcy. She wanted it badly, but maybe she should ask some questions.

Ezra huffed out a laugh and ran a hand over his hair. "Our other options are running like hell, getting every single person we love into legal trouble, and probably getting shot at the end. I know she's offering us the best possible way out. The trouble is I don't trust that she can make it work. Solo…she means well, but things go wrong. She trusts the wrong people."

"Like the president?" It was hard to believe, but according to Tucker, Solo worked with the president and his closest allies. Apparently she'd missed meeting one of the mysterious Perfect Gentlemen who surrounded the president.

"I think Hayes will back her up as long as he can, but he's a politician. He'll do what he has to do. Solo is being Solo. She's tilting at windmills, trying to be the hero, and I worry it won't end well. But I don't have another play, and being stubborn hasn't worked for me so far. I'm going along with it because there's nothing else to do."

"She's doing it for you, too." Tucker returned, a glass of water in his hand. "She's trying to get your job back."

"I don't want my job." Ezra sounded wildly stubborn again. "Why would I walk back into a nest of snakes that bit the hell out of me already?"

"Even if you don't, if the Agency restores your good status, you'll have options you don't right now," Tucker argued. "You'll be able to work in the open. By the way, when you hire on at MT, negotiate with Charlotte. Big Tag tries to pay in French fries. It almost worked on this guy named Boomer."

Ezra smiled, an expression that made him look years younger. "I'll remember that, but I don't think I'll go that route either. I don't know what I'll do."

"She's trying to give you options," Tucker said.

"She's trying to assuage her conscience." Ezra shook his head. "Hell, I don't know what she's trying to do anymore. I don't know what I'm doing either. I'm not this man. I can't think around Kim. Never have been able to. She's a force of nature. When she's around, it's like the rest of the world falls away. But then I remind myself it's hard to see anything through hurricane winds. When it goes bad, Tucker, I need you to come with me."

"If it goes bad, you know what I value," Tucker said with a solemn air.

Ezra nodded. "We all do." He seemed to shake something off. "I'll try to set up a call to New York tonight. It's going to have to be later."

She would get to see Vi. The thought brought tears to her eyes. "I'll look forward to it. And I'll try to remember anything I can about Lewis's relationship with Katie. My mom might know something more. I'll ask her about it tonight."

She glanced back at Tucker and he'd gone stock-still. "What is it? Are you okay?"

He looked like he'd seen a ghost.

"Well, hello, Veronica," an oddly familiar voice said. The German accent was soft as though the harsh edges had been rounded out by speaking all those other languages he spoke. "I didn't think I would see you again. And Steven. I certainly didn't think to see you since you were supposed to be dead. It seems Dr. McDonald stole much from you both."

A chill snaked along her spine and she turned. Arthur Dwyer stood there in his tweed jacket and pressed slacks. He looked like the young academic he was, well-groomed and confident. He'd been one of the many doctors who wouldn't give her the time of day at Kronberg unless it was to treat her like an underling.

He'd lied to Rebecca and Ariel. She'd thought the man barely noticed she was alive, but that wasn't true. He'd been watching them all those years ago. He'd known exactly where they'd been.

"What the hell is he doing here?" Tucker asked the question

before she could.

"You weren't informed?" Arthur asked. "Perhaps that's why Ms. Solomon is arguing with the intelligence officers. They're getting quite heated."

Ezra stood. "I think I'd like a word, too."

If Arthur was intimidated by all the eyes on him, he didn't show it. He merely looked around the room before settling on Roni. "I came because I made a terrible mistake before. I didn't understand what was going on. I should have known what Dr. McDonald was doing and intervened. I didn't realize Steven was playing such a dangerous game and you were caught up in it."

She felt a hand on her shoulder and knew exactly who was laying a possessive claim on her. The day had been brutal on him. She hadn't missed the fact that Levi Green had alluded to someone helping him trick her sister. It wouldn't have been Tucker. She had faith in him. He needed to know that. She reached up and put her hand over his. "No need for intervention. We're fine. And yes, Dr. McDonald stole years from us."

"But we'll move on and have many more together," Tucker said resolutely.

It was good to have a man who wanted her. Not for a second since he'd woken up had he made her question if he wanted her. His adoration was a balm for the years he'd been gone. "Many more."

Arthur stared at them for a moment as though trying to figure out how to handle them. "Well, it seems we were wrong about you, Steven. I was told you didn't remember your past and that was why we were needed."

"My name is Tucker and you're not needed at all," Tucker said. "I'd like to know why you're here. Unless you're going to tell me you're German intelligence."

Arthur shook his head and took a seat opposite Roni. "Not at all, though I am working with them. I am exactly what I've been for years, a doctor specializing in neurology, but I recently moved into a new role at Kronberg. It has come to the attention of the board of directors that Dr. McDonald continued her experiments after the board kicked her out. I'm ashamed to say my predecessor attempted to cover it all up, though I understand the impulse. When we realized we still had a problem, we immediately informed our intelligence agency."

"So when we broke in and grabbed all the files you've been hiding for years, you decided to come after your victims," Tucker said, his voice colder than she'd ever heard it.

She wasn't sure that Tucker should be admitting to breaking into Kronberg. "He's not being literal. When someone broke in. That's what he means."

Arthur chuckled. "Oh, he's being perfectly serious. Breaking into his old employer's building is a minor crime compared to what McDonald forced him to do. But you should know that Kronberg will not prosecute in any way. We're willing to ignore what happened if you help us find out who aided McDonald. We mean to clean house. If anyone on the board or still employed knew what McDonald was doing in our labs, we will deal with the problem."

"Of course you will," she said demurely because arguing with him would do nothing.

There was the sound of hurried footsteps and then Ariel and Robert were striding in the room.

"Tucker, are you all right?" Robert walked right up to Tucker and pulled him into a fierce bear hug, complete with masculine back pounding. "God, man, I was so fucking scared for you."

"I'm fine," Tucker said. "How is Jax? And River?"

Robert took a step back. "She's okay. She lost it that first night. Buster did too. I swear that dog howled the whole time she was crying. But she got to see Jax today. She said he looked good but complained about the food. She's being positive. She's hoping this is over soon and they can go home."

"She misses Bliss," Tucker said with a wisp of a smile.

"We miss you." Ariel moved in, wrapping her arms around Tucker, too.

He'd built a family from the ashes of his life. He hadn't been completely alone, and she was so grateful for that. He'd found brothers.

Who was he? Not deep down. She knew his soul, but who was waiting for him out there in the world? What had he been doing at Kronberg? She'd been so worried about whether or not he'd been lying to her all those years ago that she hadn't considered he would have a family on the other side of this. Did Violet have another grandmother waiting out there? Did she have other siblings? He was young but that didn't mean he couldn't have had a wife and kids.

"Are you all right?" Arthur was staring at her. "It doesn't seem you're part of that happy reunion."

Ariel was asking about Tucker's health and Robert had a hand on his shoulder as if he was worried about letting him go. Tucker was smiling again, looking open and happy with his friends.

"I've spent plenty of time with him over the last few days," she replied with a breezy smile she didn't quite feel. She didn't think he had a wife. At least not one he'd been married to at the time. He wouldn't have slept with her if he had. He wasn't that kind of man. Still, there could be an ex and they could have had kids together. He could have a family waiting for him. If he got his memory back, how would it work? "Hiding out from the bad guys is a great way to cement your relationship."

A single brow rose over his eyes. "Bad guys? I certainly don't see myself that way. I'm a practical man. It does no one any good if McDonald's research gets out. It would cause someone to take it up again. And it would make your boyfriend there famous. I don't know that he wants that."

"It also saves the company you work for from any number of lawsuits," she pointed out. "No one with any reputation would want their names associated with Kronberg. You wouldn't be able to recruit at all. You might end up having to hire more doctors of my caliber."

"Whatever do you mean?" Arthur asked.

"I didn't have the grades for that position and you know it. You knew it then. It was why you were such a prick to me."

Arthur shrugged. "Perhaps I'm just a prick to everyone."

She'd watched him too carefully to buy that. "You were quite polite to those you thought were worthy. Some might even say you were good at kissing ass. Why did Kronberg hire me?"

"I assume they hired you because they thought you would be a good fit. I wasn't in charge of that. Dr. McDonald asked for you specifically. I was surprised she wanted such an inexperienced nothing of an intern, but that wasn't my place."

Ah, there he was. She'd been waiting for him to show up again. "You weren't at the airport that day. I'm talking about the day Steven and I went to France. You were in the lab. So why would you tell

Rebecca and Ariel that you saw us there? That's what you told them a few weeks ago when they interviewed you."

His face went blank and then a bland expression came over him. "Memory is a funny thing. It's certainly not foolproof. Sometimes memories lie to us and then we find ourselves lying to everyone else. I wonder how your boyfriend has lied to you. Do you think committing a crime shouldn't count if you don't remember you committed it?"

Arthur stood and smoothed down his blazer as Solo and Ezra entered followed by the man she'd seen that night at The Garden, the one Tucker had identified as the new head of MI6. There was another man with him and he'd been there that night as well. He'd been standing with Arthur. German intelligence. They'd sent the big guns. Solo explained she would show everyone to the rooms they would be using for their stay here.

Still, she had an answer for Arthur. "He was forced to commit those robberies. He was under the influence of powerful drugs. He didn't know another life. So no, even if he remembers them, they don't count."

Arthur's eyes flared with something akin to victory and she knew she'd made a mistake. "Ah, but what about the crimes he committed before he ever took a drop of McDonald's drugs? What happens when he remembers why they called him Razor? And what happens when his victims were closer than he'd ever imagined? Think about that, Veronica. While you sleep beside him tonight, think about all the things he could have done. Because you don't know him."

He turned and followed Solo out. Roni tried to quell the fear his words had stoked.

It was irrational fear because she knew him. She knew Tucker for who he was deep inside and that was all that mattered.

Chapter Eleven

Tucker stared at the man in the cage. It was a small cell that contained only a cot. It wasn't meant to function as an actual jail cell, though Ezra claimed it would work for their purposes.

It was nothing like the stark white rooms he'd been kept in. His cell had been technologically advanced down to the toilet that could also give McDonald medical data. The walls had been thick glass. There had been no privacy, nowhere to hide. She could plunge them into complete darkness or blind them with light.

He'd always preferred the darkness. He could pretend in the darkness, pretend he wasn't where he was. In that bald, raw light, there was nowhere to hide.

He almost felt sorry for Green.

He knew what it felt like to be locked inside a cage with people staring at him from the outside. He knew what it was like to watch his brothers dying and to not be able to get to them. He definitely knew what it felt like to be watched, to have no privacy at all.

Green sat in the cell Clive Weston probably used for sexual games and stared right back at Tucker. "You're sure you want to do this with her in the room?"

He wasn't sure of anything. The answers he'd been waiting years for were about to be revealed and he wanted to run. He wanted to take

Roni's hand in his and leave. Fuck the past. He wanted a future.

But he couldn't have one if he didn't do this. He was trapped again. He only knew one thing for certain. "She stays if she wants to. I'm not hiding anything from her."

Good or bad, she was part of this and had every right to know.

She sat beside him, their arms brushing.

"We're all here now and you've had dinner, so could we get to talking?" Ezra wasn't sitting. He'd paced for the last hour like he was the one stuck in a cage.

Levi had made a bunch of diva-like demands that hadn't gone over well with Ezra. Solo had argued that they should just give him what he wanted so they could get things moving. What Levi had wanted was a shower, fresh clothes, a three-course meal with wine pairings, pillows and blankets made of specific materials, and access to Netflix. He'd gotten the shower and clothes, a sandwich Nina had made for him, and Solo had sat right outside his cell drinking an expensive red wine straight from the bottle and flipping the bird his way every time he talked.

Tucker thought it was a misstep on her part because Levi seemed perfectly happy to get any sort of attention from her. But then maybe that had been her point. Solo was smart enough to know she was at least part of the reason Green was here. They all needed to remember that.

Green sat back looking relaxed for a man in a prison cell, but then he'd spent the last several weeks in one. "What do you want to know? My life is an open book."

His life was highly classified, and it was obvious that there were things not even Solo had been privy to. He believed her when she said she hadn't known he'd worked for Green.

Rupert Milbern was seated on a bench that probably had been the site of many a spanking, a notepad in his hand. He'd taken off his jacket but not the tie he was wearing. He looked very British and important. "You could make it easy and tell us where the subject left the intelligence he stole from Kronberg."

The German intelligence officer was sitting close to Dwyer. He was still in his full suit. He'd been the quietest of the three. "Yes, I don't understand why we need all this drama. Mr. Dwyer has the date the intel went missing if that will help this fiasco along."

"The dates are meaningless since I have no idea where…what should we call you?" Green asked in an amused voice, staring Tucker's way.

"How about my name?" It was as good a place to start as any. His real name. It would be so odd to hear it. Would he recognize it? Or would it be one more meaningless fact that didn't connect to him in any way? That was his real fear. He would hear the truth and it wouldn't mean anything. "What's my real name and why was I at Kronberg?"

"I don't want to give away all my secrets," Green said with a smirk. "After all, the sandwich here was much better than my last prison. Bologna is another form of torture. And the view is superlative."

Ezra's face had gone red because that last bit had been directed straight to Solo. "You can talk or I'll make sure your view is of me waterboarding you. You like that, don't you, Levi? Does the Agency know how you waterboard female operatives? Did you put that in your report? Or did you leave it out like the part where you shot me?"

It was a reminder of how much evil this man had done. Tucker had gotten the full report on how Green had treated Kayla Summers during a mission in Mexico. He'd had her waterboarded the same evening he'd put a bullet in Ezra and left him for dead. He'd been trying to find a way into The Garden at the time. At the time they'd thought he simply wanted access to the Lost Boys. Now it was easy to see what Green had wanted. Access to Tucker.

"In my defense, I wasn't the one doing the torture part. I did question her, but I was gentle about it," he said, affecting an air of innocence. "The nearly drowning her over and over was the drug lord's part."

"Who you were working with," Solo pointed out.

"Allies can be found in the strangest places." Levi's head swung Tucker's way. "Rather like I found you."

"Where did you find me?" He needed answers. No matter where they led. "I wasn't working for the CIA?"

"Heavens no. You were in the last year of your residency at a highly rated hospital," Green explained.

He could feel the softness of the scrubs on his body, smell the fabric softener. He wore them pretty much everywhere. There wasn't time to do much more than sleep when he wasn't working. But it would all be worth it when he got home. He liked the city, but he missed the town he'd grown up in. He missed the way the mountains looked during wintertime.

"What hospital?" He shoved the memories away. They'd been there all day, playing and teasing at the edge of his mind. Tempting him. It would be better to view this all academically. He was investigating, nothing more.

"If I tell you what hospital you'll send one of McKay-Taggart's hackers in, and I might have missed something when I erased you from existence," Levi said with a shrug. "You're the special one, Tucker. You got erased twice. See, I went to the trouble of creating the Steven Reasor persona from top to bottom. Do you know how hard it is to create a person from nothing? It's not like the old days. I get so sick of boomers telling me how easy millennials have it. You know what those bastards had to do when going undercover? Fake ID, fake a couple of basic records, and they were in. Now I have to deal with the fact that every single record is online, and I won't even go into social media. Do you know how long it took me to fake those pictures of you summiting Everest?"

"We couldn't find any evidence of me." It wasn't like they hadn't all looked. They had facial recognition software scouring the web for any sign of him.

"McDonald erased Steven Reasor, and she did a damn fine job of it," Levi revealed. "I mean she did it with the others too, but in Robert's case he was in the military and her dad was on the Armed Services committee. That's pretty powerful. But what she did to Reasor, being able to erase my work, well, that was impressive. Of course by that point in time she knew there was something smelly going on in her lab."

"You're going to string this out as long as you can," Ezra said with a frown.

"I don't think this is what we agreed to." Arthur Dwyer looked up from his tablet. "He's supposed to give us the data we need, not turn this into some kind of weeks long holiday. It's important we do this quickly."

Green groaned. "I told you this wouldn't move fast. The data we need is stuck in Tucker's head. He's not going to simply remember if

I tell him he's from the Western United States and he was the valedictorian of his high school. Will explaining he came from a small town help him find that data? Though I will note that it made things way easier when it came to erasing him from existence. Hamilton High School was so easy to hack."

Hamilton High. He'd been a year behind his brother. There was something funny about that because he was years younger than his brother, but he knew somehow that he'd been a junior when Ace was a senior. "Tell me my brother's name. I know my mom called him Ace. I think that's a nickname."

Green's eyes lit up. "There it is. You see, it's coming back."

He really had a brother. The thought made every muscle in his body tense. *Please let my brother be alive.* "I want to know his name."

Roni sat forward. "Are his parents alive? Do we know if he was married?"

Of course she would worry about that. He put a hand on her back. "I don't think I was married, baby. I get flashes of someone who I think might be my mother, and I've had a vague recollection of a kid who I think is my brother, but there's no girlfriend or wife in my head. Only you."

"You can't be sure though," she whispered, gently biting her bottom lip. It was an easy tell that she was nervous.

"He wasn't married, but that's all I'm giving you. If I told you everything, then you wouldn't need me anymore," Levi mused. "I think I'll keep those names to myself. But how about I do tell you that you were involved in this case for more than a paycheck. I didn't have to give you the old 'do it for your country' speech. When you realized what I'd found out about Dr. McDonald, you would have done anything to bring her down."

Green watched him expectantly, as though he should do something now.

But there was no whisper along his brain. There was nothing but that sense of something veiled in his head. Like his past was hiding right under the surface of the ocean and all he needed to do was swim to find it. But the fucking water was full of jellyfish waiting to sting him.

A soft hand covered his and he immediately relaxed. He glanced to his right and Roni was there, giving him an encouraging smile. He wasn't alone.

It gave him the strength to turn back to Levi. "So you're going to pepper this conversation with hints in order to tease my brain? Or is it torture? Because it feels a lot like torture."

"Levi, you said you would cooperate." Solo stood, glaring into the cell. "If you're not going to, I can have Sparks take you home. I don't think he's left the country yet."

"I am helping." Green stood, walking to the cell bars and grasping them while he stared at Solo. "I told you it won't work if I lay it all out to him like the plot to a movie. That's not how the cure works. And you're welcome for that. Ariel, could you explain this to them? I'm surprised Rebecca isn't here treating her precious patient."

Ariel looked to Solo. "Earlier today I received a couple of documents that supposedly make up the protocols surrounding the cure Dr. McDonald may or may not have created."

"Why would I lie about that? You wound me, lovely Ariel." Green put a hand to his heart in a dramatic gesture.

"I can wound you." Robert offered the threat with a low drawl. "And none of us will let Rebecca around you. Not after what you did to her last time."

A frustrated growl came from Green's throat. "Again, not my idea. I didn't kidnap her. Minions. You can't find good ones these days, can you? But back to the issue at hand. The cure and its protocols were among the treasures we found at the former black ops site known as The Ranch."

He felt his teeth grind. The Ranch had been their op. Jax had risked everything for that data and Green had swooped in to take it, leaving a swath of destruction in his path. "You stole that."

Green shrugged. "You say potato and all that. Now, Ariel, what did the protocols require when the subject is in the first few weeks of transition?"

"To wake that part of the brain up, it's suggested that the subject be allowed to recover the memories using hints of the truth," Ariel admitted grudgingly. "What I believe the drug did was close off the pathways to long-term memory storage. It's been suggested that even though the pathways are now clear, the brain has to relearn how to use it. To rewire itself. If we simply give Tucker the full story, his mind will work with whatever we say rather than what's actually there. It's why I agree this might have come from McDonald. It's rather insidious. We could present Tucker with memories and he could potentially think they're his. I believe this was McDonald's endgame."

The ramifications hit him hard and fast. Was this what she had been working toward? "She erases our memories fully and then she cures us, gives us new identities, and we don't even know what existed before."

"Was that what she was planning to do to you?" Roni asked.

"Maybe," he replied.

"She wanted to create soldiers without ties to anyone but their commanding officers, and I believe she wanted to also create sleeper agents. He would be the perfect sleeper agent because he doesn't ever know he is one," Green agreed with what sounded like admiration. "She could rewrite a whole human life. Is that what you want me to do with Tucker here and now? Because if I fill this out like a report, he won't have nuanced memory. He'll have what I tell him."

"I want to read those protocols," Ezra announced. "Does Rebecca have them?"

"She's already sent me her notes, and our friends have read them, too." Ariel placed careful emphasis on the word *friends* to let him know exactly who she was talking about. The ones who definitely weren't friendly.

"I agree that we should attempt to follow the prescribed treatment according to McDonald's work," Arthur said. "But her work was also incomplete. I have some thoughts on a few pharmaceuticals that could help the process along."

"Yes." The intelligence officer beside him nodded. "We've talked this over between the three of us and we agree this is the best route to take."

Roni stood. "You are not giving him any drugs. Definitely not any drugs created at Kronberg. And we're going to read everything that Mr. Green sent. I might not have Rebecca Walsh's stature in the medical world, but I have a stake in this. And Tucker was an amazing doctor. He's not an experiment."

"I think reading Dr. McDonald's scholarly works could help enormously," Green agreed. "It's one of the things I was going to suggest you do. But she did mention some drugs she thought could help the process along."

"No drugs," Roni insisted.

He reached up and laced their fingers together. He would likely do anything, risk anything, to get those memories back, but he wasn't the only one making the decision. "No drugs."

He could make this work.

"We won't wait forever." Rupert stood. "You should think about that. Arthur is offering you a way to speed this process up. The longer you wait, the less patience we all have, and don't forget you have a friend in a holding cell. We can only keep him for so long before we turn him over to the proper authorities. It's obvious to me this is going nowhere tonight. Hopefully tomorrow morning will yield better results."

The German officer stood with him. "I agree. I think this is all a mistake. He shouldn't be in civilian hands."

Arthur seemed to understand the evening was over, too. "I will write up my suggestions and let you all read them. It's ridiculous to discount what the drugs could do for him. Steven, when you're ready to get serious, talk to me."

They walked out the door. Solo stood, frustration evident in the set of her shoulders. "I'll talk to them. You don't have to take anything you don't want to, Tucker. I'll make that clear."

Solo stalked out of the room, both Green and Ezra watching her the whole time.

Robert moved over, taking a place beside Tucker. "I promise I won't let them near you with more drugs."

"What did Rebecca say?" She was the expert. Roni would still make the final decision, but he thought they should listen to the doctor who was probably closest to McDonald's research. Well, the closest one who could remember anything about it.

"She said she wouldn't allow you to take anything manufactured at Kronberg," Ariel replied.

"She doesn't trust easily." Green had to throw in his two cents. "I wonder if that was because she spent that night under the influence of the time dilation drugs. I think I have your notes on that experiment somewhere. I could be coaxed into sharing. How about it, Tucker?"

Shame washed over him. He didn't even remember what he'd

done to Rebecca and he already hated himself for it. What would it be like to read his own notes on the subject?

Ezra moved in close to the cell, every movement predatory. "This is your game, isn't it? You're going to parse it out until there's nothing left and that's when you'll strike. You're a snake in the grass, waiting to sink your fangs in."

Green didn't back down. "Oh, I've been waiting for this particular game to start for years, Beck. Years. Do you understand the patience I've shown? Lesser men would have caved, would have blundered when it all fell apart. Not me. So yes, at the end of this I'm going to strike. But I assure you, you'll get everything I promised. That intelligence will come out and we'll move the game along. So what are you going to do about it, Beck? Ezra? Whatever you want to call yourself, you can't get away from the fact that you weren't strong enough to hold her."

Ezra's hands went through the bars and he pulled Levi roughly against them. "I held her just fine. I'm not the one moving heaven and earth to get her back. If I wanted her in my bed tonight, she would be there. You're the one she doesn't want."

"If that's true then why did I have her? She was good, you know. Solo's good at everything, and sex is no different," Levi replied with a smirk. "I will admit, it's hard to not compare every single woman I fuck with her."

"Ezra, please don't kill him." Ariel sounded like she was talking to a tiger who hadn't decided to pounce or not.

"I can probably figure the whole backstory thing out myself," Tucker offered. He would have slit Levi's throat by now. "And the flooring looks pretty easy to clean."

Robert gave him a nod. "If there's one thing we've learned at McKay-Taggart, it's to put down tarp if you're on carpet. This is some well-sealed wood. Go for it, man."

Ezra let go and took a step back. "He's not worth it. But I swear if you say one more vile word about Solo, I'll change my mind. Now you're going to answer a few questions and you're not going to play around."

"But playing is so much fun." Green seemed upset that he hadn't gotten the fight he so obviously wanted. "Isn't that what you all call it? Playing? I like to play."

"Did you or did you not recruit Tucker?" Ezra got straight to his point.

Green's lips closed sullenly.

Ariel crossed her arms over her chest and faced him. "Short questions and answers are in the protocols."

Green sighed. "Yes, I recruited him. I discovered something was going on with Senator Hank McDonald several years ago. The Agency had heard rumors that the senator might have sold out American military troop movements to the enemy in exchange for money and power. My investigations into McDonald led me to his daughter. I needed someone who could get close to her, someone who could speak her language. Surprisingly enough, most young doctors don't want to work for the Agency and potentially get their balls shot off. I needed someone with a brilliant medical mind who didn't mind giving it all up."

"Why? Why would I give it up?" A vision of a younger Levi Green floated across his brain. He was sitting across from Tucker at an outside café. Boston. They were in Boston. A café in the West End. "I met you in Boston."

"Yes," Levi said. "In a small café. That was where we met. Do you remember what we said?"

His whole body tightened as he searched for the memory. He could see Levi sitting there. He'd had a mug of something in his hand and he'd leaned over, an expression of concern on his face. He couldn't remember what season it had been but an overwhelming sense of hope had come over him. This was what he'd been waiting for. All the months of worry and now he finally had something he could do.

"I was worried about something."

"Something or someone?" Green asked like he knew the answer to the question. Which he did.

"Someone. It was definitely someone. I was upset and you gave me options I didn't have before. I'd almost given up when you came to talk to me. You had proof. Maybe it was a picture." A pain started in the back of his head, but he ignored it. "Why can't I remember?"

"Because you're trying too hard." Roni soothed a hand down his back. "And you've had a rough day. I think we should try this again in the morning. He's been sick once today."

"Or we could do what we'll have to do in the end." Green rolled his eyes. "We can go to Paris. The answers are there. Me telling him who he used to be won't work. He's got to see it. Hear it. Smell it."

"I'm sure you would love that," Ezra said. "Every time we move you is a chance for you to get away."

"I don't want to get away." Green's voice went low. "I'm right where I want to be." He straightened up and sounded more professional. "I want that intel. I worked my ass off for that intel. Years I spent working with him to get the intel and I think it all fell apart because of a girl. That's right, Veronica Croft. You took one of the best assets I ever worked with and cost him everything. You want to know why we're all here today? Why I'm in this cell and your boyfriend can't remember his own fucking name? It was you."

Tucker stood up and kind of wished Ezra had followed through with his instincts. "Hey, you don't talk to her like that."

"I didn't do anything," Roni whispered. "I didn't know who he was."

"Wait until you realize what she cost you," Green replied, ignoring her entirely. "When you remember what you gave up for her, that's when you'll understand why they called you Razor. I wonder what you would have done if McDonald had given you a couple of days before she wiped your mind. I think you would have shown that betraying bitch beside you how you earned that nickname."

Robert stepped in front of him, barring the path he'd been about to tread. "Hey, he's pushing you. Don't let it work. I think Roni's right. It's late. We can start again in the morning."

"Get another couple of fucks in, Tucker, because I assure you when you remember, you won't touch her again," Green taunted.

Tucker saw red and tried to plow his way to Green, shoving Robert out of the way. Levi took a step back, holding up his hands, but Tucker didn't care. He hit the cage, shoving his arms through and trying to get at the asshole. The tension of the day threatened to push him over the edge.

"Hey, hold up, brother," Robert said.

But for a moment it was another Robert he saw. He pushed back and they weren't standing in Clive Weston's dungeon. There was dirt at his feet and the bus had just pulled away. He was angry. So angry because someone had said something about him. Something nasty.

Something about all Seegers being trash and how it wasn't surprising their dad walked out.

Hey, come on. He's an asshole. What he says doesn't matter. Tim, calm down. Mom will kill you if you get suspended.

A pain flashed through him as his knees banged against the floor. Wyoming. It happened in Wyoming. They'd been in the last days of fall, a sharp snap in the air that let him know it would snow soon, and the bus ride into the high school three towns over would seem to take forever. It was only okay because his brother was with him.

This Robert was younger. He was wearing a letterman's jacket. Ace. Their mom called Russ Ace, and he was Bud because he was younger. He was Russ's little buddy. Russ was his big brother.

His brother was always there for him. Russ was the best big brother. Until he was killed in action. Except he'd known. He'd known it wasn't true. He'd known somehow that Emily was lying about what happened.

"I was looking for my brother. That's why I went into McDonald's team."

So many things fell into place. Emily. Robert's wife. She'd told him. She'd freaking told him and he hadn't been smart enough to figure it out.

"Yes." Levi Green was standing close to the bars again, looking like the manipulative asshole he was. "Imagine it. You were a brilliant resident working at one of the most famous hospitals in the world. Massachusetts General. You gave it all up because you didn't believe that report, the one that chronicled how your brother and his whole team died. It was a good report. I believed it. But there was something in the records that made you think your brother wasn't dead. You always did suspect Emily, didn't you?"

Robert gasped and his jaw dropped. "What? Emily? My ex-wife?"

"She's not really an ex. You didn't divorce her," Green pointed out. "Ariel killed her, from what I was told. That makes you a widower, not divorced."

"Robert, what's happening?" Ariel asked.

"Is it true?" There were tears in his big brother's eyes.

"I was looking for you." Flashes of his life hit him. His big brother standing up for him, never leaving him behind even though he was little and obnoxious. "I couldn't leave you behind. I couldn't let you go. Even after I knew what she'd done to you. I knew you wouldn't remember me, but I had to save you."

"You're Tim Seeger." Ezra breathed the words. "Holy shit. You went looking for your brother and you found Levi. He set you up to get on McDonald's team, gather all the intelligence on her project."

"And because of me, he found his brother. It just took him longer than expected, and that wasn't my fault. Again. You're welcome," Green replied.

Ezra started to argue with Levi, but Tucker could barely hear them. Robert was on the ground with him, staring at him with what could only be described as wonder.

"Is this real?"

Tucker nodded, reaching out for the brother he'd spent years looking for. "Is it weird that I don't think I can call you Russ? I think you'll always be Robert to me now. But Mom will definitely call you Russ. Or Ace. She called you that because when you were a kid you wanted to play baseball all the time. You wanted to be an ace pitcher." He tried to remember. It was still foggy. "Mom's alive. I think."

She'd been alive. She'd hugged him and asked him to bring his brother home.

"Alive and well and living in Wyoming," Levi answered. "I'm sure she'll be thrilled to get her sons back."

"She could have had them back years ago," Ezra argued. "You've always known, you bastard."

Robert might not remember, but Tucker did. Robert looked shocked, but it hit Tucker like a freight train. He'd done everything to find his brother, to bring him home.

A piece that had been missing, that horrible aching feeling that he could never talk away or drink away, fell softly into place.

"Hey, brother."

Robert smiled, lighting up his whole face. "Hey, brother."

He hugged his brother, wrapping him up. "I know you don't remember and I'm only starting to, but this is true and real and we missed you. Emily lied about everything. Mom and I...we missed you so much. We never stopped wanting you to come home."

Strong arms held him tight. "I knew you were special the first time I met you. Ariel. Ariel, meet my brother."

Ariel's smile was luminous, the tears on her cheeks glistening like happy diamonds. "My sweet brother-in-law. And I can't believe I get to be an auntie."

For all the tension of the day, this was worth everything he'd gone through. And there was only one person here who was missing. "Roni…"

He looked back. But she was gone.

"She snuck out," Ariel said quietly. "I think Levi got to her."

"The truth should get to her." Green stared at the door Roni had left through. "I'm absolutely certain she's the reason you got caught. You were supposed to meet me that day. You didn't make it to the drop off. You disappeared and I didn't see you again until you showed up on the Agency's radar."

"When you should have told us who he was." Ezra walked to the door. "Robert, I need to discuss the new situation with Solo and give Tag and Damon an update. That asshole is the reason we couldn't find your mother. I suspect he convinced her to hide for protection against retaliation."

His mother. God, he had a mother and she loved him. The thought made his heart feel far too tight for his chest. His mother would flip when she realized she wasn't only getting her sons back, she was getting a grandbaby to spoil.

"I thought it was best," Levi admitted. "And then I didn't care."

"I'll stay and watch him," Robert promised.

Ariel went on her toes and kissed her husband. "And I'll go make us tea. Tucker, you have to go talk to her. Unless you believe Levi."

He watched as Ariel and Ezra walked out the door. And he was left with his brother. And the man who'd given him a shot at finding his brother. The man he shouldn't trust in any way.

"You should believe me." Green's eyes had gone hard. "Everything was fine until you got involved with that woman. We were almost out. You would have met me that day and we would have left. Instead it went to hell."

He couldn't see it. "She wouldn't betray me."

"She would. She had a lot at stake. After all, her sister was involved," Green pointed out.

"How did you know her?" Her sister's death was an agony for the whole Croft family.

Green shook his head. "No. No more information tonight. I'm tired. I've been dragged across the ocean and I'm not talking again tonight. In the morning, we can renegotiate."

"Ezra will love hearing that," Robert pointed out. He turned to Tucker. "Go and talk to Roni."

Why had she walked out? For all the joy he felt at the breakthrough he'd just had, anxiety bubbled up.

Levi Green knew how to lie, but he also knew when telling a bit of the truth could be devastating.

He nodded his brother's way and went to look for the woman who should have been his wife.

To find out if she was the reason he'd been sentenced to hell.

Chapter Twelve

Roni's hands were shaking as she walked out of the house and into the gorgeous gardens. Maybe she wasn't supposed to be outside, but she couldn't breathe in that house right now. She stood under the elegant roof of the gazebo at the edge of the garden and tried to calm down.

That's right, Veronica Croft. You took one of the best assets I ever worked with and cost him everything. You want to know why we're all here today? Why I'm in this cell and your boyfriend can't remember his own fucking name? It was you.

The words rang in her ears. She'd sat and watched as Tucker had regained the precious memory of his brother and all she'd been able to do was run through a thousand scenarios where she'd tipped off Dr. McDonald.

It didn't make sense. She hadn't talked to McDonald. Not often. She'd been the lowest-level researcher there, and McDonald barely acknowledged her presence until the day she'd knocked on her door in Paris. Before that day, she would have said McDonald didn't even know her name.

But she had talked to people in the labs. She'd mentioned on more than one occasion in the beginning that she didn't think Steven Reasor was the mean guy he pretended to be. He'd had a fierce reputation and she'd told a couple of the women she'd worked with that she didn't think he was so bad. She'd even told one of her friends there that she'd spent some time with him. She'd wanted to gently rehab his image.

Had that been enough to make McDonald take a second look at him?

Would he ever forgive her if it had?

"Are you all right, Veronica?" a soft voice asked.

She turned and Arthur was standing just outside the gazebo she'd fled to. He was a shadowy figure, but there was no way to mistake his accent. "What are you doing here?"

"I was out for a walk. It was tense in there and the two intelligence agents are not great traveling companions," Arthur admitted. "I was getting a drink when I saw you running out here. I was worried. I know you don't believe me, but I really am here to save Kronberg's reputation. I'm not some undercover agent. And we used to work together."

She wasn't buying that one. "You never liked me."

He shrugged. "I didn't know you. I didn't think I needed to know you. Allow that it's been a couple of years, and discovering how McDonald used us all was a humbling experience. I'm not as arrogant as I once was. Is Steven all right? Or should I call him…what is his name now?"

"Tucker." It fit him better than Steven. Though that wasn't his name either. Tim. Timothy Seeger was his legal name, and his brother was Robert. He'd gambled his life to find his brother. And then he'd risked years of his investigation for her. How close had he been to getting out? Would he have made it if he hadn't taken her with him?

"Tucker. I will try to call him that. It's odd because he's so obviously Steven Reasor to me. Is he feeling all right? Have you examined him? I heard he was sick earlier in the day." Arthur managed to sound concerned.

"Physically he seems fine. His vitals are strong. Rebecca had been monitoring him," she explained. She knew she should walk away, but it occurred to her that Arthur had answers she needed. "He was sick earlier because he pushed a memory. How much do you know about what was done to him?"

"Enough to have nightmares about it." Arthur stepped into the gazebo and settled himself on the bench across from her. "McDonald's research is terrifying. And yet I'm intrigued. I can't help it. I'm a doctor. There are practical applications to her research that could do great good in the world."

Yes, it was the ethical quandary they all had to face in classes and seminars. Most medical professionals didn't have to deal with it in the real world. They didn't have to decide on a basic level if the horror of how an idea came to be made the idea unusable. "The end justifies the means? I think if we start down that road, you know where we go."

"Of course," he said mildly, as though they were talking about the weather and not torturing people to further medical science. "That's the argument. If we use those dark experiments, we open them up to being normalized. It's Pandora's box. We all know that on an academic level. It's different when the box is sitting right in front of you and all you have to do is open it and almost guarantee yourself a Nobel Prize."

"You truly believe you could keep a lid on where the research came from? Because I know I would go straight to the press," she threatened. He needed to understand he couldn't walk in and continue McDonald's research.

He waved her away. "Too many people know. I couldn't kill them all. I'm sorry. That was supposed to be a joke."

She stared at him. "My sister was killed because she knew about the research, so forgive me for not finding it funny."

"I'm sorry, Veronica," he said quietly. "I didn't mean to offend. I wanted to talk to you about my role in all of this. You were right that I wasn't at the airport that day."

"Yet you knew I went to Paris with Tucker." It was odd how easy it had become to think of him as Tucker. He was a new man, though she'd seen sparks of him in her Steven.

Who would Timothy Seeger be? His memory was coming back and she would have to deal with a third version of the man she'd come to love.

"After Rebecca left there were rumors about what had happened between them." Arthur's voice had gone low. "Nasty rumors. She left without notice. A doctor of her reputation doesn't do that. It was the first time I got called into the corporate offices. They were worried about a possible lawsuit."

Rebecca had told her a bit about what had happened. Tucker had told her more. "I know what happened between them. What were the rumors?"

"That Steven had done something he shouldn't have. It ranged from him saying nasty things to her to outright physical violence. It was a nightmare scenario for the company, and they wanted someone to quietly investigate. They didn't trust McDonald to tell them the whole truth. They didn't want anything on the record. I was on McDonald's periphery. They asked me to find out the truth. I hired a private investigator. He followed Steven and rapidly discovered that the two of you had a much closer relationship than you wanted people to understand. That was when the company brought McDonald in. You being close to Steven was a red flag, but it was another relationship we were truly worried about."

She was confused, but then that seemed to be her perpetual state lately. "What relationship? And why would I be a red flag?"

"For the most part Steven was boring. He went to work and went home. But he did visit your sister on occasion, and that was why we brought in McDonald." Arthur said every word carefully, as though measuring them and watching for her response.

"He didn't know my sister." She'd never heard the two connected in any way.

Except apparently, they'd both known Levi Green. Her sister had been incredibly secretive those last few months. The only reason she'd met "Lewis" had been by accident. She'd popped by her sister's place on a lark and he'd been there. He'd been the one to introduce himself as a man who dated Katie.

If she'd come a different day, would it have been Tucker who opened that door?

She shook that feeling off.

"He did know your sister," Arthur said, not unkindly. "I've got a file on Steven. I haven't shared it with the Agency because they haven't asked. They can be a bit arrogant, I've found. I'll let you read it. I've got pictures of him at your sister's flat two days before he left for Paris. When the investigator asked some of the neighbors about him, they said he frequently visited."

Tears pulsed behind her eyes, but she wasn't going to cry. There was an explanation. "My sister was working on a story about McDonald. He and Levi Green were investigating McDonald. Maybe that's how they met."

"But Steven never told you he knew her?"

She shook her head. "He was secretive about what he did. I think he was trying to protect me."

"Or he had another reason."

She wasn't going to listen to this. "I should go back to the house."

"You would have been excellent cover for him, you know." Arthur stayed right where he was. "You gave him a reason to go to Paris that weekend, and a couple traveling together is much less suspicious than a man traveling alone. I find it interesting that he never asked you to go anywhere with him before that day, the day he was planning on turning over the information he stole."

He'd kissed her before then. During those last few weeks, he'd carefully spent time with her.

Had he decided she was a good bet as cover if he needed a traveling companion? Now that she looked back, she could see how he'd drawn her in over the course of a few months. He'd stayed away for a long time. He'd only gotten truly close when he'd decided he wanted out. He hadn't mentioned he knew her sister even when she'd talked about her sister.

But something didn't make sense. "This information he stole, it was stored at Kronberg. You're telling me Kronberg didn't know what McDonald was doing, yet the information was stolen directly from Kronberg."

"Well, obviously the man they stole the information from knew," Arthur replied as though it should be evident. "The former CEO has been dealt with, as has his entire staff. But he was a careful man. He kept records of everyone who worked with McDonald, and we want to know who else at Kronberg knew. That's all we're doing. Everything will be turned over to our allies, but we need that list in order to clean house."

"You need that list in order to cover it all up." She might be naïve about a lot of things, but not this.

"I have to worry about our stock prices," he allowed. "And I have to worry that the Agency is going to screw us all over. All you have to worry about is whether or not Steven is intending to use you again." He stood. "I'm going back. I'll send you the file and you can decide for yourself."

She didn't want to see that file. She wasn't even sure if it mattered. He couldn't have had a hand in Katie's death. According to everything she knew, he'd had his mind erased days before Katie had been killed. But what if he'd given Katie up? He couldn't give her up. They'd already known. But they hadn't known how much information Katie had gathered. He could have told them everything and that could have led McDonald to kill her.

It was an endless, agonizing loop in her mind. She didn't even realize when Arthur had walked away.

"Hey, are you okay?" Tucker jogged up to the gazebo, glancing behind him to where Arthur was walking into the house. "Did he do something to you?"

He'd caused her to doubt everything she knew. "No, I'm fine."

Tucker closed the space between them and his hands cupped her shoulders, eyes shining in the moonlight. "You can't leave like that. I don't want you to be alone with that man. We have no idea what he's capable of."

"We don't know anything at all. That's the real problem." She stepped back. There was so much between them that hadn't been there before. A mere half an hour ago they'd been some undefeatable team, and now she wasn't sure what to do.

Tucker's face fell. "What's wrong?"

So much, but she settled for her original worry. "You heard what Lewis...Levi Green said. Somehow I'm responsible for you getting caught. Have you thought about that for two seconds? Have you thought about how you'll feel if you get concrete proof that I'm the reason you lost your memory?"

"No," he admitted. "Because it doesn't matter. Because I just found my brother and that's way more important than assigning blame, Roni. Come here. I don't blame you for anything. If you somehow tipped them off, you didn't mean to."

He looked so gorgeous in the moonlight, like her every fantasy come to life, and it seemed cruel that he could be taken from her twice. "Kronberg hired a PI to follow you because they were worried you'd raped Rebecca."

Even in the moonlight she could see the way he paled. "I wouldn't do that. I didn't do that. I know I didn't. Rebecca would have told me. I hurt her. I did, but I did it to save her. McDonald was going to take her to Argentina, and if Rebecca had gone, she wouldn't have come back. She would have been forced to work for McDonald or she would have been killed."

"You couldn't tell her why? You couldn't warn her? You had to torture her. Do you know how insane that sounds?" Anger was building because they were right back to where they'd been before. He'd kept secrets and it had cost everyone around him.

Tucker stared for a moment as though that had been the very last thing he'd thought she would say. "I don't know what my thinking was at the time. I can't remember, but I know I'm sorry for hurting her. I had to have thought it was for the best."

She knew it was the only excuse he could give, but she couldn't handle it right now. "How about my sister? Was it for the best that you didn't bother to tell me you knew her?"

His eyes flared in obvious surprise. "What? I thought you said Levi knew her. Are you saying you saw me with her? Sweetheart, I can't remember. I'm starting to get some of that time back, but I certainly don't remember your sister."

"That's an awfully convenient excuse."

"It's not an excuse and I assure you it's not convenient." The words that came from his mouth were practically arctic. He took a deep breath. "Look, it's been a long day. Why don't we go inside, open a bottle of wine, and talk about this? Whatever this is."

She would be in his arms before she'd emptied the glass. She wanted to be in his arms right now. She wanted nothing more than to believe everything he said and write Arthur off completely. But why would he send her a file if he didn't have proof? "I don't know that's a good idea. It seems to me we've both jumped into this relationship without thinking about it."

It had taken him exactly a week to have her madly in love with him again. Even after everything she'd gone through the first time. Even as she'd been separated from her daughter, she'd wanted to be with him.

His stare threatened to burn through her. "I think about it all the time. I think about you all the time. Roni, what is this really about?"

It was about the fact that he was too good to be true. It was about the fact that she wasn't at all sure she could trust that anything positive could happen to her. "How can I trust you when we don't know what happened?"

"What do you think happened?"

She didn't want to go there, but they had to talk about Katie. "You were involved with Levi Green. Levi Green was involved with Katie. Arthur claims he has a private investigator's report that puts you at my sister's apartment a few days before you disappeared. Why would you have gone there? Why wouldn't you have told me?"

He shook his head. "Maybe I didn't know she was your sister."

"I showed you pictures of her." He might not remember but she did. "During the last two weeks before McDonald took you, we had a couple of dates. Always away from the office. I had to meet you at the restaurants we went to. I showed you pictures of my sister and my mom one night when we were having dinner at a place in the Marienplatz. You looked at her for a long time and pointed out all the ways we looked like sisters. You even told me you didn't think your brother looked like you at all. We had a long talk about genetics."

It had been a nice night. She'd enjoyed talking about their families and the long discussion about how DNA worked. He'd been so smart, but not in a way that made her feel dumb. He'd listened to her.

He'd lied to her. If Arthur was right and Tucker had known Katie, he'd stared at that picture and not mentioned a word to her.

He seemed to think about it for a while before he finally sighed. "I don't know why I would do that, but I had a good reason."

"How do you know?"

"Because just a few days ago you made me believe in myself," he replied in a fervent tone. "You told me a whole lot about how I'm good now and that meant I had to be good then. Are you telling me one conversation with a man who is known to lie and is probably here to fuck us all over and suddenly all the sweet faith in me is gone?"

She didn't want to think like this, but she also had a hard time wrapping her head around all of it. "She was my sister."

"Yes, and Robert is my brother and I gave up everything to find him. Everything, Roni." He put his hands on her shoulders, squeezing gently as if he was afraid she would disappear if he let her go. "I was working at Mass General. That means my degree is probably from Harvard. I was a kid from small-town Wyoming and I had to have gone to an Ivy League school to have earned that residency. You know how much work that had to have been. I wanted to find my brother so much I was willing to erase my existence to do it. And I'm standing here telling you I don't care if you're the one who got me caught."

She couldn't help the tears that fell now because she felt the loss of her sister so deeply in that moment. That horrible emptiness made her reckless, and she didn't think about a thing she was saying. It was all there in her head and it spat out like a noxious poison. "And your brother is alive. My sister is dead. I won't ever see her again. My mother is missing a part of her soul and Violet won't ever know her aunt. I'm having a hard time believing that it didn't have something to do with the files you stole. You knew her. You spent time in her apartment."

He backed away, his hands coming off her like she was too hot to touch. "Have you even seen this evidence?"

She hadn't. In a lot of ways she was talking out loud, going through all the worst possible scenarios because that was what she did. She usually didn't do it with the very person she was feeling threatened by. "No. But Arthur said he was sending it to me."

His gaze sharpened and she wondered if she'd made a mistake telling him. "Yeah, he's sending it to you. Did he ask for your email?"

She shook her head.

"He doesn't have to because he's had you under surveillance for years. He works for the company that let Hope McDonald ruin lives. But he sends you some evidence that I'm a…what? I would love to know exactly what I'm being accused of."

She'd been hasty and she knew it, but she couldn't back down. "You lied to me."

"Oh, it's more than that," he said, bitterness dripping from every word. "We all know I was a liar. Let's get to the real problem. You think that if I knew your sister, then I probably slept with her. Even though from everything I've learned, I didn't have that reputation. I wasn't known as a playboy around the office. But you immediately go there. I think what you're really wondering is if I killed her."

She shook her head. "I know you didn't plant the bomb. You were in Argentina."

"Was I? Maybe I wasn't. Maybe Mother kept me somewhere closer so she could program me to kill your sister. Mother loved to play those games. She loved to pit us against one another, to show us how much control she had." He swore under his breath and turned away. "McDonald. I don't fucking call her Mother anymore."

What was she doing? She hadn't meant to take him back to that place. "I'm sorry. Arthur was pretty convincing. He makes sense. You were working with Levi and he had a relationship with my sister. We know that Kronberg probably hired me as leverage against her investigation. Why wouldn't you know her?"

"Knowing her and fucking her are two different things. And it's obvious you're questioning whether or not I got her killed. I don't even know how to defend myself. I can't defend myself because I don't remember. He could show you pictures and I can't answer them."

"This is crazy. We should take a step back and think about this." She hated the way his shoulders slumped.

"Is there anything to think about?" He took a deep breath and straightened up. "You should go and find Arthur and get the truth about me. Maybe you can write up a report and let me know how much I fucked up your life."

Tears began to fall. "That's not fair."

"None of this is fair. None of my life has been fair since the day my brother got sold out." He turned away from her. "I meant what I said. I could have found out you turned me over personally to McDonald and I would have known you thought it was best at the time. I would have believed you. The fact that you can't do the same for me merely lets me know we don't feel the same way about each other."

It had all gone so wrong. She hadn't meant for it to go this way. "Can I not have a few minutes to think this through?"

He didn't bother to turn around. "You can have all the minutes you want, Veronica. The truth is I could get my memories back and lie about them. I could tell you anything at this point and there would always be a question in the back of your head. If I had anything to do with Katie, you'll wonder if I had something to do with why she died.

I don't come back from that with you, and I definitely don't with your mom."

Her fists clenched at her sides. "I just want to know what happened."

"And I can't tell you." He turned and there was resignation in his eyes. "Since the moment I realized I was Dr. Razor I've had this sick feeling in the pit of my gut that I wasn't worthy of anything I've gotten since I was rescued. Until a few nights ago. You made me believe in myself. Like most things in my life it wasn't real, but I'm going to hold on to it."

"Damn it, I'm not trying to...I don't know what I'm doing, Tucker."

"But you do." His hands were on his hips and he was staring at her like he'd never seen her before. "You're going to look at that evidence and you think you're going to make a decision about our relationship. The truth is you've already done that. You did it the minute you asked yourself if I was the kind of man who could sleep with your sister and then make a baby with you. You said you knew my soul. You won't be with a man like that. Suspicion is an insidious thing, and there will be a whole lot of it in the next few weeks. They'll come at us from all angles and we won't be strong enough to withstand it. Maybe if we'd had more time, but we didn't."

What exactly was he saying? He was blurry in front of her, tears affecting her vision, and she worried maybe he'd always been that way, a vague dream of something she'd missed out on. "I don't understand."

"But I do. It will always be there in the back of your mind." He turned away again and was down the steps before he spoke. "I'll sleep somewhere else tonight. You should be careful around Arthur. And Levi. They've both got their own agendas and you are merely a pawn to them. When this is done, no matter how you feel about me, no matter what you decide I've done, I'm not giving up my daughter. You should understand that. I understand that you might think I'm not good for her, but she's mine, too. I have no intention of giving her up, and tell Sandra if she thinks she can hide Violet from me or scare me off, she's wrong. After all, you know how far I'll go for my family."

"Tucker." She wasn't sure how it had gone so wrong. She hadn't meant to break up with him. When she'd first walked out, she'd been terrified that he would be upset with her. How had she ended up here?

She didn't want him gone. She only wanted to understand what had happened.

"Tucker," she called out.

But he didn't turn around. She was left alone with her doubt and the aching pain in her chest that she'd lost something she could never get back.

Chapter Thirteen

"Okay, bud, how about you tell me what the hell is going on with you and Roni." Robert placed a beer in front of Tucker and sat down on the bench overlooking the front drive.

It was a long, unpaved road that led to the highway. He couldn't see it from here even if it had been light enough to see much of anything at all. The road to the country house wound through the woods. They were isolated, and it was easy to imagine a time when carriages and horses would have been the main forms of transportation. A simpler time when no one erased minds and when a man could force the woman he loved to stay at his side since she would be dependent on her husband. Yeah. Men had it good then. No one forced drugs on them, and their wives and daughters were property who couldn't change their minds because some asshole planted a seed of doubt. Hell, back then maybe he could have simply shot Arthur Dwyer and gotten away with it. No pesky CSI-types or tons of security cameras always waiting and watching and stopping a guy from having fun.

"See, when you don't talk I wonder what's going through your head, and I don't think it's good," Robert was saying. "You know you can't kill Levi. He was actually trying to be helpful today. You were the one who wasn't cooperating."

It had been a rough day, and the evening hadn't been much better. He'd gotten very little sleep the night before and it was starting to get to him. After the scene at the gazebo, he'd found a guest room and lain in bed for hours going over all the ways he hated his former self. In the morning he'd gone downstairs but Roni had been in the breakfast room and it was apparent she hadn't told anyone that they'd had a major blowout fight and broken up. She'd given him a wan smile and sat next to him during breakfast before going back to the room they'd shared. She hadn't come down to the holding room where he and the rest of the group had spent hours trying to jog his memory, with Levi Green pushing every single button he could.

Then dinner had come and while she'd cooked it, she'd announced she wasn't feeling well and had gone to bed early.

He already missed her.

"So I am going to assume that Roni's excuse that she wasn't feeling well was exactly that—an excuse to not be around today." His brother didn't seem to mind that he wasn't responding. Robert kept going. "You weren't all over her like she was your dying child, so I'll make the secondary assumption that the two of you had a major fight and that's why you've spent the entire day looking like a puppy who got kicked."

"I'm not a fucking puppy." He got enough of that shit from Big Tag.

Robert groaned and sat back. "Damn it. Ariel's right. You're being a dick. What did you do?"

He huffed and turned to his brother. "You want to play *Am I the Asshole?*"

"I want to know what's going through my brother's head. I'm worried about him because my brother can find a way to smile through the worst parts of life. He never gets dark unless he's worried he's done something wrong."

He *was* the asshole in this case. Robert was trying to help and it wouldn't work to tell him he wanted to be alone. He knew it wouldn't work because it hadn't worked when Robert had told him the same thing. He'd simply held on until Robert was ready to talk. He'd been his brother's shadow and he hadn't even realized he was Robert's brother then. Now that they knew they'd grown up together, gone through life together, he accepted that there was zero way Robert gave up. It was a miracle he'd waited this long to confront him. He could talk now or his brother would be on his ass for hours.

"We had a fight." Maybe they could handle this like men. He'd say what happened and Robert would nod and they would drink beer.

"Obviously. What was the fight about?"

"See, this is why I think Tag is an asshole. He tells us to be men and suck everything up, but he made us go to all that therapy and now we think we should talk about things. I don't want to talk about it."

Robert chuckled and took a drink of his beer. "That's the funny thing about Tag. He whines about men not being men anymore and then he's the very person who makes you talk. Because beneath that veneer of toxic masculinity beats the heart of a man who cares. I also sometimes think Tag decided he wouldn't lie to himself, so why should he bother to lie to anyone else? On a personal level, of course. On a business level, he's a spectacular liar."

Tucker went quiet for a moment but his brother never moved. Merely sat there waiting.

"She thinks I slept with her sister," Tucker admitted.

"What?"

This was why he didn't want to go into it. It was a shocking accusation and yet was it really?

"You slept with her sister?" That hadn't come from Robert. Solo stepped out from the side of the house, staring at him like her eyes were laser beams and she could cut him right there.

Robert frowned her way. "Eavesdropping is beneath you."

"Hello, spy," Solo replied, pointing to herself. "And besides, Beck is listening in on the other side. I told him my side was better but he's got to be argumentative."

Tucker stood, glaring as Ezra stepped from his place.

"Thanks, Solo," Ezra said. "You know just because you get caught doesn't mean you have to rat me out."

Solo ignored him, turning to Tucker. "I'm sorry. You weren't cooperative today and that's not like you. I had to try to figure out what's going on with you. I'll be honest, I hadn't thought about Roni. I thought she was tired. You two were fine yesterday."

Ezra shook his head. "I knew it was Roni. They didn't talk at breakfast this morning, and I'm pretty sure he didn't sleep with her. I caught him sneaking into one of the guest rooms in the east wing last night."

"I thought you went to bed." Damn, but he'd been certain he hadn't gotten caught. He wasn't sure why, but he wasn't ready to tell everyone they weren't together. Maybe he was still thinking, still trying to find a way out of the trap.

"I wanted to make sure our friends all stayed in bed," Ezra explained. He moved around to the porch. "I don't trust them."

"None of us trusts them." Solo stepped up next to her ex. "But we need them."

He had to admit, they were a good-looking couple. Solo was a statuesque blonde, an Amazon of a woman. Most men would look small compared to her, but Ezra was her male counterpart. He was taller than she was, broader, and oddly his looks complemented hers. He actually looked more handsome when he stood beside her.

He liked the way Roni fit under his arm when she cuddled up, how her head would rest against his chest. He'd missed her all night long. He was afraid he would miss her for the rest of his life.

"And that means we need Tucker to work with them," Solo continued.

Robert stood beside him, completing the standoff. "He's doing his best."

"That's not what you were saying three minutes ago," Ezra pointed out. "I believe you came out here to do exactly what we're trying to do."

"Yeah, well, he's my brother. I get to be irrational about him," Robert replied. "I don't like the two of you ganging up on him."

"We're trying to pull this thing off. That means we have to work together," Ezra argued. "Normally, unlike Tucker here, I would stay out of all the personal stuff. I would love to give him his privacy even though he doesn't deserve it."

"Hey," Robert began.

"Nah, that's fair." Despite the fact that his whole life seemed fucked, he had to concede Ezra had a point. "I watched him and Solo fight once while eating a bag of popcorn and betting on the outcome with Owen."

"Still, they should be upfront about it." Robert didn't seem as eager to be reasonable.

It was a big-brother thing.

"Uhm, I think I asked about ten times today what was wrong." Solo's boot tapped against the ground. "Look, I get that you and Veronica are having problems. Maybe you could have a couples session with Ariel. But Rupert isn't happy with how this is moving along and the Germans weren't thrilled either."

"Tell Rupert he can bite my ass," Ezra replied.

Solo's hands were fists at her sides. "Yeah, that sounds about right. Do you have any idea how hard it is to smooth things over for you? You've got the subtlety of an angry bear. We're not in a power position here and we won't be until we know where that intel is. They won't let us sit out here forever."

"And I won't let them rush my brother," Robert argued. "I won't let them push a bunch of drugs on him. It's been a day. We all knew it would take a while."

"I want to know what happens if McDonald took the intel and it's gone." Tucker had spent all day with that possibility gnawing at his gut. "It's the most likely scenario. If I had it in my hands when McDonald caught me, it's gone."

"I don't think she had it," Solo said. "If she had that information, she wouldn't have run from Kronberg."

"She's right." Ezra was softer now as he turned his focus from his ex-wife to Tucker. "If she had blackmail material, McDonald would have used it. She wouldn't have fled to Argentina. Her money dried up. She needed that money to continue her work."

"It's precisely why we started robbing banks," Robert said. "So logic points to the fact that you had to have dumped the intel somewhere. You knew McDonald was on to you and you hid it."

"I hid it somewhere in Paris." It was a daunting thought. "It's not exactly a small city. It would be like looking for a needle in a haystack."

Solo nodded. "I agree. We've also got to account for the fact that it's been years and it could have been thrown away or moved or destroyed. I know the truth is we probably won't find it. But I think they might be appeased if they know it's not out there."

"Tucker, if you remember what was on that report, I need you to never tell anyone," Ezra said, his voice low. "My worst-case scenario is you're a living record of those names."

Robert's hand came to his shoulder and he took a sharp breath. "I hadn't thought of that. You have to lie. If you remember those names, you can't talk about them."

"I don't know I'll have a choice," Tucker replied. "I have to do whatever it takes to get Jax out."

"I'll get Jax out," Ezra promised. "I won't let him rot in jail. I've already started looking at options."

"I will help." Solo moved up the steps to join them. "I've got some safe houses he can use. You, too, if you need them. But if we can find the intel or prove to them it's been destroyed, things will be much easier. We won't need safe houses or aliases. Jax and River can go home to Colorado. You can go to Wyoming if you want. We might be able to find Sasha's daughter if there's any information about him on the report."

He wasn't the only one with skin in this game. Robert had promised Sasha he would look for the daughter he'd only vaguely remembered. "I'll try harder tomorrow."

Solo sighed and there was a weariness in her eyes. "Thank you. I'm going to take the night shift with Levi. Nina needs a break."

Ezra moved past her. "No, you won't. I'll do it. I don't want you anywhere near him."

"He's in a cell." Solo started to argue and then stopped. "Thank you. I would prefer to not be around him. I appreciate it, Be…Ezra."

"Don't. It sounds weird coming from you." Ezra had a hand on the door.

The normally indomitable Solo suddenly seemed hesitant. "Thank you for handling Levi, Beck. In the morning, I'll talk to Rupert and smooth things over. I'll let him know we'll give it another shot, and maybe we can think about letting Ariel try hypnosis again."

"That would be good," Ezra replied.

They were so going to do it soon. Like hard do it soon. Despite his own problems, he kind of wanted to pop some corn and continue watching this particular show.

He deserved the eavesdropping.

"Think about what I said." Ezra looked back at Tucker and Robert from the door Solo had just walked through. "I'll do anything I have to do to protect you."

He would break Jax out of prison, help Tucker get away if he needed to. Ezra would put his own life on the line. Ezra Fain hadn't been born in McDonald's lab, but he was one of them. "Thank you, brother."

Ezra stopped for a moment as if the words had shocked him. He nodded slowly. "Always, brother."

He disappeared, following after Solo.

"I don't think you can know what that means to him," Robert said.

Tucker sighed because they were going to get back to what he didn't want to talk about. He knew it. His blood brother could be stubborn about getting to the root of a problem. "I don't think I know anything. The things I think I know prove to be false."

"Now that the peanut gallery is gone, let's get back to the part where you explain to me why Roni thinks you're sleeping with her sister," Robert insisted.

There was nothing to do but tell him the truth. "According to Arthur Dwyer, I knew Katie Croft. He claims he has proof that not only did I know who she was, I spent a lot of time with her. She must have seen it by now, and notice how she didn't come running back to me today."

"What kind of proof?" Robert asked.

Tucker shrugged. "I would assume it's photos and maybe correspondence. Apparently during the last few weeks at Kronberg, they had a PI following me."

"He could be lying," Robert argued. "Photos can be faked. That report doesn't mean anything."

"It does to Veronica since I never bothered to mention that I knew her sister." He went back to the bench and his beer because he needed that damn beer. "She showed me pictures of Katie and I never told her we had a connection. Of course now I have no idea what our connection was, so her mind has gone to the worst possible place. To say I did not take the accusation well would be an understatement. And I know what she's really worried about."

"She thinks you might have gotten her sister killed." Robert whistled and sank down beside him. "Damn. I was hoping you'd been an asshole about her potentially outing you. I could work with that. I don't know how to work with you might have killed her sister."

That neatly summed up the problem. "Katie was alive after I was taken to Argentina. But we don't know that I didn't come back. McDonald could have made planting that bomb my first assignment. And I was probably wiped a dozen times after that. I can't know. I'll probably never know, and that means this will always come between us."

"Unless I can prove who did it. Maybe the team should take a hard look at this case."

"Which team is that?" His brother wasn't thinking logically. "Because we're down a bunch of men. Sasha and Dante are dead and Jax is in jail. I think the team is pretty much you and me and Owen."

"And Ezra and Ariel and Rebecca and River." Robert stared out over the yard. "All we have to do is call Theo and he'll come with us. Don't underestimate Buster. He can distract a person with his cuteness. Or his farts. That is one gassy dog."

"Like that rescue dog we had. Mom was always complaining that we needed to change Astro's food." The memory floated over him easily now that he wasn't fighting for it. He let the vision of a big dog who always looked like he was smiling settle on him like a warm blanket. He could see the dog trying to lick him, remember how much he'd loved him. He'd walked into the shelter he'd volunteered at when he was in high school and immediately fallen in love with the massive ball of fluff.

Robert was quiet for a moment. "Do you remember her at all? Mom?"

"I remember she loved us. I remember her hugging me and begging me to bring you home." Green hadn't been willing to give their mother's name up. He'd told them they could have that information when they released him. Naturally he'd tried to run an end around on the fucker. "I gave Adam everything we've learned, including the fact that I went to Hamilton High somewhere in Wyoming. There's got to be something Green missed, some thread Adam can pull now that we know where to look."

"I should have started looking weeks ago." Robert took a long swig of his beer. "I don't know why I didn't."

"Because you bought into Emily's bullshit that we were all estranged." For a man who was married to a psychologist, he wasn't exactly self-aware. When his first wife had shown up in Munich she'd caused all sorts of chaos. One of the ways she'd manipulated Robert had been to tell him he no longer spoke to his mother or brother. All the while she'd known exactly who Tucker was to Robert and she'd kept it to herself. It was cruel, but then she'd sold her own husband to McDonald along with Robert's whole unit.

"I didn't know any better," Robert said quietly. "Kind of like you don't know what happened between you and Katie Croft. Tell me something. Did Roni ask you to leave her alone?"

Not exactly, but it had felt like rejection. "She said we'd moved too fast."

Robert chuckled. "Yeah, that ship sailed. You have a daughter. You have to deal with each other."

"That's what I said." Right before he'd walked away from her. "She was crying. A lot. I wanted to hug her and tell her everything would be all right, but I didn't think she would accept that from me."

"Did you offer it to her?"

He'd walked away because he'd been so angry. "No, but I did threaten her if she tried to keep me from seeing Violet. So there's that."

Robert finally looked at him, a frown on his face, and then he shook his head and laughed. "Dumbass. All right. Let's figure this out. You want to figure this out, right? Because if you don't, this is an excellent off-ramp. You'll have to decide how to co-parent when you're not together, but otherwise this could be a clean break."

"God, no." He'd sat up most of the night trying to find a way to take back the shit he'd said. "I don't want to break up with her. I love her. I know that deep down. I loved her then. I was willing to risk everything to take her with me. I remember the feeling of looking down at her asleep in bed and knowing we were getting out. That had to be the day I got caught."

"And if Levi's right and she's the reason you got caught?"

He shook his head. This was the easiest decision he'd made. "She didn't mean to. She might have inadvertently tipped McDonald off, but she wouldn't have betrayed me."

"You don't know her, Tucker."

"But I do." He wasn't sure how to explain it. "It's a feeling deep inside. I trust her. It's the same way I trusted you when I first met you. I didn't understand it at the time. I thought it was me being needy, but I knew you deep down. I know her, too. I reacted poorly. I can't stand the thought of her not feeling the same way about me. I'm in a corner and I don't know how to get out."

"Then we'll figure it out together," Robert promised.

He wasn't sure his brother was the best resource he had. "Or we could go to Ariel and ask her what to do."

Robert grinned. "That's what I was going to suggest. Hey, I married a smart woman. Let's go catch her before she gets in that big bathtub. I want to live like English nobility, man. I'm pretty sure every room in this house is about sex. That tub is big enough for like three people."

"My shower has shampoo, conditioner, and what I'm pretty sure is lube. Right there in the shower." He hadn't gotten to use it on Roni. It was sad. He was sad. Maybe he should do what Jax had done. Go out and buy the cutest dog he could find and they could both look miserable until Roni gave in like River had.

"The rich know how to live, brother." Robert stood up.

They hadn't been rich. They'd been comfortable, though. Their mom had made sure they had a nice house and food on the table. She'd worked hard to ensure they had good educations. Was she still there waiting for her sons to come home? "We're going to find her, you know. We're going to find Mom."

"I hope you remember more," Robert admitted. "I can barely get any of it. I worry I'm different and she won't recognize me. I don't want to hurt her."

He stood beside his brother. He got the feeling they'd done this a million times before. Brothers simply sharing space so they knew they weren't alone. Somehow, some way, they would find their way home. "She will thank God every day for bringing you back. And she'll adore Ariel. I hope I get to introduce her to Roni and Vi."

Despite what he'd said to her, he wasn't sure how much standing he would have when it came to custody of his daughter. Roni could tell the courts he was a danger to her, and given his history, it was a believable argument. That was if he could ever show his face in a court.

It was all fucked up and he had to find a way to make things right between them again.

The door came open and Ezra strode out.

"You need to come inside. We have a situation," he said grimly.

"Tucker, we need your medical skills."

He rushed in, terrified it might be too late to fix anything.

* * * *

Roni watched as Robert walked outside, two beers in his hand. She felt ridiculous skulking around like she was the spy. She wasn't. She was the woman who was trying to avoid another fight. Or maybe she wanted to avoid the fact that they might not fight at all, that Tucker might have written her off after last night's debacle. This was how she'd spent her day. Hiding out. Thinking way too much. Putting off that moment when she would have to talk to him again. Tucker was already out there. She'd seen him, staring out at the yard like there were answers there.

She had a few answers, just not the ones either of them wanted to hear.

Arthur had sent her the PI's file on Tucker's last few days in Munich. There were pictures that clearly showed Tucker walking into Katie's apartment in Munich. He'd stayed for an hour and a half and then gone home. Two days later they'd been in Paris and it had all gone to hell.

Seeing those pictures of her sister with Tucker had made her heart seize. Katie. She'd been dressed casually and she'd given him her "friends" smile. Roni had always been able to tell a lot about how her sister felt from her expression. In the picture the PI had caught, her sister had a smile that lit her eyes up. She'd liked Tucker. She'd been happy to see him.

What the hell did she do with that?

Her stomach rumbled and she made her way to the kitchen since it appeared the brothers would be out there for a while. It was good that they were talking. It really was. She was happy he'd found his brother and knew exactly who Robert was to him.

But god, it made her miss her sister.

She had to get it together because Ezra Fain had promised her a call to her mother and daughter in an hour, and she would have to sit beside Tucker and act like nothing was wrong. She couldn't bring her mom into this until she was sure of what she wanted to do. Sandra Croft could be a steamroller, obliterating everything in her path when she wanted to.

She didn't want Tucker to get caught in that. If her mom even got a hint that Tucker had a hand in what had happened to Katie, she wouldn't ever listen to reason. She needed to figure out how to handle this before she ever breathed a word of the situation to her mom.

It left her feeling incredibly alone. All through the last few years her mom had been at her side. She'd helped her make the decisions when it came to Violet. She might have felt alone, but she hadn't been.

"Hey, stranger." Nina stood in the kitchen wearing pajama pants and a T-shirt, her hair up in a high ponytail. She stood by the range, a tray of teacups by her side as she waited for the water to boil.

She wasn't alone. Arthur was there, placing some half sandwiches on the tray. He was still dressed for work. Despite the fact that they weren't in an office, Arthur dressed like he was. He'd shown up for breakfast wearing a jacket and tie and hadn't taken either off though it was almost bedtime.

Not that she would sleep.

He glanced her way. "Veronica, we missed you today. Not that you missed much. We made absolutely no progress."

Nina looked up from her task. "That's not what I heard. I was told he managed to remember something about you."

Arthur went stiff. "Well, we did work together. He claims he can remember the day we met, but that isn't meaningful at all. Levi Green tried to pull some important information out of him but to no avail. Your boyfriend seems to be having trouble focusing."

Maybe she wasn't hungry. Tucker had walked away the night before, but she'd heard the anguish in his voice. She'd known how upset he'd been. Unlike Steven Reasor, Tucker wasn't good at hiding his emotions. Or perhaps he didn't have to anymore. Perhaps he'd had to do it for so long, he simply couldn't when the reason for tamping it all down had been erased from his mind.

"I'm sorry to hear that." She'd hoped there would be a breakthrough that led them back to The Garden. Or that would allow her to go to New York to be with her mom and Violet. She wasn't sure how long she could hold out when they had to stay in the same house. She needed time to think and consider all the ramifications of Arthur's information. Instead, all she'd been able to think about was how much she'd missed Tucker. In the course of a few days he'd become necessary to her again. Maybe more necessary than the first time around since now she knew how good he was as a father.

Who was she fooling? The feeling in her heart wasn't about his skills as a dad. She liked him. Even more this time around. He was kind and thoughtful. He made her laugh. She felt more like herself when he was with her.

"Don't listen to him. Ariel isn't worried. It's a process," Nina assured her. "This could take time. Can I get you something, love? You missed your dinner. I'm making a spot of tea. Arthur and the intelligence lads are having a meeting to discuss their reports. I offered to make them some tea because I could use a bit before bed. There's some roast left if you're hungry."

"Tea sounds nice." She couldn't eat a bunch, but she'd seen some fruit, and Nina had made cookies earlier. That would do and then maybe after they'd talked to Violet, she and Tucker could talk about how to proceed. They couldn't spend their days avoiding each other.

"I brought along some excellent Schwarztee," Arthur explained.

"Like we used to have in the break room?" It was one of the only things she'd missed from Kronberg. They had tea in the break room in the afternoons, and she'd learned to love the rich, black tea they served there. The English were known as the world's tea drinkers, but the Germans weren't far behind.

Arthur smiled. "Exactly. I know I should switch to something that will help me sleep, but it's going to be a long night. I have a call back to Munich, and they won't like what I have to say. I promise, I'll let them know how important it is to not give Tucker more drugs."

No matter what went on between them, she wouldn't change her mind about that. "We don't understand how the first drugs affected him. Or what was in them."

"I still don't believe Levi Green doesn't have the formulary," Nina admitted. "I find it hard to believe there was a random dose of cure lying around."

That was a good point. "That does seem odd. From what I've been told, Green stole a lot of intelligence from the group. He did in Colorado at least."

"I think stealing is a difficult word since McKay-Taggart broke into that facility," Arthur pointed out. "It was a CIA base. At least

Green was actually working for the CIA at the time. He had some right to be there. I can't say the same for what they did at Kronberg. That was theft, pure and simple. Neither the CIA nor a group of rogue citizens had the right to come into a private company and steal documents. I would like to point out that you're all lucky my company is being patient."

"If Kronberg doesn't want to be investigated, maybe they should vet their research more carefully," Nina said as the kettle began to whistle. "And perhaps they should stay away from Illuminati-like groups who try to influence politics in a way that corporations shouldn't."

"If the CIA truly believed my company was a part of…what was it called?" Arthur asked.

Oh, she knew this one. It was exactly what her sister had been investigating. "The Collective."

Arthur's eyes rolled behind his glasses. "Yes, The Collective. It's ridiculous to think a group of corporations who are normally at war with one another could ever cooperate long enough to take over the world."

What had Katie told her?

They don't need to take over the world. Just push it this way or that. Just enough to keep them in economic power. All they need is a few of the right people in the right places to make things happen for them.

The words played through her head as Nina and Arthur argued. Nina poured hot water into two separate pots.

"We'll have to agree to disagree," Arthur said. "I find arguing with conspiracy theorists to be wearing. Facts don't matter to people like you. Veronica, I bid you good night. Perhaps you'll join us in the morning. It seems Steven needs something other than the good of the world in order to actually focus on the job at hand. Maybe you can be that for him."

He picked up his tray of late-night treats and walked back toward where the English and German operatives would be waiting for him.

"There's an unctuous prick if I ever saw one," Nina said with a sigh. "Sometimes those big words come in handy." She placed some cookies on her tray and picked it up. "Let's sit and have a chat. Arthur might be an arrogant nob, but he's right about one thing. Tucker was off today. I suspect you had something to do with that. What's he done?"

Nina was so nice it could be easy to forget she was a trained investigator. She'd spent years with Interpol running down some of the world's worst criminals. If she was still there, she would likely be looking for Tucker.

Was she treating Tucker like a criminal? Had she lost faith because her grief had stricken out like a viper she'd thought was gone?

"We had a fight," she admitted. It might be good to talk to someone. If she couldn't talk to her mom, it might as well be Nina. She didn't seem particularly close to Tucker. From what Roni understood, Nina had only been with the team for a few months. The only other person she might be able to talk to would be Solo, but she was oddly intimidating. There was a core to Solo that seemed a bit untouchable despite how warm the woman could be. Ariel was Tucker's sister-in-law, so she was a no go. She didn't think Ezra Fain would appreciate being made a relationship sounding board.

Nina it was then.

"I assumed so since you both looked utterly miserable," Nina said, pulling out a chair. "He didn't sleep in your room last night."

"How did you know? I thought he snuck into another room." He hadn't seemed to want anyone to know they were having trouble. He'd smiled her way when he'd come down for breakfast and she'd noticed he'd come in from the direction he would have had he slept in their room, rather than the easiest route from the room he'd stayed in.

"It's my responsibility to know everything that goes on in the house. Ezra is too preoccupied with Solo and vice versa. Robert can't think about anything but his brother and Ariel. I'm the only one who can think straight here, so I have to be careful." She stood up and walked to the doorway, glancing the way Arthur had gone before returning to the table and picking the tray up again. She walked right back to the sink.

"Uh, is something wrong with the tea?" She'd been looking forward to it.

"Yes, it comes from Arthur, who happens to travel with his own tea." Nina poured the pot out. "Like I said, I have to be careful and I would be an idiot if I let you drink something that man gave us. Right now, we don't eat or drink anything we're not one hundred percent sure is fine. There are two spies in this house I don't trust, and Arthur Dwyer works for an evil pharmaceutical corporation."

Put like that it did seem ridiculous. She wasn't built for the conspiracy life. She wanted…she wanted what he'd promised her that day in Paris. A quiet practice where they cared for their patients, a life where they raised their children. She wanted more kids and she wanted them with Tucker. But how could they go on?

Nina dumped the tea but came back with something better. "I can assure you he hasn't put anything in this."

She held up the bottle of wine before opening it and filling two glasses.

"You think he tried to poison us?" The idea sent a shiver down her spine. Were they not safe here?

Were they safe anywhere? She hadn't felt safe for years, but now she realized she'd reached next-level anxiety.

Nina shrugged and passed her a glass of the rich red wine. "I'm not taking the chance. But I'm also not going to accuse him of anything. I've found it's best to smile and let whoever your opponent is completely underestimate you. What did Tucker do?"

Arthur was the opponent. Why had she forgotten that? It didn't mean he was lying, but it did mean he didn't have pure motives for showing her that report. "He knew my sister."

"The one who was killed? From what I've read about her, she was possibly investigating The Collective."

Roni took a sip. "She was. At the time I thought she was crazy."

"She definitely wasn't, though I can understand how it would look that way," Nina admitted. "Let me see if I can guess how this plays out for you. So either Arthur or Rupert showed you something that links Tucker with your sister, hoping that he didn't say anything back then when he was pretending to be Steven Reasor. If Tucker never mentioned to you that he knew your sister, naturally your brain will put two and two together. If Steven knew your sister and didn't tell you, he might have had a hand in her death. At the very least Levi might have. Since Levi is connected to Steven, you have to consider that he might have had something to do with it even though she died after Steven had already become Tucker."

Well, that succinctly summed her up. "Why wouldn't he have

told me he knew Katie?"

Nina chuckled, likely at how naïve she sounded. "Well, in the first place he was working for the Agency. They tend to be tight lipped. He didn't tell you his real name. There's a possibility that he didn't know she was your sister."

"No, he knew," Roni explained. "I showed him pictures of her and he never said a thing."

Nina nodded. "All right, then it might have been important you not know anything. I can't be sure. I might not be the best person to give you advice about this."

"Because you like Tucker?"

"No, because I've been used for information before. It's why I left Interpol," Nina admitted. "I was seeing a man there, another agent. I was on the biggest case of my career, investigating an international arms dealer. Unfortunately, he was working the case too. From the arms dealer's side. He slept with me to get information for his real boss. Is that what you think Tucker did? Slept with you to get information about your sister?"

"He never asked about her." He'd listened to her talk about Katie, but he certainly hadn't pressed her for anything beyond asking about stories from her childhood. Now that she thought about it, she wasn't sure hearing about the great soap debate of their teens would have done anything to help his cause. "Not anything serious. Like he didn't ask about her work. Obviously because he knew what she did."

Nina nodded as though she'd expected that was the case. "Then you've got two options for why he did what he did. Option A—he formed a relationship with you in hopes of eventually using you against your sister. I would assume they would have threatened you to get her to hand over her research or something like that."

That was definitely a scenario that had gone through her head. "And the other option?"

"He fell in love with you," Nina said simply. "He was in a position where he could have gotten you killed. He thought the less you knew, the better. I know that sounds harsh, and every person who's ever been on the other side of this argument thinks they had a right to know what was going on, but they're wrong."

Roni didn't understand why. Knowledge was always better than ignorance. "At least I would have known what was coming for me."

"What was coming for you, Roni? McDonald? According to what you told Solo, she did come for you and as your mind is still completely your own, she must have decided you didn't know anything," Nina pointed out. "Otherwise, you would either have found yourself without a memory, or more likely without a life. According to your report she showed up at that Paris flat you were staying at the same day Tucker went missing."

"Yes." She could remember how carefully McDonald had studied her, questioning her and finding her utterly harmless. "She came by to pick up Tucker's computer and his tablet." Her stomach clenched as she realized who else had shown up. She'd known, but she hadn't realized the cruelty of it. It made tears threaten. "She brought Robert with her. Robert was there. He took Tucker's computer and his things. Do you think…"

Nina took a long sip of wine. "Do I think that she brought Robert with her to taunt Tucker? To show him exactly how close he came to saving his brother right before she took it all away from him? Perhaps. I also think if you'd shown even a hint that you knew what was going on, she might have taken you to Argentina and let her boys have fun with you. She liked to let them sleep with women as rewards for good behavior and then they would wake up next to a corpse in the morning. You could have been that for Tucker had she not believed you."

A fine tremble went through her. Tucker had known how cruel McDonald could be. It was why he'd done what he'd done to Rebecca. If he'd told Rebecca, she would have confronted McDonald. It was her nature. So he'd done something bad to stop something far worse from happening. He'd taken the sin on himself.

She wasn't a great actress. She didn't lie well. If he'd told her what was happening, she likely would have given herself away that day when she was in the same room with McDonald. She would have come off as scared and anxious instead of sad that her boyfriend had used her. "He really was protecting me. He promised he would tell me everything when he was done. I think he was planning on us leaving from Paris."

"Yes, I believe he was." Nina sighed, sitting back. "Believe me when I say I know how a man who's using a woman acts. He doesn't keep her safe. He puts her up as a shield to save himself. I don't know what Tucker was doing with your sister, but I don't think that man is capable of what you're accusing him of. Have you considered the fact that he might have been working with your sister and they were both trying to protect you? That you had two people who wanted so badly to look out for you? What did Katie say when you told her Tucker had left?"

The tears flowed freely now because in this she was absolutely the guilty party. "I never told her. She knew I was seeing him, but I avoided her after he left me. I dodged her calls and then she died."

Would her sister have known something had gone wrong and saved herself if she'd talked to her about what happened to Tucker?

Nina shook her head. "No. You can't go there. You can't. McDonald took her out. Or maybe Kronberg did for all we know. They would have found you and then you and Katie would be dead. Violet wouldn't have been born. Can't you see that was exactly what they were both trying to stop?"

She'd been wrong. She didn't have a lick of proof, but the scenario Nina had put out was the correct one. He hadn't betrayed her. He hadn't used her. He'd done everything he could in the best way he'd known how.

She'd betrayed him.

She stood up. "I have to go talk to him."

Nina smiled. "I'm glad. I honestly believe if he knows you're with…"

Nina's words were cut off with the sound of a single ping. It was so quiet, nothing more than a brief puff of air whispering around her as the bullet entered Nina's chest. Bright red blood bloomed.

Up and left of her heart. But it might have gotten her lung. She needed to seal the wound. It wouldn't be fatal if she could seal it and keep Nina breathing.

"Well, you obviously didn't drink the tea as I had planned. She was a bit too smart for her own good," Arthur said, staring down at Nina as she fell to the floor. He glanced back Roni's way. "If you scream I'll put one in her brain. I'm not good with the shooting business. I'm not a damn spy. I missed her heart. She might still live, but only if you come with me. Come now, Veronica. You're not so out of practice you don't know that what I'm saying is true, are you?"

He was so close. He wouldn't miss this time. He couldn't. Nina wouldn't survive.

"You should hurry or I'll shoot anyone who walks in here. Don't think I won't. I already drugged the head of MI6 and a German intelligence agent. I have nothing to lose. You have ten seconds to make your decision," he said, his eyes lit with something that scared the hell out of her.

Truth. He was telling her the utter truth.

"I'll come with you." She didn't have another choice. There was no way she could stand here and watch him kill Nina. He wouldn't stop there. If she screamed, he would kill her, too.

Arthur grimaced as he approached her. "I think you'll likely comply until we're far enough away that I won't be able to hurt your friend. I told them I didn't want this job."

She barely managed to gasp before he brought the gun down on her head and the whole world went dark.

Chapter Fourteen

"She's stable. You got to her in time and managed to keep her breathing," Ariel said over the phone two hours later. "The doctors here say she was lucky."

"What about the intelligence officers?" Tucker asked. He'd had a lot to deal with and he was only now starting to completely understand how fucked they all were.

"They're both still sedated," Ariel replied. "But the toxicology came back and the doctors assure me they're going to be fine. No word on Veronica?"

His stomach rolled and Ezra nodded, holding his hand out to take the phone.

"We're working on it. I've already sent copies of the security tapes to Dallas. They'll go over it with a fine-tooth comb for anything that might help," Ezra was saying. "We couldn't chase after that massive ass because we had to deal with Nina and then our sleeping friends. I suspect Arthur planned to drug Nina as well, but she chose wine over tea."

He'd seen Arthur carrying an unconscious Veronica into the woods. It had been right there on the security cameras. They would have been minutes behind but he hadn't been able to chase after them because he'd had a dying Nina and he was the only one with medical expertise. Now it was too late and she was gone.

She was gone.

They were supposed to be talking about how good Violet looked and awkwardly trying to broach the subject of what had gone wrong between them, but he didn't even know where she was. Had she been drugged, too? What did Arthur Dwyer want?

If he'd thought to kidnap Veronica Croft, there was only one thing Dwyer could want.

Him.

"I found where he had a car hidden in the woods." Robert strode in, Solo hard on his heels. "We followed the tracks to the road and lost him there."

"I've already talked to Damon and he's got someone working on the traffic cams," Solo explained.

He could already see a problem with that scenario. "You don't know what kind of car he's driving."

"No, but we can make some educated guesses." Solo had her phone out again. "We can check and see if a new car shows up between cameras. It's not foolproof, but we have to give it a shot. I'm also trying to figure out if anyone is scheduled to fly out of one of the private airfields. There aren't many around here. We're fairly isolated so we have a shot."

They wouldn't find Arthur. He would be well-funded and he would have a plan. "Who will he call with the ransom request?"

Ezra hung up with Ariel. "I suspect it will be Damon, or maybe me. I don't know, man. You know what he'll want, right?"

"We don't know anything yet," Solo argued.

He hadn't thought she could be naïve. "At some point he'll call and he'll be willing to make an exchange. Me for Roni. Once he has me, I'll be taken to some lab Kronberg owns and he'll give me all those drugs he's wanted to from the beginning. They'll do whatever they can to find that intel."

"And keep us out of the loop," Robert surmised. His brother was thinking along the same lines. "I'm certain they'll say something about how Arthur was acting as a rogue agent and they have no idea what's going on."

"Then why would Arthur do it?" Solo asked.

There was only one real reason he could think of. "His name is on the list. Or he knows whose is and he thinks getting that list will give him all the power he needs. The question is what will he do with Roni. I can't see him actually giving her up."

"Which is why this is an irrational plan," Robert said. "He has to know there's zero way we give you up. Not when he'll kill Roni anyway. You have to know that. He can't let her live."

Nausea threatened to overtake him. "He can't think he'll get away with this if she dies. I won't stop, and Big Tag won't let him get away with killing me."

"It's got to be bad," Solo said with a shake of her head. "Whatever is in the intel you stole, it has to be damning if he's risking this much."

Her cell buzzed and she grimaced. "It's DC. I have to take this. Ezra, will you please check on Levi? He was fine when I left, but it's been a while."

She stepped out of the room and after a few seconds, he heard the back door open and close.

"You have to give me up," he said. He couldn't see a way around it. "You have to be careful and make sure you get Roni out of there. I'll make it a condition of turning myself over."

He couldn't leave Violet without her mom. He couldn't let her die out there for him. He would do anything it took to make sure she got out of this alive and whole, and then his brothers would take care of her. All of his brothers. The blood one and the ones he'd chosen.

How funny was it that when they'd been separated, they'd found their brotherhood again without ever knowing there was an ounce of blood between them. He trusted Robert would see to Veronica's and Violet's health and happiness. He could do what needed to be done because his brothers would make sure the people he loved were okay.

Ezra glanced outside, his eyes on his ex-wife as she paced. "Or we could negotiate."

"How?" Robert asked.

"We do something truly shitty to Solo because she would never go for this plan." He frowned. "I know I talk crap about her all the time, but I don't want to do this to her. I can't think of another way out. I'm worried she's telling her boss what happened, and they'll come pick up Levi in the morning and our shot will be gone. She won't have a choice. Come with me."

Ezra turned and started down the hallway. It was the one that led to Levi Green's cell.

But then didn't all the roads of his life lead back to that asshole?

He followed along. How far away was Veronica now? Had they gotten her on a plane? Was she already en route to Germany? Would he ever see her again?

"This is going to be all right," Robert was saying as he walked down the hall. "I'm going to make sure of it. I've already contacted Owen. He knows what's happening and he's monitoring things back in London. I think Damon's giving MI6 some serious hell."

"And that will work in our favor," Ezra added, taking the steps down to the dungeon. "But I don't think it will work fast enough. We've got to move before dawn if we're going to do this."

Tucker had a good idea of what Ezra was saying. It was dangerous, and he wasn't sure they could pull it off. "You think Green will go along with it?"

Ezra slid his key into the door and unlocked it. He'd been down here when all the chaos had started, and Tucker was happy he'd been watching over Green or they might have lost him, too.

He and Robert had heard nothing, seen nothing, until Ezra had come running.

"What the hell is happening?" Green was on his feet, his hands wrapped around the bars. "You think I can't hear down here? I might not be able to make out what you're saying, but I know when something's gone to hell. Don't you forget you need me. You let some fucking foreign agency take me and you get nothing. Where's Solo?"

There was a wild look in his eyes that almost convinced Tucker he cared about the outcome. He supposed obsession was a kind of caring. "She's safe upstairs. Roni's the one who's gone, and Nina has a bullet in her chest because she preferred wine to tea."

Green cursed under his breath before slamming his palm against the bars. "I knew this would happen. Was it MI6, or did that fucker Dwyer show his colors?"

"Rupert is sleeping off a roofie," Robert explained.

Green shook his head. "Kronberg is touchy. You know what they want, right?"

"Me." But maybe he could find something they wanted even

more.

Green looked to Ezra. "What's Solo doing?"

"She's out talking to DC," Ezra replied, his eyes stony. "I'm sure they'll have your transport logistics figured out in no time at all. Unless we can come to an agreement."

Green was back at the bars, a fierce look in his eyes. "You know we can. You know exactly what we need to do. Solo won't go for it. She'll play it safe because she won't want to get you in trouble. Everything she's doing right now is to put you in a position to get your job back. She'll sacrifice this whole operation to do it. But you don't want that, do you?"

Robert seemed to grasp what Ezra was offering them. "You want to break Green out before Solo's boss can come?"

Tucker stared at the man who'd recruited him and left him behind when the tide had turned. He didn't want to have to depend on Levi Green, but it looked like he didn't have a choice. "We need to go to Paris. Green was right that first day. I need to be in the city. I need to stand where it all started and let myself trust my instincts. You remember what it was like when I got inside the Kronberg building a few weeks ago."

He'd known where to go, known where the safe would be hidden. It had been as though his feet could remember what his head couldn't. It might be the same in Paris. His body might recall the terrible things that happened that day. But he would need Green to set him on the path. There might be a way around it though.

"You can give me everything you know about where I was in Paris. Roni didn't know the address, but she gave me some landmarks. I think you know exactly where I was. Tell me," he said. "I'll take it from there."

After all, he hadn't needed anyone with him in the Kronberg building. He'd made that happen. Maybe he could mitigate the risk.

Green shook his head. "No. I'm going with you."

Ezra's eyes narrowed. "Or I could beat it out of you."

"You think I can't take a beating? How long do you have? A few minutes before Solo shows up again and you have to get physical with her? You won't like that. She will fight you on this. You ready for it? Because I survived weeks with some of the best torturers imaginable, and guess what? I. Didn't. Break. I won't break because I've waited too long for this. I'd rather die than stop now. How about you, Timmy? You got your brother back so it's okay for the girl to die?"

"I swear to god, I'll kill you if you stab me in the back," Tucker swore.

Ezra's head fell forward with a groan. "She's going to kill me, but I don't see another way out. Call Owen. Leave Damon out of it. He needs plausible deniability, but tell Owen to get his ass to Paris. You'll need support. I'll get to France if I can."

But he might not be able to because Solo might take him into custody for what they were about to do. They were fucking her over and hard. She might lose her job over it. And he would do it to save Roni.

He would do anything to save her. But Ezra was missing one important point. "How will they contact us? He didn't leave a note. Rob and I dumped our cells. Won't he have to contact Damon?"

Ezra reached into his pocket and came up with a cell phone. It was the cheap kind that wasn't registered. "I found it by Nina's body. I slipped it in my pocket or Solo would have insisted on keeping it."

"You knew exactly what you were going to do the minute you realized someone had taken Veronica Croft," Green said in a silky tone. "You might have been out of the game for a while, but you haven't forgotten how to play. Now go and do what you need to do. I'll take care of this. I promise on my honor I'll do everything I can to help Tucker find that intelligence. And bring it back to you."

"You don't have any honor," Ezra said.

"But I do, and I mean what I say," Green shot back. "I won't even try to get away, and you know why. Because you're about to distract her, and she won't ever forgive you for that. She'll understand exactly what you did, and it will break her in a way you haven't yet. That's where I'll slip in. I'll come back and give her what she needs, and I'll be the hero."

Ezra's hands fisted. "Somehow I doubt that. Not that she'll be angry with me, but that she'll turn to you."

"But that's exactly what she does when she's upset with you," Green crooned.

"Do you want him to murder you, asshole?" He needed to shut this down.

Green's eyes slid to the floor. "No. I'm sorry. I can't help it around him. I meant what I said. I will help you, Tucker. I owe you. I was the reason you were in Paris. Let's finish this op once and for all."

Tucker nodded. He couldn't find it in him to speak. He knew he was making a deal with the devil, but he was out of options.

"Ariel's going to kill me," Robert said with a sigh. "I'll make the calls. There's a Land Rover in the garage and I know where the keys are. We have to move before my wife gets back. She won't like this."

"I'll go alone. I don't want to come between you and your wife," he said.

"I said she wouldn't like it, not that she won't understand. I'll ask forgiveness not permission," Robert said resolutely.

"And I'll handle Solo." Ezra moved to the stairs again, a grim look on his face. "Contact me on the secure line when you can. I'll be back in London by morning. If I'm not on my way to DC."

Because Solo would have every reason to turn him in for betraying her. "If there was any other way…"

"There isn't and we have very little time. Keep that phone on you at all times," Ezra ordered. "It's how Arthur Dwyer will contact you. I'll work on getting Jax out in case we need to go to ground."

In case they failed. If he failed, he took a lot of good people with him.

"I'll meet you out back in ten," Robert promised.

Ezra handed him the keys to Levi's prison. "Good luck."

He was alone with the devil. He was going to need it.

* * * *

Roni's head throbbed but she kept as quiet as she could because no blow to the head could possibly make her forget the nightmare she found herself in. Misery swamped her, but she forced herself to focus.

What had her mother taught her? Assess the situation.

She was moving. She could feel the motion of a car, but she was in complete darkness. Her hands were tied, but she could move her feet. There was a faint hint of gasoline and the muffled sound of a man speaking.

Trunk. She was in the trunk of a car, likely whatever Arthur had waiting for him.

How long had she been out? Were they still in England? Or had he made the crossing into France, from where he would have the ease to go almost anywhere in Europe a road connected to.

Did Tucker know she was gone? Did he care? Or had she killed whatever he'd felt for her with her doubt?

It was funny that now she didn't have a single doubt in her mind. She knew Nina was right. Tucker and her sister had been trying to protect her as best they could. They'd been the ones who had paid and they'd managed to spare her. She couldn't be angry. When she thought about it, she likely would have done the same thing.

But none of that mattered now because she was being driven away from him. Fast.

She'd assessed her situation. Fucked. That was the only way to describe it.

Now it was time to figure out what her assets were. Was there anything she could use to help get herself out of the situation?

Suddenly having a locator in her butt actually did seem like a plus. If this was Tucker being stolen away, she could find him. He'd sounded insane that first day when he'd told her it was one of the things he brought to the table, but now she got it. He'd been in this position more than once, and having a GPS locator inserted into his body was a must.

She breathed in, trying to find a calm place. Panic wouldn't serve her in any way. She needed a cool head. They wouldn't kill her right away. They would try to get Tucker to turn himself over or turn over the intelligence she was absolutely sure he didn't have.

Did they think he was lying?

How old was the vehicle she was in? Newer vehicles had trunk releases in case someone got caught. If she could locate it, she might risk rolling herself out of the car when it slowed down.

It was so dark she couldn't tell what direction she was facing. She reached out, trying to get a sense of how big the trunk was. She was facing inward. As gently as she could, she turned her body, head aching with every move.

Arthur was speaking in German. She didn't hear a response. He was likely on the phone. She listened for a moment, but it was hard to hear over the hum of the engine and the drone of tires beating against the road.

He was saying something about how he had to do it. The situation was getting out of hand. It wouldn't work without the drugs and…she lost part of the conversation. Arthur mentioned her and how she was the key to getting Reasor to play ball.

Playing ball meant submitting to the drugs they wanted him to take. They wanted to be in control of his memories. He said something about what would happen if Tucker remembered and named names. They wouldn't have anywhere to hide. They needed control.

She reached out, trying to feel for the release latch. Tucker would trade himself. There was no question in her mind he would do it. Even if he was angry with her, he would be there, trying to ensure her safety. He would do it for his daughter.

Hell, he would do it for the woman who'd accused him of being a bad guy. He would do it because he was a good guy.

The car started to slow and Arthur said something about being close.

Close to what? Were they near whatever place he intended to keep her in? Or was he turning her over to even worse people?

They wouldn't let her live. Any more than they would let Tucker live after he gave them what they wanted.

Her heart was beating in her chest, so hard she worried he would be able to hear it. The car was rolling to a stop. She worked, feeling for anything that might help her. She would run. It didn't matter that her hands were tied. She would run and hide and find a way to survive.

It was all that mattered. Getting back to Tucker and Vi was all that mattered.

The car rolled to a stop and she still hadn't found the lever. It was hard to maneuver her body. She twisted but couldn't get her hands where she needed them to be. Frustration welled, threatening to merge with the panic she hadn't quite banished. It made a big comeback as she heard the door come open and close.

One shot. She would have one shot at this. Her legs were the only weapons she had. She would have to kick out and get to the ground, run as fast as she could without even knowing where she was going.

She had to take the chance. There was nothing else to do except fight. Tucker needed her.

She had to force herself to breathe as the trunk started to come open. She tried to kick her legs out, but strong arms caught her and she felt the pain of a needle penetrating her leg, and the world immediately went fuzzy.

"Sorry, Veronica," Arthur said. "I can't allow you to leave. My name is on that list."

As she started to go under, she knew she'd been right. They would never let any of them live.

Chapter Fifteen

Tucker looked up and down the street, praying he recognized anything at all.

Nothing. It was a lovely morning in Paris and the people were already out en masse, walking into the gardens that ran the length from the Place de la Concorde to the Louvre. Tourists with cameras mingled with locals carrying their coffees and walking their dogs.

He wanted to walk through the park with Veronica. They might not be able to come back to Europe for a long time. Of course if they did take a nice traipse through the park, it might be the last thing they did.

How did he explain to his newly committed girlfriend that he'd just made a drop to a CIA agent and they had to run because all of their old colleagues would want to kill him now and hey, how about a June wedding? Wyoming was nice that time of year.

Tucker stopped, the feeling so clear in his head that it could have happened yesterday. He'd stood in front of the gardens and known that it was almost over.

"Don't," a familiar voice said. "He's got the scent of something."

"It would be easier if you would point out the damn apartment building," Robert groused.

"And then he wouldn't have these lovely moments where he looks like a zombie," Green shot back.

Levi Green was an asshole but he hadn't tried anything.

Yet.

He shook his head, letting the feeling go because he was on a clock and he couldn't afford to get sick. He had less than four hours to turn himself over to Arthur Dwyer or they would start sending him Veronica's body parts.

They'd already sent him a video of her. She'd been tied up and unconscious, only the faint rise and fall of her chest reassuring him that she was alive.

Would she still be alive at this time tomorrow? Would he?

"Hey, you okay?"

His brother had been with him the whole way. Robert had driven hours during the long night it had taken to get them to Paris. Much of that time had been spent with Big Tag screaming at them over a cell phone. He'd used words Tucker hadn't ever thought could be intimidating, but when Tag got going, he could really let his rage flow.

He nodded his brother's way. "Yeah, but Green's right. I'm starting to get a sense of the place. I've definitely been here before. I've been in this park. We're close to the apartment I took Roni to. I think it was Levi's place."

Green was wearing jeans and a T-shirt he'd borrowed from Robert. They were both slightly too big for him, and he'd complained endlessly about how basic they were. Tucker wasn't sure why basic was a bad thing, but it was the height of horror for Green. All in all, as road trip partners went, Green was an asshole. The man loved to listen to himself talk, but not about what they wanted him to talk about. He'd refused to divulge anything important, but he'd talked a lot about his many missions and how smart he was.

If he got shot, Tucker wasn't going to save him. Well, he would try because he'd taken a Hippocratic oath, but he probably wouldn't try too hard. Was it wrong to call time of death while the patient was still breathing?

"We should find the hotel." Robert was looking down at his cell phone. "Owen said he's already here and he found a place for us to

Long Lost

stay."

"Or we could stay at my flat," Green offered. "It's close."

Robert's eyes rolled. "Yeah, look, man, I've been up for hours and my wife is ready to hand me my balls. I'm not up for playing Where's Waldo's French Flat. I know we don't have long, but we all need a nap and some food. MI6 is pissed, and according to Damon, they think they might have a lead on Dwyer."

He didn't need a lead on Dwyer. Dwyer would find him. Dwyer might already be here, following him as he proved to be completely useless.

He stared out at the entrance to the garden for a moment. There was a merry-go-round just inside the gates with happy children bouncing on their seats as it went around and around.

Violet would like that.

Violet had been conceived in this city. Not far from here. He was close, but they were on the wrong side of the gardens. Yes. They were very close. He needed to stop thinking about it and let himself go.

"Any word from Ezra?" He moved down the steps, certain his brother would follow him.

"Hey, I thought we were going..." Robert sighed and fell in step beside him. "He texted a few minutes ago. He's going to try to get here later today, but Solo is pissed. She hasn't had him arrested though."

"She won't," Green said, taking up on the other side of Tucker. "I was lying about that. I don't think she could ever be angry enough with him that she would put his life at risk. I often think Solo's childhood led her to a bad place as an adult. She's not able to recognize real love."

"When it slaps her in the face?" Robert asked pointedly.

"I regret that." Green managed to sound remorseful but then again, if there was one thing he'd learned about the man it was that he was an excellent actor. "Solo and I can be quite passionate when it comes to our relationship. It's a bit twisted but it's real. Far more real than anything she has with Beck."

He'd talked about his girlfriend back then. Kim. They'd gotten to know each other during the training sessions Green had insisted on. Tucker had bemoaned the fact that his residency didn't leave much time for a romantic life, and Levi had countered with what happened

271

when two CIA agents were in love and on different continents.

How long had the man been delusional?

How long had he been plotting to get Solo?

It was starting to come back to him, those months he'd spent prepping. Being around Green without bars between them was doing something to him. It was making it far easier to be back in those moments.

"We prepped for the op. You and me," he said, the path crunching beneath his feet.

"Yes, we did." Green's voice remained perfectly calm. Of the three of them only Green seemed unaffected by the drama playing out around him. "You were in physically good shape, but I thought you needed some defensive training. You knew how to use a rifle, but you weren't good with a handgun."

"We didn't have handguns at home." Though he remembered the gun case where his mom kept two shotguns and their granddad's rifle. They lived outside of town where it was beautiful and quiet and there were far more animals than people, some of which wouldn't mind eating him.

"What's your impression of how long we trained?" Green asked.

Tucker let himself walk as his mind roamed. He didn't think about where he was going. "It was a couple of months, I think. I know we met in Boston. I can remember that meeting. I remember how I felt." It flowed over him easily now. He didn't have to fight for it. He could feel the breeze coming off the river and he'd wondered if it was cool where Russ was. "I was hopeful for the first time in months. For the first time since I'd been told my brother died."

"I had been investigating some incidents surrounding classified intelligence getting out. I won't go into it too much, but troop movements were being leaked or sold. That investigation led me to Senator Hank McDonald, and that's when I started watching his daughters. Faith was of no interest to me, but Hope was."

Green had showed him a picture of Hope McDonald that day. The first time he'd seen her. "I thought she looked harmless."

"And I told you that was precisely why she was so dangerous," Green confirmed.

He turned down a path, the memories whirling in his brain. "You were the first person to believe me when I said I thought my brother was alive."

"How did you know I was alive?" Robert asked. "I've looked at the report on how my unit died. I didn't see anything that would raise a red flag. Emily did a good job."

"Oh, she didn't fake that report," Levi corrected. "That was all Hank McDonald's doing. He had connections in the military, corrupt individuals who sold out their fellow soldiers for the cash he was offering. I took care of them, by the way. It was a fun weekend project."

He stopped and stared at Levi.

"Hey, I'm a lot of things, but I don't sell out soldiers, and before you say anything Ezra isn't a soldier and we're at war," Levi said with a shrug. "I keep telling you I'm not the bad guy here. Taggart and his crew might have handled the McDonalds, but there were plenty of people they missed. Retribution shouldn't simply be saved for the head of the snake. There was a body and a tail to chop up, too."

"But not Emily. I find it interesting that she was still hanging around." Robert's arms crossed over his chest.

"She had a role to play. When Tucker didn't show up for our meeting, I realized it had gone to hell and McDonald had him and she had the intel. I had nothing without that intel," Green admitted. "I wasn't exactly working on the books."

"The Agency wouldn't have approved sending me in." It was the only reason he could think of.

"There were members of the Agency who were well versed in what McDonald was doing. I found that out fairly quickly," Levi admitted. "I had to work around people in my own group. I did not agree with the methods McDonald used, and I really didn't like American soldiers getting treated like guinea pigs."

But he seemed to have changed his mind. "You've been chasing down her research ever since. Somehow I don't think you're going to destroy it."

Another negligent shrug of his shoulders. "Destroying McDonald's research won't bring back the dead. It's out there and someone will use it. I'll feel safer if it's in the right hands."

"Yours," Robert surmised.

"Mine are better than most. Tucker, do you want me to apologize for abandoning you? Should I have invaded McDonald's compound to rescue you? First off, you wouldn't have even known who I was."

If you do this and things go bad, I'll have to disavow any knowledge of you. You'll be on a tightrope, Tim, and there won't be any kind of safety net for you.

He'd been warned and he'd done it anyway. He'd had to. "I don't need an apology. You were upfront about what could happen. You didn't sugarcoat anything. You needed someone who wasn't on the agency's radar to infiltrate McDonald's operation. You had solid proof that Robert was with her. You showed me surveillance footage. And Robert, I knew you weren't dead because I went to the site of where your supposed accident occurred and talked to some of the locals. There was no accident that day."

It was coming back in rapid flashes now. He'd gone into a damn warzone because he'd needed to feel close to his brother, needed to be where he'd died.

"He went in with a charitable group." Green sounded almost proud. "He used the fact that he was a doctor to get into a place no one else could have gone. I got a report about an American in that area causing trouble. I investigated and when I realized what he was looking for, I knew I had my guy."

"What happened to the rest of my unit?" Robert asked.

"I can't be completely sure," Levi began. "But I believe they went into McDonald's program. They were some of her first subjects. You were the only one who survived. I think that's why you were her favorite. You were one of the first to handle the therapies well."

"I wish I could have saved them." He hated the idea that his brother's friends had been dying while he'd been working or sleeping or doing anything at all normal.

"When I think about what you gave up," Robert began.

He shook his head. "I would do it all again." He found himself on the other side of the park. He'd walked across, not lengthwise but through the middle.

He was here.

"It's on the second floor." He stared up at the elegant building with stone steps. He could see Roni there. She'd stopped at the top of the stairs and he'd had his breath taken away because she'd been so beautiful, and he'd known that his job was almost done.

Green nodded. "Yes. I don't own it anymore. I gave it up after you went missing. The heat was on when McDonald left Kronberg. I had to cool my heels for a while. I knew what had happened when you didn't show up for our meeting. I knew she had you. I honestly figured she'd gotten the intelligence and that was why she left Kronberg so quickly after."

"You didn't bother to look for him?" Robert was staring up at the building, too.

"I knew where he was. I knew he was in Argentina. Again, should I have stormed the building and given up everything for a man who no longer remembered who I was?" Green glanced down at his watch. "We're down to three hours now. I personally don't care if we get Veronica back, but it seems like a deal breaker for you."

You did what? You do understand if she sees me the whole fucking thing could blow up in our faces. She's met me before. She thinks I'm fucking her sister. Do you even remember why you're here?

"We were supposed to meet here, but I brought Veronica." Green had been angry with him, but he couldn't have left her behind. He'd intended to tell her everything when they got free. "Katie Croft was working with us."

"Yes, she was. She had a lot of information about Kronberg, but she had no real idea what to do with it. She couldn't corroborate it enough to report it, but she could give it to us to help our investigation. You were key to getting her to talk to us." Green leaned against the half wall that separated the building from the sidewalk. "You did an excellent job convincing her. You played the 'do it for your country' card. I think the fact that her mother was a soldier helped her along. She was trying to make Mommy proud."

"I told you there was no way you slept with her," Robert said.

"Of course he didn't," Green agreed. "No, he had a professional relationship with Katie. She wasn't the problem."

"If you say one more word against…"

He could feel the cell phone in his hand. It was early. The sun wasn't up. He'd stood right here and argued with Levi Green about where they would meet since he'd fucked everything up.

In a heartbeat, he was back in the past.

Three years before

Timothy Seeger held the phone to his ear and glanced back up at the building, wishing he didn't have to leave. The night before had been everything he'd thought it could be. Roni was the one.

His brother would love her. So would his mom. God, if this worked, they would be a family again soon.

Russ would have problems. Given what he knew about the drugs McDonald had used on his brother, he wasn't fooling himself. They would face an uphill battle when they got Russell back, but they *would* get him back.

"Do you even remember why you're here?" Levi did not bother to hide his irritation with the situation.

"I know I changed the plan, but after what happened with Rebecca Walsh, I couldn't leave Veronica behind." It still made him sick to think about what he'd done to Dr. Walsh, but he'd had to step in. Dr. Walsh had been ready to leave. Hope McDonald had given her a dose of the time dilation drug in a mad attempt to convince Walsh to stay. She'd needed Rebecca's genius. For all her cold ruthlessness, McDonald lost her shit from time to time. She'd panicked at the thought of Rebecca leaving and tried a partial memory wipe. It hadn't worked and that was when they'd started to talk about killing the pretty doctor. He'd offered them an alternative.

It had been up to him to ensure Rebecca ran and never looked back. He'd used a virtual reality headset to simulate hurting the doctor. He'd known the memories would be vague and murky, and they wouldn't jive with her physical health, but it had worked. Rebecca was safely back in the States.

He couldn't put Roni through the same thing.

A long sigh came over the line. "McDonald doesn't give a damn about your girlfriend. She couldn't care less. Do you know who she does care about? You. And now we have to meet in the open because I can't show up at my own damn safe house."

He couldn't help it. He wasn't going to risk Roni. He was too close to getting everything he wanted. What he wasn't about to tell Levi was that he wasn't going back to Munich. McDonald was acting suspicious, and he wasn't entirely sure she didn't know something was going on with him. It was there in the way he caught her staring at him—like she had plans. McDonald's plans always involved pain. "Tell me where to meet you. I've got a flight back this evening. I would like to spend some time looking like the tourist I'm supposed to be."

"Meet me at Père Lachaise Cemetery. Go in the main entrance and walk straight up the main street. It will take you to a monument. You can't miss it. It's quiet at this time of the morning. We should be able to talk without being overheard. Take the Métro. I'll be waiting for you there at nine. And watch your back. McDonald isn't in Munich right now."

"She's getting the lab in Argentina ready." She'd been planning on moving Dr. Walsh there. If she'd accepted the job, Rebecca Walsh would have found herself a prisoner. She would have been forced to work or die. McDonald thought she was close to a breakthrough, and she wasn't about to let a thing like ethics keep her from getting what she needed.

Was his brother in that lab in Argentina?

"I hope so. I don't like not having eyes on her," Levi admitted. "I'll see you in an hour and maybe we can talk about how to use this to get your brother. Things are shaking out in a way I hadn't planned. There's a group in Dallas I'm worried is about to make a move."

Levi had been talking about some ex-military guys getting involved because their brother had gone missing. "I thought the Taggarts believed Theo is dead."

He wasn't. Tim had seen the man not a few weeks before. McDonald had brought him in to work with Dr. Walsh.

"It would have been best for me if they did," Levi admitted. "I don't need that group fucking things up. I've had this planned for a very long time."

"I don't see why we couldn't do this back in Munich." Things would have been far easier if he'd made the handoff and gone straight to the States.

"Well, I'm sorry my day job is inconveniencing you," Levi shot back. "I've got more than one operation I'm working on. You're lucky I could get into Paris today."

The line went dead and he took a deep breath. He glanced back up to where Veronica was sleeping. She'd looked so delicious wrapped up in the blanket, her hair spread out across the pillow.

He would tell her everything this afternoon and pray she forgave him.

Forty minutes later, he jogged up the steps that led him out of the Père Lachaise Métro station along with what seemed like half of Paris. It was easy to get lost in a city this size, but it was also why it was good cover. He'd dressed for the occasion, a ballcap covering his head and plain T-shirt, jeans, and boots. He could be anyone.

He glanced at the café across the street and realized why Levi hadn't picked it as their meeting place. It was mobbed. Sometimes chaos was good, but not in this case. They needed to talk. He had a flash drive to pass off. The last thing he needed to do was drop the drive in the crush of bodies.

The flash drive in his pocket was the most important thing he'd ever done. It was proof of what was happening at Kronberg. Everything he'd observed and documented was in his report. The whole of Katie Croft's investigation was documented there. Conversations he'd managed to record were on that flash drive. All those names, all the people, companies and politicians who supported the McDonalds. There were even a couple of CIA agents' names in there. Levi had made sure his people got called out, too. Levi had been open and honest about the corruption in his own organization.

He was going to owe Levi Green so much.

He oriented himself and started walking toward the main entrance of the famous Paris cemetery. Tall white stone walls rose to the sides. He glanced down at his watch. He was early but he still found himself walking to the entrance. The minute he walked past the main gate it was like the world receded. The bustle of the street outside was replaced with an odd quiet.

An almost eerie quiet.

Levi had been right. The place was almost empty at this time of the morning. It wasn't tourist season, though there were always tourists in Paris. A chill was in the air as he started up the stone path that promised to lead to the monument known as the *Au Morts de la Commune*. He'd had some time on the Métro to look it up.

On either side of him were monuments to the dead. They looked like small stone rooms in the middle of the forest, some ornate, others much simpler.

It was utterly unlike anything they had in Wyoming. His grandfather's grave was a simple thing. The cemetery there was small. It was pretty, but nothing at all like the lush garden that was the Père Lachaise.

Russell had a headstone there. Beloved Husband, Son, and Brother. If he was right about Emily, he was damn glad there wasn't a body buried there because he would have to change that stone. Emily had ties to the McDonalds. He was almost certain she'd had a hand in what happened to his brother. She hadn't loved Russ at all.

Veronica would love him. He was going to marry her and have kids with her. Three would be good. He'd loved having a brother, but sometimes brothers got in trouble and it would have been awesome to have another one to have shared this particular load. So three it was.

He felt a goofy smile cross his face. He was stupid in love.

She might like this place. It was peaceful. He could hear birds calling. Their sound split the silence in an eerie way. Even the people around him seemed to move solemnly.

There was a road wide enough for cars that seemed to lead to the monument where he would meet Green. There was a single van parked to his left. He moved quickly past it. It was likely a service van of some sort, though he noticed the tinted windows.

He should have grabbed a cup of coffee.

He trudged up the road as it gently ascended. He would make this as quick as possible, get back to Roni, and get to the airport where they would find the first flight that could get them to the States. It would be so fucking good to be Tim Seeger again. How fast could Levi Green turn his real identity on? He wouldn't be able to go back to Mass General, but he could finish out his residency in Laramie and be close to home. Be close to his brother.

When they took down McDonald, he would get his brother back. He had to believe that. He had to trust that Green would do what he'd promised and save Russ.

Up ahead he saw the place he would meet Levi in about twenty minutes. He took a deep breath and tried to banish the anxiety playing in his brain. He felt like someone was watching him, but then he'd felt that way ever since the day he'd accepted the job at Kronberg and gone undercover.

He didn't like that van.

He moved off the main road, taking a right and walking on one of the smaller paths. The path here wasn't cobbled. It was well-worn dirt and gravel, the graves and tombs seemingly hundreds of years old. Some of them were phone-booth sized, the doors on the front mostly closed and locked, though he could see through the fronts. There was no glass in the windows so a person who wanted to could see inside to the stones that marked the actual grave. Some of the tombs had chairs inside or old planters where once flowers had grown. The spaces were dark, disuse apparent.

His mother kept Russell's grave perfect, despite the fact his body wasn't there. She went to the headstone once a week and laid out flowers as though she needed the connection to her son no matter what it was.

He was getting maudlin.

"Hello, brother."

The sound made him turn and then his heart threatened to stop in his chest.

Tall, with broad shoulders and a jaw that could have come from a comic book hero. His brother. "Russ?"

Was he dreaming? Had all of this been one long dream and he was back in bed with Veronica?

Russell's lips turned up in a grim smile. "No. My name is Robert. I'm sorry you've been neglected, brother. Mother told me you were left behind on a mission. It was an accident. Apparently, it was my fault. You know how the meds can be. I forget things. I won't do it again."

What the hell? His brother was standing right there and yet every word that came from his mouth sounded wrong. "Russell. Your name is Russell Seeger and I'm your brother, Tim. You are from Wyoming. You were in the Army when a woman named Hope McDonald kidnapped you."

He wanted to reach out and get a hand on him. If he could just put a hand on his brother, he could know he was real. He looked leaner, his body more sculpted than it had been even during his Army days.

"I know what you're trying to do," Russ said with what sounded like sympathy. "It's hard when you haven't had your meds for a long time, but I'm not leaving you alone. I promise, it's going to be fine when we get back to base. And please, call me Robert."

His body seemed to go cold. This was his brother, but he didn't know this man. This man stared at him like they hadn't spent their lives together, like they hadn't built pillow forts and chased each other across the lawn, like they hadn't sat up at night and wondered where their dad had gone.

"Your name is Russ," he said as though he had to remind himself. This was his brother. This was Russell and he could save him. He could find his way back. "Mom misses you so much."

His brain had started to function again, the shock of seeing his brother giving way to questions. Why the hell was his brother here?

He glanced behind him and sure enough, they weren't alone. A big man with dark hair was walking up the path behind him. They'd been following him, waiting for a chance to get him in between them.

McDonald was here and she'd sent her boys after him.

"Please, Russ, you have to listen to me. You don't understand what's going on," he pleaded, his heart rate tripling. This couldn't be happening. Not now. Not when he was so fucking close to getting out.

He couldn't be killed by his own brother.

"Mother can't miss me. I'm with her all the time," the man in Russell's body said with a humorless chuckle. "It's you she misses. I know you don't remember it but you're part of a team, and it's time for you to come home now. You're off your medications and it's making everything seem confusing."

That was her game? He stood in the middle of the path, the dead all around him. It was the living that he was worried about. The big man who'd come up at his back was still, a predator waiting for the right time to pounce. "I'm not the one who's confused. She's feeding you a ton of drugs. She's lying to you both. She took away your memories. Do you honestly believe you were born fully grown in a lab?"

If he could reach his brother, make him see some reason, there might be hope.

"Of course not." Russell started to move his way. "Everything is going to be so much clearer when you're back on your meds. Dante, don't you dare hurt him. You know Mother wants him brought in alive."

"She said alive," Dante replied with a shrug. "She didn't say we couldn't play with him a bit."

Dante lunged and Tim took off, leaping over a stone tomb and hitting the ground on the other side. His knees hit the soft earth and he forced himself up. He had to move and keep moving until he could find a way out. There weren't enough people here and he would bet anything his brother and Dante had continued their training. They would be lethal, and they likely wouldn't mind hurting a few tourists to complete their mission.

He needed to get back to the street where he could lose himself in the crowd. They wouldn't want to bring attention to themselves.

He had to shove his way between tombs to get to a parallel path.

He turned to his left, but Dante was already there. He took off to the right as his brother managed to make it through the thicket. He shoved at Russell, rushing past him and turning the first chance he got. Where was he? He had to get back to the main road. It was his best chance, but he could hear them running behind. He cut through another set of graves, scrambling over low tombs. He was confused and probably heading the wrong direction since the path he found himself on started to climb.

"Don't do this, Tucker." Russ's voice rang out. "That's your name, you know. Mother said you likely don't even remember your own name."

He slowed down because they hadn't caught up to him yet. He slid his body between two standing tombs. They were so close together he could barely manage it.

"Which way did he go?" Dante asked in what sounded like a thick Eastern European accent. "You know what she'll do if we fail."

"I'm not going to fail," Russ replied. "I won't let another brother down."

Emotion welled inside him at those words. He was letting his brother down by hiding, but he needed more time. He couldn't let McDonald take him.

If McDonald knew about him…had she already taken Veronica? Had she been waiting when he walked out?

Don't let her be dead. She can't be dead.

He bit back bile. How soon would Levi be here? He needed to find the monument. That's where Levi was supposed to meet him.

Levi would be ready for this. All he had to do was get away.

And if he didn't?

He reached into the pocket of his jeans and felt the thumb drive.

If she got it, there would be no need for him. If he hid it, he had something to hold over her. He could buy himself time, time to save Roni.

"He's hiding," Dante said. "He didn't get away. He's in one of these bushes or he's gotten inside the tombs."

The standing tomb in front of him had elaborate grating. If he went up on his toes, he could push the drive through. If this was one of the older tombs, there might not be maintenance to sweep the inside. The little drive might survive.

He might survive. He couldn't get caught with that drive on him. McDonald would have everything she wanted and no reason at all to keep him or Roni alive. If she thought Roni knew anything at all, she would take her out or use her in her experiments. That couldn't happen.

He could hear someone moving behind him. He had to run again or they would be on him.

He pressed up and let the drive slip through the grate.

He turned and started to run.

And was tackled from behind. He hit the ground with a sickening thud, all the air leaving his lungs.

"It's going to be okay. You'll see."

His brother. He was getting taken down by the very person he'd come to find. So close.

"Very good, Robert," a familiar voice said. "Though you could have taken him closer to the van. Now we have to get him all the way back. Or you could go and ask Tomas to move the van a bit closer. That would be best."

"Dante can do it," Russell said. He could feel his brother's knee on his back, keeping him right there in the dirt.

"That's not what I asked, Robert." McDonald stepped onto the path. He could see her shoes. High heels even in the middle of a deadly chase, but then she hadn't really been the one chasing. She'd done what she loved to do, ordered someone else to do her dirty work.

The knee on his back eased up and he found himself hauled to his feet by the big dark-haired man his brother had called Dante.

"Russell," he started to shout but felt something hard against his spine.

"I can shoot you and you'll still live," Dante whispered.

It didn't matter because his brother never looked back.

"Hello, Steven," McDonald said, looking him over. "I was surprised to hear you came to Paris. I was even more surprised to hear you talking to that man on the phone. Who is he?"

She'd duped his phone? He was usually careful about it, but phones weren't allowed in the labs, and she could have gotten to it in the locker where he left it. That explained how she'd known where he would be. "He's a friend of mine."

"He's a CIA agent, I suspect," McDonald said.

"I don't know what you're talking about." He couldn't give Levi up.

She waved it off. "If you think I don't have my own CIA contacts, you're more naïve than I thought. So the Agency has some leaks it seems. I'll have to deal with that. It's harder since that bastard killed my father, but I'll make it work."

"How long have you been watching me?" He wanted to know how long he'd been fucked.

"Oh, Kronberg has had someone watching you for days now," she said. "Ever since that incident with Rebecca. It was kind of you to handle that for me. I didn't realize how seriously they would take her defection. You probably saved me a major headache. I was going to kill the bitch. I think that would have gotten me in trouble. Instead you're the one who got in trouble. The man they put in charge of investigating is a smart man. He came to me when he realized you were talking to that reporter. You know she's Veronica's sister, right?"

"Of course." He had to protect Veronica. She was completely innocent in all of this. God, he loved her and she didn't even know his real name. "I've been seeing Veronica on the sly. Wouldn't do to let anyone know I'm fucking the underlings." He smirked, an expression he'd perfected over his time as Steven Reasor. "Her sister lives in Munich. She's a kook, a crazy conspiracy theorist, but she's harmless enough. Now let's negotiate. I'm meeting with another pharmaceutical firm. You're right about the CIA guy. He wants information about Kronberg. He's going to use his influence to get me on somewhere else. All I have to do is a little espionage. I'm sick of Kronberg and I'm sick of you putting women like Rebecca Walsh above me."

She stared at him for a moment. "You fooled me. Not many people can manage to do that. I will admit, I find it fascinating. The man on the phone told you to remember why you're here, but he didn't mention the reason. I'm curious."

That wasn't a good thing since she was a woman who liked to study the things she found fascinating. Usually by cutting them up and examining the pieces. "I told you. I'm here to trade information about Kronberg for a new job. Are you going to kill me over it?"

He was trying to be as cool as he could. He wasn't going to give up information if he didn't have to. It was obvious she hadn't been listening in for long. He'd been careful. Not careful enough, but perhaps she truly didn't understand what he was doing here today.

"He called Robert Russell," the man with the gun to his spine said. "Isn't that his real name?"

Shit. He'd forgotten he'd already given himself away. Maybe he could still work this. "Sorry, he looked like someone I used to know. And then he attacked me. I didn't realize you were sending your...who are these assholes? Bodyguards? Henchmen?"

"Dante handles certain problems for me," she explained. "As far as Robert knows, Dante is just like him and Victor and Tomas. I've got another site. One not even Kronberg knows about. I keep a few of my boys there. Robert is special. But then you know that, don't you? So you're his brother. That's how the CIA agent got to you. How did you find him?"

"I told you," he started, but Dante's hand twisted his arm.

"It doesn't matter. I'll figure it out one way or another," she promised. "I believe Robert has the car here. It's time for you to meet Tomas, though I suppose you'll try to call him Theo."

He started to struggle, but Dante wrapped a meaty hand around his throat. "I heard you. I know the truth. If you don't get into the van quietly, I'll kill Robert. Will you watch your brother die?"

He knew the answer to that. He couldn't do it. McDonald had questions and that meant he would have a shot to get out. Levi would know something was wrong when he didn't show up for their meeting. Levi would find him and save both him and his brother.

He forced himself to get into that van.

It would be all right.

It had to be.

Tucker blinked into the bright light of the midday sun. That day so long ago had come back in vivid color. His heart was racing as it had done that day, beating against his chest until he'd been knocked out. When he'd come to, he'd found a whole new world of agony.

"Hey, you okay?" Robert asked.

He looked to his brother who would never know he'd been the one to turn him over. He wouldn't put that guilt on him. Both Robert and Levi were looking at him expectantly.

"Yes, and I know where to schedule the meeting with Arthur Dwyer."

He would get his girl back and then he was going to take them all down.

Chapter Sixteen

Veronica had learned a lot about Arthur Dwyer in the day she'd been held by him. He was a brilliant doctor. He was a terrible criminal.

Unfortunately, even terrible criminals could get in a lucky shot from time to time.

"You're staying here," Arthur said from his seat in the front of the vehicle. He wasn't driving. Kronberg had sent two security team members with Arthur and they had become her watchers. One of them had been with her every moment of the day. She'd woken up on a bed and it hadn't taken her long to figure out she was in Paris. She'd listened to her captors, who seemed to think they could talk all they liked in German. Kronberg kept the apartment for their executives and they were awaiting the outcome of Arthur's endeavor. But the bed was nice and she would have been entirely comfortable if she hadn't had her wrists and feet bound.

"I'll take Kurt with me," Arthur continued. "Your boyfriend claims he remembers where he hid the thumb drive he stole. When we have the data, we'll bring Reasor back here."

The man named Kurt frowned. "How will we be sure he doesn't have a copy of the data?"

"Well, I wasn't planning on giving him the girl. I was planning on letting him see the girl, then you'll give him a dose of the sedative, and we'll have a long talk about corporate espionage," Arthur explained. "I'll have to figure out how to deal with our own intelligence agency. According to the CEO, they're not happy with my play. If I can clean up the data and give them a sanitized version with all the proper scapegoats, perhaps they'll forgive my hasty actions."

She would have said something about how it wouldn't work because there was no way Tucker hadn't shared what he'd found with his group before turning it over, but she was gagged. She didn't think he would appreciate her logic anyway.

But she was worried because Tucker would absolutely turn over whatever he had, and he would come to this car looking for her. He would put himself at risk. For all Arthur was a moron when it came to criminal enterprise, if he managed to get Tucker in this car, he would be able to pass him off to more competent people and they would both be in trouble.

She'd been so wrong. It had been all she could think about since the moment Arthur had captured her. She'd been stupid to doubt Tucker. If only she'd had a little faith, Nina wouldn't have been shot and they wouldn't be in this position.

She would have to find a way to warn him what Arthur was planning.

She glanced out the tinted windows of the van they'd placed her in. She couldn't tell where they were except that the streets were crowded. It looked like some kind of park.

"Keep her quiet," Arthur instructed. "If she makes trouble, dose her again, but don't kill her. I'm going to need her alive. I think our friend will speak much more freely if we've got the mother of his child as a hostage. It's too bad we couldn't nab the kid."

She hated that man.

"I'll be back soon." Arthur and Kurt got out of the car and she was left alone with the guard they'd called Oskar.

He sat in the driver's seat and stared straight ahead.

Her hands were bound on her lap and she was pretty sure she'd lost all feeling in them. She might have nerve damage. They hadn't cared about her circulation the way Tucker had.

God, would he ever forgive her? She'd put them in this position. She'd made him risk everything he'd worked for. Had he been able to find the data or was he lying?

He would lie to save her. He might walk away from her afterward, but he would never leave her in this position.

How long would it be? How long would she be sitting here waiting for him?

Damn it, she had to do something. She couldn't sit here and let him sacrifice himself for her. She was not this girl.

The back door was child locked and the windows were heavily tinted. If she kicked at the door, would anyone on the street notice? Could she make the vehicle move enough that someone realized something was wrong?

Oskar was in a bad position. He couldn't simply turn and get his hands on her. It would be awkward to get to her while he was sitting in the front seat.

Another way they'd underestimated her.

She was about to start moving when there was a knock on the car door.

"Hey, you can't park here," a masculine voice said.

A familiar voice. She would have gasped had it not been for the gag in her mouth.

"Hey, I'm with the police. You can't park here," he insisted. "You're going to have to move."

But French police officers didn't have Scottish accents.

Oskar started to lower the window and that's when Owen's hand reached in, shoving a rag at his face. He was stuck there, caught between the seatbelt and what was likely a very potent form of chloroform. He slumped over quickly. Owen unlocked the doors and Damon Knight was at her side untying her hands.

The minute her hands were free, she pulled the gag from her mouth. "What are you doing here?"

"Tucker forgot Tag…well, Tag tagged him," Damon admitted. "I've been following the little bugger since he left the country house. I knew he would bring Owen in."

Owen was grinning as he made his way around the car. "I actually went to the boss when Tucker called me. MI6 was so angry with Kronberg that they're willing to work with us. So is German intelligence. We might get out of this after all."

"Only if Tucker's right and we can find that data." Damon seemed far less optimistic as he went to work on her feet.

She became very aware that they weren't alone. Several men wearing suits surrounded the car. One of them pushed Oskar over and took his seat.

"Don't mind them," Damon said. "They're French intelligence. Yes, we are the whole bloody world today. Let's get you out of here. Tucker's going to try to get Dwyer to admit what's going on at Kronberg before we arrest him."

"Is he all right? Is Nina okay?" She had a million questions, but she remembered something important. "Arthur has a gun. So does Kurt."

"And Tucker's got backup, too," Owen said. "We couldn't move into place fast enough to get Green out, but we've stuffed him in a van. We've got people stationed at all the entrances and exits. He won't get away this time."

"I don't think he wants to," Damon admitted. "I think he believes whatever's on that thumb drive will get him back at the Agency."

She slid out of the car the minute her feet were free. Blood started to rush back into her hands and she winced from the pain.

"Come on," Owen said. "We've got a couple of cars parked inside the cemetery. You can wait for Tucker there."

"Or she can go back to the hotel," Damon countered. "Rebecca and Penny are there. As soon as we can manage it, we're going back to London, but we've got a bit of clean-up to do. Firstly, we'll have to debrief with the French since we're doing all of this in their backyard. You have no idea how happy I am that Tag is in Dallas. Getting him to sit through a debrief with four bloody intelligence agencies without starting a war would be a miracle."

"What is going on?" She didn't understand a thing. One minute she'd been sure everything would go to hell and now they were joking?

Owen stopped. "It's all right, Veronica. We've got everything under control."

"Well, that's not exactly true." Damon moved to her other side so she was surrounded as he herded her along. "We're not entirely sure Tucker knows where the data is. He says he stashed it somewhere in the cemetery. It's been over three years. We're not sure it's still here. If it's not, we'll have some work to do. Tucker remembers what happened, but without solid proof, we'll have to maneuver our way out."

"Tucker's all right? I don't even understand what's going on. Arthur got scared. His name is on that list. Kronberg never wanted it found. I think the drugs they were going to use on him would have done the opposite of what they said." She hurried to keep up with the taller men.

"Yes, I think when Dwyer realized no one would let him use his drugs, he panicked, and Kronberg likely did, too," Damon concurred. "From their end this whole thing is a mess. German intelligence was working with them and now I suspect they won't listen to anything Kronberg tells them. They've got agents watching the houses of the board of directors in case one of them attempts to flee the country."

"They'll throw Dwyer under the bus," Owen said with a shake of his head. "No doubt about it. Those big companies know how to survive."

"Why let Tucker meet with him at all?" She didn't like the idea. "Why not simply arrest Arthur when he shows up at the meet site?"

Damon stopped as they reached the massive entryway to the Père Lachaise Cemetery. She recognized the twin pillars that marked one of the entryways because she'd come here years before with her sister. She and Katie had spent the weekend in Paris, and a whole afternoon wandering the peaceful grounds of the cemetery.

"That's about you, I suspect," Damon said. "He wants to get as much information as he can out of Arthur before the Germans take him. We had to agree that they got custody of Dwyer and any Kronberg employees. Tucker is recording everything the man says."

"He's alone out there?" She didn't care how many agents were in that cemetery, she didn't want Tucker going up against Dwyer and the big guard without someone directly at his side. Hell, she didn't want him in there at all.

"Robert is with him." Owen gestured to the main road through the cemetery. It wasn't a thoroughfare and was supposed to be used only for special occasions, but there were several vans parked inside now. "Levi Green turned himself in. Ezra's watching him in one of the vans. I don't like it, boss. Green is planning something."

"I don't see what he can do. Don't think I haven't gone over it again and again in my head. He can't steal the data. He won't be allowed close enough to it," Damon explained. "That is if it's even here. Anything could have happened to it over the years."

"Happened to what?" she asked.

"The day he was taken he was supposed to pass off a thumb drive to Levi Green," Owen explained. "He was supposed to meet Green here at the cemetery because you were back at the original meet spot."

"The apartment." God, it really had been her fault. If he hadn't taken her with him, things might have been different.

"Yes, that's where they had been planning to meet," Damon agreed. "Unfortunately, Tucker didn't realize that they'd tagged his phone. It was a rookie mistake, and I blame Green. He should never have sent in a civilian."

"McDonald knew he was going to be in Paris and she followed him," Owen continued. "Green and Tucker discussed where they were going to meet over their mobiles, and she set up an ambush. She didn't even realize he'd stolen the intelligence from Kronberg. She thought he was passing off your sister's research. And this is why I think something's up. Why didn't Green let him copy the drive and send it to him? All of this could have been avoided with a simple email."

"That's not how spies work, Owen," Damon said as though they'd gone over this. "I don't know what his thought process was, but I know I've worked operations this way from time to time. If the material was sensitive enough, they wouldn't want any chance that it could have been hacked. There's also the possibility that there are Agency names on that list."

"It still doesn't seem right to me." Owen put a hand on her shoulder. "Come on, Roni. You can stay with me until Tucker's got what he needs."

There was the sound of a shot splitting the peace of the cemetery and then shouts.

"Bloody hell," Damon cursed and took off running.

"I would tell you to stay behind, but we might need a doctor. You stay close to me," Owen ordered.

But she was already following Damon and praying she got there in time.

* * * *

Tucker took a deep breath as he realized he was in the right place.

"You do understand that all I have to do to end Veronica's life is send the text that's on my phone." Dwyer had his phone in one hand and his other was in the pocket of his coat where he was carrying a semiautomatic pistol. He'd flashed it when they'd first met, before he'd had Kurt frisk them both.

"You've said that a couple of times." He wasn't sure how they'd done it, but this part of the cemetery was quiet. Oh, there were enough people walking by that he was certain Dwyer wasn't suspicious, but Tucker knew an agent when he saw one, and the pair that had just passed them while arguing over a map of the cemetery had definitely been agents.

Damon had worked quickly, but then the whole London team had been monitoring his ass. Literally. He was fairly certain the tracker was in one of his butt cheeks.

He was going to put one in Roni's.

Except she likely would hate him because from what he could tell, he had been involved in her sister's death. He'd been the reason Kronberg decided to kill Katie Croft. "Do you want the actual data I stole or not? Rob, can you check this one? Shine a light in there."

Robert stepped up and pulled out the small flashlight he was carrying for just this occasion. He'd been frisked by the big guard Dwyer had called Kurt. "This one has nothing at all in it."

They were moving down the row of tombs. The "cure" hadn't crystalized his memory down to the actual tomb he'd shoved that drive into. But he was sure he was on the right path. It was one of these. He remembered the grave he'd had to scramble over to get away from his brother.

"Of course I want that data," Dwyer replied. "But we can't spend the afternoon here. We should come back when it's dark."

"I'm not leaving Roni with you." He knew exactly what would happen if he allowed himself to be taken into custody. He wouldn't ever leave it again. "Give me fifteen minutes. If I can hand it to you, we can make this a clean break."

"You remembered where it was. How do I know you don't

remember what's on it?" Dwyer asked.

Robert sent him a knowing look as he moved on to the next tomb.

They'd already figured out that Dwyer's name was on that list. Kronberg had panicked when he wouldn't take the drugs they'd offered to "help" his memory along. "I never looked at it. I had a mission. I was supposed to break into that safe and get the thumb drive. I then went to Katie Croft's house and I uploaded the information she'd found during her investigation. I read neither report. I uploaded Katie's information with her permission. She'd been working with my CIA contact for months."

"You could be lying," Dwyer countered.

"Do you honestly believe I memorized a list of names?" He was glad Damon had been in the city. It made him perfectly safe to do what he needed to do. And there would be none of these questions when he did find the drive because someone had been watching him all along. It would make it far easier for him to have a normal life if the world's intelligence agencies believed they had what he'd stolen that day. He could fade into the background and find a normal life. He would move to where Roni wanted to raise Vi and be a part of their lives. If she would let him.

Dwyer looked around, his anxiety apparent. In some ways he felt sorry for the bastard. He knew what it was like to be shoved into a job he hadn't been prepared for at all. Green might have given him some training, but there was far more to the spy business. After all, he'd proven to be bad at it. He hadn't even known he was being followed those weeks before that fateful day in Paris.

"I would have tried," Dwyer said, looking around again as though he were starting to understand something was wrong. "I think we should go. You've already broken our agreement once."

By bringing Rob with him. "He's my brother. He wouldn't let me come alone."

The tomb in front of him made the hair on his arms stand straight. The grating on the dilapidated door was so familiar.

"How can I know you didn't bring someone else?" Dwyer looked to Kurt, who was guarding his back.

Kurt simply frowned. "I didn't see anyone else, boss."

"Robert, I think this might be it." He pointed to the door. "I was in between these two tombs, hiding from McDonald. I made the decision to dump the thumb drive because I didn't want her to get her hands on it."

"It's here?" Dwyer moved forward.

Robert shined the light inside. "There's a statue. I'm sure it's some kind of memorial."

"Open the doors," Dwyer ordered. "It could have fallen on the floor and been missed. I doubt they do more than basic maintenance on these. Some of them are covered with leaves and vegetation."

He had to hope that was the case here. He would hate to think someone had found it and it had sat in a lost and found or been dumped in the trash.

"It's locked." Robert gently pulled on the ornate doors that locked the tomb off from the world. "Does anyone have something I can use as a pick?"

He'd come prepared. After a heinously long lecture where Damon used some very British threats, they'd prepped with the flashlight and a couple of paperclips he'd manipulated. "Here. Try this."

Rob took the paperclip and went to work on the lock.

"I don't like this," Kurt said. "It's too quiet."

Kurt proved he was far better at this game than Dwyer.

He wouldn't have long to get the information he wanted. He turned to Dwyer. "Did you have a hand in Katie Croft's murder? I mean we're sharing, right?"

The question seemed to shake Dwyer. "She was close to putting together some details we didn't want connected."

That sparked his memory. Katie had done excellent work. He hadn't read her final report, but she'd walked him through her research. She'd managed to get financial records that tied Kronberg to a man named Nieland. He ran a vast corporate empire. "She connected Kronberg to the Nieland Corporation. She thought Al Nieland was the head of The Collective."

Simon and Chelsea Weston had taken him down with the help of the McKay-Taggart team long before McDonald came on the radar, but the connections had been there for a brilliant reporter to find.

Katie had been putting together the labyrinthine arms that connected The Collective.

She'd given him her data because she'd worried about reprisals.

She hadn't trusted anyone with the story because The Collective owned many media outlets. She'd put all her hard work in Tucker's hands because she'd believed he loved her sister.

He'd failed her so badly.

The gun made an appearance. "Yes, the board knew about her investigation. It was precisely why we brought Veronica onto the team. We thought she would be a good tool against her sister. She turned out to be one for you, too. McDonald didn't understand how bad it was getting. She should have handed you over to us, but she was arrogant. She thought she was the only one in danger. She didn't think about the company at all. Instead of learning your secrets, she dosed you with the drug and anything you knew was lost to us."

How odd to think that McDonald's mistake had very likely led to Roni's relative freedom. If she'd known he had valuable intel, she would have used Roni against him. She would have tortured her and given her any number of drugs that could have hurt their baby. Losing his memory had saved his daughter.

He would take that. "Rob, I think we can finish this now."

He had enough. He knew what had happened.

"I've been here before." Rob had gone an ashen shade and he stood in front of the door, the makeshift lockpick in his hands.

He hadn't counted on this. Not for a second had he thought Rob might remember. "Hey, let it go. You can't get sick now."

"Open that door," Dwyer insisted.

Kurt moved in. "I'll do it and then we have to go. Something is wrong. I think we're being watched."

Robert had a hand to his head. "I was here and you were here."

"Let it go, Rob. It doesn't matter." The last thing he needed was his brother to lose his shit.

"You tried to tell me. You begged me. God, you begged me," Rob said.

There was a loud bang as Kurt kicked the door to the tomb in.

He had to pray he'd given Damon and Owen enough time to get Roni out. They'd promised they would do it the second Dwyer walked away.

"What's wrong with him?" Dwyer glanced around like a man who knew something was about to happen.

That was the moment the intelligence agencies made their play.

The couple who'd argued moments before were back, guns drawn and shouting in German for Arthur to put the gun down.

The head of MI6 rushed in from the right with a couple of his people. "Stand down, Dwyer. You're not going anywhere."

"Oh, he will come home with me and face what he has done," the German intelligence officer said.

Dwyer looked like a deer in the headlights. He started to turn, but Solo was there. She frowned at Dwyer, cutting him off.

She looked Tucker's way, her eyes narrow with irritation. "You're going to get a spanking, little boy."

Yeah, he'd known he would be in trouble with Solo, but they would have to work that out later. Robert was standing by the doors of the tomb, and the man who'd just walked in had a gun.

"Robert, get out of the line of fire," he said.

Kurt stepped out of the tomb, holding the drive in his hand. "It was there."

The moment he realized he was caught, he brought up his gun and fired at the first person he could. Solo.

Luckily Solo moved fast. She ducked and rolled, and before the shot had stopped ringing through the trees, she'd taken her own.

Dwyer turned Tucker's way as his guard hit his knees, a hole in his chest.

"Why couldn't you have stayed dead?" Dwyer asked.

And Tucker knew what he was about to do. Dwyer raised his weapon and he heard Solo shout out. The world seemed to slow down and he knew Dwyer wasn't going out alone. But then Arthur had always been that way. Arthur had been far closer to McDonald than he'd let on. Yes, now that he was staring at Dwyer, he remembered how the man had worked with her, had been the bridge between her and the higher-ups.

This was what he'd been trying to protect. He'd panicked when he'd realized Tucker might actually remember working side by side with him.

But it didn't matter now because Dwyer pulled the trigger.

He heard a roar and suddenly he was tackled, his body slamming against the rocks and dirt. His head hit and the world went woozy. His breath was knocked out of his chest and pain flared through him. He could hear the sound of another gun going off. He saw Dwyer hit the ground not far from him. And then his brother was staring down at him.

Robert. Robert had thrown himself in front of Dwyer's bullet.

"Rob?" He could barely speak. His head was throbbing.

Robert's head came up. "Couldn't do it again. Couldn't let them take you. I'm so sorry, brother. Forgive me."

"What? Are you okay?" He was pretty sure *he* was okay since he hadn't felt a bullet hit his body.

"Tell Ariel I love her," Robert said.

What the fuck was happening? His brother was draped across him, dead weight on his body. But he couldn't seem to make his brain work. His vision was in and out.

Concussion. He'd hit his head. But something worse had happened to Rob. He was sure of it.

"Hey, Tucker." Solo was above him, staring down. "I'm not great with the medical stuff. He's got a bullet in his abdomen. Should I wait for an ambulance?"

"Rob?" He was so woozy. What was happening to Rob?

His brother stared down at him. "We almost made it. Almost made it all the way home."

Robert's head dropped down and Tucker's heart threatened to explode.

"Move him off now," a familiar voice said. "Lay him out and I'm going to need something to stop the bleeding."

Roni. Roni was here and she was taking charge. In a group of intimidating people, all of them with guns, his Roni was handling them, ordering them around.

He prayed his Roni could save his brother.

They'd almost made it. It was his last thought as the darkness took him.

Chapter Seventeen

"Is he here yet?"

Roni turned at the sound of her mother's voice. It had been a week since that horrible day in the cemetery and it felt like everything had changed. Not all of it for the better.

One thing was fantastic though. Her mom and daughter were back. Her mom walked out of the apartment with Violet on her hip.

"He's supposed to be here any minute." Tucker hadn't left Paris when the rest of them had. He'd stayed at his brother's bedside while he recovered. "He texted me that they were in London finally."

"Texted you?" Her mother's brows rose. "He can't call?"

"I told you we're in a weird place." She'd saved his brother and he'd been profuse in his appreciation of that act. But he'd also been distant. He'd been diagnosed with a concussion and he hadn't complained when she'd stayed with him that first night. When he'd been released, however, he'd explained that he could take care of himself and she should go to New York to be with their daughter.

Instead, she'd come to London and brought her family here. To wait for him.

"Physically he's all right?" her mom asked.

She reached out to her baby, who grinned that adorable, way-too-like-her-father grin and came into her arms. Roni breathed her in, so grateful to have her back. "He's fine. Robert's fine. They wanted to hold him for a few days because he started to develop an infection, but it's cleared up now."

Her mom put her hands on her hips, her general pose. "Then what's the problem that he can't call? Does he even know Violet's here?"

She grimaced as Vi started bouncing up and down in her arms. "He doesn't know I'm here so he wouldn't know about Vi, either. Or at least I'm not sure he knows. The last time we talked in person I was going to New York to be with you. It's what he suggested."

"Because he thinks you turned him in to McDonald?"

She shook her head. Despite her mother's attempts to get her to talk, she'd worked her way around this subject. "No. He knows that's not what happened."

"According to Taggart it was Tucker's relationship with Katie that got him in trouble," her mother said flatly. "That and a true clusterfuck of a situation. It seems to me everything happened at once and that led to him being caught. I don't understand why he would blame you."

She felt her eyes widen because she'd been trying for days to figure out how to tell her mother Tucker had known Katie. "Mom, I don't think he was using Katie."

A frown crossed her mother's face. "Of course he wasn't. I'm a little worried Katie was using him. She was always ambitious. If anything, it was that CIA agent that used them both. What is that look about?"

"I didn't think you knew about the connection between them. I've been trying to figure out how to explain it to you. And you're right about Green. We had this big debrief and Solo got Levi Green to admit he was the reason Katie didn't think anything was wrong. When she didn't hear anything from Tucker, she called him and he told her to hang tight."

Anger welled fast and true. She hated Levi Green. When everything had gone to hell, Levi Green hadn't tried to save Tucker. He'd shut everything down, including leaving her sister in the dark about the fact that McDonald and Kronberg were on to them. He'd planted that bomb as surely as whichever Kronberg paid assassin had.

Her mom reached up and gently wiped away the tears she hadn't realized she was shedding. "I know about that, too. I'm angry, but anger isn't going to help us today. We'll get that bastard in the end. I promise."

She sniffled, shoving the rage down because her mother was right. "How did you know?"

"Taggart's been keeping me up to date on everything," her mom explained. "I've been playing this online war game with the Dallas boys. Taggart's a fairly good tactician, but no matter what he says, his hand eye coordination could use some work. In the middle of shooting the shit out of each other, he gave me updates on what was happening. I also know way too much about his wife's pregnancy cravings. They are not all food."

"I'm still trying to process the fact that Katie had this whole thing going on in her life that she never talked to me about. I really thought Green was a guy she was dating. I'm kind of shocked my sister thought she needed a cover with me."

"She was obviously trying to protect you," her mother pointed out. "She knew she had something dangerous and she tried to turn it over to a professional. And don't start in on how you probably could have saved her. She didn't talk to me about it, either, and I had connections that could have helped. Your sister was always independent. I would give anything to have her with us today, but I'm not going to play games with what could have been. That's the way to waste your life."

The thought of her mother finally moving on brought tears to her eyes. "I think Tucker was trying to help her. But Mom, when I first found out about their connection, I accused him of a whole lot of things that weren't true. I don't think he's going to forgive me for that."

"Have you asked him to?"

She'd tried to connect with him. She'd sat at his bedside while they'd diagnosed his concussion. When they'd gone to the debrief, she'd been beside him as she'd told her side of what had happened. But after it was over, he'd sent her away. "Not directly, but he's been so worried about his brother that I didn't want to push him."

There was the sound of a door closing and then Nina Blunt was walking down the hall. The lovely redhead looked like she'd never taken a bullet to the chest. She was coming out of the apartment

Tucker had once shared with Robert. She locked it behind her and smiled as she caught sight of them. "Hey, you two, I was wondering if you were going down to greet our lads. Ariel texted me to say they're almost here. I wanted to make sure Tucker's place was ready for them."

"He's staying in his apartment." The minute the words were out of her mouth she realized how dumb they sounded. Of course he was. As far as she knew, he wasn't aware she was home. When had she started to think of The Garden that way? It wasn't truly. Tucker was home and wherever he was—that was her home.

Nina's bright expression dimmed a bit. "Yes. He didn't say anything about moving you in. He told me he needed to make sure he had some clean sheets because he'd left so quickly. We all did. I made sure it was comfy for him. I checked on Rob and Ari's place too. Rob's being a massive baby about getting shot. It's surprising since it happens so frequently to him. You would think he would be used to it by now. Men. They should think twice about getting dangerous jobs if they're going to whine every time someone shoots them. Me? I was up the next day. I had my surgery and then it was back to work."

Her mom nodded. "Males are always the worst patients. They're all as soft as their mommas made 'em. And it sounds like Tucker's being a whiny manbaby. He got his feelings hurt and like all men, he's extra sensitive."

Nina looked Roni's way. "I thought for sure you would have worked it out. Usually watching a loved one be kidnapped does the trick. Is he making you work even harder? Have you pointed out that you were kidnapped and that means everything should bloody well be forgiven?"

She kind of thought Nina had been reading too many romance novels. "I don't think it works that way."

There was noise from down below and she watched as a massive ball of fur barreled across The Garden's floor. Buster barked wildly and his whole body wriggled and squirmed and jumped as Jax Seaborne walked in followed by the rest of the party.

River was right behind her dog, running to her husband and jumping into his arms. She couldn't hear what they were saying—well, what the humans were saying—but she knew the words.

I love you. I missed you. Let's never be apart again.

"Pup pup," Vi said, looking down at the happy reunion.

Her girl was going to be a dog person. No doubt about it. She loved watching Buster's antics. It wouldn't be long before she would want a pup pup of her own.

Tucker walked in and smiled at his friends, his brother right behind him. Ariel had a hand on both of them.

Ariel was part of Tucker's family. She'd been the one he was comfortable with. Roni was the one who'd been left out. He hadn't wanted her there.

He looked up and their eyes caught. A look of complete shock hit his face. Tucker dropped the bag he'd been carrying and said something to his brother, who looked up, too.

Robert caught her gaze and put a hand over his heart as though touching the place where the bullet had almost killed him. He nodded her way and said something to his brother.

Tucker took off. He jogged to the elevator and pushed it several times as though he could force the thing to come open.

He was coming for her. Her heart was in her throat because he hadn't looked like a man who was unhappy to see her.

Maybe he'd forgiven her in the days they'd spent apart.

"He doesn't look like he's mad at you," her mom said with a shake of her head.

She felt a smile cross her face as the doors to the elevator opened and Tucker strode out.

"I thought you were in New York," he said, opening his arms. "I thought it would be weeks before I saw her. Hey, baby girl. God, I missed you."

She felt like someone had tossed a vat of freezing water her way. He was talking about Vi. All that sweet energy and enthusiasm had been for their daughter. Not for her.

Vi was already reaching out for her dad, and she had to move fast so she didn't fall. Father and daughter hugged, fitting together like two puzzle pieces. He wrapped her up in his strong arms and she snuggled against him.

His eyes closed like this was what he'd been longing for.

Tears welled hard and fast because it was a beautiful sight and it also made her heart ache.

When his eyes came open he looked her way. "Thank you for

bringing her here."

All she could do was nod. Words completely escaped her.

"Can I take her for a while?"

She nodded again and then watched as he walked back to the elevators.

"You want to go see Buster, Vi? Pup pup?" he was saying as he whisked her away to show her off to his family.

Vi was bouncing happily in her father's arms as the doors closed.

"That was cold," Nina said with a frown. "He does remember you got kidnapped, right? I heard he took a blow to the head."

"He knows." She wiped away tears. They wouldn't do her any good. At some point she would have to sit down with him, and they would be adults about the situation. They would calmly and patiently talk about how best to raise their daughter. They would have to decide if they were going to try to live in the same city. Maybe even the same country. Her mom was going back to the States. She'd already accepted a job at McKay-Taggart in Dallas. If she was going to stay a single mom, she would need to be close to her mother. Would Tucker be satisfied seeing his daughter a few times a year?

"Or he's a dumbass," her mom pointed out. "Like I said, men are sensitive and sometimes they need to be taken in hand. You just let him walk out. You didn't even try, baby. That's not who I raised you to be. I know you want a knight in shining armor to come and sweep you off your feet, but sometimes a woman has to put that armor on herself and fix the situation."

"Oh, I don't think she should put on armor," Nina disagreed. "I think she should take it all off."

"Boobs can be like armor at the right time," her mother mused.

Maybe she shouldn't try to live too close to her mom. "What are you saying?"

Nina moved beside her mom, a united front. "Do you want him?"

"Yes." She wanted him more than anything. And not for his fatherly skills. Not for his hot bod. Not even for the tracker in his buttocks that came in handy. She wanted him because no one in her life had ever had a stronger heart, a more open and loving soul. She wanted him because she'd never loved anyone the way she did him.

"Then fight for your man," Nina said. "And by fight I mean let's tempt him until he can't see straight. You see everyone will tell you the way to a man's heart is through his stomach."

Her mom shook her head. "It's his penis. It's always his penis."

Yep, her mom was a bad influence.

Was she brave enough to try it?

"What are you thinking?"

Nina got the brightest smile on her face. She leaned in and they began to plot.

* * * *

Hours later Tucker looked around his brother's apartment and realized he would have to go to his own soon.

"That woman is incredibly intimidating," Robert said, closing the door on Sandra and Vi.

She'd been the one to come down to take Violet to bed. She'd been the one earlier in the evening who'd dropped off Violet's bag with a smirk and told him not to let her explode. He hadn't been sure what that meant until about thirty minutes after he'd fed her dinner. Robert and Ariel were definitely putting off the baby making for a while.

Sandra had facilitated his evening with Violet. She'd also facilitated Roni not having to see him. They hadn't spoken at all. She'd nodded twice and then he'd walked away.

He'd been shocked to see Roni. He truly hadn't believed that she would be waiting here for him. Seeing her standing there with Violet had made his heart threaten to stop.

And then he'd remembered all the accusations, all the suspicion. Every reason he'd sent her away had come back to slap him in the face and he'd forced himself to focus on Violet.

"She is," Tucker agreed. "That's probably why Tag hired her. She's going to work at McKay-Taggart. I'm not sure what she's going to do there."

"Amuse Big Tag, I suspect," Robert said, easing into the chair across from him. "You sure you didn't want to go with her and help put Violet to bed?"

"She was already asleep." She'd drifted off while he'd rocked her and talked to Robert.

"I think you were trying to avoid Roni."

Ariel walked out from the kitchen and put a mug of tea in front of them both. "He was definitely trying to avoid Veronica. He hasn't even walked into his flat because he would have to walk past hers and he's afraid he'll knock on the door. Or maybe that she'll be there, waiting for him. She's not, by the way."

Of course she wasn't. "I'm not afraid of Roni. I'm giving her space."

"You're giving yourself space," Robert argued.

Maybe he was. "I thought she would be in New York. Someone should have told me she was here."

Ariel sighed and leaned over to kiss her husband's forehead. "I think they were worried you wouldn't come home. Or maybe they thought it wasn't a terrible thing to have your daughter waiting here for you. You can't ignore Veronica forever."

"I'm not going to." But a few days wouldn't hurt. "I'll talk to her in my own time."

"Fine. I know when I'm not wanted," Ariel said. "I'll be in the bedroom reading. You take it easy. I don't want you to overdo it. The docs are going to look you over tomorrow. You should know I told them to be very pessimistic about your outlook."

Rob smiled up at his wife. "I'm sure you did. Love you."

Ariel winked and walked away.

"What did that mean? Why would they be pessimistic?" Had his brother been holding back on him?

"Because Ariel wants me to take a couple of weeks off," he replied. "She thinks I need the excuse to relax, but she's wrong. I'm seriously thinking about heading to Loa Mali for a nice long vacation before we decide what to do with the rest of our lives. We're done. I'm still having a hard time believing it. I mean, I know we still have work to do, but we're all free."

"Nothing's been decided yet. They're still analyzing the data. Solo hasn't even seen it yet," Tucker pointed out. "With all the chaos, we weren't able to make that copy I was planning on."

"The Agency has a copy and so do the Germans, MI6, and the French," Robert said. "Connor Sparks said he's going to make sure we get to see that data, too. He's also assured us the president will do everything Solo promised. He's working on getting you a proper passport."

With his real name. He still wasn't used to Tim. Tucker might be his nickname for life. But it was damn good to be a Seeger again. "I believe that."

"You and Jax are going to get your lives back and we have some decisions to make."

"I want to find Mom." It was distressing that he'd remembered so much, but he couldn't remember her name. He couldn't remember the name of the town they'd grown up in.

"I do, too," Robert said. "And I suspect now that Green is back in custody, he won't be giving us any more information. I don't know. I'm hoping Solo will find something. She's supposed to be back here in a couple of days to update us. If Green won't tell us, then we'll go to Wyoming. We both seem to remember best when we're in the actual places the events took place. We'll rent a car and go to every single small town we can."

"About remembering things," he began. "I didn't tell you what happened that day because I don't blame you."

Robert picked up the tea Ariel had left. "I wish this was a beer but I'm on tons of meds and that means no alcohol." He took a quick sip and grimaced. "And it's herbal. That day has been haunting me ever since I got a hint of what happened in that cemetery. I remember you begging me."

Tucker shook his head. "You didn't know who I was."

"I didn't even listen." Guilt flavored every word that came out of his brother's mouth. "Maybe if I had I could have saved all of us."

"You were trained not to listen." He'd been thinking for days about how to handle this particular conversation. Luckily, he had history on his side. "Hey, you remember what happened after you got out?"

A wary look came into his brother's eyes. "I went to Dallas."

"Yes, you went to Dallas with Theo and you both worked with that team for a while. You used to go grab lunch with him. Do you remember? You and Theo were grabbing lunch at a park and what happened?"

"McDonald tried to get us back," Robert replied, his jaw tightening with the memory.

McDonald had given her B-team a mission. They were to recapture the A-team at all cost. And it had cost them much. He'd lost two of the men on his team that day. "I was there. I was one of the men who tried to drag you back to hell and I did it because I genuinely believed it was my job. Jax was there."

Robert sat back, shaking his head. "God, I hadn't even thought about that."

"If it hadn't been for the guys from MT, you and Theo would have gone back into the program and it would have been me taking you there." He needed to press this point home because he didn't want this guilt to come between him and his brother. "I'm going to ask you a question and I want you to be honest with yourself and with me. Would you have blamed me?"

"Absolutely not," Robert said as quickly as he could. "That was not your fault."

"And it wasn't yours either," he replied, making his point. "But saving me in the cemetery was, and we need to make sure we never do that again. I don't think your wife can handle you getting shot a third time."

"Oh, I've been shot way more than that. But I guess it has been a bad run lately." Robert sighed, a relieved sound. "Okay. I promise to try to never get shot again. I've got too much to live for. And so do you. What are you going to do about Roni? Did she ask you to stay away?"

He shook his head. "Not at all. She tried to stay with me in Paris. I asked her to leave."

A brow rose over his brother's eyes. "Really? Why would you do that? I thought you wanted to get back together with her. Did you change your mind?"

"No, but think about it. She doesn't mean it. She went through something traumatic and I look safe to her. When things calm down she's going to still have all those questions." He didn't think he could handle living with her and being a family only to have this all come back up again a few months down the line.

Robert shook his head. "She won't have questions because now we have answers. She knows you didn't sleep with her sister. She knows Green was the reason Katie was still sitting there when Kronberg decided to take her out. If he'd given her a heads-up, she would likely have taken Roni and run."

He would love to pay Green back for that bit of business. He hoped the asshole was getting tortured again but feared turning that data over meant Green might get out free and clear. "Yeah, but I was still working with her. I still got Katie into a situation that ended up getting her killed. Roni will always remember that."

"Do you honestly believe Sandra doesn't know what happened?" Robert asked. "Because I happen to know she talks to Big Tag on a daily basis. She didn't kill you when she saw you. She took Vi, said you looked like hell, and told you to come by for breakfast in the morning if you found your balls. That was practically a declaration of love from one of the toughest women I've ever met. She doesn't blame you and that means neither does Roni."

"I don't know. She didn't talk about it back in Paris. We didn't talk about anything really. She told me about Violet and what she's been doing," he admitted. "And we talked about you and your recovery. We pretty much avoided anything personal."

"We or you?"

"I don't know." But he did. Roni wasn't good at hiding her feelings. She wore them all over her face. He'd seen the hurt in her eyes when he'd explained he thought she should go to New York to be with Violet. "Okay, yeah, it was me. I avoided it because I didn't want to hear her say she wanted me again. I know she knows now. She knows she was wrong about me betraying her with her sister. She might even be okay with me lying about knowing her sister. But she didn't believe me. Shouldn't she have had faith in me?"

That was what gnawed at him. He could still remember how she'd looked at him, like she hadn't known him at all. He'd felt so small, and coming from her it had been awful.

"You know relationships are rough, and they're especially rough in the beginning. What Roni's been through…I can't imagine that it's easy for her to trust anyone. I know you're the weirdo who can go through all the pain in the world and still not expect to get kicked again, but the rest of us aren't like that. I held Ari off forever because I didn't think I deserved her."

"It's not the same," Tucker argued.

"But it is. I know you had a good reason, but you lied to her. It might have been a good thing at the time, but it impacted her and she needed time to process it. You think she shouldn't have a single doubt about a relationship that's already devastated her once?"

Put that way, it did seem like he was being sensitive. "I didn't mean to hurt her."

"And it sounds like she was trying to forgive you. I don't think Sandra is that kind to you if she believes her daughter wants to cut you out of her life."

Kind? What conversation had his brother overheard? "She asked if I needed a cream for my vagina."

Robert snorted. "Yeah, she's not the most politic of mother-in-laws. She's going to be a blast at Thanksgivings. Mom will think she's funny."

His family life would be interesting. And yet he wanted it. Turning Vi over for the night had been rough. He'd wanted to take her back to her mother himself and lay down the law. They were going to be a family. They were going to be together, and he would spend the rest of his life showing her how much he loved her.

"You should go to her," Robert said.

"He really should." Ariel popped out from behind the bedroom door. "I think he'll find she's downstairs."

"Why would she be downstairs?" It was late. Damon had closed down the club for a few nights while they all recovered.

Ariel's eyes glittered with mischief. "I think you should go find out. And it took you long enough."

He stood up. Maybe it was time to be brave.

Chapter Eighteen

The ground floor of The Garden was quiet, and he started to get suspicious that this was a setup. Ariel had known something was going on, but she wouldn't say a word.

Roni was making her play, and he didn't think it was to shut him out.

He wasn't completely foolish. He'd seen the way her eyes lit up when he'd walked out of the elevator. And he'd seen the way she'd shut down when he'd taken Vi and left her behind.

Could he trust that she wouldn't change her mind? That these feelings for him weren't the result of almost dying?

No one was down here. Had she gone back to her place?

He glanced to his right and realized where she would go. The privacy rooms. He stepped up and the doors opened with their high-tech swish.

Nina sat at the security desk. She gave him a brilliant smile and hopped off the stool, her arms open in greeting.

"Hey, you look amazing for a woman who was recently shot." He hugged her, grateful he'd been able to have a hand in saving her.

"Well, I had some very good doctors, and I suspect I had an angel who sacrificed herself to save me." Nina stepped back. "She won't admit it but I'm almost certain she went with him when she had a chance to run. She did it because he threatened me."

"I can believe that." Roni was good deep down, and that was why he worried she would have trouble forgetting the past once the glow of surviving the storm had passed.

"She's in room four, of course," Nina said. "I'm going to leave you two alone for the evening. Unless you're planning on telling her you're done. Then I think I should go back there. She's not exactly dressed for the breakup conversation, if you know what I mean."

Every muscle in his body tightened at the thought of what she was—or wasn't—wearing. She was waiting in that room where they'd made love, and he wanted so badly to walk back there and take her, imprint himself on her. But he had to be careful, for both their sakes.

"It's not my intention to hurt her, but she was having second thoughts," he said, hating the fact that he couldn't make this simple. It felt like it should be simple, but he'd learned that nothing in life was.

"She's not having them now, I assure you."

"She's been through a lot."

Nina shook her head. "No. You don't get to do that, Tucker. You don't get to decide how she's feeling. You don't get to know better than her. If you're hesitating, be honest about why you're doing it. You got hurt and you're scared you'll get hurt again."

He needed to see her. Maybe he would walk in that room and it would all be clear to him. "I don't know. I guess I've been through a lot, too. But maybe she's right. Maybe this is how we should work things out." They could talk and talk and not get to the heart of the problem. Sometimes words got in the way. "Go ahead and go. I know the security code. I'll take care of her."

"See that you do," Nina said with a jaunty salute. "She's a smart lady. She knows what she wants."

The doors opened and then closed as Nina left and he was alone with the only woman in the world he wanted.

She'd hurt him. He'd hurt her. He hadn't meant to. He hadn't meant to leave her but he had. She'd spent years believing that he'd dumped her and left her pregnant, and she'd still come back to him, still found a way to shove that ache aside.

He'd asked her to have some faith. Shouldn't he have some, too?

He strode down the hall and opened the door to number four.

And stopped entirely, his breath held for a moment because she was on the bed, her arms tied down, her body completely naked. She was soft and vulnerable, and what had it taken for her to open herself up like this when he'd basically rejected her hours earlier?

"Hey, gorgeous." He loved her. In the end, it really was simple. He loved her. If she had doubts, he would put them to rest. If she questioned his devotion, he would give her answers with his lips and his tongue and his cock. He would love her so long and so well, she would know he would never leave her again.

Her head came up and she gasped before settling back and attempting to look like she wasn't nervous. She was. He could tell by the way she bit her bottom lip. "Hi. Uhm, is Vi asleep?"

All of his own doubts slid away. Robert was right. A relationship would always have its troubles, but it was up to them to stick together, and they couldn't do that if he was off somewhere nursing his hurt feelings. Roni was offering him everything and he wasn't about to turn her down because it might—somewhere down the line—get difficult. It would get difficult. And they would fix it. "Yes, but I don't think you brought me down here to discuss our daughter. Did I mention how happy I was to see you earlier?"

Now that he was here with her, a peace overtook him. And an amusement. She wanted to discuss their parenting duties when she was all tied up and ready for play? No. They did have things to discuss, but it wouldn't be Vi and it wouldn't be polite. It would be dirty and sweet.

Her lips turned down in the most delicious pout. "I got the idea that you weren't happy to see me."

"Oh, I was happy." He walked over to the small table someone had kindly set up for him. At least now he knew where Ariel had disappeared to after dinner. She and Nina seemed to have set up an array of treats for their friend. "I was also surprised. You were supposed to be in New York."

"I didn't want to be in New York."

When he'd suggested she should go to be with their daughter and she'd agreed, he'd been disappointed. It was perverse, but he'd wanted an argument out of her. "You didn't tell me that."

"You didn't want to hear it."

"Fair," he agreed. "But not because I didn't want you, baby. I was hurt and I didn't talk to you about it. I was scared because you mean everything to me. Getting my memory back, getting my life back, means nothing if you're not in it."

"I'm sorry I doubted you. It all happened so fast," she began.

He shook his head. He didn't need to have some big fight with her. He'd thought he did, but all he'd truly needed was to give up his own insecurities. Of course she'd worried. He would have worried, too. "No apologies. It did happen fast, and we were both caught in it. Here's the thing. I love you. Do you love me?"

Her eyes were steady on his, emotion shining in them. "So much. I loved you as Steven. I loved you as Tucker. I'll love you as Timothy Seeger."

He picked up the deerskin flogger. The falls were buttery soft and perfect to warm her up a bit. But then he wouldn't be touching her. He wanted his hands on her skin. Toys might have to wait. Then a little jar caught his eye and he thanked the universe his sister-in-law understood how fun torture could be.

He didn't need a damn thing to get warmed up. He was already hot for her. He could fuck her hard right that second; however, she'd set this scene up and he wasn't about to fail her. But he had made a few decisions. "I think I like Tucker. I consider it a nickname, and I earned it. I like the way you say my name."

"Tucker." A smile settled on her face. "I love you, Tucker."

The words were a balm to his soul. "I love you, Roni. I'm sorry I hesitated back in Paris. Like I said, I was scared."

"You were worried I would change my mind. I won't."

"And I won't either." He pulled his T-shirt over his head and tossed it aside before picking up the jar they'd left for him. Well, for him to use on her. "I think, though, that you forgot something."

"What's that?"

"I'm in charge in this room." He moved to the bedside and opened the jar, getting a dab of the cream on his fingers. "Spread your legs."

Her eyes widened and he was pleased with the bit of trepidation he saw there.

"What is that?" she asked, the question a breathy huff.

It wouldn't do for her to be completely comfortable. "The main ingredient is menthol. Can you guess what it does and how I'm planning on using it?"

Her nipples had tightened. "You're going to put it on my clitoris. It's going to stimulate the nerves there, make it easier for me to orgasm."

He loved the fact that she could barely get the words out. "Precisely. Now do as I asked and spread your legs."

Her knees came apart, giving him access to what he wanted. Her pussy was lovely and soft. His cock thickened further at the sight of that sweet part of her. He palmed her, easing his hands across the soft, smooth skin of her pussy. He slid his fingers between her labia, loving how wet she already was. "What have you been lying here thinking about?"

Her eyes closed as she obviously reveled in the contact. "Mostly about the fact that Nina was sitting here talking about her favorite books, and how weird it was that I was naked and she wasn't. You took your time."

That hadn't been all she'd thought about. Either that or he'd had a quick effect on her.

He rubbed the cream on her clitoris, taking his time and watching how she responded, how her breath deepened, her toes curling as he worked the cream all over her clit. Her hips moved, pressing herself up against his fingers.

He set the jar down because a little of that stuff went a long way, and he wasn't ready for her to come yet. Not until he'd had a bit of fun. He reached over and undid the tie on her right hand. "I want you on all fours. I think you earned a spanking."

"Earned? How?"

He could come up with a million ways she'd scared the hell out of him, but one was enough. "Well, let's see, you got yourself kidnapped."

Her eyes flared. "I did not get myself kidnapped."

"Play with me. I spent hours and hours worried you were dead. I should get to spank that pretty ass." She wasn't used to the lifestyle, so he had to coax her. He knew if she tried, she would enjoy it.

Her eyes went gorgeously wide and innocent. "I was terrible. I got myself kidnapped and worried my poor husband."

He felt a brilliant smile cross his face as he released her other hand. "I like the sound of that."

"See how I worked that in," she replied with a grin and then she gasped. "Oh, that stuff works fast."

She turned over and suddenly that pretty ass was in the air, waiting for his caress.

She was all his. This was what he'd wanted as he'd walked through the streets of Paris that day. He'd wanted a life where she was waiting for him, where she trusted and loved him.

They had a shot at it now.

"You are so beautiful." He ran his hand over her back, tracing the graceful line of her spine from her neck all the way down to her ass. He cupped a cheek before bringing his hand up and back in a sharp arc.

Her whole body shuddered.

"Do you have any idea how scared I was I would lose you?" He spanked her again, easy slaps to her flesh meant more to sensitize than to punish. He didn't want to punish her. He simply wanted this connection with her.

And he had been scared. Terrified. He'd come close to getting what he'd wanted once before, and that bastard Dwyer had almost taken everything from him again.

"Did he hurt you?" The question was accompanied by another smack.

"He hit me with a gun. He properly surmised that the minute I thought Nina was safe I would scream my head off. That's why he knocked me out with the gun," she admitted. "After I woke up in the trunk of his car, he dosed me. The sedative was surprisingly easy. Good rest. No nausea afterward. I think Kronberg has a winner there."

This smack was harder because he didn't need her sarcasm. Except he did. It brought a smile to his face. "I wouldn't go buying stock. I think that company is going to undergo some big changes soon."

They would burn to the ground if he had any say in things.

"Okay, but that was seriously good stuff," she replied, giving him a wiggle of that gorgeous ass.

He spanked her again, loving the way her skin pinkened. He set in on his task, smacking her cheeks over and over again. He watched her carefully, studied how she responded. Every smack and caress made his cock ache.

"Never again," he swore. "You are not allowed to be kidnapped again. I'm not going to be shot at again or mind erased. We're going to find someplace nice and quiet and raise our kids and life is going to be boring."

And he would love every second of it. He would love every boring, normal not getting shot at or under threat of arrest moment.

"I promise. God, I promise, Tucker. I'll promise you anything if you'll please fuck me. I'm dying. And I like the spanking thing, but it's got to stop because I'm dying here."

He slapped her backside one last time and then lifted her with ease.

It was time to please his woman.

* * * *

She could medically explain what that damn cream had done to her clitoris, but academic words couldn't possibly express what she felt.

Fire. Want. Desperate need.

It had taken the normal desire she had for him and turned the dial up to one hundred, but then it fit. She'd already been at the extremes of need on an emotional level. Since the moment she'd decided to make her play for him, she'd been a bundle of nerves, knowing this might be their last shot. Nina had brought Ariel into their plot. It had been Ariel who convinced her to show Tucker how much she trusted him.

Naturally Ariel's way had been to tie her up naked and make her wait until Tucker came down and found her and all of his doubts magically drifted away at the sight of her naked boobs. Nina had sat in the room, chatting as though it wasn't abnormal at all to hang out with a naked chick. She'd only left when Ariel had texted her Tucker was on his way down.

Tucker lifted her and rolled her over, moving her onto her back. There was soft material under her, caressing her slightly sore backside. That spanking had been a revelation. The minor pain had been overwhelmed by the sensitivity she'd received. It was like every slap of his hand went straight to her pussy. Even now she could feel how warm her skin was. The thought that she might feel it the next day made her perfectly happy.

She watched as his hands went to his waistband, shoving down his jeans and showing off that body she craved. He was a stunning man, even more so than he'd been years before.

She let go of all the time that he'd been gone. They'd been taken from her, but she wouldn't let those lost years cost them their future.

Not that she was thinking of the future. Nope. She wanted the right now.

He climbed on the bed but didn't fall on top of her, and that was annoying.

She started to reach for him, but that was the moment he pounced. He pinned her hands above her head and pressed her into the mattress with his body. Even the feel of his skin against hers was almost enough to make her shout out in pleasure.

"God, I missed this," she managed to breathe.

He lowered his head to hers. "I missed you."

He took her mouth in a long, luscious kiss that had their tongues tangling. After a moment, he released her wrists and she let her arms wind around him. Everywhere he touched her, she was warm, her skin tingling like it had been asleep without his to press against.

"Did I say thank you for saving my brother?" He whispered the question against her ear as his hands smoothed back her hair. He leaned over and dropped light kisses on her nose.

Her hips moved restlessly, trying to make harder contact with him. She was so hot, desperate to have him. "That's wonderful. You should reward me."

His lips curled in the sexiest smirk. "I should. I'll reward you with kisses. Lots of kisses."

His mouth covered hers again and she moaned. It wasn't enough, but she couldn't force him to move faster. Every kiss drugged her with pleasure, with connection. He held her still, forcing her to focus on him. She let her legs tangle with his, moving against his muscular ones.

"Do you know what else I should reward you for?" He kissed his way over her cheek and to her ear where he licked the shell. "I should reward you for everything you had to do for our daughter while I was gone. For being the best mom."

"You should reward me with your cock." It would be the perfect way to celebrate motherhood, doing the very thing that had caused it in the first place.

"I'll get to that." His hips were moving, gently rocking against her, making her light up. "I have to find a condom first. I think your friends forgot them. They weren't on the table. But I did spy a pretty butt plug."

She would have to thank Nina and Ariel for that. She intended to avoid the butt plug for the evening. It would have to wait. "They didn't put condoms out because I told them we didn't need them. I think Violet would make a great big sister, and you owe me."

He stopped, his whole body going still. His blue eyes were wide as he stared down at her. "What are you saying?"

Oh, she had him now. She could see it plainly. He'd likely had plans to keep her on the edge as long as he could, but she was going to make that impossible for him. She was going to make him totally lose control. "I'm saying I want you with me this time. I'm saying you're going to rub my feet and get me Chinese takeout when I can't go another minute without cashew chicken."

He smiled, an expression of pure joy. "I will. I'll have to have it brought in from somewhere else because Jennings only has two restaurants and they're both burger joints, but I'll make it work."

There had been something wrong about what he'd just said, but he'd moved down her body and taken a nipple in his mouth. Sparks seemed to shoot through her and she lost her train of thought. He licked and sucked her nipples, moving from one to the other. She let her hands roam across the smooth skin of his shoulders and back, reveling in the muscles she found there.

"I'll give you everything you need this time. I won't miss a minute," he vowed as he nestled beside her and his hand skimmed down from her breasts to the apex of her thighs. "I love you so much. You won't regret it."

She never would. Even during the dark times she hadn't been able to regret being with this man because he'd given her Vi.

The minute his finger slid over her clitoris, she could barely breathe.

"I need you to give me one because I'm already close. I lose all control when I'm with you. Maybe after we do this a couple of hundred times, I'll be able to make it last," he whispered. "You drive me crazy in the best way possible."

He'd told her to give, but he was the one giving. His fingers pressed and rotated, igniting a spark she couldn't deny. Sensation swamped her and every inch of her flesh seemed lit from within as the orgasm took her.

Then he was moving, turning over and offering himself up. Even through the haze of her pleasure, she could see he was in the same position she'd been in when he'd entered the room, on his back, giving himself to her the way she had.

"I want to watch you," he said. "I want to watch us."

He wanted to watch as she sank onto his cock? She could make that happen. Every limb felt loose but she straddled him. She gripped him, stroking that big dick of his and watching as he gritted his teeth and his eyes threatened to roll to the back of his head.

"Roni, please."

Everything about him pleased her, but she knew what he wanted. She lined his cock up and let herself sink on. He filled her up, every inch a new decadent sensation to be had. She lowered herself onto his dick, going slow and watching his every move. His hands came to clutch at her hips, but she wouldn't hurry this. He was a gorgeous sight, his stark blue eyes watching her body. Nothing in the world had ever made her feel as powerful as when Tucker looked at her like that, like she was a goddess, like he needed her more than air or water or food.

She began to move, lifting her body up and letting it slide back down. Over and over she impaled herself on his cock.

"That's what I want," Tucker groaned and his hands tightened around her. He moved against her. He never took his eyes off her, his gaze shifting between watching her face, moving to her breasts, and then down to the place where he could watch her take his cock. She tightened around him, feeling the orgasm about to take over again.

It sent a shudder through her and then she felt Tucker's body go taut beneath her, felt him shake as he came deep inside her.

Peace overwhelmed her as she let herself fall forward against his chest, listening to the thundering beat of his heart.

His hands wound around her, holding her tight. "Oh, we're going to have to practice that a lot. I mean a lot, baby. Maybe I don't always have to be in control. You seem to take the reins nicely."

She was so happy. "I can do that. Especially if we move back to your hometown. It sounds like we won't be going out…" She rolled to the side and sat up, her heart thumping for a different reason. "Jennings. You called it Jennings."

He smiled and reached up to cup her cheek. "I know. I remember where it is. I remember that it's beautiful when the snow falls. I remember we used to keep horses. I remember what our cabin looked like and how good it was to be warm and safe inside it."

"When did you remember?" Shouldn't he have led with that information? "Have you called her?"

"I didn't remember until you called me your husband and I thought about how we could get married in the mountains," he said quietly. "I saw you standing there on our big front porch. You and Vi, dressed for a wedding. Our wedding. My mother's name is Sharon Seeger and she will be waiting. She won't have moved. She won't have given up. In that cabin in the woods where I grew up, she's going to bed tonight and she'll pray that I come home. She'll do it every day until she gets her sons back."

Her tears began at the thought of her future mother-in-law waiting for her babies. She'd been apart from Vi for a few days and it had seemed like forever. "We should call her."

He tugged her back down. "We will. We'll go upstairs and get my brother and we'll call Mom. You know why I really remembered?"

She looked down at him, at this man she was going to spend the rest of her life with. "You remember best when you're in the place, so no, I don't."

He held her tight. "I was thinking that you're my home. I was settled and happy and I realized no matter what, I'm home with you. And that's when I remembered."

She laid her head on his chest and held him, her whole soul complete.

Chapter Nineteen

Jennings, Wyoming
Four days later

"Stop. I want to look at it for a minute," Robert said, his voice going hushed. "I remember this."

Tucker parked the car at the beginning of a long gravel road that led to the house he and his brother had grown up in. It was the road that would lead them home, but then they'd been on it for a long time when he thought about it. Ever since that day when he'd realized his brother was alive, he'd been driving them right back here.

"It's beautiful," Ariel said. She was seated behind her husband, leaning forward, her hands on his shoulders as she looked out the window at the sea of trees around them. In the distance, snowcapped mountains marked the horizon. Those mountains always had snow on the top, even in the middle of summer.

"It is." Roni sat behind him, Vi in a car seat between her mom and her Aunt Ari.

"This is where the bus would drop us off," he said to his brother. Robert was remembering more and more, but Tucker's memories of this place had practically flattened him the minute he'd heard his mother's voice over the phone. So much of his life had rushed in, overwhelming him with precious memories.

The smell of her banana bread. The way she kissed his boo-boos before putting a bandage on them. The way she'd leaned over and kissed his chest, right over his heart when his first girlfriend had broken up with him because she'd said a broken heart was far worse than a skinned knee.

The way she'd loved them.

It had come back in a wave of emotion that had left him shaking and happy. Roni had sat up all night listening to stories about his childhood. About his mother and grandfather, and how he and his brother had run wild through the Wyoming wilderness.

Up ahead they could make out the big log cabin they'd called home.

Rob unhooked his seatbelt and got out of the SUV they'd rented in Laramie. He stepped out and looked around, taking in his home once again. "It was thirty minutes into town, but longer in the winter. God, this place is beautiful in the winter."

Rob might remember some things, but he was selectively forgetting a few. He eased out of the vehicle and moved to stand by his brother, looking out over the long drive that led from the road to the big cabin their grandfather had built with his own hands back in the fifties. "It was cold, Rob. So freaking cold. We complained bitterly during our high school years."

Rob's face lit up. "I didn't. You were the whiny one. I was built for the cold. And Mom would stand out here with us. She would have a thermos of hot chocolate to keep us warm. God, we're about to see our mom."

He put a hand on his brother's shoulder. "We are."

"Hey, why don't you two walk down there and Roni and I will follow you," Ariel suggested.

Roni had gotten out of the SUV and leaned against the side. "Vi's asleep anyway. And you said the walk after school from the road to the house was a special time for you two. You're home. Take that walk with your brother."

He strode to her, closing the space between them. That space meant nothing since she was always in his heart, no matter where she was. "Give us a couple of minutes and then join us. It's not that…"

She went on her toes and kissed him. "No explanations are necessary. That woman has waited a long time. She deserves a couple of moments with her boys. You should enjoy the attention because once she gets a look at her grandbaby, it will all be over. She'll fall madly in love with Vi."

God, he loved this woman. It had all been worth it because she was here with him. "She will indeed. See you in a few."

He handed her the keys as his brother kissed Ariel and joined him at the top of the drive.

"Grandad didn't want to pave this because he said it would make it easier for people to get to the house. You know for a small-town doctor, he was a little curmudgeonly." Rob stared straight ahead.

It was good his brother was remembering on his own. "He was a character."

"I'm nervous," Rob admitted.

The hard dirt and gravel crunched under his feet in a beautifully familiar way. "Why? If anything, I should be nervous. I believe I promised her I would have you home soon. It took me a long time. She might make me sit in the corner."

Rob snorted, an amused sound. "She was a terrible disciplinarian. All we had to do was look sad and she gave in. I loved her. I loved her so much. She was always worried that she wasn't enough after Dad left but she was."

"She was everything and there's nothing to worry about. I'm glad it happened and I'm going to tell her that. I'm glad because we're here," he admitted.

Rob nodded. "I'm glad we're here, too."

Here meant Roni and Vi and Ariel. *Here* might not have been where they had thought they would end up. Something terrible had happened, but they'd survived. They'd lived and sacrificed and built families.

"Even though we couldn't remember her, she was with us," Tucker said, emotion welling as the door to the cabin came open and a petite woman with steel-colored hair walked out, her hand to her heart.

Rob stopped and stared. "Mom." Tears started streaming down his brother's face. "Oh, I missed her. I missed her so much."

"Last one home has to do the dishes." Tucker felt a fierce smile cross his face. It had been their game. It had taken him years to beat his brother, though Rob had always winked and helped him after supper anyway.

Because he'd been the best big brother.

Tucker took off, jogging to meet the woman who had waited so faithfully for her sons to come home. All the years they'd been gone, she'd hoped and prayed and never given up.

Rob fell in beside him, racing toward their mom.

And when her arms were around him, when they were finally together, his job, the one he'd begun so many years before, was done.

He was home.

* * * *

London, England

The man who called himself Ezra Fain sat back and wondered how bad this particular meeting was going to go.

Because it was definitely going to go bad. He could feel it. There had been something in Levi Green's eyes as they'd hauled him away that day in Paris. He hadn't been upset. There hadn't been worry or even hope in his eyes.

There had been something far more frightening stamped on his face.

Triumph.

"I hear the lads are happy." Damon Knight sat across from him looking like he fit perfectly well in the efficient conference room. Though it wasn't the one at The Garden, Knight still looked like he owned the place. Of course, at one point he'd belonged here since this was MI6 headquarters.

"Yes, I talked to Tucker and Rob last night. They're thrilled to be home. I think Rob will come back to work, but you've probably lost Tucker. He's already talking about finishing up his residency as soon as he can. He and Veronica are both looking to restart their medical careers."

Damon nodded at him from across the conference table. "I always knew I would lose some of them. Most of them, really, since

Sasha and Dante are gone. Jax and River are already on their way back to Colorado. Owen and Rebecca are spending some time in Scotland, but he's assured me he's coming back. Of course, at some point Rebecca will need to move and we'll lose him, too. Funny, isn't it? When Tag first foisted that crew on me, I couldn't wait to get rid of them. I suppose we all get attached to strays. Makes it hard when they find their homes."

"I think they'll always come back for a visit. You won't get rid of them so easily, but damn it's good to see them happy," he admitted. Although it left him wondering what the hell he was going to do next. The Lost Boys had found their places in the world, but he was still floating, still completely unanchored.

Because she was always the one who grounded you. Or rather, you grounded her and that was your place in the world. Watching her fly.

He shut that voice down because he wasn't giving in. Being around her so much in the last few months had softened him up. Being around her smile and all that freaking blonde hair that ended up everywhere, and the way she could look at him like he was a god on earth.

"Solo really came through," Damon was saying. "Once we turned over that data, she got pardons for Tucker and Jax within hours. I have to say I'm impressed with how quickly she worked. Especially since she was rather annoyed with you."

Annoyed wasn't the word he would use. Kim had felt utterly betrayed by him. His plan to distract her had worked. He'd started a fight. She'd never been able to back down, and he could keep it going forever.

Of course, he'd considered distracting her another way. He'd thought about backing her up against the wall and pressing his body to hers. Kim was the single most sensual woman he'd ever met, and she'd always responded to him like he was the only man she wanted to touch her.

Unfortunately, he definitely wasn't the only man she'd wanted.

"Yes, she seems determined to do this right," he replied. And then it would be over. That's what she'd told him. She'd told him he'd finally gone too far when she realized he'd distracted her and let Levi Green escape with Tucker and Rob. The look on her face…he'd thought he was over such silly notions as shame, but he'd felt it in that moment. He glanced toward the doors. "Where is everyone else?"

Damon looked down at his watch. "They should be here soon. I was disappointed we were left out of the initial meetings."

"Have you been out of the game so long you forgot how this works?" He'd known damn well the minute the Agency got their hands on that thumb drive that they would only see the information the Agency wanted them to. "We're private citizens. We're lucky they're willing to talk to us at all."

Damon frowned, a supremely arrogant look. "I don't like being on the outside. I don't like not controlling things. I know Rupert has been accommodating since that bloody Kronberg employee he brought along went rogue, but I have a bad feeling about this."

It was good to know he wasn't the only one. "I do, too. Something's off about this whole thing."

The door came open and there she was. Kimberly Solomon, used to be Kent. His one-time wife. The only woman he'd ever loved, and the only one he'd ever hated. Sometimes he thought he clung to the hate with every bit as much vigor as he'd held on to the love.

"Hello, Beck." She moved to the seat furthest from him, putting her ridiculously expensive handbag on the table in front of her. "Damon, it's good to see you."

"And you, Solo," Damon returned. "I want to say thank you for everything you did for the lads. I suspect you're the only reason we're here today, too. I appreciate it all."

She sank into her seat, not looking his way. "I'm glad it worked out. But I've got to admit they've been stonewalling me about that drive. I tried to go back to DC to help analyze the data and I was told to stay here in London to liaise with MI6. I think someone convinced the big bosses that I'm too close to the subject. I have to wonder if that was you, Beck."

He shook his head, rather hurt at the suspicion in her eyes. Even when he was horrible to her, when they fought like cats and dogs, she didn't look at him like he was the bad guy. "No. Why would I try to put you on the outside? We kind of need you on the inside. Are you telling me you haven't seen the report?"

He didn't like the sound of that. This had been Kim's op. She should have been the one trying to decrypt the data, or at least it should have been her team doing it.

Damon seemed to have the same concerns. "Who is running the op now?"

She shrugged. "No idea. I suppose it's one of the big guys. I'll find out when they walk through the door."

"Kim, whose name is on that list?" A chill crept up his spine. There was supposed to be a list of everyone who'd worked with McDonald.

What had Levi said? That he'd been waiting. That he'd been patient.

What if this had been Levi's play all along?

She blinked as though thinking. "What do you mean?"

The doors came open and his worst fear walked right in wearing a three-piece suit and looking like a complete douchebag. Levi Green was back and he'd prettied himself up for the occasion. And he'd brought friends. Friends who probably had lots of guns.

Fuck. He was caught and he was about to be arrested because that fucker had stacked the deck. Anger flushed through his system and he thought seriously about going down in a blaze of glory.

This was what Levi had waited for, why he hadn't broken under torture. He'd known this was coming because he'd set it up years ago.

He'd set up his worst enemy to take a fall no one would see coming. Somehow, Levi had put his name on that list. He just knew it.

Levi smirked as he stood at the head of the table. "Hello, all. It's so good to be back."

Kim stood, a look of horror dawning on her face. "What are you doing here? Why have you been released?"

"My darling, not only have I been released, I'm back to my full duties, and unfortunately the first is a bit distasteful," Levi said, his voice silky smooth. He glanced back at the small army he'd brought with him. "Gentlemen, it's time."

Ezra stood, ready to fight.

"Mr. Knight, I invited you here because someone should be a witness," Levi said as four large men walked into the room. "Don't make me regret it. You'll have full access to the data after I do what needs to be done."

Arrest him. Take him out of the country and put him at Green's mercy.

"Kimberly Solomon, I'm placing you under arrest for treason," Green said as his men put hands on her.

Damon had moved quickly and gripped Ezra's arm, stopping him from what he wanted to do—tear apart the men who were manhandling his wife.

Ex-wife.

"Don't," Damon whispered. "You have to let her go. We're outnumbered. There's a reason he's doing it here. He's got the full cooperation of MI6."

"What is happening?" Kim tried to pull away but they held her tight.

"Be careful with her," Levi barked. "I told you I'll kill the first person who hurts her. She's an important prisoner."

"Levi, I swear if you take her, I'm going to kill you," he said, his heart racing. He'd thought he'd found the worst-case scenario, but Levi had taken it a step further.

"I'm sure you'll try," Levi replied with a calm that unnerved Ezra. "Damon, I wish you hadn't stopped him. I wouldn't mind shooting him right here. Solo, your name was on the list. We know you were working with McDonald. What a pity."

Kim had gone completely white. "That's not true. You're lying."

Damon's hand tightened as they began to haul her out. "There's nothing you can do now. Patience. We'll get her back if we need to. I promise, brother. Don't make things worse right now."

It was the word *brother* that did it, that calmed him and made him believe every word Damon was saying.

Kim looked to him. He waited for her to plead with him to save her, but then her shoulders straightened and her chin came up. She didn't believe he would fight for her.

Because he'd given her no reason to think he would.

She walked out, the betrayed queen on her way to the execution, her head held high, her whole demeanor defiant even as she complied.

His queen.

He watched as Green turned and walked after her, but not before he'd winked his way.

"I'm going to kill that man," he vowed.

"I'm going to help you," Damon promised.

He was left shaken. Now that she was gone, he knew beyond a

shadow of a doubt that he couldn't let her go.

* * * *

Ezra, Solo, and the whole McKay-Taggart team will return in *No Love Lost*, now available.

And don't miss Nina finding her very own billionaire when she meets JT Malone in *Charmed*, now available.

Author's Note

I'm often asked by generous readers how they can help get the word out about a book they enjoyed. There are so many ways to help an author you like. Leave a review. If your e-reader allows you to lend a book to a friend, please share it. Go to Goodreads and connect with others. Recommend the books you love because stories are meant to be shared. Thank you so much for reading this book and for supporting all the authors you love!

No Love Lost
By Lexi Blake
Masters and Mercenaries: The Forgotten Book 5
Now available.

When Ezra Fain joined the ranks of the CIA, the last thing on his mind was romance. After meeting Kim Soloman, it was difficult to think of anything else. A tragic mistake drove them apart, leaving him shattered and unable to forgive the woman he loved. But when his greatest enemy threatens her life, Ezra leaps into action, prepared to do anything to try to save her.

Solo accepted long ago that she won't get over Ezra. She's worked for years to get back into his life, looking for any way to reignite the love they once shared. Unfortunately, nothing seems to penetrate the wall he has built between them. When she's arrested for a crime she didn't commit, she believes she's on her own.

Racing across the globe, Ezra and Solo find themselves together again, caught in the crosshairs of the agency they sacrificed so much to serve. Days on the run soon turn to steamy nights, but Levi Green isn't about to let them find their happily ever after. And when the smoke clears, the men and women of McKay-Taggart will never be the same again.

Charmed
Masters and Mercenaries Book 20.5
By Lexi Blake
Now available.

JT Malone is lucky, and he knows it. He is the heir to a billion-dollar petroleum empire, and he has a loving family. Between his good looks and his charm, he can have almost any woman he wants. The world is his oyster, and he really likes oysters. So why does it all feel so empty?

Nina Blunt is pretty sure she's cursed. She worked her way up through the ranks at Interpol, fighting for every step with hard work and discipline. Then she lost it all because she loved the wrong person. Rebuilding her career with McKay-Taggart, she can't help but feel lonely. It seems everyone around her is finding love and starting families. But she knows that isn't for her. She has vowed never to make the mistake of falling in love again.

JT comes to McKay-Taggart for assistance rooting out a corporate spy, and Nina signs on to the job. Their working relationship becomes tricky, however, as their personal chemistry flares like a wildfire. Completing the assignment without giving in to the attraction that threatens to overwhelm them seems like it might be the most difficult part of the job. When danger strikes, will they be able to count on each other when the bullets are flying? If not, JT's charmed life might just come to an end.

About Lexi Blake

New York Times bestselling author Lexi Blake lives in North Texas with her husband and three kids. Since starting her publishing journey in 2010, she's sold over three million copies of her books. She began writing at a young age, concentrating on plays and journalism. It wasn't until she started writing romance that she found success. She likes to find humor in the strangest places and believes in happy endings.

Connect with Lexi online:

Facebook: Lexi Blake
Twitter: authorlexiblake
Website: www.LexiBlake.net
Instagram: www.instagram.com

Sign up for Lexi's free newsletter at www.LexiBlake.net.

www.ingramcontent.com/pod-product-compliance
Lightning Source LLC
LaVergne TN
LVHW092314211225
828271LV00039B/320